COLLECTION FOLIO

Philippe Delerm

La tranchée
d'Arenberg

et autres voluptés sportives

Gallimard

Philippe Delerm est né le 27 novembre 1950 à Auvers-sur-Oise. Ses parents étaient instituteurs et il a passé son enfance dans des « maisons d'école » à Auvers, à Louveciennes, à Saint-Germain.

Après des études de lettres, il enseigne en Normandie où il vit depuis 1975. Il a reçu le prix Alain-Fournier 1990 pour *Autumn* (Folio n° 3166), le prix Grandgousier 1997 pour *La première gorgée de bière et autres plaisirs minuscules*, le prix des Libraires 1997 et le prix national des Bibliothécaires 1997 pour *Sundborn ou les jours de lumière* (Folio n° 3041), le prix Aliénor d'Aquitaine 2007 et le prix Sport scriptum du meilleur livre de sport 2007 pour *La tranchée d'Arenberg et autres voluptés sportives* (Folio n° 4752).

Ce livre est dédié à Roger Gicquel,
qui cavalait dans les couloirs du métro
après son boulot pour venir nous entraîner
sur la piste en herbe du Pecq.

Légende aux Tuileries

Un livre vert pomme, sans photo sur la couverture, sans dessin. Il n'y avait plus de distribution des prix officielle, mais on donnait un livre à chaque élève, et en cinquième j'avais eu celui-là. Une autobiographie de Georges Carpentier. Ce nom me disait quelque chose, car j'avais dû lire quatre pages de bandes dessinées sur lui dans « Les belles histoires de l'Oncle Paul », de *Spirou*, ou l'équivalent dans *Le Journal de Tintin*. Dans le livre vert, toutes les cinquante ou soixante pages, étaient distillées quelques photos noir et blanc. L'une d'elles me reste en mémoire. On y voit Carpentier, plutôt petit, mince, à peine décoiffé au milieu du ring. À ses pieds, un géant en short noir couché de tout son long : Bombardier Wells. Une autre aussi, dans un océan de public, avec les deux boxeurs minuscules, comme écrasés par l'enjeu de leur rencontre mythique : Carpentier-Dempsey.

Carpentier racontait son enfance pauvre dans

le Nord, et le plat que sa mère lui préparait les jours de fête : du lapin aux pronnes, aux pruneaux. Quant à la boxe, les pages déclinaient sous toutes ses formes le mythe de David et Goliath. Carpentier était le petit qui terrassait les grands, en général d'un crochet à la pointe du menton. Jusqu'au jour où Dempsey...

D'autres aspects de sa vie intervenaient sur la fin du récit : sa participation à la guerre, dans l'aviation je crois, et aussi toute une vie mondaine, qui m'étonnait : on le voyait au côté de Douglas Fairbanks ou de Charlie Chaplin. Les succès féminins n'étaient pas évoqués, mais on les devinait sans peine. Carpentier était beau, d'une beauté d'époque, la raie pas tout à fait au milieu, les cheveux soigneusement lissés. Il portait le smoking avec un naturel étonnant pour un enfant du peuple ; bref, il avait changé de monde, et dans le second, il semblait une sorte de chouchou. Je l'imaginais dansant le charleston avec une star de cinéma très fine, au long collier, à la coiffure un rien garçonne.

Et puis en 1970 un jour je l'ai revu, aux Tuileries. Pas difficile de le reconnaître : on le voyait souvent dans les journaux, parfois à la télé. Un vieux monsieur tout seul en pardessus, mains dans les poches, qui en fin d'après-midi fait sa petite promenade hygiénique. Je l'ai suivi. Il a traversé la rue de Rivoli, s'est engagé dans la rue du Marché-Saint-Honoré. Je suis revenu aux Tuileries plusieurs soirs à la même heure, et presque à chaque fois j'ai retrouvé la même silhouette très droite. La même distinction. La même solitude. La rumeur de Paris me semblait comme un vertigineux silence, si loin de la foule de Carpentier-Dempsey. En France, à l'époque, tout le monde avait attendu le résultat du match. Personne en apparence n'attendait plus le vieux monsieur qui empruntait à petits pas la rue du Marché-Saint-Honoré. Je restais à distance. Surtout ne pas effaroucher l'écho d'une légende. Je n'ai pas retrouvé mon livre vert.

You'll never walk alone

Un frisson vous parcourt l'échine. Le kop d'Anfield s'est mis à chanter. C'est quelque part sur les rives de la Mersey, au nord de l'Angleterre. Les Reds de Liverpool ont davantage que des supporters : des milliers d'officiants pour une messe en l'honneur du dieu Football, qui sublime toutes les cheminées d'usine, et les mélancolies poisseuses du chômage.

Les plus chanceux ou les plus débrouillards réussirent à faire le voyage d'Istanbul en mai 2005. Ils étaient assez fous pour y croire encore quand Liverpool s'est vu mener par Milan 3-0 en finale de la Ligue des champions. Ils avaient raison. Steven Gerrard leur a rendu l'espoir à la cinquante-quatrième. Le reste fut comme un rêve noyé dans une brume de bière. Les Reds ne pouvaient plus perdre aux tirs au but.

« You'll never walk alone. » La symbolique de la chanson est d'autant plus prenante qu'on se demande toujours à qui elle s'adresse vraiment. Qui ne marchera jamais seul ? Chacun des joueurs, sans doute. Mais peut-être aussi les supporters de Liverpool eux-mêmes, abandonnés par la beauté du monde, mais trouvant dans l'énergie de leur souffle vital la ferveur de croire en quelque chose. Et cela devient chant, et nous donne la chair de poule.

Croire en Steven Gerrard ? L'enfant du pays, arrivé au club à huit ans, couvé au collège de West Derby jusqu'à seize, porteur du brassard de *captain*, semble incarner la pure tradition des Reds. Mais à l'intersaison, on a dû se résigner à envisager l'incroyable. Gerrard a failli partir chez les Bleus, les milliardaires de Chelsea, l'ennemi absolu : un club bâti seulement sur l'argent. Combien a-t-il fallu de cet argent maudit pour que Steven finisse par décider de rester à Liverpool ?

Le kop d'Anfield évite de se poser la question. Dans les clubs anglais, les spectateurs sont tout près du jeu, au ras de la pelouse. On croit aux joueurs pour croire un peu en soi. Quand ça va mal, on chante. « You'll never walk alone. »

Classiques du Nord

Classiques flandriennes, ou ardennaises. Tour des Flandres. Gand-Wevelgem. Amstel Gold Race. Flèche Wallonne. Liège-Bastogne-Liège. Ce n'est plus tout à fait l'hiver, mais c'est tellement au nord. Tous ces noms installent à la fois une distance et une familiarité, liée à la succession rapprochée de ces rendez-vous. L'alternance ville-campagne nous y prend souvent au dépourvu. On passe du mur de Grammont pavé à une portion d'autoroute, d'une forêt des Ardennes à la banlieue de Liège. Le concept même de classiques flandriennes ou ardennaises est ambigu. Il a pour nous la connotation d'un apéritif de l'année cycliste, mais nous savons que, pour beaucoup de coureurs flamands, il est l'apothéose de la saison. Cela nous plaît d'y frôler une mythologie que nous maîtrisons mal, et dont la figure de proue, en dépit de ses récents succès, ne saurait être Tom Boonen, trop policé, trop souriant, trop bien

17

coiffé. Bien davantage Johann Museeuw, un champion brusque, anguleux, trop fermé pour susciter la sympathie, assez mystérieux pour provoquer la vénération.

Un flahute. Les journaux ont beau nous proposer ce raccourci débonnaire, nous ne pénétrons pas l'intimité de ces coureurs du plat pays, si costauds pour s'opposer au pire ennemi du cycliste : le vent. En les regardant tirer des bordures dans l'abstraction grise d'un paysage que le printemps envahit à regret nous reviennent les allitérations lancinantes du poème de Verhaeren « Voici le vent, le vent sauvage… » Mais le français ne traduit pas les sensations de course. On s'y empoigne sur des accents flamands, une langue résolument étrangère, avec ses astringences, son hypocrite fluidité qui nous éloignent.

Petit taureau fonceur, compact, Bernard Hinault s'engouffrait sans états d'âme dans les stratégies autochtones et les faisait exploser. Parfois, un Italien s'impose aussi, comme si sa méridionalité le rendait insensible aux sortilèges locaux. Mais le plus souvent, l'impression demeure d'un espace réservé. Il y a comme un quota mental, sous peine de dénaturer l'essence du propos. On ne saurait faire injure à ce public fervent disséminé le long des routes qui attend la victoire d'un des siens avec moins de chauvinisme qu'un sens de l'équité peu remis en question : ici, l'âpreté de la vie veut un vainqueur à la rugosité de sa mesure.

Filmer sa peur

En 1924, aux Jeux olympiques de Paris, Mussabini, l'entraîneur de Harold Abrahams, restait dans sa modeste chambre d'hôtel pendant que son poulain anglais disputait la finale du 100 mètres. On imagine à quel point le couvre-lit, le papier peint, l'armoire, devaient, dans leur silence et leur anonymat apparents, prendre la forme vertigineuse du stade tout proche, s'habiller de sa clameur.

Dans les années soixante, Joseph Maigrot, le magicien du 4 × 100 mètres, réglait au millimètre les courroies de transmission du relais national. Mais il ne pénétrait pas dans le stade à l'heure des finales. Berger, Genevay, Piquemal, Delecour, Laidebeur ou Bambuck connaissaient par cœur son message. Sans doute n'eussent-ils pas couru différemment en présence de leur mentor. Mais voilà. Superstition ? Peur, plutôt, et désir de vivre seul ces quelques secondes où tout va se jouer.

On a tout préparé et l'on ne peut plus rien, c'est effrayant.

Aujourd'hui, les entraîneurs fébriles ont trouvé un subterfuge. Bien placés dans l'enceinte du stade, au-dessus de la ligne d'arrivée, ils filment la course. Ils filment. À quoi bon ? Que l'on enregistre une séance d'entraînement, pour disséquer ensuite avec l'athlète la moindre de ses imperfections, cela s'impose. Que l'on filme encore, à la rigueur, un tour préliminaire afin de discuter à chaud d'une ultime correction technique à apporter, soit. Mais filmer une finale, un aboutissement, quand les images de télévision donneront à satiété et perfection tous les ralentis possibles ?

Bien sûr on devine. L'œil dans la caméra, les entraîneurs font semblant d'être là. En se focalisant sur leur athlète, ils effacent une part de l'enjeu. La perception vivante du stade entier serait trop forte. Alors ils partent ailleurs ; dans une boîte dérisoire ils se protègent. Le voyeurisme toutefois se pratique en abyme. Souvent, une autre caméra les filme en train de filmer. Des images pour après, diffusées aux actualités le lendemain en cas de victoire, ou plus tard dans un reportage.

Ce que l'on voit alors est étonnant. La personne la plus concernée par le spectacle est la seule qui ne réagit pas à l'unisson du stade. Pendant que la foule se dresse, l'entraîneur continue à filmer quelques secondes. Caméra : « chambre ». L'étymologie épouse l'objet au plus près. La caméra devient une chambre de pudeur où l'entraîneur démiurge exorcise sa peur.

Ils connaissent le film

Il le sait tout de suite. À l'intensité de la rumeur du public de Roland-Garros, à l'impavidité maladroite du juge de ligne qui feint de n'avoir rien vu, mais que l'on sent troublé, il sait qu'il doit descendre sur le court. Ça n'a l'air de rien, mais ce n'est pas évident de descendre rapidement d'une chaise d'arbitre quand tout un central, quand toutes les caméras de la télévision se focalisent sur vous. Il faut se lever, se retourner, aborder les échelons sans se casser la figure. La silhouette a beau être honorablement déliée, elle fait contraste avec les chassés-glissés des virtuoses de la terre battue.

Une fois qu'il a touché le sol, il trottine vers le lieu du litige, et là encore la maîtrise est subtile : assez rapide pour manifester son sens des responsabilités, sa certitude ; assez lent pour ne pas avoir l'air de succomber à la pression populaire ni à l'ire du joueur prétendument spolié qui l'attend de pied ferme. Alors le scénario devient délectable, tant on a déjà deviné quelle en sera la substance. L'arbitre court encore. D'une main, il maîtrise la fermeture de son blazer, de l'autre il indique d'un doigt comminatoire la trace de l'impact, puis sa main s'aplanit pour signifier que la balle était bien dans le court. Juste à côté de lui, le réclameur ne l'entend pas de cette oreille. Avec le bout de sa raquette, il indique une autre trace, qu'il entoure d'un cercle suffisamment vaste pour ne pas risquer de l'effacer. Déjà l'arbitre s'en revenait vers son perchoir, de la même foulée apparemment paisible. Mais il ne peut faire mine de ne pas entendre la vocifération plus ou moins anglophone du joueur à la fois furieux de l'injustice de la décision arbitrale et vexé de cette ébauche de dialogue qui n'a pas cru bon d'en venir aux mots.

Alors l'arbitre se retourne. Quelques secondes à peine ils se regardent, et l'on connaît l'issue de ce face-à-face gratuit. Le grand juge va confirmer sa décision, avec un hochement de tête qui se voudrait très calme. Puis il tourne le dos, reprend sa course, grimpe les échelons de la chaise, se dandine un peu pour reprendre son assise. L'essentiel est de bien réinstaller son micro, car, dans ce rapport de force phonique, il ne sera pas de trop pour rivaliser avec la bronca qui monte des tribunes, et quelques noms d'oiseaux bien détachés, tout en haut. Et pendant tout ce temps, le joueur s'est installé, mains sur les hanches, au bord du carré de service, comme s'il ne devait jamais en bouger. Pour devenir victime jusqu'au bout, il attend que tombe le verdict. Et puis il s'en revient si lentement vers les bâches du fond de court, avec un accablement de tout l'être que le service adverse va vite dissiper. Quarante-quinze. *Forty-fifteen*.

Chat écorché

Un entraîneur quadragénaire lui tend sa veste
de survêtement. Un ancien gymnaste, sûrement.
La gamine lui arrive à la poitrine. Il la félicite avec
un enthousiasme mesuré, juste deux mots, penché vers elle. Crainte de paraître trop satisfait, et
de déplaire ainsi aux juges ? Mais ces derniers,
inaccessibles, ont les yeux rivés sur leur écran. La
petite championne passe devant le banc de ses
compatriotes. Chacune lui tend la main pour une
tape furtive, presque mécanique. Elles ne prennent pas même le temps de se regarder. Elle va
s'asseoir elle aussi, garde un moment la veste jetée
sur ses épaules.

Elle est vraiment jeune, quatorze, quinze ans
au plus. Mais surtout très maigre, très pâle. Ses
cheveux tirés en arrière par une petite queue de
cheval glissée dans un élastique. Elle semble ne
pas se détacher de tout cet univers à la fois sonore et feutré. Il y a du public, des applaudisse-

ments, mais si lointains, si raisonnables qu'ils soulignent l'immensité creuse de la nef, s'évadent en abstraction vers le plafond.

Rien ne vient troubler ce cérémonial drastique. On voudrait que ce soit seulement de l'admiration, du respect, mais il y a aussi comme une chape militaire déployée sur ce jardin d'enfants. Elle étouffe la singularité de toutes ces petites filles si explosives sur le tapis, sur le cheval, aux barres asymétriques, et puis si tristes et résignées dans l'immobilité. Leur corps osseux, pas même musculeux, n'a le droit de bouger que dans l'intensité barbare de la presque perfection.

Elle enfile sa veste maintenant. Elle sait bien que cette fois encore c'était seulement presque. Quand la note s'est affichée, elle n'a pas cillé. Une très bonne note, et cependant rien n'est gagné, car la poutre l'attend. Elle fouille dans son sac. Il y a un vieux nounours et de l'eau minérale.

Au départ d'la balle

« Au départ d'la balle, j'suis pas sûr ! » Parmi les connivences et les coquetteries qui émaillent les conversations des amateurs de foot, il faut faire un sort à cette phrase. Il pourrait s'agir d'un commentaire télévisuel, mais la forme contractée indique plutôt un propos villageois, proféré contre la main courante qui entoure le terrain, et suivi d'un regard périscopique sur l'assistance proche. À côté des « À l'aile, bon Dieu, à l'aile ! », des « Non, y a rien, m'sieur l'arbitre ! » et même des « Alors, Jeanjean, qu'est-ce que t'as fait cette nuit ? », le « Au départ d'la balle, j'suis pas sûr ! » nous fait passer dans un registre supérieur. La forme syntaxique apparemment modeste – « j'suis pas sûr » – n'est là que pour mieux souligner un non-dit très explicite : « Y a une chose dont j'suis sûr, c'est que j'connais la règle du hors-jeu ! »

La phrase une fois prononcée, le coup d'œil périphérique opéré, la bonhomie du groupe social concerné se mue quelques instants en gravité sagace. On peut deviner chez les autres membres un léger regret de n'avoir pas prononcé eux-mêmes ces mots, car certes cette connaissance d'un point délicat du règlement est partagée par tous. Le mieux est de s'en tenir à une moue légèrement dubitative ou à un hochement de tête discrètement approbatif. Chacun sait bien en effet qu'un « Si, il y est, hors jeu ! », pour aussi sincère et lucide qu'il soit, déclencherait aussitôt un « Mais j'te dis au départ d'la balle ! » délibérément vexatoire, qui reprocherait à l'interlocuteur une perception sommaire des choses – a-t-il bien eu comme son jouteur oratoire une vision panoramique de l'événement ? –, voire une pleutrerie de mauvais aloi : ne ferait-il pas par hasard partie des frileux suiveurs du juge de touche, dont les levers de drapeau impérieux, le dos tourné au peuple, ont une brusquerie infamante ?

Silence, donc, de préférence, et respect. Non pas pour celui qui a parlé, mais respect jubilatoire pour cette règle du hors-jeu qui fait de tous des subtils, ce dont au départ on n'était pas si sûr.

Héroïsme pendulaire

L'un a franchi 8 mètres en longueur, un autre a couru le 400 mètres en 46 secondes, un troisième a sauté 5,40 mètres à la perche. Mais les voilà réunis à présent près de la ligne de départ du 1 500 mètres. L'ultime épreuve, le sommet du décathlon. C'est là que va se dénouer la pièce, dans la scène où ils sont tous les plus humbles, les plus faibles. Leur façon de se congratuler avant le départ installe déjà une atmosphère atypique, légèrement pagailleuse, comme si l'éthique de leur discipline effaçait les solitudes rectilignes, comme si des ondes chaleureuses pouvaient suspendre et relativiser l'idée d'un classement.

Certes, ils ne sont pas des spécialistes du demi-fond. Il y a même une espèce de perversion à les faire se départager dans une course qui va à l'encontre de leurs qualités athlétiques. En général, l'un d'entre eux, qui n'a aucune chance de médaille, s'échappe dès le départ. Il semble très mince, court sur une base de 4 min 10 s environ. Sa fuite légère n'est là que pour mieux souligner la lourdeur pendulaire du peloton où va se gagner le titre, quelque part autour de 4 min 30 s, parfois davantage. Trois minutes aux 1 000 mètres. Un temps synonyme d'effort aérien pour la silhouette d'un marathonien. Mais, à ce rythme, la puissante carcasse d'un décathlonien semble faire du surplace.

Une souffrance en apparence dérisoire, comme si tout se jouait au ralenti. Bientôt le groupe éclate, et chacun fait sa propre course aimantée par le chronomètre, dans une solitude résignée. La plupart n'ont même plus la force de sprinter dans les derniers cent mètres. Ils s'affalent sur la piste, ou dans l'herbe, s'étreignent quelquefois avant même de connaître le résultat. C'est cela qui est beau, cette reconnaissance de l'effort de l'autre à travers sa propre douleur. Dans quelques minutes, il y aura place pour le bonheur, la tristesse. Mais maintenant, ils sont ensemble. C'est ça le décathlon.

Quitter l'enfance

Par leur pureté, certains gestes sportifs nous disent autre chose. Elle est presque allongée sur la glace, en fente avant, le genou gauche sous l'épaule, la jambe droite étirée en arrière. Elle glisse lentement, si lentement. Mais c'est la position de son bras droit, étiré vers l'avant, qui donne une sensation de douceur, de confiance et d'abandon. Elle est en train de lancer cet objet étrange qu'on appelle une pierre, au curling. Une pierre, oui, peut-être. Un énorme palet poli, cylindrique, aplati, curieusement surmonté d'une poignée rudimentaire, un peu comme un potiron et son pédoncule. Une chose presque ménagère – c'est la présence des balais qui renforce cette impression, mais aussi la propreté clinique de la piste couronnée d'une cible, tout au fond.

Au bout de l'élan, son bras droit s'avance ; elle garde encore la pierre dans la main. C'est ce moment qui est très beau, juste avant qu'elle ait abandonné la pierre, et juste après, quand son regard l'accompagne, et sait déjà si le cheminement obéit à son envie. Rien à voir avec un lâcher de boule de pétanque, si retenu, si calculé soit-il. Ce geste est plus beau quand c'est, comme ce matin, une épreuve féminine, juste un deuxième tour qualificatif aux Jeux olympiques de Turin, un match Suisse-Angleterre. Peu importe qu'elle soit anglaise ou suisse, dans la patinoire étonnamment déserte où quelques spectateurs supporters n'osent même pas crier tant ils sont seuls. Mais l'œil de la télévision est là, qui suit et reproduit à l'envi son avancée du bras droit, cette métaphore parfaite de la maternité. Il s'agit de guider avec une infinie patience, puis d'abandonner à regret, de suivre du regard : mélange de certitude et d'appréhension, émouvant vouloir de tout tenir et de tout libérer.

Le curling est un sport bizarre. On l'a vu pratiqué sur des photos anciennes, qui montraient le pont d'un paquebot à la Belle Époque. Le curling est un sport bizarre, car à la hiératique perfection du geste lent succède le frotti-frotta ridicule et surexcité de deux autres joueuses qui tentent de guider avec leur balai la pierre livrée au destin de sa glisse. On sent que le frotti-frotta ne peut tout changer. Ce qui compte vraiment, ce ne sont pas les péripéties dramatico-comiques du milieu de parcours, mais l'enfance du mouvement, et cet instant si douloureux, si fragile, où l'abandon se résigne à l'espoir.

À la cinquante-sixième

Séville, jeudi 8 juillet 1982, stade Sánchez-Pizjuán. Il fait nuit. Cinquante-sixième minute de la demi-finale Allemagne-France. Encore une ouverture lumineuse de Michel Platini. Patrick Battiston s'est engagé de toutes ses forces pour reprendre la balle. Il l'a touchée. La France va mener deux buts à un, mettre un pied en finale. Mais non. Le ballon poursuit sa course tout doucement et roule juste à côté de la cage allemande. Obnubilé par cette occasion magnifique, Battiston n'a pas vu fondre sur lui le gardien allemand Harald Schumacher. Celui-ci le percute de plein fouet. Patrick Battiston reste allongé sur la pelouse, et bientôt c'est la panique dans le clan français. Le docteur Vrillac, craignant une fracture des vertèbres cervicales, fait des signes de détresse en direction de la touche. Vite, on apporte la civière. Et c'est là... Michel Platini, un peu voûté, a pris la main de Battiston, escorte la civière jusqu'à la ligne de touche. On voit qu'il parle à son coéquipier, on devine qu'il lui parle. « T'en fais pas, ça va aller », ou bien « Ce match, je te promets qu'on va le gagner ! »

Peu importe ce qu'il dit, ce que Battiston peut entendre. L'attitude de Platini traduit tout cela, et plus encore. C'est un très joli soir d'été, un soir de chaleur, de vacances. Ce 8 juillet, sans avoir eu vraiment le temps d'y penser, on se retrouve dans le grand, le vrai, l'historique. Ça commence juste là, à la cinquante-sixième. C'est fort, cette attitude de Platini courbé qui tient la main de son copain. Il est complètement avec lui, mais en même temps on sent qu'il a dans le dos, sur le terrain, tout un destin à assumer, une tragédie à jouer. Le prof de français au lycée avait toujours une petite lueur de triomphe dans les yeux, quand il expliquait : « C'est ça, c'est seulement ça, la tragédie : une pièce qui finit mal ! »

Pourtant, on va tous espérer. Comment ne pas espérer, quand Trésor puis Giresse marquent pendant les prolongations ? Mais on n'est pas autrement surpris de voir l'Allemagne revenir à trois buts partout. Et quand Bossis, le joueur modèle, manque son tir au but, on sait : c'était écrit. Le lendemain, au lieu de son « Fabuleux ! », *L'Équipe* aurait pu titrer : « Si près du Paradis ».

Le Paradis. Oui, peut-être. Mais peut-être aussi

que c'est bien ennuyeux, le Paradis. Deux ans après, la France qui perd de justesse est devenue la France qui gagne, au Championnat d'Europe des nations. Platini marque le coup franc le plus foireux de sa carrière (on dira désormais une « arconada » pour désigner une toile aussi spectaculaire que celle du gardien espagnol). Tout le monde est joyeux, bien sûr. Mais pas aussi joyeux qu'on était triste le 8 juillet 1982. Normal. C'est tellement fort, la mélancolie – un peu comme l'adolescence. Et toutes les choses qu'on a manquées de justesse sont tellement plus grandes que celles qu'on a réussies.

Le 8 juillet 1982, Battiston s'en tire avec un traumatisme crânien, trois dents cassées. La balle a roulé à côté du but de Schumacher… Quand Platini lui prend la main, il ne sait pas que toute une époque se termine là. À la cinquante-sixième minute de la demi-finale Allemagne-France meurt la France de Poulidor, celle où le cœur bat plus fort pour celui qui perd en beauté. On n'ira jamais plus loin dans la tristesse que ce soir-là, alors… Alors il va falloir gagner, il va falloir aimer gagner.

Le prof avait raison : c'est beau, la tragédie.

On la tente

Dès que le coup de sifflet a retenti, le demi de mêlée s'est précipité sur le ballon, n'hésitant pas même à écarter du bras le pilier mastodonte adverse pour s'en emparer plus vite. Cette pénalité, il veut la jouer à la main. Toute sa gestuelle dynamique va dans ce sens. Raffûter, surprendre, se faufiler dans des forêts de jambes comme il devait le faire aux gendarmes et aux voleurs dans la cour de l'école. Et puis son équipe est menée de huit points, il reste six minutes à peine, il faut à tout prix marquer un essai. À côté de ce numéro 9, le numéro 10, son frère en construction tactique, en relais entre les tâcherons de la mêlée et les trois-quarts chevaliers de l'espace, devrait apporter aussitôt son soutien, sa disponibilité complice pour jouer le coup en douce, à la barbe du chronomètre.

Mais non. Le demi d'ouverture est resté trop droit, trop loin, pour que son attitude ne manifeste pas une explicite désapprobation. Furibard, le numéro 9 est bien obligé de renoncer à son impulsion. Le public, qui s'enflammait déjà pour un exploit possible à la Fanfan la Tulipe, marque sa déception par des sifflets. En une fraction de seconde, le demi de mêlée, le demi d'ouverture et le capitaine se consultent du regard. Mais la décision est déjà prise. Le capitaine montre à l'arbitre les poteaux : ils vont la tenter au pied.

Pusillanimité ? Mesquinerie ? Dans un premier temps, tout le monde semble le croire. Mais le numéro 10 s'est emparé du ballon avec un tel détachement, une telle indifférence à la rumeur publique qu'on va bientôt changer de bord. Au fond, c'est lui qui a raison. Un essai transformé ne suffirait pas, de toute façon. Alors, la véritable ambition, c'est de grappiller ces trois points apparemment dérisoires, mais qui préservent jusqu'au bout l'espoir de la victoire. C'est là que la sérénité du demi d'ouverture prend une dimension héroïque. Ce coup de pied, c'est lui qui va le donner, et son échec serait rédhibitoire, impopulaire de surcroît. Quand il pose le tee par terre, y dresse la balle, prend ses quelques pas d'élan, il sait qu'au-delà de ces rites une responsabilité presque philosophique tombe sur ses seules épaules. À lui de prouver que son avarice était généreuse. À lui de démontrer qu'en stratège lucide il préservait une chance de folie. Les autres ont fait semblant d'être d'accord, mais il est si seul à présent. Il se concentre si longtemps. Il y a des matchs gagnés qui ne sont rien d'abord qu'une petite réticence.

L'odeur du Figaro

Contrairement à ce qu'on pourrait penser, le parfum du Figaro n'était pas l'eau de violette ou de fougère. Une puissante odeur d'embrocation plutôt, liée à une sensation de froid et d'inconfort fébrile. La tribune de l'hippodrome d'Auteuil servait de vestiaire au cross, et c'était assez drôle de se retrouver à la mi-décembre dans ce temple chic des courses d'obstacles soudain privé de connotations équestres et livré à une humanité débonnaire, populaire, les banquettes encombrées d'un amoncellement de sacs, de serviettes, de survêtements et de maillots.

Faire le Figaro. Dans ce concept, les options politiques, économiques ou sociales d'un journal, pour traditionalistes qu'elles fussent, s'effaçaient devant une autre tradition : se retrouver un samedi matin d'hiver dans la foule anonyme des non-licenciés puis des vétérans qui se donnaient rendez-vous pour faire le Figaro, dans des catégories d'âge suffisamment précises pour étalonner un niveau sportif : 20-25 ans, vétérans I (40-46 ans), jusqu'au tout mêlé des « vieilles pointes » – à partir de cinquante-six ans, on ne comptait plus. C'est fou ce que les gens qui ont le même âge sont physiquement différents.

J'ai commencé le Figaro en minimes, le dimanche, car j'étais licencié du Stade Français. Dans la course des as, le gratin du cross national se retrouvait alors : Jazy, Wadoux, Bernard, Nicolas, Fayolle, Martinage. Plus tard, j'ai disputé la course en seniors, très modestement, puisque je préparais le 400 mètres. Puis je suis devenu plus dilettante, coureur du dimanche donc. Ah ! cette année où j'ai perdu une chaussure à pointes à mi-parcours ! Je n'arrêtais pas de remonter, un copain m'avait crié « Soixante-dixième ! » au passage du premier tour. 224e quand même, sur une chaussette. Sans cette chaussure engluée dans la boue, la face du monde athlétique eût été changée.

Préparer le Figaro était devenu un objectif à la fois simple et prestigieux, qui supposait un entraînement décent tout au long de l'automne dans ma forêt normande, suivi d'un déplacement à Paris. Se retrouver en survêtement métro Porte d'Auteuil, sac à l'épaule, avait quelque chose de délicieusement rajeunissant. Quand on a supprimé le Figaro, l'année des Twin Towers, je n'ai pas été le seul, je pense, à prendre un petit coup de blues. Une odeur d'embrocation dans l'hippodrome d'Auteuil a remonté. Le souvenir des files d'attente pour récupérer son dossard avec les épingles, la fausse décontraction des gestes préparatoires, et même, mine de rien, une bonne petite trouille, au milieu de ces gars réunis par l'envie de terminer devant moi. Une petite trouille qui sentait l'embrocation. Un rendez-vous perdu au coin du Bois. Je ne m'en consolerai pas.

Sourire après

C'est à la fin de la première minute. Le patineur a négocié son premier enchaînement de sauts. Une salve d'applaudissements synonyme de délivrance est montée des tribunes. Alors, une diagonale d'élan : pour le quadruple boucle piquée, il va prendre tous les risques, avec la vitesse de la confiance. C'est le moment d'emporter tous les suffrages, au moins le podium. Peut-être un petit peu trop près de la rambarde. Et puis voilà. Il est par terre. Cela dure une fraction de seconde. Déjà il est debout, le sourire aux lèvres. Sourire légèrement forcé, cette infime crispation qui fait mal. On imagine. Les heures blêmes, la solitude caverneuse de la patinoire, la diagonale cent fois reprise, au bout le quadruple qui passe de mieux en mieux au fil des mois, qui passe à chaque fois. Chaque fois.

Bien sûr, il reste presque tout le programme, encore bien des choses à sauver, une concentration extrême à préserver. Il n'a pas le temps d'y penser. Mais quand même. C'est désormais écrit en filigrane dans chacun de ses gestes, la pathétique élégance des bras qu'il sublime dans le passage lent comme pour invoquer la clémence des dieux. L'énergie si juste qu'il déploie pour les derniers sauts, parfaitement réussis. Mais parfaitement réussis parce qu'il est beaucoup trop tard, que la cadence enfin acquise est celle du détachement, presque du désespoir.

Tomber n'est rien. Mais continuer, sourire, saluer comme si tout avait été voulu. Ramasser un bouquet, quitter la piste, affronter la pénible promiscuité du « kiss and cry ». Et tant et tant d'heures si blêmes à retrouver.

Elles portent des noms slaves...

Grâces soient rendues à Dick Fosbury. En découvrant le saut sur le dos, ce héron américain planeur n'a pas seulement inscrit dans nos mémoires l'image stupéfiante de sa victoire aux Jeux de Mexico. Il a tout simplement inventé un nouveau type de beauté féminine : la sauteuse en hauteur. Bien sûr, les hommes ont hérité eux aussi de sa technique. Mais le rouleau ventral ne leur seyait pas si mal, par son équilibre de puissance engagée suivie d'un enroulement félin de la barre. Avec les femmes, la révolution ne fut pas de même nature : le Fosbury flop leur a donné une autre essence.

Les foulées de leur course d'élan, caracolantes, un peu piaffantes, presque saccadées parfois, ne sont là que pour attester leur énergie musculaire, en dépit de leur minceur extrême, et faire contraste avec ce qui va suivre. Le dernier contact presque brutal du pied sur la piste signe la fin des contingences. L'envol commence. Il n'a rien de systématique, c'est ce qui fait son prix. Souvent, les omoplates heurtent la barre qui peut retomber dans une vibration métallique désolée, ou bien être emportée sur le tapis de réception, et la posture du corps n'est plus alors qu'un recroquevillement apeuré, absorbé par la crainte d'un douloureux contact avec ce rigide témoin qu'il voulait abolir, et qui prend sa revanche. Mais quand les épaules sont engagées, le temps s'arrête. Peut-on pratiquer à la fois la lévitation et la vitesse ? Les sauteuses en hauteur ont la réponse, le secret. Elles portent souvent des noms slaves, l'idée de blondeur leur va bien, et celle d'une maigreur sublimée qui devient la beauté parfaite. Mais il y a des lianes brunes aussi, qui ôtent leur bandeau juste à la fin du saut, secouent leur chevelure quelques secondes, pour nous faire croire qu'elles sont de jolies jeunes femmes comme les autres. Mais personne n'est dupe. Lorsque l'on sait voler aussi longtemps, on ne fait que semblant de vivre sur la terre.

Les inédits de Zidane

On peut appeler ça comme on veut. Des râteaux, des coups du sombrero, des passements de jambe, des talonnades, des virgules, des contrôles orientés. Il faudrait inventer d'autres noms, des enroulements, des encorbellements, des trompe-l'œil, et peu à peu glisser vers le vocabulaire de la magie : car tous ces grigris de Zizou ont pour essence et pour but la mystification. De l'adversaire évidemment, mais aussi du public, et parfois même des coéquipiers, déroutés par un nouveau sortilège.

Pour s'en convaincre, il suffit de regarder sur une cassette ses gestes au ralenti. Mais on peut aussi s'allonger sur une plage, et observer les ados d'aujourd'hui : on ne jongle plus désormais avec un ballon comme on le faisait avant Zidane. Il faut certes une sacrée technique pour reproduire proprement un de ses tours de passe-passe. Mais au-delà de la réussite absolue, on voit que la recherche va dans ce sens, dans ces effleurements de la balle avec la plante du pied, dans ces déroulements caressants. Cela ressemble à du brésilien de la grande époque, mais c'est autre chose. Une langue nouvelle.

Combien de joueurs laissent-ils ainsi une trace non seulement dans les mémoires, mais aussi dans les gestes ? Bien sûr, Pelé, Maradona ou Platini ont eu leurs coups de génie, liés à des séquences de jeu qu'on rediffuse à l'envi. Mais pour Zidane, c'est différent. Il a laissé l'exploit, mais aussi un mode d'emploi, une possibilité de s'inspirer de lui pour essayer de reproduire. Son tutoiement avec la balle peut se détacher syllabe par syllabe, comme un manuel de lecture du cours préparatoire, quand on a renoncé à la méthode globale. Des coups de maître.

Une ligne sur une ardoise

C'était dans les années trente. Les gens se rassemblaient rue du Faubourg-Montmartre, devant le siège de *L'Auto*. Ils attendaient, en fin d'après-midi. Un employé du journal apparaissait, et écrivait sur une ardoise le résultat de l'étape au blanc d'Espagne.

J'aurais bien aimé partager cette scène. Vivre de cette manière le Tour de France. Les discussions avec des voisins inconnus, en supputant les chances des champions, en évoquant le profil plus ou moins maîtrisé du parcours dans une France paysanne, si loin de la poussière des Grands Boulevards aux soirs d'été.

Bien sûr, le sport n'est pas qu'un résultat. Pour nous, il est devenu spectacle, sur les lieux mêmes des compétitions, ou plus souvent devant l'écran de la télévision. Mais une ligne dans un journal donne parfois autant de plaisir, en réveillant le pouvoir d'imaginer qu'on croyait avoir abandonné avec l'enfance.

Il y a quelques années, je me rappelle avoir savouré ainsi dans la *Gazzetta dello Sport* le résultat de Diagana au Meeting de Paris que j'attendais. J'étais en vacances à Venise, où les kiosquiers reçoivent *L'Équipe* avec un jour de retard. Je pensais bien que le résultat du 400 mètres haies parisien auquel ne participait aucun athlète italien ne tiendrait guère de place dans les pages roses du quotidien transalpin. Mais pour Stéphane Diagana, qui relevait de blessure, le test était capital. Je finis par découvrir dans un coin de page sa performance, très encourageante, une deuxième place en un peu plus de 48 secondes. J'ai dégusté ce verdict apparemment bien sec sous les frondaisons de l'esplanade de Burano, à côté de l'embarcadère, assis sur un banc rouge au bois écaillé. La suite de la saison de Diagana prenait les perspectives de l'île aux maisons bigarrées, dans la chaleur étale de juillet.

Comme l'amour, le sport a le pouvoir de s'intégrer au paysage, de nous faire vivre un peu plus large. Il suffit pour cela qu'il ne se livre pas trop. Pénétrer dans les vestiaires avant, après un match, suivre le déroulement d'une compétition dans le moindre détail, interviewer les acteurs quelques secondes après leur prestation. Oui. Peut-être. Mais une ligne sur une ardoise, quelques mots dans un journal, c'est fort aussi.

La marche lente

17 mars 1990. L'Angleterre et l'Écosse, invaincues jusqu'alors dans le Tournoi, vont se disputer le grand chelem à Murrayfield. Le contexte politique est des plus brûlants. Margaret Thatcher a eu la bonne idée d'expérimenter dans un premier temps la très impopulaire *poll tax* au détriment des seuls Écossais. Au cas où ceux-ci auraient eu tendance à oublier la haine viscérale qu'ils vouent à leurs voisins anglais...

Quand les deux formations s'alignent devant la tribune officielle, le ton est vite donné. Pendant que les Guscott et autres Andrew s'époumonent courageusement, les caméras de télévision montrent les visages impavides des joueurs écossais, figés dans un silence provoquant. Pour la première fois de leur histoire, les hommes au chardon ne chantent pas le *God Save the Queen*. On sent que leur mutisme va bientôt lâcher la bonde. De fait, ils ont obtenu le droit de lancer deux strophes de *Flower of Scotland*, ce chant dont les paroles ne font pas dans la dentelle pour évoquer les antagonismes ancestraux entre les deux pays : « Toi qui résistas contre la fière armée d'Édouard Et la renvoyas d'où elle venait… »

Après l'indifférence hostile réservée à l'hymne britannique officiel, la flamme avec laquelle le stade entier attaque *Flower of Scotland* est impressionnante. Le match sera à l'image de ces paroles historiques. Contre une brillante équipe anglaise et les courses dévoreuses d'espace des arrogants trois-quarts Carling et Guscott, les Écossais résistent, résistent… et renvoient les Anglais d'où ils étaient venus, aidés par le talent de leur arrière Hastings, mais surtout par l'âpreté d'un pack farouche qui ne lâche pas un pouce de terrain.

13-7 pour l'Écosse au bout du compte. Mais la victoire s'était jouée avant le match, avant même les hymnes. Une inspiration géniale et symbolique. Au lieu de gagner la pelouse en courant, suivant la tradition, les Écossais avaient décidé de sortir du tunnel des vestiaires en marchant. Une marche ostentatoire, hiératique, au milieu du stade hurlant. L'affirmation d'une certitude, le défi dans la lenteur. Pénétrés de solennité, implacables dans leur apparent détachement, les Bleus marine avançaient sans hâte vers leur triomphe revanchard.

Le 17 mars 1990, ils ne pouvaient pas perdre.

La tranchée d'Arenberg

C'est très tôt dans la course. Peu d'incidence sur le résultat final de Paris-Roubaix. Un secteur pavé dans la forêt. Des spectateurs nombreux, qui se méfiaient depuis quelques années – une bonne partie des coureurs avaient conçu une filouterie frustrante : échapper aux pavés en s'élançant dans le dos du public, sur la droite. Mais la foule quand même, pourquoi ?

La réponse est dans le nom lui-même : tranchée d'Arenberg. Tranchée, bien sûr : c'est du cyclisme à l'épique, une histoire de guerriers qui rêvent d'entrer dans l'histoire. Les couleurs bariolées ne sont là que pour contraste. Au-dessus du mouvement machinal des pédaliers flotte dans l'air brumeux la mélancolie des âmes grises. C'est un Nord indécis, quelque part entre la Scarpe et l'Escaut. Pour les autochtones, un lieu de fierté sans doute, peut-être même de plaisir aux beaux jours. Mais pour tous les autres, c'est juste un nom pour se faire une petite peur, un espoir de drame – il y en a eu, déjà – à consommer sur écran, dans le confort coupable des débuts d'après-midi dominicaux qui s'ennuient. Autour de la forêt de Saint-Amand-Wallers, les autres noms n'ont rien de rassurant : Wandignies-Hamage, Hornaing, les Trieux-d'Escautpont.

C'est un Nord indécis, aux marches de l'enfer, dans une glaise mentale qui prend à contre-pied les velléités pascales du sous-bois. S'y enfoncer, ne pas s'y enliser pour faire partie des rescapés, ceux qui se retrouveront en tête au presque bout du bout : le carrefour de l'Arbre. S'il pleut, la boue, s'il fait beau, la poussière. Les cuissards, les maillots fluo vont s'effacer dans le brun cendre, le sépia ; les photos seront d'autrefois.

Alors tranchée, mais d'Arenberg : une bouffée de belgitude où dormiraient des connotations germaniques. Le râpement dans le gosier a des arrière-goûts de bière, de no man's land guerrier. Les commentateurs n'ont pas besoin d'en rajouter :

« Dans dix kilomètres, nous serons dans la tranchée d'Arenberg ! »

Fini de rire. Il est beaucoup trop tôt pour s'échapper. Le peloton entier accepte de se faire scarifier ; la tranchée d'Arenberg, c'est un vaccin pour l'épopée.

Loulou dans la piscine

Les caméras de « Téléfoot » aiment traquer ce moment-là. Souvent, le président concerné est sur le plateau dès le lendemain pour le regarder en différé, après une petite nuit, comme disent les commentateurs avec un sourire entendu. Une victoire en Coupe de France, ça se fête.

Ça se fête apparemment toujours de la même manière. Crise de folie au déroulement prévisible dans les vestiaires. Puis la soirée qui se prolonge, et finit immanquablement dans un cabaret parisien, avec du champagne et des girls qui posent pour l'objectif ou la caméra près du staff, des joueurs, une main posée sur l'épaule, à peu près nues, souriantes mais distantes. Ils ont l'air un peu gênés, elles font leur boulot. De temps en temps, une énième chanson boy-scout s'élance et retombe comme si elle avait sommeil.

Mais le grand moment du reportage, c'est dans les vestiaires, disons une heure après l'issue du match. Certains joueurs sont encore tout nus, d'autres commencent à se rhabiller. Après les tchicatchicatchics en tout genre, les « vraiment phénoménal », quelques chahutages respectueux avec la coupe, une seule issue pour les débordements jubilatoires s'impose.

Suivant la personnalité de l'entraîneur ou du président, elle va revêtir des formes différentes. On se demande bien comment les Lyonnais pourraient s'y prendre avec Jean-Michel Aulas, comptable austère d'une entreprise où l'on sourit du bout des lèvres. Avec Luis Fernandez, il n'y avait pas de bile à se faire, c'est lui qui devançait les familiarités. En dépit de sa rondeur, de son paternalisme, Guy Roux ne doit pas être si facile à manier.

Mais la cible idéale pour cette transgression faussement redoutée par l'impétrant, c'était Louis Nicollin. Louis Nicollin et ses vapeurs, ses sueurs, son accent à la Raimu, son entreprise de ramassage d'ordures, son embonpoint affectif. Tout le monde aurait été déçu de ne pas voir cela au moins une fois. En 1990, le Racing, après prolongations, a eu le bon goût de se faire battre par Montpellier. Nicollin seul était conçu pour prononcer à la perfection le « putain les mecs » attendu du dirigeant qui s'ébroue, ridicule et ravi, cheveux collants, costume dégoulinant, triomphant et résigné. On aura vu Loulou dans la piscine.

Le Grave et le Sérieux

« Je n'aime pas les gens graves, ils ne sont pas sérieux. » Jamais cette phrase ne s'est mieux imposée que durant l'été 2005.

D'un côté, nous avons eu le visage inflexible de Lance Armstrong, lancé sur les pentes alpestres aux commandes de sa moulinette à pédales, en quête de son septième titre dans le Tour. Dans son cas, on aurait aussi bien pu aller jusqu'à dix ou quinze, il suffisait de programmer le disque dur. Condescendance avec les flagorneurs, les courtisans, coéquipiers et adversaires réduits à une domesticité rampante, rancune tenace vis-à-vis des insurgés. Certes, celui-là n'aura pas été le premier à triompher par le dopage, mais il l'aura fait avec une froideur de despote, liée à une désagréable utilisation médiatique de son cancer pour faire vibrer la corde sensible.

Avec lui, l'été semblait bien morne et gris. Mais du soleil nous est venu, du Meeting de Paris jusqu'aux orages d'Helsinki. La discipline de Ladji Doucouré n'est pourtant pas une partie de plaisir. Pour qui s'est déjà trouvé face à une haie de 1,05 mètre, pour qui a eu l'occasion de mesurer l'amplitude qu'il faut déployer pour avaler l'intervalle entre les haies en trois foulées, l'exercice a même quelque chose d'austère et de rugueux. Mais tant de champions ont effleuré, enveloppé l'obstacle avec une souplesse de puma. Colin Jackson, Allen Johnson n'étaient pas les moins fauves. Il a fallu que Doucouré devance ce dernier pour s'imposer au monde dans la course la plus relevée et faire oublier sa chute des Jeux d'Athènes.

Autant que la victoire, la manière m'a ravi. Interviewé par le speaker de la réunion après son premier succès à Paris, Ladji s'est lancé dans une analyse très lucide : « C'est surtout à Helsinki qu'il faudra être le plus fort. J'ai fait une faute sur la deuxième… » Et tout à coup, il a abandonné cette rhétorique d'enfant sage pour pousser un grand cri de victoire, incapable de ne pas donner une dimension physique à la joie qui le submergeait. Il a refait le coup à Helsinki. Quelques mots polis jetés au micro, mais en même temps des pas de danse esquissés dans la jubilation totale.

On dit qu'il est très mûr, la suite l'a prouvé – on ne l'a pas vu se commettre dans les émissions à paillettes. Mais il est fou, aussi. Quand il va parler, son petit sourire expectatif et doux semble hésiter entre les deux attitudes. Raison n'empêche pas folie. Sérieux, Ladji.

Quand on a joué aux boutons

Quand on a ouvert la boîte ronde Biscuits Gondolo, plongé ses mains dans l'océan des boutons dépareillés de toutes tailles, de toutes formes. Avant, on demandait la boîte simplement pour regarder les pièces les plus extraordinaires – ah ! ces petits boutons rouges en forme de serrure, avec un minuscule cache doré qu'il fallait écarter pour y passer le fil ! Mais à dix ans, onze ans, c'est autre chose qu'on s'est mis à chercher. Dix boutons de même taille, cinq de chaque couleur, en bois mat pour qu'ils ne glissent pas trop sur la table de la chambre. Deux plus gros pour les gardiens. Quand on a pris deux crayons pour faire la barre transversale des buts, et pétri dans la pâte à modeler quatre poteaux. Un bouton de chemise tout léger pour le ballon.

Quand on a disposé les boutons sur la table. Deux arrières, trois avants, cela suffit : après, c'est la bousculade. Un miracle à chaque fois s'est produit. La chambre n'a plus été la chambre, la table n'a plus été la table. On s'est retrouvé au Parc des Princes ou au Maracanã. On a délivré des pichenettes, de préférence avec le pouce, sur le côté, pour toutes les phases subtiles, les passes, les centres – on a utilisé le majeur pour les tirs au but.

On a joué seul, souvent, et c'était comme une fièvre de faire les commentaires à haute voix. Douis cherche un partenaire démarqué, le trouve en la personne de… Avec un copain, c'était plus drôle. Au début, on était davantage intimidés pour commenter, et puis, après quelques passes, on se complétait. Celui qui ne jouait pas était le speaker – on jouait tant qu'on touchait la balle, mais parfois on la manquait, et surtout on éprouvait au bout d'un moment la nécessité de perdre un coup pour replacer ses joueurs en position stratégique satisfaisante.

Quand on a organisé une Coupe du monde complète, avec résultats sur un petit carnet noir et cela a duré des semaines, poule par poule, avant d'entamer la voie royale des quarts de finale.

Après, il peut se passer n'importe quoi. On apprend qu'il y a des matchs truqués, on vit en direct à la radio la catastrophe du Heysel, les supporters piétinés, des dizaines de morts, et partout la bêtise, des arbitres frappés pour des matchs amateurs, les insultes racistes et même le salut fasciste de Di Canio devant tous les crétins de la Lazio. On a beau savoir tout cela. On croit toujours au foot quand on a joué aux boutons, avec des buts en pâte à modeler et en crayon.

Courir vers l'immobilité

Pourquoi s'inventer cette peur-là ? C'est effrayant d'être dans les starting-blocks, parfaitement immobile, le corps tendu. Dans quelques fractions de seconde on va souffrir. Mais ce n'est pas cela qui fait peur. C'est cette idée de se préparer méticuleusement à basculer dans l'action absolue. Au « À vos marques », on affecte encore la décontraction, on s'essuie les mains lentement sur la ligne, pouce et index écartés au maximum, avec d'infimes ondulations dans la ligne des épaules. Mais le « Prêts ? » est terrifiant. On voudrait être loin, libéré de ce couloir où tout va se jouer dans une solitude obsédée par toutes les solitudes parallèles qui vont marteler la piste et vouloir vous devancer. Le silence qui précède le coup de feu n'arrange pas les choses. On sent son cœur battre si fort – pourquoi a-t-on effectué cette dernière ligne droite d'échauffement un peu trop vite, juste avant le départ ? Et puis ça y est, on est parti. Avant même de se sentir dans la course, on entend quelques encouragements de copains, comme si on en avait déjà besoin. Le reste est souffrance, sur quatre cents mètres. Il faut partir presque à fond, ne ralentir qu'à peine et, à la fin du second virage, sentir cette asphyxie progressive de tout le corps qu'il faut maîtriser dans un effort factice de relâchement.

Je récupère, mains sur les hanches, souffle court, parfois même accroupi sur la piste. Alors vont commencer des choses délectables. Enlever les pointes. Fouler la pelouse, d'une incroyable fraîcheur. Aller s'asseoir à côté de son sac, là-bas près du sautoir en hauteur. Il fait chaud, on n'a pas besoin d'enfiler son survêtement tout de suite. On s'assoit jambes écartées, les bras loin en arrière. La tête renversée, on boit le ciel, le soleil de juin. Des nuages se baladent tranquilles, et chaque seconde qui passe efface un peu la brûlure au creux de la poitrine. La réunion d'athlétisme devient une rumeur composite volant dans le ciel, vibration métallique de la barre de saut tombant sur le sol, éclaboussures légères de la rivière du 3 000 mètres steeple, fous rires chahuteurs. Que c'est bon d'avoir juste encore assez mal pour cueillir toute la paix de l'après-midi soudain révélée. On est bien, si bien d'avoir eu peur, d'avoir souffert pour rien. On se moque du chronomètre, à présent. L'obsession du temps à battre s'est diluée en volupté du temps gagné. Garder les pieds nus est bon, mais enfiler ses chaussettes, remettre son bas de survêtement et un sweat-shirt est bon aussi. Les gestes prennent une lenteur, une saveur inexplicables. On trottine un peu pour récupérer plus vite, pour sentir surtout son corps obéir en sourdine. On existe à peine, tout léger. On n'a aucune envie de regagner les vestiaires. C'est tellement bon sur l'herbe du terrain de foot, après.

Pays d'avant

On connaît mal les coulisses. Certains sports n'en révèlent à peu près rien. Parfois, c'est sur le lieu même de l'épreuve qu'on découvre une séquence d'échauffement. À travers l'aisance, la souplesse, la facilité gestuelle des athlètes, leur énergie d'autant plus spectaculaire qu'elle se manifeste avec un évident retrait, une réserve difficile à estimer, on mesure davantage encore que dans la compétition à quel point leur corps est différent.

Il en est ainsi du ballet des gymnastes au-dessus du cheval d'arçons. Leurs entrecroisements de jambes, leur survol de l'agrès sont juste un peu moins précipités, un peu moins agressifs que dans la recherche de la note, et la sensation d'une agilité aérienne trouve paradoxalement son accomplissement maximal alors qu'ils ne vont pas au bout de leur effort.

Le stade d'échauffement d'athlétisme est étonnant aussi. Les sauteurs, les sprinters y déploient une variété d'assouplissements, de contorsions élégantes, de mises en jambes différées, qui leur donne une dimension féline et fait contraste avec la suite, infiniment plus heurtée. Combien d'entre eux savent préserver dans la course ou le saut cet impérial relâchement ? Quelques-uns des meilleurs seulement, et le plus grand au plan technique : Carl Lewis, dont chaque saut en longueur, chaque ligne droite de 100 mètres savait préserver magiquement dans l'intensité absolue la chatterie veloutée des rituels préparatoires.

Mais la différence la plus étonnante, parfois presque comique, est fournie par les joueurs de football qui sont appelés à entrer en jeu tardivement, le milieu de la seconde mi-temps dépassé. À lorgner du coin de l'œil leur frénétique envie d'entrer dans le bal, leurs étirements dynamiques, leurs sprints forcenés, leurs montées de genoux conquérantes, on se dit qu'ils vont tout casser. Mais à peine ont-ils ôté leur survêtement, furtivement montré leurs crampons à l'arbitre de touche, franchi la ligne blanche, que leur apport au jeu réel devient dérisoire, comme s'ils changeaient d'essence, devaient se résoudre à jouer les utilités, eux qui semblaient détenir les clés du match.

La musique du sport est singulière : plus forte, plus belle encore quand elle joue ses gammes.

Le multiplex

On connaît le générique par cœur. Pom pom po pom… « Le multiplex football, une émission du service des sports présentée par… ce soir en direct du stade de la Beaujoire, à Nantes ! »

C'est bien à écouter, quand on est en voiture. La nuit d'hiver est tombée tôt. Dans la maison qui roule, on se sent protégé. Le multiplex, c'est juste ce qu'il faut pour éviter de basculer vers le sommeil. En quelques minutes, on voit se dessiner une France familière, avec le tour des stades : « Ici le stade Bonal à Sochaux… Ici le stade Gerland à Lyon… Ici le stade de la Route de Lorient… Ici le Stade-Vélodrome à Marseille… » Des lieux mythiques, où l'on s'embarque dans un faux présent riche de connotations, constellé de légendes, d'exploits anciens.

D'ailleurs, le présent du speaker n'existe pas. « Penalty à Bordeaux ! » hurle-t-il pour réclamer l'antenne. Un penalty à vivre en direct, ou presque. Car la clameur du public vous indique l'issue du tir bien avant son commentaire. C'est ce petit décalage qui est bon. On est au secret de l'action, dans le faisceau des phares. On pressent, on devine, on imagine. Rien à voir avec la passivité des matchs à la télévision. Le multiplex, c'est comme un livre. On se la crée, cette petite pluie qui crachine sur les tribunes de Geoffroy-Guichard, cette moiteur maritime qui souffle sur la Beaujoire quand le correspondant garde l'antenne pour le corner.

Et puis l'excitation, l'emphase des journalistes sont délicieuses. C'est la dix-huitième journée du championnat, il en reste vingt, mais chaque but est commenté comme si la face du monde allait en être changée. Tout ce cérémonial de voix apoplectiques, d'engouements pathétiques pour célébrer le presque prévisible, le tout à fait infime… On met en route les essuie-glaces. Nice vient de réduire le score à Lyon.

Affinités électives

Ces deux-là, on sait qu'une tendresse particulière les a liés. Le sommet médiatique en a été le jour où Jean-Pierre Rives, « Casque d'or », a offert son maillot ensanglanté à Roger Couderc. Mais, au-delà de ce que nous avons eu le droit de voir, il nous plaît d'imaginer les liens secrets qui unissaient ces deux hommes.

Il y a un mystère de la voix humaine. Quand le narrateur de *À la recherche du temps perdu* évoque l'approche de la mort de sa grand-mère, il est frappé par l'extrême fatigue qui se dégage de sa voix au téléphone, alors que dans la réalité visuelle elle arrive à lui donner le change. La voix de Roger Couderc, si chantante et si voilée, recelait une humanité, une générosité qui en faisaient certes « le seizième homme de l'équipe de France », mais aussi un ami personnel de chacun des téléspectateurs. C'est un peu comme le lien des Français avec Bourvil : ça ne s'explique pas, mais on sait que c'est vrai.

Pas étonnant que Couderc ait eu le béguin pour le style de jeu de Jean-Pierre Rives. Si la métaphore « Casque d'or » s'adressait à la chevelure de ce dernier, le flamboiement évoqué semblait concerner plus encore son rayonnement sur le terrain. Troisième ligne centre : avec lui, ce poste devenait la clé de voûte de l'édifice. Il faisait partie de la mêlée, se dévouait sans compter dans les tâches obscures, mais, les mains dans le cambouis, le garagiste se tournait déjà vers les demis, les lignes arrière, et toute son attitude semblait leur dire : que vos courses soient aussi belles que notre travail l'a mérité.

Alors Roger Couderc malade, fatigué, trouvait un fils spirituel dans ce jeune capitaine amoureux comme lui d'un rugby chaud, ouvert, vivant. Couderc le lyrique aimait ce garçon si peu prolixe devant les micros. Il y avait entre eux un peu du rapport de Bernard Pivot avec Patrick Modiano. Ils ont écrit les belles lettres du rugby.

Passing-shot

Depuis quatre échanges, il est complètement dominé, contraint de faire l'essuie-glace en fond de court. Sans se précipiter, son adversaire dirige la manœuvre, assène avec de plus en plus d'intensité son coup droit. À plusieurs reprises déjà, ce dernier a été tenté de monter au filet pour parachever le massacre, même s'il n'est pas attaquant dans l'âme. Mais cette fois, le coup, presque dans l'angle, a été tellement dominateur qu'il n'a pu s'empêcher de l'accompagner. Avec un peu de chance, il va faire le point d'emblée, au pire il n'aura qu'à négocier une petite volée sur un renvoi aléatoire.

Et c'est là, dans une fraction de seconde suspendue, que se dessine la possibilité du passing-shot. On pense d'abord que, exténué, le joueur dominé va courir cette fois pour rien, ne pourra qu'effleurer la balle, qu'à la limite il aurait pu renoncer plus tôt afin de préserver ses forces. Mais il trouve dans sa course de défense des ressources inattendues qui le font arriver sur la balle un centième avant qu'on ne l'ait envisagé. À la limite de la rupture, il semble esquisser un geste de désespoir – peut-être même va-t-il lâcher sa raquette.

Là se fomente le miracle. Le pantin désarticulé amorce on ne sait trop comment un geste réflexe du bras vers l'arrière – c'est du côté gauche, il est gaucher. Cette balle dont on pensait l'instant d'avant qu'il avait peu de chance de la toucher, il trouve on ne sait comment le moyen de la gifler, le plan de raquette à l'horizontale, de s'appuyer sur la violence du coup adverse pour lui imprimer un effet sidérant. Le mouvement est magnifique. En un éclair, la défense hasardeuse se métamorphose en claque maîtrisée, ample, déjà dominatrice, et le contraste est incroyable entre le bras impérial qui semble voler seul dans l'espace et le reste du corps empêtré dans sa hâte éperdue, sur le point de chuter.

Le passing-shot rase le haut du filet, finit sa course sur la ligne de fond. À la volée, l'autre a déjà compris, n'a pas même esquissé un geste, assume ce coup de balancier du destin. Contre la perfection des causes perdues, il n'y a rien à faire.

Vikash un peu ailleurs

Jean-Michel Larqué ne doit pas l'aimer : je ne me souviens pas de l'avoir jamais entendu souligner positivement une action de Dhorasoo. Mais peut-être suis-je de mauvaise foi. Car Vikash, c'est mon préféré. Je ne connais pas ses origines. Mauriciennes, indiennes ? Mon fantasme pencherait pour la seconde solution : je l'imagine bien drapé dans un sari, au bord du Gange, silencieux, retiré, laissant couler le flot de l'incompréhension.

Il est très beau mais différent, un peu à côté du monde du football. La barbe naissante lui donne la finesse d'un artiste, la barbe quelquefois rasée la tête d'un enfant. Frêle en apparence, pas bien grand. Son style physique, son allure sont la métaphore de son jeu, de son talent. Le type de joueur qui peut complètement passer à travers un match, paraître transparent. Mais ce qui est en cause alors, ce sont les autres autant que lui. On ne l'aura pas utilisé parce qu'on ne l'aura pas compris. À Lyon, Paul Le Guen avait sous la main ce trésor fragile : la possibilité de faire jouer ensemble Carrière et Dhorasoo, le bonheur absolu de l'intelligence. Mais il a préféré des malabars et, bien sûr, au plan comptable, il n'aura pas eu tort.

Pour choisir Dhorasoo, il faut aimer le risque de l'art. Il peut illuminer un match à lui tout seul, par l'explosivité de crochets courts suivis de passes en profondeur d'une précision millimétrique. Il semble incontournable. Le match suivant le verra disparaître. Présent sur le terrain, mais étrangement diaphane, farfadet exilé ; son gabarit semble alors dérisoire. Il s'éloigne. Ces jours-là, lorsque l'on happe son regard au retour des vestiaires, on sent qu'il n'est pas tout à fait d'ici.

On ne pourra dire de sa carrière qu'elle a été ratée ni réussie. À plus de trente ans seulement il s'est imposé en équipe de France. Et encore… imposé… non, ce terme n'est pas pour lui. Il gardera toujours quelque chose de l'adolescence, je dirais le génie, et d'autres l'inconstance. Mais il n'est pas conçu pour la sérénité fade de l'accompli. Vikash, c'est le football de la mélancolie.

L'éloignement du samouraï

Chacun sa peur. Les dernières foulées des demi-finales n'ont rien livré. Celui qui s'est relevé ostensiblement deux mètres avant la ligne n'en conçoit aucune supériorité. Plutôt le sentiment d'avoir joué avec le feu. Un autre a eu la certitude de terminer en dedans, sobre et léger, mais il serait bien incapable à présent d'affirmer qu'il a ralenti. Tout de suite, cette infime sensation au mollet droit. Pas même une gêne. Peut-être pas.

Entre eux, cette poignée de centièmes qui n'a pas confirmé les résultats de l'année écoulée. Et puis c'était il y a trois heures. Une éternité. Ils se sont effacés très vite au plus secret du stade, ont presque réussi à se faire oublier. Mais deux heures après, ils sont déjà en train de trottiner sur le terrain d'échauffement, superbement absents et routiniers en apparence, transis d'inquiétude au fond d'eux-mêmes. Cauchemar de la chambre d'appel. Installation des starts. Enlever le sweat-shirt, le bas du survêtement. Les dernières accélérations, en collant et tee-shirt, encore une peau à ôter, comme une ultime protection. Les plus extravertis peuvent rouler des yeux fous, se déhancher, tanguer des épaules ; l'indifférence des autres semble toiser ces pitreries, mais peu importe désormais. Chacun sa peur.

Les marathoniens disent qu'ils pensent à ceux qu'ils aiment, à Dieu ou au destin. Mais les coureurs de 100 mètres ne peuvent songer qu'à eux-mêmes, cristalliser dans de minuscules rituels techniques l'espoir, l'attente accumulés depuis des années. L'épreuve reine, sans doute à cause de cet isolement de samouraï qu'il faut assumer la gorge sèche, parfaitement immobile avant de tout donner. Le silence angoissant descend par vagues sur le stade. La plus haute des solitudes. Un présent absolu.

Le dernier mot pour le rétiaire

Combien de temps sont-ils restés au coude à coude dans l'ascension de ce puy de Dôme 1964 ? Cela ne se compte pas en minutes, en secondes. Ce coude-à-coude-là, c'est de l'éternité. Pour la première fois vraiment, on sait qu'Anquetil peut perdre le Tour de France contre Poulidor. Après cette étape, il ne restera presque rien : le contre-la-montre le dernier jour, avec l'arrivée tradition-nelle au Parc des Princes. Si Poulidor prend plus d'une minute d'avance dans la montée du Puy, tout est possible. La configuration de la course accrédite cette éventualité : pour une fois, ils sont seuls, et cette simplicité stratégique semble devoir profiter à Poulidor, que l'on pense meilleur grim-peur – un peu meilleur grimpeur, davantage puncheur en tout cas. Pour une fois, les roublar-dises d'Anquetil sont mises au rancart. Voire.

Pédale contre pédale, ils se frôlent, se touchent du bras à plusieurs reprises. Le Normand. Le Limousin. Deux France qui s'opposent. Leurs origines ne sont pas si antagonistes pourtant : entre les champs de fraises d'Anquetil et la ferme de Poulidor, les racines sont pareillement rurales. Mais ce qui compte, ce sont les choix d'après : d'un côté, champagne, voiture de sport, hors-bord, blonde voyante ; de l'autre, vouvoiement réciproque avec le directeur sportif, respect de bon élève en provenance du certif, épouse inconnue à *Paris Match*. Pâleur arrogante contre humilité tannée. Chance contre malchance surtout, calcul contre naïveté.

Et puis voilà qu'on est dans la vérité de la route, pour un défi qui dépasse le puy de Dôme, et même le Tour de France : la France qui perd peut-elle devenir la France qui gagne ?

On va le croire. On veut y croire. Mais Anquetil résiste tellement. Est-il exsangue ? On sait que nul n'a son pareil pour le cacher. Et Poulidor attaque-t-il à fond ? Si longtemps, les deux silhouettes rapprochées ne livrent pas de réponse. Et quand Anquetil finira par lâcher, on sent déjà que ce sera juste trop tard. Poulidor enfin délivré ne prendra pas sa minute. Car Anquetil ne va pas s'écrouler, mais concéder raisonnablement du terrain, mètre à mètre. Dans ce combat de gladiateurs, il n'était nu qu'en apparence, et le rétiaire aura le dernier mot. Le glaive de Poupou n'aura pas su trancher.

Champion déchu

Trois lignes de faits divers dans un journal généraliste : « L'ancien attaquant de l'équipe de France… a été interpellé à son domicile vendredi soir dans le cadre d'une affaire… »

Ça arrive souvent. Ça ne surprend pas. Pourtant, on n'imagine pas que tous les anciens champions soient devenus des malfrats. Mais cette forme de déchéance fait partie du système. À chaque fois, on revoit une silhouette, quelques exploits. Et puis on imagine un peu… Le succès, l'argent, l'ennui, le mal de vivre, l'alcoolisme, un premier divorce. Un jour déjà, une rixe dans un bar que les journaux ont évoquée. C'est un ancien footballeur, un ancien boxeur, ou un cycliste. Des sports contaminés par les enjeux financiers. Un manager recommandé par des amis, des niches fiscales véreuses, et très vite la dégringolade.

C'est comme si ça collait au sport, cette pente grise de la vie sociale. Comme si l'absence de consistance morale accompagnait paradoxalement quelqu'un qui avait su se plier à la rigueur d'un entraînement draconien, au respect de règles exigeantes. Comme si, après la plénitude volontariste de la jeunesse, le prix à payer était cette veulerie rampante qui finissait par tourner mal pour se trouver au moins un semblant d'identité, après beaucoup de rien. Une philosophie de bistrot accompagne cette dégénérescence bistrotière : « C'est normal, ils sont mal conseillés, et puis ils se prennent pour des dieux, ils se croient tout permis. »

C'est une petite vengeance mesquine de tous ceux qui n'ont jamais fait rêver personne. Car il y a de la grandeur dans ces destins ensoleillés qui passent à l'ombre au presque début de leur vie adulte, malades du silence et de l'oubli. Leur vie d'après voudrait solder les comptes. Mais ils n'ont pas de vie d'après.

Belle fêlure

Je n'ai jamais rencontré Patrick Montel ni Bernard Faure. Longtemps, je les ai simplement appréciés. Mais depuis août 2005…

C'est un matin pour les mordus. Championnats du monde d'athlétisme, qualifications. Helsinki entre deux orages, deux coups de froid, deux averses. Et puis la nouvelle qui vient de tomber, Colette Besson est morte, et la volubilité de Montel a beau prendre un élan professionnel, la phrase tout d'un coup se casse, de vrais sanglots montent dans sa gorge. Faure essaie de prendre le relais, mais il n'est pas en meilleur point. Les yeux s'embuent, et pour une fois on ne se sent pas voyeur. D'habitude, la tristesse à la télé, c'est du cousu main pour l'audience. Et quant aux sports, on en a tellement entendu, de ces commentateurs vedettes qui s'émeuvent, oui, sur eux-mêmes, au moment de quitter leur place, ou de faire semblant.

Mais en ce matin d'Helsinki, les caméras nous ont découvert autre chose. Une petite part d'humanité qui tout à coup déraille hors des chemins balisés. Ils étaient tristes, et plus que tristes, malheureux, ça se voyait, mais ce n'était pas gênant car on avait envie de l'être avec eux. Pas étonnant quand même que cela ait pu être autour d'une figure de l'athlé. Colette Besson. L'incarnation d'une forme de pureté, une de ces personnalités auxquelles on se raccroche pour croire au sport, avec en mémoire l'intégrité d'une longue ligne droite à Mexico où Colette remontait toutes ses adversaires, sans dopage, sans fric en perspective, sans même une titularisation dans l'enseignement.

Patrick, Bernard, je ne sais combien de téléspectateurs vous ont vus tout à coup bouleversés comme on l'est par surprise, avec la jolie pudeur de vouloir continuer. N'ayez pas peur que ces quelques instants aient pu paraître de faiblesse, ou qu'au contraire ils aient pu sembler appuyés. C'était vrai, simplement, et triste et bon de pleurer avec vous. Merci pour ce vrai-là. Vos commentaires ont désormais le goût de l'amitié.

N. B. Du coup, on n'en voudra pas à Patrick Montel de n'avoir jamais réussi à prononcer le nom de la coureuse de 400 mètres américaine Jearl Miles, qu'il a toujours appelée Jearles Miles.

Kiss and cry

Le voyeurisme télévisuel s'y exerce avec une intensité sans égale. Un minuscule studio-salon où les patineurs des deux sexes se succèdent après leur prestation. La dominante kitsch vivement ressentie tient moins à la décoration et au mobilier – large canapé où patineur, entraîneur, chorégraphe viennent s'asseoir ensemble – qu'à l'accumulation dans un endroit aussi exigu de nombreux bouquets de fleurs glanés à leur sortie de piste par les champions, mêlés à la kitscherie non moins certaine de leur tenue – supportable quand elle incarne l'élégance sur la glace, mais d'un pailleté-décolleté-vaporeux délibérément ringard quand elle habille le corps d'une personne assise sur un canapé. Le contraste avec les manteaux, toques de fourrure et autres vêtements hivernaux des membres de l'équipe est lui aussi assez croquignolet. Pour peu qu'on y ajoute quelque mascotte au col enrubanné, le tableau est complet.

À cet ensemble visuellement hétéroclite mais plutôt cosy se surimprime, quand la championne ou le champion est arrivé, une dimension sonore redoutable : on y entend son halètement exténué avec une intensité des plus désagréables. Dès qu'il ou elle commence à pouvoir déglutir, il lui faut faire un petit coucou de la main, destiné sans doute à une famille particulière, quelque part à Moscou, Tokyo ou Chicago, mais qui semble s'adresser aussi à des millions de téléspectateurs témoins seconde par seconde d'un moment délicat : celui où les patineurs se voient contraints de se composer une attitude socialement conviviale, alors qu'ils sont dans l'imminence d'un verdict, et presque du destin.

Échanger alors quelques mots avec son entraîneur, son chorégraphe, pendant que ce dernier vous tapote la cuisse d'un geste parfois rassurant et plus souvent consolateur, tient du prodige. On sait que dans quelques secondes les caméras feront mieux encore en détaillant en gros plan les moindres de vos battements de cils et crispations zygomatiques à la lecture des notes qui vont s'afficher. C'est plus que du direct ; on est beaucoup, beaucoup trop près, mais on reste là, fasciné. De l'inhumanité sur canapé.

« *Mesdames et messieurs...* »

Le speaker était Raymond Boisset. Agrégé de lettres, si je ne m'abuse, et auteur en son temps d'un remarquable record de France du 400 mètres en 47 s 6. Sans doute possédait-il mieux que personne les vibrations pour sentir tout ce que ce soir de juin 1970 allait avoir d'exceptionnel. Mais quand même. La façon dont il a détaché les mots dans son micro reste un grand moment, qui a participé de la fête et lui a donné une dimension à la fois prémonitoire et historique.

400 mètres haies. Première course de ce France-États-Unis. Jean-Claude Nallet, qui s'essaie depuis le début de la saison dans cette discipline, a déjà réalisé 50 s 4, à un souffle du record national de Robert Poirier. Mais cette fois, pas question de piétiner entre les haies : il rencontre Ralph Mann, qui vient de battre le record du monde du 440 yards haies en 48 s 9. Nallet part bien, mais Mann le rattrape à l'entrée de la dernière

ligne droite. Et là, au lieu de se dérégler, de se bloquer, notre Jean-Claude repart de plus belle, creuse l'écart avec l'Américain. Le soir commence à tomber, on allume les projecteurs. Dans le bleu de la nuit commençante, on sent que quelque chose vient de se passer. On ne va pas attendre longtemps.

J'ai en mémoire chaque inflexion de la voix du speaker, avec ce faux détachement, cette objectivité apparente, qui ont dû lui paraître délectables, tant il savait qu'il allait faire chavirer un stade entier par ce constat, tout juste précédé d'une phrase qui en disait long :

« Mesdames et messieurs, la réunion est lancée. » Petit temps de latence pour ménager son effet. Reprise : « Le temps du vainqueur du 400 mètres haies : quarante-huit secondes… »

Le « huit » est monté très haut, souligné à la perfection dans le soir de Colombes. Le reste s'est perdu dans une ovation folle. Cette voix-là, ce soir-là, c'est une petite madeleine qui ne se délitera jamais dans l'eau d'une tisane. En écrivant, j'en ai encore la chair de poule.

Emballez, c'est pour offrir

Celui-là, vraiment, je crois qu'on ne fera jamais mieux. Les circonstances ? Au Mondial de rugby, la France vient de perdre sa demi-finale, contre les Springboks, dans un champ de boue, et de justesse – ah ! cette main de Benazzi qui pose la balle peut-être un poil avant la ligne, mais on n'en sera jamais sûr. Des regrets, mais des regrets aussi dans la manière : les Bleus n'ont pas déployé le jeu dont ils étaient capables. Il reste donc le match pour la troisième place, peut-être pas un immense événement en soi, mais contre l'Angleterre, ce qui change les perspectives. Et voilà que *L'Équipe* nous la joue plus que fine avec ce titre. Emballer, oui, ça ne serait pas trop tôt de lâcher un peu les chevaux, de revenir aux cavalcades du panache. Mais emballer pour offrir, c'est fort dans la polysémie : un petit cadeau comme ça, juste avant de partir, disons un bouquet d'anémones. Et mieux encore, « c'est pour offrir ». Même si ça ne coûte pas très cher, vous seriez gentil de mettre un joli papier autour, bref de soigner le style. Difficile de dire davantage dans la concision complice.

D'autres me reviennent. Certains, plus anciens, pouvaient s'abandonner à un lyrisme qui ne passerait plus guère aujourd'hui. Mais quand même, quand on s'appelle Jean-Pierre Lux, qu'on a été au côté de Claude Dourthe le trois-quarts centre sublime d'une après-midi colombienne où les rosbifs ont frôlé le ridicule, cela doit faire quelque chose de voir le lendemain le journal balafré à la une de ce titre incroyable : « Le bonheur de s'appeler Lux quand c'est samedi de lumière ».

Il y a aussi les grandes tristesses cristallisées, le décalé mais finalement si juste « Fabuleux ! » de Séville 82, la désinvolture inattendue, « C'est leur truc », pour les victoires à répétition du Paris-Saint-Germain en Coupe de France. Et puis tous les calembours plus ou moins signifiants, l'esprit à la Blondin, cette façon de pratiquer la dérision légère à l'égard de ce qu'on trouve tous si important.

Les titres de *L'Équipe*, c'est un genre littéraire. Je m'en suis inventé pour le plaisir. À propos de Marco Pantani, qui triomphe à l'Alpe d'Huez, et se moque alors du classement général : « L'étape, l'étape, oui mais c'est Pantani ». Ou, davantage pour initiés, après un début de championnat euphorique pour les Corses : « Bastia en tête : un feu de paille, ou un peu de Faye ? » Peut-être plus risqué, pour dire la générosité avec laquelle le grand champion éthiopien a su passer le relais à son compatriote Békélé : « La branche sur laquelle il est assis, Gébré sait la scier ».

Ce n'est pas un métier, et c'est pourtant celui dont j'aurais rêvé : titreur à *L'Équipe.*

À la cuillère

C'est une expression péjorative, liée le plus souvent à une étape enfantine de l'apprentissage du tennis.

– Tu sers à la cuillère ?

Une ligne de partage. Si la réponse est positive, c'est qu'on en est encore à peine au stade de pouvoir compter les points. Bien sûr, on peut disputer un set, mais on ferait mieux de se contenter de frapper des balles, ou même de faire du mur.

Il est peut-être alors opportun de se demander si la plus colossale surprise sportive de tous les temps n'a pas été cette scène vécue en 1989 à Roland-Garros : un joueur de dix-sept ans a battu le numéro un mondial Ivan Lendl en servant à la cuillère. Une seule fois, entendons-nous bien. Mais quelle fois ! Au moment le plus dramatique du cinquième set, quand l'irritation du champion tchèque commençait à devenir palpable. Chang renvoyait tout, trouvait des angles impossibles, courait comme un lapin équipé de piles Duracell.

Il y a cuillère et cuillère. Le service à la cuillère de Chang fut presque une antithèse de son principe : une balle vive, décochée avec une incroyable rapidité d'exécution. Il n'y avait pas encore de compteur indiquant la vitesse du service, mais on imagine que cette cuillère-là n'était pas intrinsèquement si dérisoire. Psychologiquement dévastatrice en tout cas. Dérouté, presque écœuré, Lendl se tapa l'index contre le front. Un geste dangereux, ambivalent : c'est lui qui était en train de devenir fou.

Il le fut plus encore sur la balle de match contre lui. Lendl au service. Première balle faute. Et sur la seconde… Chang se rapproche avec une insolence inouïe, s'installe tout près de la ligne du premier carré. Lendl s'énerve, invective l'arbitre, et le stade entier, ravi et médusé, se pose la question : a-t-on le droit de faire ça ? Et après tout, pourquoi pas ?

C'est peut-être à ce moment-là que Chang atteint le sommet de la ruse. Au lieu de risquer l'affrontement verbal, la palabre, il se recule d'un mètre. Lendl se sent obligé de jouer. Il sert. Il perd. Coup de génie et coup de bluff. Il perd comme on perd au poker. Contre un enfant. À la cuillère.

Cocotte nerveuse

Tout un gymnase bourré de tables de ping-pong – une trentaine au moins. Tout un gymnase résonnant seulement du son cristallin et comme fêlé à l'avance de la petite balle blanche. Soixante minimes et benjamins qui jouent ensemble. Et ça joue. La plupart ont déjà le geste, l'ampleur du top spin, qui fait monter le bras très haut pour mieux frotter la balle. C'est seulement chez les seniors, en club, en série départementale ou régionale, qu'on voit de petits pépés venir à bout des jeux sophistiqués avec une poussette de revers implacable et simplette. Mais chez les jeunes, on utilise la technique fraîche, sans prudence ni garantie. De temps en temps on peut entendre un « Allez ! » ou un « Joue ! » adressé par un compétiteur à lui-même. Mais cela sonne snob aux oreilles des autres. On n'est pas au tennis ici, on n'est pas censé s'invectiver. La plupart sont venus seuls ou dans la voiture d'un entraîneur, mais il y a pas mal de pères aussi. Stressés, stressants. J'ai fait partie des pires, ceux qui doivent quitter la salle pour que leur progéniture recouvre ses moyens.

Chaque table est séparée de la suivante par un carré de jupettes de plastique vert montées sur une frêle structure métallique, parfois renversée lors d'un échange lointain. À chaque instant, le match est interrompu par l'arrivée inopinée d'une balle étrangère venue d'un smash voisin. Entre deux matchs, les joueurs en arbitrent un troisième dans leur propre poule. Les rapports sont plutôt sympathiques. Beaucoup se connaissent, et savent leurs chances respectives. Entre la poule et les matchs de barrage, ils partagent leur goûter, et la conversation quitte parfois le tennis de table pour évoquer les profs.

Mais quand même. Il règne sur tout cela une éprouvante nervosité, et presque une sensation d'étouffement. Les scores très serrés, l'obsession du résultat contaminent l'effort et la dépense physiques. Chez les plus jeunes, les pleurs sont fréquents. Chez tous, une tension dévorante. On a du mal à penser que dans cette cocotte-minute du gymnase sous pression ils puissent atteindre la sérénité de la fatigue, la délivrance d'être allé au bout de soi. Une impression de manque flotte et reste suspendue, comme un malaise.

Les conformistes et les rebelles

Les Anglais ont le chic pour nous proposer ces oppositions de style, de caractère, de milieu social. Même si on peut y trouver des connotations politiques, il ne s'agit pas d'une guerre travaillistes contre conservateurs – d'autant que les options de Tony Blair ont quelque peu fait évoluer le concept de travailliste. C'est plus viscéral et plus fondamental chez eux. D'un côté, il y avait Sebastian Coe. Il suffit de le revoir vingt ans après, coiffure impeccable, aisance absolue dans le port du costume de bonne coupe, défendre victorieusement la candidature olympique de Londres 2012 pour se faire une idée de ce qu'il était sur la piste. De l'autre, Steve Ovett, qui dominait également à la même époque le demi-fond mondial. Ovett aussi cockney que Coe pouvait être BCBG, Ovett buveur de bière au fond des pubs, râleur, agressif en course comme en interview, peu coquet, la bretelle lâche du maillot toujours prête à quitter l'épaule. Deux foulées admirables, peut-être un peu plus d'amplitude chez Ovett, un peu plus de vélocité et de puissance chez Coe. Deux palmarès éblouissants, mais à l'évidence une façon différente de s'imposer par l'athlétisme. On voit toujours Sebastian Coe, homme de dossiers et de pouvoir. Qu'est devenu Steve Ovett, individualiste libre, sans doute peu enclin à pactiser avec la société ? Le conformiste et le rebelle.

Nous avons les nôtres. Ceux qui digèrent toutes les couleuvres et ceux qui font le coup de poing. Ceux qui ratissent les ballons et les capes tricolores – le sélectionneur est toujours à leur goût, puisqu'il est le sélectionneur. Ceux qui poussent un coup de gueule quand ça leur fait du bien, et quelquefois sur la pelouse un coup de génie, dans le vestiaire un coup de folie. Les Deschamps et les Cantona.

Pourtant, je crois que les rebelles du sport aujourd'hui n'ont pas le profil d'Ovett ou de Cantona. Ils semblent lisses, presque transparents. Ils ne sont pas les plus spectaculaires ni les plus doués. Mais une force morale pointilleuse les voit se dresser tout à coup contre un système qui parviendra bien sûr à les broyer. Avant de les oublier, on leur aura reproché de cracher dans la soupe – comparaison n'est pas raison, et la méta-

phore parfois confine à l'imbécillité. Basson, Glas-
smann, j'aime ces rebelles discrets que l'on appelle
Monsieur Propre en ricanant. Car dans le sport,
hélas, les vrais conformistes s'appellent Monsieur
Sale désormais.

En somnambule

Il est tombé au tapis à la fin du deuxième round. Pas une glissade, mais un crochet court qui lui a ébranlé soudain la mâchoire, à la sortie confuse d'un corps à corps. Depuis, il s'est repris tant bien que mal, un peu flageolant. Le sautillement de son jeu de jambes n'a été pendant toute la reprise suivante qu'un artifice puisé au fond de ses réserves pour donner le change. Et voilà que le premier gong de fin du troisième round a retenti. Il a gagné son coin sans hâte – surtout ne pas manifester à quel point ce repos est devenu vital. Et le voilà assis sur son tabouret, le visage en arrière, buvant l'air à longs traits, les bras enlaçant les cordes du ring. Le soigneur s'affaire sur son arcade sourcilière. L'entraîneur lui déverse dans les oreilles une logorrhée fiévreuse. Le hochement de tête du boxeur semble approbatif, mais que pense-t-il vraiment ?

On a l'impression que ce discours tout fait

l'agace davantage qu'il ne le réconforte, et contribue même à l'oppresser. Il doit s'entendre dire qu'il a encore toutes ses chances, qu'il faut juste être patient, que le temps joue pour lui. Mais dans son souffle court, son visage tuméfié, on sent qu'il est seulement en recherche d'absence, de repli. Il faudrait que cette pause dure à l'infini pour lui rendre les forces vives qui l'habitaient hier encore devant le miroir, contre le sac de sable ou son sparring-partner. Sa dernière chance pour un titre mondial. Que c'est dur de risquer sa carrière sur un match et de savoir déjà que tout est fini. C'est au-delà de la volonté, du bichonnage dérisoire du soigneur, du harcèlement verbal de l'entraîneur.

Il se sent loin, si seul et comme inerte au milieu de toute cette électricité factice qui se déploie autour de lui. Au milieu du ring, la lumière est si crue, si blanche. Au coup de gong il se lèvera d'un bond, comme s'il était pressé d'y revenir. C'est la vraie vie qu'il faut jouer en somnambule.

Triomphe à l'ombre

C'est un instant mythique. Quelques secondes pour la vie. Certes, le marathon est devenu une course presque comme les autres – tant de joggers du dimanche ont fini par en boucler un, parmi des milliers de concurrents. Certes, lors des grands championnats, on n'attend plus les marathoniens avec cette inquiétude admirative qui régnait à l'époque d'Alain Mimoun ou encore à celle d'Abebe Bikila – si le vainqueur manifestait quelque fraîcheur, tous les suivants étaient emmaillotés dans de grandes serviettes et couvés comme s'ils revenaient de l'enfer. Certes, la course elle-même, passionnante et familière, a quelque peu perdu de son mystère, depuis que les caméras de télévision en traquent le moindre hectomètre.

Mais il y a ce moment, juste avant d'entrer dans le stade. Le gagnant sait qu'il va gagner. Une zone d'ombre se dessine, tunnel anonyme sous les tribunes. Un arc de triomphe en béton brut de décoffrage. Au-delà, un haut rectangle de lumière éclabousse l'avenir si proche, une rumeur encore imperceptible et dont il sait qu'elle va s'enfler, déferler dès qu'il apparaîtra.

Il est seulement lui-même, pour ce passage du tunnel. Dans quelques secondes, il appartiendra au stade entier qui se lèvera. Il sera le vainqueur du marathon. C'est drôle. Il semble que rien ne presse désormais. Plus tard, devant les journalistes, il parlera de son arrivée dans le stade. Il gardera pour lui la délicieuse obscurité. Que durent pour toujours ces quelques foulées sous l'arche où il tient tout, mais où tout reste devant. Que l'ombre fasse belle la lumière.

L'angoisse du tireur

*L'Angoisse du gardien de but au moment du pe-
nalty.* Tout le monde a ce titre de Peter Handke
en tête, sans forcément savoir ce que le livre re-
cèle par ailleurs. Un titre accrocheur par le contre-
sens affiché. On sait bien qu'à propos du gardien
de but et du penalty on ne peut parler d'angoisse. Dans le duel gardien-tireur, le goal n'a pas
le temps d'être angoissé. C'est lui qui joue le rôle
actif, qui fait plus ou moins mine de rien son
petit cinéma. Cela peut aller jusqu'à un signe à
l'arbitre pour indiquer que la balle n'est pas cor-
rectement posée sur le point blanc, ou se limiter
à une façon goguenarde de regarder bien en face
le tireur qui s'approche en s'efforçant de ne pas
croiser les yeux du gardien. Pour le goal, l'alternative est simple : il va plonger à gauche ou à
droite, en espérant que ce sera le bon côté.

Quant au tireur, c'est beaucoup plus délicat.
Il sait que sa réussite est attendue, normale. La

pression sur lui est maximale, surtout quand le penalty est sifflé sur la fin de la partie, et plus encore quand il s'agit d'un tir au but, aux conséquences parfois définitives. Il lui faut alors quitter le rond central en marchant lentement, comme dans un western, entendre toute la rumeur d'un kop, agaçante quand elle prend la forme des lazzis des supporters de l'équipe adverse, mais peut-être plus éprouvante encore lorsqu'il s'agit de la ferveur exacerbée de ses propres supporters. D'habitude, il la met du plat du pied à gauche, à ras de terre, mais ne serait-il pas opportun cette fois de tirer en force du cou-de-pied ? À gauche, ou à droite ? Et pourquoi pas en hauteur au centre, puisque le gardien va plonger ?

La dramaturgie reste prégnante, mais elle a tendance à s'adoucir, depuis quelques années. Tant de titres capitaux se sont joués récemment dans l'épreuve des tirs au but qu'un certain fatalisme accompagne désormais le sacrifice. À l'évocation de la Coupe du monde 98, qui se rappelle tout de suite le tir au but italien sur la barre qui propulsait les Bleus en demi-finale ?

Restent ces quelques secondes où la gorge se noue. Le tireur vit, le gardien joue.

Les flambeurs funambules

Ils sont d'une autre race. Athlètes, bien sûr — quand l'un d'entre eux s'essaie au décathlon, ses résultats sont loin d'être dérisoires. Mais pas seulement. Il y a en eux un mélange subtil entre l'austérité du gymnaste et la désinvolture sexy du surfer ou du véliplanchiste. Cette connotation maritime est liée peut-être aussi à la présence virtuelle d'un casino, dans un coin de leur tête. Car ce sont des flambeurs. Ils jouent pour le jackpot, et misent gros. Tout dans leur attitude traduit le mépris pour la sagesse épargnante. Combien de fois, après une Coupe d'Europe des nations, n'a-t-on pas entendu : « Il aurait quand même pu assurer une barre à 5,40 mètres ? » Combien de fois avant n'a-t-on pas redouté : « Il va encore nous faire un zéro ! », histoire de conjurer le mauvais sort en l'invoquant ?

Ils ne font pas souvent des zéros. Mais une mesquinerie persistante nous pousse à les leur reprocher longtemps. Parce que nous sommes un peu jaloux des perchistes. Trop beaux, trop déliés, trop indépendants. Des anarchistes de luxe, qui jouent avec nos nerfs : « Il a fait l'impasse à 5,80… Il garde un dernier essai pour 5,95… » Ces stratégies dilatoires s'imposent, à la fin du concours. Mais elles nous agacent quand même, à cause de cette lenteur distante avec laquelle ils enlèvent leur survêtement. En bout de piste, la perche nonchalamment posée sur l'épaule, ils ne semblent pas voir défiler à rebours le temps qui leur est imparti, sur l'écran de contrôle. Un soulagement nous saisit quand ils empoignent la gaule à deux mains. Alors le dilettante surdoué se mue en chevalier, puis en acrobate, puis en funambule. Fregolis du geste parfait, ils foncent, attaquent, esquivent. Comment peut-on être à la fois si puissant et si mince, si audacieux et si technique ? Sur le tapis de réception, ils manifestent enfin leur dépit ou leur joie, se tournent vers le public, saluent. Nous existons pour eux. Et cela nous rassure.

Remembrances

C'est le mot de passe absolu, la complicité immédiate : « Théo. Le pied gauche de Théo… Sivori… Les chaussettes baissées de Sivori… Les chaussettes baissées. Il y avait Bonnel, aussi… Omar Sivori… Et les frères Lech… Georges Lech… Première sélection à dix-huit ans… Oui, contre la Bulgarie… Goujon en met deux, ce jour-là… Pendant tout le match on ne le voit pas, et il en met deux… »

C'est un dialogue. On ne se souvient jamais exactement des mêmes choses, mais, une fulgurance en appelant une autre, on se fait la courte échelle à la mémoire. C'est rarement avec un ami proche. Plutôt dans une relation professionnelle, ou pour créer une intimité plus étroite dans un échange qui risque de rester épisodique. Il n'empêche. Ça fonctionne. À chaque fois, les quelques mots sont suivis d'un hochement de tête, d'un sourire satisfait, d'une espèce d'acquiescement plein de gratitude à l'égard du passé. Oui, la vie nous a donné ça, et quelque part on l'a gardé. Ce ne sont pas tout à fait les remembrances des vieillards idiots, mais quand même, c'est rassurant. Si un jour on a l'infortune de s'ennuyer dans une maison de retraite, on pourra toujours se trouver un partenaire pour partager ces bribes nostalgiques de hauts faits pas oubliés.

Seul le sport a ce pouvoir. Pourquoi ? Il y a une fausse humilité dans ces rappels glorieux qu'on se lance à la tête. Bien sûr, on se parle des autres, on semble s'effacer. Mais d'une certaine manière, on est partie prenante de ces attitudes, de ces performances, de ces styles enviés. Si on les a préservés dans sa tête avec autant de précision, c'est qu'on entretient avec eux un rapport privilégié, que les chaussettes baissées de Sivori, le maillot sorti du short de Rocheteau ou de Platini incarnent une désinvolture élégante qu'on revendique sans l'avouer, c'est qu'on espère bien qu'une part infime de soi se reflète dans l'admiration que l'on voue à l'aérienne foulée de Wilson Kipketer.

Les enfants jouent à « On aurait dit qu'on serait ». Adulte, en parlant sport, on joue à « On aurait dit sans le dire qu'on aurait été un peu… » C'est comme ça que je voudrais finir gâteux.

Débordement de tendresse

La natation nous a souvent offert des champions charismatiques. Sans remonter jusqu'aux années 1920, à Johnny Weissmuller, premier homme sous la minute au 100 mètres nage libre avant de devenir Tarzan au cinéma, les anciens se souviennent de Mark Spitz, sept fois médaillé d'or à Munich et physique de star, minceur profilée, œil sombre, moustache noire. Et qui a oublié la fraîcheur de Kiki Caron, deuxième sur 100 mètres dos à Tokyo, et auteur de ce joli geste : quand la gagnante américaine Kathy Ferguson verse des larmes d'émotion sur le podium, c'est Christine qui lui prend la main, pour la consoler en quelque sorte de son bonheur ? C'est la même spontanéité qu'on aime aujourd'hui retrouver dans les réactions de Laure Manaudou, qui donne envie à des milliers de petites filles de s'inscrire dans des clubs de natation.

Mais au plan populaire, la natation souffre d'un

déficit rédhibitoire : la nature de son théâtre. Pour aussi bleu qu'il soit, ce rectangle dur y propose des luttes toujours un peu abstraites, cloisonnées par de larges couloirs. Le téléspectateur n'en reçoit qu'une image à peine déchiffrable, le gros plan empêchant toute idée précise de la compétition, le plan large se révélant bien lointain. Quant aux visages filmés sous l'eau, c'est la pagaille à bulles bleues.

Un seul geste, une seule impulsion, une seule folie a su un jour bousculer la linéarité des rites natatoires. Aux Jeux olympiques d'Helsinki, en 1952, un monsieur d'un certain âge a trompé la vigilance d'un service d'ordre sans doute peu consistant pour plonger dans la piscine tout habillé, et saluer ainsi comme il ne se doit pas la victoire de son fils, Jean Boiteux, vainqueur du 400 mètres nage libre en 4 min 30 s 7. On n'a pas retrouvé depuis un vainqueur français masculin dans une épreuve de natation aux Jeux olympiques. Mais on n'a pas revu non plus un papa dans l'eau, de quelque nationalité qu'il fût. Pour aussi singulière qu'elle ait pu sembler, cette manifestation d'enthousiasme a suscité partout la sympathie. Comme quoi il faut parfois jeter par-dessus bord les pudeurs inutiles. La photo est restée. Tous les papas du monde aimeraient y figurer avec leur rejeton, sauf moi qui ne supporte pas les bassins où je n'ai pas pied. La piscine d'Helsinki ne s'est pas sentie violée, ce jour-là. Et seule la tendresse a débordé.

Raisonnables Barjots

Les Barjots ont gagné. C'est Jackson Richardson qu'on interviewe. Il est assis sur le banc, dans
les vestiaires, torse nu. Il essaie d'analyser posé-
ment les dernières minutes du match, l'instant
où la victoire a penché pour la France. Mais déjà
une serviette a volé par-dessus la caméra pour
tomber sur les dreadlocks du meneur de jeu. Il l'a
écartée avec un petit sourire, mais on se rend
compte qu'il n'est plus vraiment à ce qu'il dit.
Autour de lui, on entend des imitations de cris de
poule, et même des débuts de phrase qui le cham-
brent : « Monsieur Richardson… » Tout d'un
coup, un paquet entier de serviettes lui tombe sur
la tête, et le commentateur lui-même est obligé
de prendre en compte le chahut qui menace l'en-
tretien.

Pas difficile. Ce sont les Barjots, on connaît
leur philosophie du sport, leurs pitreries de cara-
bins en goguette, on peut intégrer tout cela dans

ces instants dérobés à leur joie du vestiaire. Mais l'équilibre, bon enfant de part et d'autre, est homéopathique. La télévision pourrait être franchement mal venue dans un pareil moment à fêter entre soi. En même temps, ces joyeux bidasses sont aussi des professionnels et mesurent au plus près les enjeux médiatiques. Le statut du handball ne peut leur permettre une désinvolture complète à cet égard. Ils lancent des serviettes, mais ils ne vont pas bousculer la caméra.

Quant au rapport des autres joueurs avec Richardson, c'est encore autre chose. Bien sûr, il tente de dire au cœur même de l'interview bousculée qu'il n'est qu'une pièce comme les autres sur l'échiquier. Mais son talent, son allure lui donnent malgré lui une position à part, qu'il assume en répondant tant bien que mal aux questions, et que tout dans son attitude renie par ailleurs. Ses coups d'œil à l'entourage, ses sourires, son absence d'agacement devant les potacheries de ses coéquipiers montrent qu'il est avec eux, que sa patience vis-à-vis du journaliste est seulement de la politesse.

Il y a beaucoup de choses dans ces quelques secondes de télévision confuse : un véritable élan collectif qui n'empêche pas une pointe de jalousie, une folie qui se doit de s'exprimer à la hauteur du mythe naissant des Barjots, avec en même temps un sens aigu de la limite. Même la joie n'est pas si simple.

Corner à la rémoise

Ça pourrait être un nom de dessert. En fait, c'est presque le cas, puisque c'est un mystère. On est tenté de lancer le défi, avec prime à la clé. Qui a jamais vu un but marqué à la suite d'un corner à la rémoise ? Cette option, *a priori* séduisante, coupe court à tous les ceinturages, toutes les prises de maillot, les courses de chien fou pour échapper au marquage qui s'électrisent dès que la balle est posée sur l'arc de cercle, à côté du poteau, du drapeau blanc.

La plupart du temps, le corner à la rémoise n'est pas dans l'intention du tireur. C'est la disponibilité ostentatoire d'un partenaire qui provoque ce choix. Ce dernier arrive à toutes jambes, fort du règlement qui interdit à son adversaire direct de le suivre aussi près du poteau. Alors il s'ébroue, manifeste sa présence à grands gestes fébriles qu'il faut traduire ainsi : passe-la-moi vite en douce, on va le jouer à la rémoise.

Devant cette gesticulation impérieuse, le tireur se sent influencé. Refuser serait considéré comme un affront. C'est ce qu'il fait parfois pourtant, confiant dans la force de son pied droit, de son tir brossé rentrant. Mais plus souvent il obéit à l'invite, moins par conviction que par lâcheté. C'est drôle car, vu des tribunes, le corner à la rémoise est tout l'inverse : un raffinement dans la complicité. On ne va pas se livrer à la traditionnelle bataille de chiffonniers de la surface, on va jouer dans la subtilité.

Subtilité dans ces cas-là rime cruellement avec inefficacité. C'est tellement latéral, tellement confiné, cette disposition stratégique promise à l'étouffement, au mieux à un centre trop vite délivré sous la menace du contre – et si souvent contré. Mais quand même, sur le coup on se laisse prendre. Un dessert, après tout, pourquoi pas ? Plaisir sucré sans importance, et l'on verra plus tard pour l'addition. Comme on commanderait un sorbet aux fruits rouges, on se laisse tenter : je prendrais bien un petit corner à la rémoise.

Le rouge est mis

Le travail de sape est bien amorcé. Le rugby professionnalisé nous livre ses beaux bébés body-buildés dénudés sur calendrier papier glacé qui donnent des idées, paraît-il. Le terrain surtout nous offre les déboulés laborieux, tamponnés, de tous ces gabarits formatés – quelle différence désormais entre un troisième ligne et un trois-quarts ? Les chantres de la métaphore symphonique – le rugby, c'est le sport où tous les gabarits trouvent à s'exprimer — doivent en rabattre. La tunique ras-du-cou-près-du-corps des Bleus souligne ce pseudo-modernisme stéréotypé. Juste pour comparer, regardez une photo d'André Boniface en mouvement sous l'ample maillot à rayures de Mont-de-Marsan.

La France et l'Angleterre sont désormais monolithiques, et l'hémisphère Sud leur fait cortège. La petite flamme de révolte contre la standardisation existe cependant. Il faut aller la chercher dans les prairies sauvages et les décors usiniers abandonnés des territoires britanniques en marge.

Le pays de Galles ouvre, et tout d'un coup un petit vent de folie renaît. L'espace existe encore. Davantage que du panache, c'est une espèce de colère généreuse qui se moque de toutes les précautions, les fixations. Avec les Gallois, le terrain ne semble plus quadrillé, symétrique. L'inspiration de la percée, l'espoir du décalage soulèvent le couvercle. Les gros plans révèlent des visages pâles, des rousseurs de cheveux en bataille, des oreilles décollées, étonnantes au milieu de tous les lobes tuméfiés, une énergie surtout qui ne calcule pas. Avec eux, la balle brûle sur les charbons ardents de l'impatience. Bien sûr, en fin de compte, ils se font souvent contrer, manipuler par les machines implacables et tout le poids de l'argent amassé, la culture du résultat.

Triste culture. Du rugby au moins, on espérait qu'il garderait l'idée que son essence était le jeu, la manière, le risque aussi. Comme il est loin le temps où Gachassin se faisait contrer à l'Arms Park sur une dernière attaque sans doute pas nécessaire – et le grand chelem s'envolait sur l'interception, la course de quatre-vingts mètres de l'ailier gallois Watkins. Aujourd'hui, la France ne perdrait plus un match comme celui-ci. Mais comme à la voir gagner, le plus souvent je m'ennuie. Je vois rouge.

À Tokyo, il pleuvait

C'est un dimanche matin d'octobre 1964. Tout le monde a oublié le temps qu'il faisait en France ce jour-là. Mais à Tokyo, ce jour-là, il pleuvait. Et ça, tous ceux qui s'intéressaient un peu au sport à l'époque s'en souviennent. C'était tôt le matin. La télé ne retransmettait pas d'épreuves avec un tel décalage horaire. Debout dans les cuisines, près du gros poste de radio à œilleton vert phosphorescent dans le salon, ou bien l'oreille collée au transistor dans les chambres, on s'est tous fait une belle petite tristesse. Ensemble. On voulait entendre que Jazy allait gagner le 5 000. On en était presque sûrs. Un peu trop sûrs, c'est ça qui commençait à nous inquiéter.

Jazy, tout le monde ne l'aimait pas. Dans sa rivalité avec le coureur d'Anzin Michel Bernard, beaucoup préféraient Bernard. La gueule et la silhouette du gars qui a souffert, qui souffrira toujours. Celui qui rigole quand il se pince. Jazy, lui, il souriait en couverture des magazines. Beau gosse, œil clair, blondeur crantée, shorts satinés, et puis cette foulée. L'élégance, ça ne s'achète pas. La foulée de Jazy, c'était du concentré de perfection aérienne, le pied qui va chercher loin loin derrière, et le corps frêle reste si longtemps en équilibre sur la poussée. Et plus Jazy planait à l'aristo céleste, plus Bernard nous la faisait au besogneux déhanché rugueux, au coureur du fond de la mine. Pourtant, c'est dans le Nord aussi, à Oignies, que Jazy avait passé une enfance très peu bourgeoise, élevé par ses grands-parents, jouant pieds nus au foot, en attendant que sa mère trouve un bon boulot en région parisienne. Mais depuis, Jazy était devenu un gagnant. À *L'Équipe*, Gaston Meyer le protégeait, il n'effectuait qu'à mi-temps son travail de linotypiste. Dans la France de ces années-là, ça paraissait presque un statut à l'américaine. Sur la piste, Jazy gagnait. À Rome, en 1960, Bernard menait un train d'enfer sur le 1 500, c'est grâce à lui que le record du monde était battu, mais c'est Jazy qui allait chercher la médaille d'argent. Et puis Jazy battait ses premiers records du monde. Les pisse-vinaigre disaient qu'il n'était qu'un suceur, un finisseur. Mais sur un trottoir, quand quelqu'un courait, on disait : « Vas-y, Jazy ! »

Le 5 000 à Tokyo, c'était du cousu main. Sur

le papier, la concurrence ne pesait pas lourd. L'Allemand Norpoth (Norpoth le gitan, comme disait Jazy), l'Américain Bob Schul ? Soyons sérieux. Le Néo-Zélandais Peter Snell, là on aurait pu craindre. Mais il courait le 1 500. Les pistes étaient encore en cendrée. Et quand il pleuvait longtemps... Au fil des tours, la foulée de Jazy s'est alourdie dans la pâte mouillée de Tokyo. Pourtant, Jazy se sent bien. Mais s'il attaque un tout petit peu trop loin de l'arrivée, aux trois cents mètres, c'est sans doute qu'il veut dissiper une secrète appréhension. Il fait le trou. Enfin, pas tant que ça. À l'entrée de la dernière droite, les genoux ne se lèvent plus, derrière, la meute rapplique. Schul, et puis Norpoth, et même Dilinger. Jazy est quatrième. « Capitulation de Jazy » titrera *L'Équipe*, avant de devoir se justifier devant la réprobation générale : « Il y eut des capitulations glorieuses. » Car tout a changé ce jour-là. La nature humaine est ainsi faite : souvent, on attend que les gens soient tristes pour se rendre compte qu'on les aime. Désormais, Jazy on l'aime tous et pour toujours. Il ne sera jamais champion olympique. Bien sûr, il nous fera une magnifique année 1965, battant tous les plus grands, et même le record du monde du mile. Mais c'était pour nous remercier d'avoir été si fort avec lui, juste après l'arrivée, par un petit matin français dont personne ne sait même s'il était vraiment gris. On est partis acheter les gâteaux du dimanche, une petite mort dans la tête. À Tokyo, il pleuvait.

C'est celle-là

C'est la balle de match. La balle du match Forget-Sampras. La balle du match France-États-Unis. La balle de match de la finale de la Coupe Davis. Quatrième set. Tant d'ondes électriques ont déjà passé sur cette rencontre, depuis l'incroyable victoire d'Henri Leconte contre Sampras le premier jour. Forget, battu par Agassi, meilleur dans le double, n'est pas franchement dominateur. Mais il a remporté le troisième set. Toute l'équipe s'est précipitée en courant dans les vestiaires pour une pause frénétique. Boetsch, remplaçant, n'en finit pas de sauter partout. Yannick Noah joue les gourous. On voudrait se convaincre qu'il diffuse autour de lui cette sérénité qui lui manquait souvent, lorsqu'il était joueur. Sa pratique zen du capitanat ne fait que souligner par contraste la formidable fébrilité de tous les autres, maintenus par le grand chef dans un état de fausse décontraction proche de l'implosion.

Et puis voilà. Balle de match. On sent qu'il n'y en aura pas cinquante. Forget jette un regard vers le banc. Vers Noah, bien sûr. En une seconde, on sent tout l'écrasement de cette responsabilité. Sur une balle, donner la Coupe Davis à la France. Et cela tombe sur ce grand échalas livide, mort d'angoisse. Il regarde Noah, puis il hoche la tête en fermant les yeux. Oui, c'est celle-là, je la joue, c'est une balle normale, mais c'est celle-là. Et il la joue, comme s'il n'avait pas peur. On sait qu'il est absolument terrorisé, mais il domine l'échange. Au filet, il n'a plus qu'à pousser la balle dans le court. Ce n'est pas un coup smashé, plutôt un accompagnement prudentissime de ce point immanquable. On a l'impression que la balle ne veut pas se détacher de la raquette. Derrière, il y a un bras qui tremble, un cœur exsangue. Et tout le courage qu'il faut pour aller au bout extrême de sa peur. Oui, c'est celle-là.

Zatopek à l'étude

À l'étude, les soirs d'hiver, au cours moyen deuxième année. Après la longue récré de quatre heures et demie, nous revenions dans la salle de classe. Ce n'était plus pareil. Nous étions moins nombreux, dehors la nuit venait. Je faisais mes exercices de trains et de baignoires, j'apprenais mes leçons, noblesse, clergé, tiers état, étamine et pistil. À son bureau, l'instituteur – mon père – corrigeait nos cahiers. Plus besoin de faire de la discipline. Une bonne volonté un peu sommeilleuse et engourdie gagnait les pupitres. Vers six heures moins le quart, moins dix, j'avais fini.

Nous avions deux livres de lecture. On leur donnait le nom de leur auteur, Renaud pour l'un, Duru pour l'autre. Lire, pour demain, Duru p. 232… Il y avait des textes qu'on n'étudierait jamais en classe, parce que leur sujet n'intéressait guère M. Delerm.

Est-ce cela qui donnait tant de prix à l'évocation du 5 000 mètres d'Helsinki, aux Jeux de 1952 ? Duru… j'ai oublié la page, 155 ? Mais j'ai gardé des phrases par cœur. « Mimoun suit, Mimoun remonte… » La course – je crois qu'il s'agissait d'un extrait de *La Quinzième Olympiade* de B. Cacérès – était évoquée avec un envoûtant lyrisme. La chute de l'Anglais Chataway à l'entrée de la dernière ligne droite en constituait le sommet tragique. Une photo en noir et blanc, brouillée par la mauvaise qualité de sa reproduction neigeuse, illustrait ce moment précis. Sortie du dernier virage. L'implacable Zatopek lancé vers la victoire avec son masque de souffrance, Mimoun, puis l'Allemand Schade, et, couché contre la lice, le malheureux Chataway.

Je l'ai faite cent fois, la course d'Helsinki, dans la tiédeur des soirs d'étude, juste avant six heures. Le sport, c'était ce qu'on n'expliquerait pas en classe, et devenait du coup si désirable. Un monde pour moi seul. Des mythes à enfourcher, à amplifier au creux de soi. Des silhouettes en noir et blanc, des phrases. La gloire et la tristesse. Toute la vie devant pour aimer ça.

139

DU MÊME AUTEUR

LE MIROIR DE MA MÈRE, en collaboration avec Marthe Delerm (Folio n° 4246).

AUTUMN (prix Alain-Fournier 1990), (Folio, n° 3166).

LES AMOUREUX DE L'HÔTEL DE VILLE (Folio n° 3976).

MISTER MOUSE OU LA MÉTAPHYSIQUE DU TERRIER (Folio n° 3470).

L'ENVOL.

SUNDBORN OU LES JOURS DE LUMIÈRE (prix des Libraires 1997 et prix national des Bibliothécaires 1997) (Folio n° 3041).

PANIER DE FRUITS.

LE PORTIQUE (Folio n° 3761).

Aux Éditions Milan

C'EST BIEN.

C'EST TOUJOURS BIEN.

Aux Éditions Stock

LES CHEMINS NOUS INVENTENT.

Aux Éditions Champ Vallon

ROUEN (collection « Des villes »).

Aux Éditions Flohic

INTÉRIEUR (collection « Musées secrets »).

Aux Éditions Magnard Jeunesse

SORTILÈGE AU MUSÉUM.

LA MALÉDICTION DES RUINES.

LES GLACES DU CHIMBAROZO.

Aux Éditions Fayard

PARIS L'INSTANT. Photographies de Martine Delerm.

TRACES. Photographies de Martine Delerm.

THE GREEKS

H. D. F. KITTO

PENGUIN BOOKS

BALTIMORE · MARYLAND

Penguin Books Ltd, Harmondsworth, Middlesex

U.S.A.: Penguin Books Inc., 3300 Clipper Mill Road, Baltimore 11, Md

AUSTRALIA: Penguin Books Pty Ltd, 762 Whitehorse Road,
Mitcham, Victoria

—

First published 1951
Reprinted 1951, 1952, 1954, 1956
Reprinted with revisions 1957
Reprinted 1958, 1959, 1960, 1961

Made and printed in Great Britain
by R. & R. Clark Ltd
Edinburgh

CONTENTS

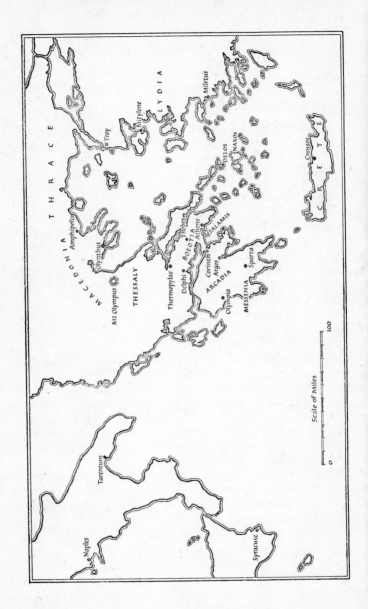

INTRODUCTION

THE reader is asked, for the moment, to accept this as a reasonable statement of fact, that in a part of the world that had for centuries been civilized, and quite highly civilized, there gradually emerged a people, not very numerous, not very powerful, not very well organized, who had a totally new conception of what human life was for, and showed for the first time what the human mind was for. This statement will be amplified and, I hope, justified in what follows. We can begin the amplification now by observing that the Greeks themselves felt, in quite a simple and natural way, that they were different from any other people that they knew. At least, the Greeks of the classical period habitually divided the human family into Hellenes and barbarians.[1] The pre-classical Greek, Homer for instance, does not speak of 'barbarians' in this way; not because he was more polite than his descendants, but because this difference had not then fully declared itself.

It was not, in fact, a matter of politeness at all. The Greek word 'barbaros' does not mean 'barbarian' in the modern sense; it is not a term of loathing or contempt; it does not mean people who live in caves and eat their meat raw. It means simply people who make noises like 'bar bar' instead of talking Greek. If you did not speak Greek you were a 'barbarian', whether you belonged to some wild Thracian tribe, or to one of the luxurious cities of the East, or to Egypt, which, as the Greeks well knew, had been a stable and civilized country many centuries before Greece existed. 'Barbaros' did not necessarily imply contempt. Many Greeks admired the moral code of the Persians and the wisdom of the Egyptians. The debt – material, intellectual and artistic – which the Greeks owed to the peoples of the East was

1. I shall use the term 'classical' to designate the period from about the middle of the seventh century B.C. to the conquests of Alexander in the latter part of the fourth.

rarely forgotten. Yet these people were 'barbaroi', foreigners, and classed with (though not confused with) Thracians, Scythians and such. Only because they did not talk Greek? No; for the fact that they did not talk Greek was a sign of a profounder difference: it meant that they did not live Greek or think Greek either. Their whole attitude to life seemed different; and a Greek, however much he might admire or even envy a 'barbarian' for this reason or that, could not but be aware of this difference.

We may note in passing that one other race (not counting ourselves) has made this sharp distinction between itself and all other foreigners, namely the Hebrews. Here were two races, each very conscious of being different from its neighbours, living not very far apart, yet for the most part in complete ignorance of each other and influencing each other not at all until the period following Alexander's conquests, when Greek thought influenced Hebraic thought considerably – as in *Ecclesiastes*. Yet it was the fusion of what was most characteristic in these two cultures – the religious earnestness of the Hebrews with the reason and humanity of the Greeks – which was to form the basis of later European culture, the Christian religion. But Gentile and Barbaros were very different conceptions; the one purely racial and religious, the other only incidentally racial and not in the least religious. What then led the Greek to make this sharp division? And had it any justification?

It would be one answer, a true and sufficient one, to say that while the older civilizations of the East were often extremely efficient in practical matters and, sometimes, in their art not inferior to the Greeks, yet they were intellectually barren. For centuries, millions of people had had experience of life – and what did they do with it? Nothing. The experience of each generation (except in certain purely practical matters) died with it – not like the leaves of the forest, for they at least enrich the soil. That which distils, preserves and then enlarges the experience of a people is Literature. Before the Greeks, the Hebrews had created religious poetry, love-poetry, and the religious poetry and oratory of the Prophets, but literature in all its other known forms (except the novel) was created and perfected by the Greeks. The difference between 'barbarian' historical chronicles and Thucydides is the difference between a child and a man who can not only understand, but also make his understanding available to others. Epic poetry, history and drama; philosophy in all its branches, from metaphysics to economics; mathematics and many of the natural sciences – all these begin with the Greeks.

Yet if we could ask an ancient Greek what distinguished him from the barbarian, he would not, I fancy, put these triumphs of the Greek mind first, even though he was conscious that he set about most things in a more intelligent way. (Demosthenes, for example, rating his fellow-citizens for their spineless policy towards Philip of Macedon, says 'You are no better than a barbarian trying to box. Hit him in one spot, and his hands fly there; hit him somewhere else, and his hands go there.') Nor would he think first of the temples, statues and plays which we so justly admire. He would say, and in fact did say, 'The barbarians are slaves; we Hellenes are free men'.

And what did he mean by this 'freedom' of the Greek, and the 'slavery' of the foreigner? We must be careful not to interpret it in political terms alone, though the political reference is important enough. Politically it meant, not necessarily that he governed himself – because oftener than not he didn't – but that however his polity was governed it respected his rights. State affairs were public affairs, not the private concern of a despot. He was ruled by Law, a known Law which respected justice. If his state was a full democracy, he took his own share in the government – and democracy, as the Greek understood it, was a form of government which the modern world does not and cannot know; but if it was not a democracy, he was at least a 'member', not a subject, and the principles of government were known. Arbitrary government offended the Greek in his very soul. But as he looked out upon the wealthier and more highly civilized countries of the East, this is precisely what he saw: palace-government, the rule of a King who was absolute; not governing, like the early Greek monarch, according to Themis, or a law derived from Heaven, but according to his private will only; not responsible to the gods, because he was himself a god. The subject of such a master was a slave.

But 'eleutheria' – of which 'freedom' is only an incomplete translation – was much more than this, though this is already a great deal. Slavery and despotism are things that maim the soul, for, as Homer says, 'Zeus takes away from a man half of his manhood if the day of enslavement lays hold of him'. The Oriental custom of obeisance struck the Greek as not 'eleu- theron'; in his eyes it was an affront to human dignity. Even to the gods the Greek prayed like a man, erect; though he knew as well as any the difference between the human and the divine. That he was not a god, he knew; but he was at least a man. He knew that the gods were quick to strike down with- out mercy the man who aped divinity, and that of all human qualities they most approved of modesty and reverence. Yet he remembered that God and Man were sprung of the same parentage:

'One is the race of Gods and of men; from one mother[1] we both draw our breath. Yet are our powers poles apart; for we are nothing, but for them the brazen Heaven endures for ever, their secure abode.'

So says Pindar, in a noble passage sometimes mistranslated by scholars who should know better, and made to mean: 'One is the race of Gods, and that of man is another'. But Pindar's whole point here is the dignity and the weakness of man; and this is the ultimate source of that tragic note that runs through all classical Greek literature. And it was this con- sciousness of the dignity of being a man that gave such urgency and intensity to the word that we inadequately translate 'freedom'.

But there is more than this. There were 'barbaroi' other than those living under Oriental despotism. There were for example peoples of the North, living in tribal conditions from which the Greeks themselves had not long escaped. What was the great difference between these and the Greeks, if it was not merely the superior culture of the Greeks?

It was this, that the Greeks had developed a form of polity

1. The Earth-Mother.

which we clumsily and inaccurately translate 'city-state' – because no modern language can do any better – which both stimulated and satisfied man's higher instincts and capabilities. We shall have much to say about the 'city-state'; here it will be enough to remark that the city-state, originally a local association for common security, became the focus of a man's moral, intellectual, aesthetic, social and practical life, developing and enriching these in a way in which no form of society had done before or has done since. Other forms of political society have been, as it were, static; the city-state was the means by which the Greek consciously strove to make the life both of the community and of the individual more excellent than it was before.

This certainly is what an ancient Greek would put first among his countrymen's discoveries, that they had found out the best way to live. Aristotle at all events thought so, for that saying of his which is usually translated 'Man is a political animal' really means 'Man is an animal whose characteristic it is to live in a city-state'. If you did not do this, you were something less than man at his best and most characteristic. Barbarians did not; this was the great difference.

In compiling this account of a people about whom such a lot might be said I have allowed myself the luxury of writing on points that happen to interest me, instead of trying to cover the whole field in a systematic and probably hurried way; also, I have stopped short with Alexander the Great, that is with the end of the city-state: not because I think the Greece of the next few centuries unimportant, but on the contrary because I think it far too important to be tucked away in a perfunctory final chapter – which is often what happens to it. If the gods are kind, I shall deal with Hellenistic and Roman Greece in a second volume.

I have made the Greeks speak for themselves as much as I could, and I hope that a reasonably clear and balanced picture emerges. I have tried not to idealize, though I deal with the great men rather than the little ones, and with philosophers rather than rogues. It is from the mountain-tops that one gets the views: and rogues are much the same everywhere – though the Greek rogue seems rarely to have been dull as well as wicked.

II

THE FORMATION OF THE
GREEK PEOPLE

XENOPHON tells an immortal story which, since it is immortal, can be retold here. It concerns an incident in the march of the Ten Thousand through the awful mountains of Armenia towards the Black Sea. These men were mercenary soldiers who had been enlisted by Cyrus the Younger to help him drive his half-brother from the Persian throne – not that Cyrus told them this, for he knew very well that no Greek army would willingly march three months from the sea. However, by deceit and cajolery he got them into Mesopotamia. The disciplined and well-armed Greeks easily defeated the Persian army, but Cyrus was killed. An awkward position for everybody. The Persians suddenly had on their hands an experienced army that they could do nothing with, and the Greeks were three months' march from home, without a leader, paymaster or purpose, an unofficial, international body, owing allegiance to no one but itself. They might have run amok; they might have degenerated into robber-bands to be destroyed piecemeal; they might have been incorporated into the Persian army and empire.

None of these things happened. They wanted to go home – but not through the length of Asia Minor, of which they had seen quite enough. They decided to strike north, in the hope of reaching the Black Sea. They elected a general, Xenophon himself, an Athenian country-gentleman, and he was as much Chairman as he was General, for they decided policy in concert. With the self-discipline that these turbulent Greeks often displayed, they held together, week after week, and made their way through these unknown mountains, conciliating the natives when they could, and fighting them when conciliation failed.

Some perished, but not many; they survived as an organized force. One day, as we read in Xenophon's quite unheroic *Anabasis*, Xenophon was commanding the rearguard while the leading troops were climbing to the head of a pass. When they got to the top they suddenly began to shout and to gesticulate to those behind. These hurried up, imagining that it was yet another hostile tribe in front. They, on reaching the ridge, began to shout too, and so did each successive company after them – all shouting, and pointing excitedly to the north. At last the anxious rearguard could hear what they were all shouting: it was 'Thalassa, thalassa'. The long nightmare was over, for 'thalassa' is the Greek for 'sea'. There it was, shimmering in the distance – salt water; and where there was salt water, Greek was understood, and the way home was open. As one of the Ten Thousand said, 'We can finish our journey like Odysseus, lying on our backs'.

I recount this story, partly on Herodotus' excellent principle, that a good story never comes amiss to the judicious reader, partly because of the surprising fact that this eminently Greek word 'thalassa', 'salt-water', appears to be not a Greek word at all. To be more precise: Greek is a member of the Indo-European family of languages, akin to Latin, Sanskrit, and the Celtic and Teutonic tongues: languages carried by migrations from somewhere in Central Europe south-east to Persia and India, so that the Indian 'raj' is akin to the Latin 'rex' and the French 'roi', southwards into the Balkan and Italian peninsulas, and westwards as far as Ireland. Yet the Greek for so Greek a thing as the sea is not Indo-European. Where did the Greeks find it?

A companion-picture to Xenophon's may explain that – though the earliest authority for this story is the present writer. Some ten, or maybe fifteen, centuries before the march of the Ten Thousand a band of Greek-speaking people was making its way south, out of the Balkan mountains, down the Struma or Vardar valley in search of a more comfortable home. Suddenly they saw in front of them an immense amount of water, more water than they or their ancestors had ever seen before. In astonishment, they contrived to ask the natives what that was: and the natives, rather puzzled, said, 'Why, thalassa, of course'. So 'thalassa' it remained, after nearly all the other words in that language had perished.

It would of course be very rash to base upon a single word any theory of the origins of a people: foreign words are adopted, and can strangle native words, with great ease. But in the mature Greek civilization of the fifth and subsequent centuries (B.C.), there are many features which are most easily explained if this civilization was the direct offspring of two earlier ones, and there is some evidence that in fact it was.

Let us examine a few more words. There are in Greek two classes of words which are not Greek by origin, words ending (like 'thalassa') in -assos or -essos, mostly place names – Halicarnassos, Herodotus' birthplace, is an example – and words ending in -inthos, such as 'hyacinthos', 'Corinthos', 'labyrinthos', all of which are familiar to us. Foreign importations? Corinth originally a foreign settlement? Possibly. What is more surprising than 'Corinth' is that 'Athens' is not a Greek name, nor the goddess Athena. Sentiment at least rebels against the idea that Athens owes her name to foreigners intruding upon Greeks – and so does tradition, for the Athenians were one of two Greek peoples who claimed to be 'autochthonous', or 'born of the soil'; the other one being the Arcadians, who were settled in Arcadia before the birth of the moon.

Now, there is reason, as we shall see presently, for treating traditions with respect, and there is at least some plausibility in these Arcadian and Athenian legends; for Arcadia is the mountainous heart of the Peloponnese, difficult to conquer (as the Turks found later), and Attica, the territory of the Athenians, has thin soil not very attractive to invaders or immigrants. Athena then is non-Greek, and there is some reason to think that she and her people are also pre-Greek, which is a different thing.

Another Athenian legend may take us a little further. One of the best known of Athenian stories was that there was once a contest between Athena and the god Poseidon for the possession of the Acropolis. Athena came off best, but the god also obtained a footing there. Now, Poseidon appears to be a

Greek god – it might perhaps be less confusing to say 'Hellenic': Athena is non-Hellenic. The interpretation of legends like these is not a matter of certainty, but it is tempting to see in this one the memory of the collision, in Attica, of an incoming Hellenic people with the indigenous worshippers of Athena, a collision which found a peaceful issue, with the natives absorbing the incomers.

The later Greeks themselves believed in an original non-Hellenic population which they called Pelasgian, remnants of which still remained pure in classical times, speaking their own language. Herodotus, who was interested in nearly everything that came to his notice, was interested in the origin of the Greeks; and of the two main branches of the later Greek people, the Ionians and the Dorians, he asserts that the Ionians were Pelasgian by descent. Indeed, in distinction to the Ionians he calls the Dorians 'Hellenic'. He goes on to say 'What language the Pelasgians used I cannot say for certain, but if I may conjecture from those Pelasgians who still exist ... they spoke a barbarian language' – meaning by 'barbarian' no more than 'non-Hellenic'.

This tallies well enough with what we have conjectured about the Athenians, for they claimed to be the leaders and the metropolis of the Ionian Greeks, and they also claimed to be indigenous.

This then would be the picture, if we could trust the traditions. An indigenous non-Hellenic race inhabited Attica and the Peloponnese. At some time that cannot be determined Greek-speaking peoples from further north migrated into this region – no doubt very gradually – and imposed their language on them, much as the Saxons did on England. This was not a sudden, catastrophic invasion: the archaeological records show no sudden break in culture before the Dorian invasion of about 1100. Pelasgian 'pockets' which escaped the influence of these incomers continued to speak a language unintelligible to Herodotus.

I have said that the date of these migrations cannot be determined; it is, however, possible to set a lower limit. It is quite certain that these Dorian Greeks of about 1100 were not the first bringers of the Greek tongue to Greece, for they were preceded, by at least two centuries, by Achaean Greeks, about whom we know something, though not enough. Some of these have, to generations of Englishmen, been more familiar than our own Egberts and Egwiths and Aelfrics, for Atreus' sons Agamemnon and Menelaus were Achaeans, and Achilles and the other heroes of whom Homer was to write, three hundred years or so later.

Were these Achaeans then the first Greek-speakers in Greece? Nothing obliges us to think so; indeed, nothing but the tradition really obliges us to think that anything other than Greek was ever the dominant language in Greece, for it is conceivable, though not perhaps very likely, that non-Hellenic names like Athens are intrusions.

But is there any reason to believe these traditions? A hundred years ago historians said no. Grote wrote, for example, that the legends were invented by the Greeks, out of their inexhaustible fancy, to fill in the blank space of their unknown past. To believe that a King Minos had ever ruled in Crete, or that a Trojan War had ever been fought, would be foolish: equally foolish to deny the possibility. An earlier historian of Greece, Thucydides, treated the traditions quite differently, as historical records – of a certain kind – to be criticized and used in the appropriate way.

His account of the Trojan War, given in the early chapters of his history, is a fine example of the proper handling of historical material – for it never occurred to Thucydides that he was not dealing with historical material. On Minos the legendary King of Crete he writes:

Minos is the earliest ruler we know of who possessed a fleet, and controlled most of what are now Greek waters. He ruled the Cyclades, and was the first colonizer of most of them, installing his own sons as governors. In all probability he cleared the sea of pirates, so far as he could, to secure his own revenues.

Thucydides, like most Greeks, believed in the general truth of the traditions: modern writers disbelieved. But Grote's admirable history had not passed through many editions before

Schliemann went to Mycenae and Troy and dug up something uncommonly like Homer's two cities: and subsequently Sir Arthur Evans went to Crete and practically dug up King Minos and his island-empire. It is at least abundantly clear that from early in the third millennium to about 1400 B.C. – a period as long as from the Fall of Rome to the present day – Crete, especially the city of Cnossos, was the centre of a brilliant civilization which gradually spread in all directions over the Aegean world. Since Cnossos was unfortified, its masters must have controlled the seas, just as Thucydides said.

This is the outstanding example of the general reliability of tradition – in the Greek world: parallels elsewhere are not hard to find. Sometimes legends have been corroborated to an almost absurd degree. The story of the Minotaur is an example. There was a story – which Thucydides is too austere to mention – that each year the Athenians had to pay the tribute of seven youths and seven maidens to a dreadful monster, the Minotaur, who lived in a labyrinth at Cnossos, until they were set free by the royal prince Theseus, who slew the Minotaur, aided by Ariadne and the ball of string which she gave him to guide him out of the labyrinth. Such was the legend: here are some facts. Of the name 'Minotauros', the first half is obviously Minos, and the second half 'tauros' is the Greek for a bull; and from what Evans found at Cnossos – friezes, statuettes and the like – it is quite clear that these Cretans worshipped the bull. Then, if anything ancient looks like a labyrinth it is the ground-plan of the vast palace which Evans dug up. Further, there is abundant evidence that these Minoan Cretans used, as a symbol of divinity, or of authority, a double-headed axe of the kind that the later Greeks called 'labrys'. Finally, Attica certainly came under Cretan influence culturally, quite possibly then politically as well: it is therefore not at all unlikely that the lords of Cnossos did in fact take hostages for good behaviour from noble Athenian families, just as the Turks did many centuries later. Theseus seems to be a mistake, as he comes from a later period, and so far no one has substantiated the romantic Ariadne or found the string: otherwise the legend emerges with credit.

Similarly with Troy. Of the nine superimposed cities on that site, Troy VI was destroyed by fire at about the traditional date of the Trojan War (1194–1184). One of Homer's standing epithets for Troy is 'of the wide way': Troy VI did have a wide street running around the city just inside the walls. These walls were built by two gods and one mortal, and the sector built by the mortal was weaker and proved vulnerable: the walls of Troy VI were weaker at one point (where access was more difficult), and this corresponds with Homer's description.

So it is with many of the genealogies. Of the Homeric heroes most could trace their line up through three generations, then comes a god. With some irreverence this has been suggested as meaning 'And who *his* father was, God only knows': with more reverence, one may suggest alternatively that it represents a claim to divine favour made by the founder of a dynasty: 'By the grace of God, your new King'. In the other direction, these genealogies peter out two generations after the Trojan War, which would bring us to the traditional date of the Dorian invasion, about 1100, at which time (as excavation has shown) all existing cities on the mainland were destroyed. Again, the longest genealogies known were those of the royal houses of Attica and Argos; these would take us back to about 1700 B.C. We have already seen that the Athenians, with some plausibility, claimed to be oldest inhabitants, but there is also this point: Athens and Argos were conspicuous among Greek cities in the Classical Age in having as their chief deity not a god but a goddess, Athena and Argive Hera. Now, many cult-images have been discovered in Crete, and they make it fairly clear that this people worshipped a goddess. If there was a god, he was subordinate. The goddess was evidently a nature-goddess, symbolic of the fertility of the soil. The Hellenic deities were predominantly male. It is at least suggestive that these two people, the Athenians and the Argives, which had the longest genealogies, worshipped female deities, one of whom, and probably both, had non-Hellenic names. Zeus (Latin *deus* 'god') is purely Hellenic. He had a very shadowy Hellenic consort Diône, whose name is akin to his own. But in Greek mythology his consort was Argive Hera, and we are assured by a Homeric Hymn that Argive Hera had been reluctant to marry him – not unreasonably, as it turned out. Once more an obvious interpretation lies to hand, in the fusion of two peoples of different cultures, apparently of different languages, and possibly therefore of different race.

We see then that traditions which profess to be historical are by no means to be dismissed out of hand. Herodotus, an avid and not uncritical enquirer, regarded the Ionian Greeks as a 'barbarian' people who had been Hellenized: it may yet be shown that he is right. If so, we should certainly expect to find that the process was a very gradual one: only the Dorian Invasion presents the appearance of a general conquest.

Our brief discussion has touched on another point: gods and goddesses. In the religious observances of classical Greece there is a kind of dualism. This is rather surprising in so philosophic a people, and is most easily understood on the assumption that Greek culture is the offspring of two profoundly different ones. From a distance the Olympian Pantheon of the twelve gods, presided over by Zeus, looks impressively solid, but on closer inspection this solidity dissolves. The goddesses, as we have seen, turn out not even to have Greek names, and the keystone of the whole arch, the marriage of Zeus with Hera, looks very like a dynastic marriage. Moreover, there was a whole region of cult and belief that had only an adventitious connexion with Olympus. The true Olympian cults were based on the ideas of a god who protected the tribe or the state or the family, and took the guest or the suppliant under his care; the god was, in fact, intimately connected with the social organism. He was also a nature-god, but only in the sense that he explained certain natural forces: Zeus sent the rain and lightning, and Poseidon stirred up the sea and shook the earth. Into this system Athena was entirely absorbed: she became the daughter of Zeus, the armed protectress of the city, the giver of social wisdom. But her Owl reminds us of her origin – a nature-goddess, not a goddess of the tribe. Cults based on the mysterious life-giving powers of nature existed in Greece side by side with the Olympian cults and in sharp contrast with them; for instance, these mystery cults appealed to the individual, the Olympian concerned the group: these admitted anyone, bond or free, the Olympian admitted only members of the group: these taught doctrines of rebirth, regeneration, immortality; the Olympian taught nothing, but were concerned with the paying of the honours due to the immortal and unseen members of the community. They are entirely different conceptions of religion, and it is roughly true to say that the god-conception is European and the goddess-conception Mediterranean; the goddesses come down in straight descent from Minoan Crete.

It is time now to say something about this age-long civilization which was a dim memory to the historical Greeks and pure fancy to our grandfathers. Chronologically, it begins in the Neolithic stage at about 4000 B.C., has reached the Bronze Age by 2800, and thereupon flourishes, with periods of great brilliance alternating with periods of relative stagnation, until Cnossos is finally sacked and destroyed at about 1400. Geographically, it begins in Cnossos, then spreads to other sites in Crete, then gradually to the islands of the Aegean and to many parts not only of southern and central Greece but also to the coasts of Asia Minor and to Philistia. From 1600 certain places on the Greek mainland begin to rival Crete herself as centres of civilization, and after the destruction of Cnossos become its heirs: among these the chief is Mycenae, whence this late branch of the old Minoan, or Aegean, culture (though the first to be rediscovered) is known as the Mycenaean civilization. It is a late stage of this, imperfectly remembered, which is the background of the *Iliad*.

It is impossible to say much here about this civilization. The absence of fortification attests that it was politically based on sea-power; the vast palaces attest its wealth. The extremely complex plan of the palace at Cnossos suggests that it was a centre of administration rather than a stronghold. We may safely attribute a palace-government to these ancient Cretans; it is impossible to fit any kind of popular government into the ruins. The painted vases, friezes, statuettes and other material remains show that this civilization was one of great elegance, vigour, gaiety and material well-being. There is the often quoted remark of the French scholar contemplating the Cretan ladies on a frieze: 'mais ce sont des Parisiennes!' And – to turn to a rather different aspect of human culture – the drainage system of the great palace was hailed as 'absolutely English'. The pottery, big and little, shows in its best periods a marvellous craftsmanship and sense of design. It can indeed be fussy, filling with ornament what should be empty space; on the other hand it sometimes uses empty space with an assurance and security reminiscent of Chinese art at its best. In general, we get the impression of a gay, aristocratic culture, with hunting, bull-baiting and acrobatics well to the fore.

But other sides of their civilization were, presumably, as important to these Minoans as their art – possibly more so. In books about past civilizations art is commonly given undue space – for two reasons. In the first place, it is easier to photograph a temple or a painting than a moral creed or a political philosophy; and in the second place, many peoples have been inarticulate except through their art. In fact, the Greeks and the Jews are the first ancient peoples who were not. So it is with the Minoans. Their art speaks to us directly, nothing else speaks at all, except indirectly, through inferences. Their remains are abundant, and, in both senses of the word, unquestionable. But what they thought about life, how they faced its problems, we do not know. They did indeed know the art of writing; we have something of what they wrote – but we cannot read it. We must hope that someone, sometime will succeed in deciphering and translating it – to tell us, it may be, why an official was angry with a subordinate, or what, in the seventeenth century before Christ, was the price of beef.

But though we know nothing, except by inference, about their ideas and experiences, we know something about their ancestry. They have left representations of themselves, and these make it quite clear that they were of the slight, dark-skinned, black-haired 'Mediterranean' stock which originated in North Africa. This people had already passed out of the palaeolithic stage when they came – some of them – to an uninhabited Crete. Did others of them push further, and settle in parts of Greece? That is what we do not know.

The latest Cretan art leads directly into the 'Mycenaean' culture of the mainland, almost without a break, though with the addition of new features. The typical palace-plan was different. Not only was the palace more of a fortress (which the more turbulent conditions of the mainland would explain), but also the rooms seem to have been less open, as if the style had originated in a harder climate; moreover, as the style developed it achieved a symmetry unlike anything in Cretan architecture. Another difference is the greater prominence, in vase-painting, of the human figure. Cretan artists had used, in the main, linear patterns, and designs (whether naturalistic or stylized) derived from animal or plant life; the Mycenaean artists continued the linear designs, but used the human figure more frequently, as in processional scenes and chariot races.

Who were the people who made this Mycenaean culture? Artists and craftsmen who abandoned a Crete in decay and settled in a new home, among rude Hellenes, and made art for them? Or have we (as seems more likely) a predominantly non-Greek population, already deeply influenced by Crete, and possibly akin to the Cretan people, but having over them a newly-arrived, charioteering Greek aristocracy? Is it possible, if the latter supposition is true, that Herodotus is right, and that the mass of the 'Mycenaeans' were Ionians, whether already Hellenized or not? – These are questions that may be answered, some day. Meanwhile, whatever be the picture that we attempt to draw, we should probably be wise not to try to make it too tidy, for no doubt casual immigrations and local conquests had been going on for a very long time: and somewhere in this picture room must be found for Homer's 'brown-haired Achaeans', brown-haired (Xanthoi) in evident distinction from the black-haired people over whom they ruled. For Homer's Zeus-born kings were a quasi-feudal aristocracy lording it over inert subjects who played a very small part either in fighting or in politics. An obvious parallel is the Norman aristocracy which planted itself on Saxon England: the 'palace' which Atreus built at Mycenae and bequeathed to his son Agamemnon was a fortress rather than a palace, the centre of a system of strategic roads which gave ready access to various parts of the Peloponnese and Central Greece: and in these parts of Greece there were other fortresses of the same kind. Achaean iron weapons had proved themselves superior to Mycenaean bronze, but in general the Mycenaean culture was the higher one. From this point of view it is interesting to note one of the inaccuracies of the tradition on which Homer worked, three or four centuries later. In some respects this tradition reproduces the Mycenaean Age with remarkable fidelity, notably in its political geography. When Homer wrote – perhaps somewhere near 850 – the Dorian Invasion of about 1100 had completely changed the map of Greece. Mycenae itself, for example, had become a place of no importance, and the Asian coast, Homer's own home, had become Greek. Yet the *Iliad* preserves with complete fidelity a picture of Greece as it had been in the thirteenth century; nothing in it implies the Ionia in Asia which Homer himself knew. But the interesting inaccuracy is that the art and the articles of luxury which Homer describes are attributed to the Phoenicians. The fact that they were of native workmanship was completely forgotten, and must have seemed incredible. The Achaeans were rude conquerors with no art: still more so the Dorians who followed them. They have been compared to a man who succeeds to an estate and spends all his capital.

Other inconsistencies point in the same direction. In Homer the dead are cremated, but the native practice – and indeed the usual classical practice – was burial. In Homer we meet the Olympian religion of sky-gods; there is no trace of the Cretan and Aegean earth-goddess. In Homer there is hunting in plenty, but no sign of the bull-baiting so prominent in Mycenaean art. So one might continue. The Homeric tradition is accurate so far as it goes, but it is the tradition of a small conquering class, separated by a wide gulf from the life of the more civilized subject-people, yet not suddenly destroying or even seriously modifying that civilized life.

When did the Achaeans arrive? To put the question like this implies, probably, over-simplification. Cnossos was destroyed, certainly by raiders from oversea, at about 1400, and contemporary Egyptian records say that the 'islands of the sea' were being disturbed and the coasts of Egypt raided by 'Akhai-washi' – who are near enough in name to the Homeric 'Akhaivoi' to make the identification certain. Rather later we hear from Hittite sources of marauders in Asia led by a man whose name is suspiciously like 'Atreus'. Agamemnon's father was called Atreus. There is no need to try to identify the two. The Atreus whom we know was the King of Mycenae, son of Pelops who gave his name to the Peloponnese ('island of Pelops') – not perhaps a very likely person to be chasing Hittites in Asia Minor. 'Pelops' is a Greek name, meaning 'ruddy-face' – and he came from Lydia in Asia Minor, so that the other Atreus may have been of the same family.

All this suggests widespread disturbances during the late fifteenth and the fourteenth centuries, with people called Achaeans taking the lead. If we can rely on the genealogies, Pelops crossed the Aegean and married into the royal family of Elis, near Olympia, in the first half of the thirteenth century, since his grandson Agamemnon led the united Achaeans to Troy very early in the twelfth (traditionally, 1194). Moreover – if the genealogies are to be trusted – it was during the same thirteenth century that other Achaean dynasties were founded.

But they all fell, and the decaying Mycenaean Age came to an end, at the end of the twelfth. Other conquerors, the Dorians, came down from north-central Greece, this time not successful adventurers seizing or harrying small kingdoms, but a destroying flood of men, making a sudden end of a long civilization, and beginning a Dark Age, three centuries of chaos, after which Classical Greece begins to emerge. The Ionians have taken refuge across the sea (except the Athenians), the name 'Achaea' is confined to the narrow plain along the southern coast of the Gulf of Corinth, and the 'brown-haired' Achaeans – and for that matter the brown-haired Dorians, if they also were of this colour – have been absorbed into the dark-haired type which Greece produces, much as the fair-haired Celts of Gaul became dark Frenchmen.

A hundred years ago this Dark Age was completely dark, but for the sudden and inexplicable blaze of Homer, and the Classical Age that followed was the miraculous first flowering

THE FORMATION OF THE GREEK PEOPLE

of civilization and art in Europe. Now the darkness is a little less
dense, since we can follow through it the arts of the potter and
the metal-worker. The latter art actually progressed, stimulated
by the introduction of iron, and the painting of pottery, though
it lost the elegance, freedom and invention of the earlier age,
produced in the ninth century the splended 'Dipylon' vases of
Athens. Like the earliest Minoan pottery, they are decorated
with geometrical patterns; but again, we find a *motif* which
had not been so common in Crete: the human figure. We
find subjects like warriors with their chariots, funeral scenes,
men rowing a warship; the figures stylized, with thin lines for
arms and legs, a blob for a head, and a triangle for the upper
body: primitive in technique, but extremely successful in
general design, and showing, like some of the Mycenaean
vases, the typically Hellenic interest in man and his works.

This has been a long and necessarily inconclusive survey, but
it has brought out one important point, that the art of Classical
Greece was not an entirely new creation, but rather a Renaissance. It is, however, a Renaissance in very different conditions
and of a very different temper. To the earlier art something had
been added; the confusion which we have just described produced a fusion – a new people with the gifts of both its parents.
I have suggested, perhaps a little rashly, that we have signs of
this in the interest shown, first by Mycenaean, and then by
Athenian, painters in the activities of man, and indeed this
interest in man is one of the dominant characteristics of Greek
thought. But we may perhaps go deeper. The greatness of
Greek art – and let us use the word in its most inclusive sense
– lies in this, that it completely reconciles two principles which
are often opposed: on the one hand control and clarity and
fundamental seriousness; on the other, brilliance, imagination
and passion. All Classical Greek art has to a remarkable degree
that intellectual quality which shows itself in the logic and the
certainty of its construction. Intellectualism in art suggests to
us a certain aridity; but Greek art, whether it be the Parthenon,
a play by Aeschylus, a Platonic dialogue, a piece of pottery,
the painting on it, or a passage of difficult analysis in Thucydides, has, with all its intellectualism, an energy and a passion

which are overwhelming precisely because they are so intelligently controlled.

Now, if we compare the art of Classical Greece with Minoan or Aegean art, we find a significant difference. The best of Minoan art has all the qualities that art can have – except this consuming intellectualism. It is difficult to imagine Greek architects evolving, even by accident or under pain of death, a building so chaotic in plan as the palace at Cnossos. Greek art won some of its most brilliant victories in the hardest and most serious of all the arts, big-scale sculpture: it can be no accident, at this time of day, that no Minoan sculpture has been found other than quite small works. It is of course true that all art worthy of the name must be serious – and reflective: nevertheless, there is a sense in which one would attribute these qualities to Greek art and not to the Minoan: brilliant, sensitive, elegant, gay – these are the adjectives which one instinctively uses of the Minoan – but not 'intellectual'.

For the intellectual strain in Classical Greek art we must turn to the Hellenes – and not without evidence. When they descended from the northern mountains they brought no art with them, but they did bring a language, and in the Greek language – in its very structure – are to be found that clarity and control, that command of structure, which we see preeminently in Classical Greek art and miss in the earlier. In the first place, Greek, like its cousin Latin, is a highly-inflected language, with a most elaborate and delicate syntax, and the further back one can go in the history of the language, the more elaborate are the inflections, and (in many ways) the more delicate is the syntax. Greek syntax is much more varied, much less rigid, than Latin – as the young student of Classics soon discovers, to his joy or his sorrow, according to temperament. Consequently, it is the nature of Greek to express with extreme accuracy not only the relation between ideas, but also shades of meaning and emotion. But closer to our present point is a consequence of this – unless indeed it is a cause – the periodic style. Both in Greek and in Latin, if a statement happens to be complex, consisting of one or more leading ideas accompanied by any number of explanatory or qualifying ideas, the whole complex can be set out, and normally is, with perfect clarity in a single sentence. That is to say, both languages have a markedly architectural quality. But there is a significant difference between them. The Romans seem to have achieved the periodic style by sheer determination and courage: the Greeks were born with it. Not only has Greek many more ways of slipping in a subordinate clause – for example, the regular Greek verb has ten participles (if I have counted correctly), the Latin only three – but also Greek is well stocked with little words, conjunctions that hunt in couples or in packs, whose sole function is to make the structure clear. They act, as it were, as signposts. The reader must often have had the following embarrassing experience: reading aloud, he has embarked on an English sentence, and at a certain point has dropped his voice, under the impression that the sentence was coming to an end: but at the critical point he has found not a full-stop but only a semi-colon or a comma, so that he has had to retrace his steps for a word or two, hitch up his voice, and continue. This could never happen to him in Greek, because the Greek writer would have put at the very beginning the word which I must write as 'te' meaning 'This sentence (or clause or phrase) is going to have at least two co-ordinate members, and the second (and subsequent ones, if any) is going to be a simple addition to the first', or the word 'men', meaning precisely the same thing, except that this time the second (and subsequent) members will be not a continuation but a contrast. English of course can do this: an English sentence can begin 'While, on the one hand ...'. But Greek does it with much more ease, by instinct, and always. We have indeed no direct transcripts of Ancient Greek conversation, but we have passages, in the dramatists and in Plato, in which the writer is striving to give the effect of unpremeditated speech, and in these a fairly elaborate periodic structure is not uncommon, but even if we do not find this we always find a perfectly limpid and unambiguous ordering of the sentence, as if the speaker saw the ground-plan of his idea, and therefore of his sentence, in a flash, before he began to put it into words. It is the nature of the Greek language to be exact, subtle and clear. The imprecision and the lack of immediate perspicuity into which English occasionally deviates[1] and from which German occasionally emerges, is quite foreign to Greek. I do not mean that it is impossible to talk nonsense in Greek; it is quite possible – but the fact that it is nonsense is at once patent. The Greek vice in language is not vagueness or woolliness but a kind of bogus clarity, a firm drawing of distinctions which are not there.

The mind of a people is expressed perhaps more immediately in the structure of its language than in anything else it makes, but in all Greek work we shall find this firm grasp of the idea, and its expression in clear and economical form. With this clarity and constructive power and seriousness we shall find a quick sensitiveness and an unfailing elegance. This is the secret of what has been called 'the Greek miracle', and the explanation – or an important part of it – lies in the fusion of cultures, if not of peoples too.

III

THE COUNTRY

THIS perhaps is the place to consider briefly the geography of Greece. What is the nature of the country that attracted these successive bands of rude Northerners, and occasionally Easterners, and what did it do for them?

The reader will be familiar with the general configuration of Greece – a land of limestone mountains, narrow valleys, long gulfs, few rivers and many islands – the surviving eminences of a drowned mountain-system, as a glance at the map at once suggests. There are a few plains – not large ones, but extremely important in the economy and the history of the country. Of these, some are coastal, like the narrow and fertile plain of

1. When I say 'English' I do not mean the English of administrators, politicians and important people who write letters to *The Times*. Imprecision would be the chief quality of this language, but for its weary pomposity and its childish delight in foolish metaphors.

Achaea that runs along the southern coast of the Gulf; others lie inland, like Lacedaemon (Sparta); perhaps almost entirely barred from the sea by mountains, like the plains of Thessaly and Boeotia. The Boeotian plain is particularly lush,[1] and with a very heavy atmosphere; 'Boeotian pig', the more nimble-witted Athenians used to call their neighbours.

Greece is a region of great variety. Mediterranean and sub-alpine conditions exist within a few miles of each other; fertile plains alternate with wild mountain country; many an enterprising community of seamen and traders had as neigh-bours an inland agricultural people that knew the sea and commerce hardly at all, traditional and conservative, even as wheat and cattle are traditional and conservative. Contrasts in Greece today can be startling. In Athens and the Piraeus you have at your disposal – or had, before the war – a large modern European city, with trams, buses and taxis, aeroplanes arriving every few hours, and a harbour crammed with ships going everywhere – to Aegina across the bay, up the east coast, up the west coast, through the Canal, to Alexandria, to the chief ports of Europe, to the Americas; but in a few hours you can make your way to parts of Central Greece or the Peloponnesus where for miles around the only roads are bridle-tracks and the only wheeled vehicle is the wheelbarrow. In Kalamata I was taken over a large, up-to-date flour-mill, into which the corn was brought directly, by suction, from the holds of the ships that had carried it; two days before, and not twenty miles away, I had seen threshing being done, in Old Testament style, by horses or mules careering around a circular threshing-floor in a corner of a field, and the winnowing done on the same spot with the never-failing help of the wind. In antiquity the con-trasts are perhaps not so great, but they are still very striking. Variety meets us everywhere, and is a fact of great significance.

It is of great importance to the development of Greek cul-ture that most states had their strip of fertile plain, of upland pasture, of forested mountain-slopes, and of barren mountain-summits, and in many cases access to the sea as well. There was

1. The name Boeotia means 'cow-land'. Not many parts of Greece have pastures good enough for cows.

no Birmingham, or Wiltshire; no community, that is, with a uniform way of life; less uniformity even than in medieval England. States that we think of as pre-eminently commercial and industrial, like Corinth and Athens, were at least as much agricultural as commercial. The brilliance of the civic life of Athens in the fifth century makes us forget too easily that most Athenian citizens were in the first place farmers. It is evident from the earlier comedies of Aristophanes that Athens remained very much of a country-town, and Thucydides expressly says that those in Attica who had land lived on it until the Peloponnesian War drove them into the city for safety. It was the Spartan invasions that turned them into city-dwellers.

If this is true of Athens, it is much more true of the other Greek states. Town and country were closely-knit – except in those remoter parts, like Arcadia and Western Greece, which had no towns at all. City-life, where it developed, was always conscious of its background of country, mountains and sea, and country-life knew the usages of the city. This encouraged a sane and balanced outlook; Classical Greece did not know at all the resigned immobility of the steppe-mind, and very little[1] the shortsighted follies of the urban mob.

Having such variety of soil and climate, the normal Greek state was reasonably self-sufficient, and could enjoy a balanced corporate life. The Greek word for Self-sufficiency, Autarkeia or Autarky, we have learned to use in recent years, but in a more dismal context; to the Greek, as we shall see later, it was an essential part of the idea of the State – and the physical conditions of Greece enabled him to realize it.

There was another important consequence of the constant variety found within this small Greek world. Though most states could be reasonably self-supporting, thanks to variations of altitude, many had their special products – for example, the olive of Attica, the marble of Melos, the wine of the small island of Peparethus. This encouraged brisk trade and constant

1. Certain follies committed by Athens during the Peloponnesian War make this qualification necessary – but by then, as we have just seen, Athens had been largely urbanized.

intercourse. Moreover, communications by sea were easy and – except in winter – safe. With this, we may consider another fact of decisive importance, that Greece as a whole faces south-east. The mountains run in that direction, consequently the valleys and harbours face that way, and the chains of islands, continuing the mountain-ranges, guide the voyager in a small ship, without a compass, in perfect security to Asia and Egypt, the homes of earlier and richer civilizations. The result was that in prehistoric days Greece lay invitingly open to traders and others from Crete and then from Phoenicia, while in historical times, when the Hellenes had themselves taken to the sea with enormous success, the sea-lanes took them to lands older than their own. The contrast with Italy will make the point clear. The Apennines lie near the east coast; the rivers and valleys therefore run westwards, and the fertile plains and the harbours are on the west coast. To the east, Italy presents her most in-hospitable coast-line. Civilization therefore came late to Italy; Minoan influence was not great, and the Greeks, when they planted colonies, worked their way around the south coast and up the west. The great differences between Greek and Roman civilization must be due largely to the fact that the Latins, un-like the Hellenes, did not find the old culture of the south-eastern Mediterranean well established in the peninsula that they invaded: the Apennines had been too much of a barrier.

Another contrast suggests itself, that between the Greek Archipelago and the Hebrides. The differences in climate and in fertility between the two are obvious enough, but there is also this, that the products of one Hebridean island are much the same as those of another – or, for that matter, of the main-land as well. Therefore, in primitive conditions trade was slight, and there were no sharp contrasts to enlarge the mind; moreover, the sea-ways led, not to a Phoenicia or Egypt, but either to a mainland which was but little different, or into the North Atlantic, where a man would either drown, or come back no wiser than he had set out.

Another factor of importance is the climate. This is, on the whole, very agreeable, and it is steady. Greece, in fact, is one of those countries which have a climate, and not merely weather.

Winter is severe in the mountains; elsewhere, moderate and sunny. Summer sets in early, and is hot, but, except in the land-locked plains, the heat is not enervating, for the atmosphere is dry, and the heat is tempered with the daily alternation of land and sea-breezes. Rain in summer is almost unknown; late winter and the autumn are the rainy seasons.

Among the Greek medical writings attributed to Hippo-crates is a short treatise entitled *Airs, Waters, Places*. This gives a gloomy impression of the Greek climate. The unknown writer tells us that if a place has a south-easterly to a south-westerly exposure, being open to the hot winds and sheltered from the north, the waters will be hot in summer, cold in winter, and full of salts, because they will be near the surface. The inhabitants will suffer from phlegm, and consequently digestive troubles: they will be poor eaters and drinkers; the women will be unhealthy, and liable to have abortions; con-vulsions, asthma and epilepsy will attack the children; and the men will be liable to dysentery, diarrhoea, ague, chronic fevers, eczema and haemorrhoids, and, after the age of 50, will be paralyzed by humours descending from the head. However, pleurisy, pneumonia and a few other diseases rarely occur. If your exposure is northerly, you have the contrary troubles. The water will be hard, and consequently your physique too. You will be lean and sinewy, will eat a lot but drink little, 'since it is impossible to be at once a big eater and a heavy drinker', and will be liable to pleurisy and to internal lacerations. Childbirth will be difficult, while the rearing of children sounds next to impossible. An easterly exposure is best; the westerly is the worst of all.

Not a cheerful picture; but medical text-books are always horrifying, and in any case this writer is obviously a man with a bee in his bonnet – not the best type of Greek scientist.

Let us take evidence of a different kind. From a recent cen-tury I set down at random the following names: Haydn, Mozart, Beethoven, Goethe, Schubert, Mendelssohn, Words-worth, Coleridge, Keats, Shelley. From a Greek century, a comparable list of names: Aeschylus, Sophocles, Euripides, Aristophanes, Socrates, Plato, Isocrates, Gorgias, Protagoras,

Xenophon. The age at death of the first list is, respectively:
77, 35, 57, 83, 31, 38, 80, 62, 26, 30; of the second, 71, 91,
78, at least 60, 70, 87, 98, 95(?), about 70, 76. Shelley, of course,
was drowned; but Aeschylus and Euripides (apparently) both
met with accidental deaths, Socrates was executed and Protagoras died in a shipwreck; the three tragic poets were active,
and still at the height of their genius, when they died (which
no one would say of Wordsworth), and death interrupted
Plato in the task of writing *The Laws*. If anyone interested in
the topic will look through the quite entertaining *Lives of the
Philosophers*, by Diogenes Laertius, he will be astonished at the
general picture of longevity. Some of the dates are obviously
legendary; no one will believe that Empedocles really lived to
be 150; but he is hardly a historical figure anyhow. There is no
reason at all to doubt the accuracy of most of the figures
stated. It is quite clear that Greece was favourable not only to
long life, but also to sustained energy. By the side of Sophocles,
composing his magnificent *Oedipus Coloneus* at the age of 90,
we can set the figure of Agesilaus, King of Sparta, campaign-
ing hard in the field, not merely directing battles, at the age of
80. Vigorous old age seems to have been commoner in Greece
than in any modern country, at least until recent times.

Regimen no doubt had much to do with this. Greece is a
poor country today; she was undoubtedly richer in antiquity,
and supported a much larger population – but not in any
luxury. The Greek muleteer today can keep going for days on
a loaf of bread and a few olives, and his ancestor of classical
times was just as frugal. Barley-meal, olives, a little wine, fish
as a relish, meat only on high holidays – such was the normal
diet. As Zimmern has said, the usual Attic dinner consisted of
two courses, the first a kind of porridge, and the second, a kind
of porridge. It was a spare diet – though suitably interrupted
by drinking-parties – but, together with the active out-of-door
life of the ordinary Greek, it bred a vigorous race of men.

Why was Greece so poor? For at least a partial answer we
may turn to the very interesting description of Attica which
Plato gives in the *Critias*. Attica, he says, is only the skeleton of
what it was in the past, 'for it runs out from the mainland far

into the sea, like a cliff' – which is indeed what the name 'Attica' means—'and the sea all around it is deep'. During these nine thousand years[1] many severe storms have occurred, and the soil swilled away from the higher regions has not formed, as it has in other places, any alluvial plain worth mentioning, but has been washed away everywhere and lost at the bottom of the sea, so that what is now left, just as in the small islands, compared with what existed then is like the bones of a body wasted with disease: the fertile soil has fallen away, leaving only the skeleton of the land. When it was still unravaged, it had high hills instead of bare mountains, and the plain now called Phelleus[2] was a plain of deep, rich earth. And there were great forests on the mountains, indications of which are still to be seen: there are mountains which now support nothing but bees, but it is not long since timber was cut from them for the roofing of the largest buildings, and these roof-timbers are still sound. Moreover, there were tall cultivated trees in abundance, and the mountains afforded pasture for countless herds.'

Hence, no doubt, the startling difference between the Homeric and the classical Greek diet; in Homer, the heroes eat an ox every two or three hundred verses, and to eat fish is a token of extreme destitution; in classical times fish was a luxury, and meat almost unknown.

Plato mentioned storms. The Greek climate has indeed its dramatic aspects: Zeus, the sky-god, was irascible, and Poseidon, the Shaker of Earth whether by waves or by earthquakes, was a formidable being. Hesiod, the second oldest surviving Greek poet, is describing how Heracles felled the giant Cycnus, and he says that he fell 'as falls an oak or a beetling crag when smitten by the smoking thunderbolt of Zeus'; and the present writer has seen something of the furious work of Zeus. I was making my way up a valley in Arcadia, which was so luxuriant as to be almost oppressive. Suddenly I came to a piece of ground, possibly a dozen acres in extent, which was so strewn with boulders, large and small, that no soil was visible. It looked like a rocky seashore. In the middle was a house, half

---

1. Not to be taken too literally. Plato was fond of a sort of mathematical mysticism.   2. Meaning 'Stony'.

buried in debris. Two days before this had been a farm; but a storm had burst some miles way on Mt Tourtovano, and this was the result. No doubt it was a farm again, two years later, for the hard-working Greek peasant knows what is the only remedy against Zeus.

Hesiod himself had no great love for the climate of his native spot, and, as we have so far given the Greek climate high marks, it is only fair that so distinguished an authority should be heard on the other side. Hesiod disliked the sweltering heat of summer, and he hated the winter – 'the month of Lenaeon, evil days, cattle-flaying days, when the frosts that appear for men's sorrow cover the earth as the breath of the north-easter from Thrace bloweth on the wide sea and stirreth it, and earth and wood bellow aloud. Many an oak of lofty foliage and many a stout pine in the mountain glens doth his onset bring low to the bounteous earth, and all the unnumbered forest crieth aloud, and the wild beasts shudder and set their tails between their legs, even they whose hide is covered with hair. Yea, even through these, shaggy-breasted though they are, he bloweth with chill breath. Through the hide of the ox he bloweth, and it stayeth him not, and through the thin-haired goat: but nowise through the sheep doth the might of Boreas blow, because of their abundant wool. But he maketh the old man bent.' Of the eight winds Hesiod hated four. The others 'are of the race of gods, a great boon to mortal men. But these are random winds, blowing fitfully on the sea; they fall on the misty deep, a great bane to mortal men, and rage with evil tempest. Different at different times they blow, and scatter ships and destroy sailors. And there is no defence against woe for men who meet those winds upon the deep. And those again over the infinite flowery earth destroy the pleasant works of men, filling them with dust and grievous turmoil.'[1]

But Hesiod was a farmer, and a Boeotian, 'of Ascra, a sorry place near Helicon; bad in winter, hard in summer, never good' – and a man should not write like this of his home, even though his father has come there from Asia Minor, and no doubt told Hesiod times without number how much better it had been in Asia.

1. Transl. A. W. Mair.

An Athenian, we may be sure, would have told him that it served him right for living in Boeotia. In Athens, they held the first dramatic festival of the year – in the open air – in February; the rainy season was now over, though the sailing-season had not yet begun. It was therefore a domestic festival, homely in comparison with the splendid City Dionysia in early April, when visitors from any city in Greece might be expected. Evidently, Athens had a better climate than the one Hesiod describes – but we have said already that Greece is essentially a land of contrasts.

We ought not to leave this matter of the Greek climate without considering its effect on Greek, especially on Athenian, life.

In the first place, it enabled the Greek to live with extremely little apparatus. In Greece one can lead an active life on much less food than harsher climates make necessary; but there is also the fact that the Greek – the Greek *man* – could and did spend most of his leisure hours out of doors. That in itself meant that he had more leisure; he did not need to work in order to buy settees and coal. – After all, the reason why we English have invented 'le confort anglais' is that we cannot be comfortable and warm except indoors. The leisure which the Athenian enjoyed is popularly attributed to the existence of slavery. Slavery had something to do with it,[1] but not so much as the fact that three-quarters of the things which we slave for the Greek simply did without.

So, spending out of doors the leisure which he earned largely by doing without things which we find or think necessary, the Greek, whether in town or village, was able to sharpen his wits and improve his manners through constant intercourse with his fellows. Few people have been so completely sociable. Talk was the breath of life to the Greek – as indeed it still is, though somewhat spoiled by a serious addiction to newspapers. What society but Athens could have produced a figure like Socrates – a man who changed the current of human thought without writing a word, without preaching a doctrine, simply by talking in the streets of a city which he never left but twice – for the battlefield? In what other society is one so little

1. See below, p. 131 ff.

conscious of a chasm between the educated and the uneducated, between those with taste and the vulgar? The real education of the Athenian, and of many another Greek, was given in the places of assembly – in the hours of talk in market-place, colonnade or gymnasium, in the political assembly, in the theatre, at the public recitals of Homer, and at the religious processions and celebrations. For it was perhaps the greatest boon conferred upon Attica by her climate that her big assemblies could be held in the open air. However democratic the instincts of the Athenian might be, Athenian democracy could not have developed as it did – nor for that matter Athenian Drama – if a roof and walls had been necessary. In our conditions of shelter, privacy and admission-fees, the life of the well-to-do must be potentially richer than the life of the poor, and only six hundred can have direct access to the business of the nation. In Athens all these things could be open to all because they could be open to the air and the sun. To explain Athenian culture simply as the product of the Athenian climate would be foolish, though not unfashionable; nevertheless it is demonstrable that in a different climate it could not have developed as it did.

This discursive survey of the physical conditions in which the Greeks lived may well conclude with some remarks on the natural resources of the country and the nature of its economy in primitive conditions.

Today, four-fifths of Greece are barren: in early times (as we have already seen) the mountain-slopes were well forested, a rich source both of timber and of game, large and small. It is a fair inference that rainfall was both heavier and less catastrophic, and that therefore there was more and better pasture-land than there is now. From the evidence available – mainly Homer and Hesiod – it seems clear that Greece was practically self-supporting so far as primary goods are concerned. Apart from agricultural products, there was building-stone in abundance, and good potters' clay. The olive was an important crop, then as now, providing cooking-fat, oil for burning in lamps, and the ancient equivalent of soap. The vine too was cultivated freely.

It was in minerals that Greece was poor. Gold, silver, lead and copper were found, but in no great abundance, and there was no iron at all. Above all, there was no coal. The simple fact that no ancient civilization had coal has not, I think, been sufficiently considered by social historians. Honey is a satisfactory substitute for sugar; abundant wine at least does something to make up for the absence of tea and coffee. Tobacco one can live without – provided that one does not know that tobacco exists – but what can replace coal? The answer is that coal, merely as a source of warmth and light, can be replaced by the Mediterranean sun and by wood: for cooking, charcoal serves excellently: but for coal as a source of power there was no satisfactory substitute – only slave labour, which is mechanically a wasteful use of power, and for other reasons evil.

Of the economic life of this Dark Age, we can learn something from Homer and Hesiod. It is clear that agriculture was quite intelligently managed: in particular, the culture of the vine – no simple matter – was thoroughly understood. In the *Odyssey*, in the description of the city of Phaeacians Homer gives a picture of very well-tended orchards and gardens, very rich, and very neat.

You will see near the path a fine poplar wood sacred to Athene, with a spring welling up in the middle and a meadow all round. That is where my father has his royal park and vegetable garden, within call of the city. Sit down there and wait awhile till we get into the town and reach my father's house. When you think we have had time to do so, go into the city yourself and ask for the palace of my father, King Alcinous. It is quite easy to recognize: any little child could show it you. For the houses of the rest are not built in anything like the style of Lord Alcinous' mansion. Directly you have passed through the courtyard and into the buildings, walk quickly through the great hall till you reach my mother, who generally sits in the firelight by the hearth, weaving yarn stained with sea-purple, and forming a delightful picture, with her chair against a pillar and her maids sitting behind. My father's throne is close to hers, and there he sits drinking his wine like a god.[1]

1. From the *Odyssey*, VI, transl. E. V. Rieu.

So does the princess Nausicaa instruct the shipwrecked Odysseus. When Odysseus reaches the palace, this is what he sees:

Outside the courtyard but stretching close up to the gates, and with a hedge running down on either side, lies a large orchard of four acres, where trees hang their greenery on high, the pear and the pomegranate, the apple with its glossy burden, the sweet fig and the luxuriant olive. Their fruit never fails nor runs short, winter and summer alike. It comes at all seasons of the year, and there is never a time when the West Winds' breath is not assisting, here the bud, and here the ripening fruit: so that pear after pear, apple after apple, cluster on cluster of grapes, and fig upon fig are always coming to perfection. In the same enclosure there is a fruitful vineyard, in one part of which is a warm patch of level ground, where some of the grapes are drying in the sun, while others are gathered or being trodden, and on the foremost rows hang unripe bunches that have just cast their blossom or show the first faint tinge of purple. Vegetable beds of various kinds are neatly laid out beyond the furthest row and make a smiling patch of never-failing green. The garden is served by two springs, one lets in rills to all parts of the enclosure, while its fellow opposite, after providing a watering-place for the townsfolk, runs under the courtyard gate towards the great house itself.[1]

The land of the Phaeacians has about it a touch of fairyland, but, however much Homer may have touched up his picture, it is obviously a picture of something that he has seen.

We hear of another vineyard in the last book of the *Odyssey*, and there is no magic here. After slaying the suitors, Odysseus goes off to find his old father, who in his despair has removed himself from the town:

As he made his way down into the great orchard, he fell in neither with Dolius nor with any of the serfs or Dolius' sons, who had all gone with the old man at their head to gather stones for the vineyard wall. Thus he found his father alone on the vineyard terrace digging round a plant. He was wearing a filthy, patched and disreputable tunic, a pair of stitched leather gaiters strapped around his shins to protect them from scratches, and gloves to save his hands from the brambles:

1. From the *Odyssey*, VII, transl. E. V. Rieu.

while to crown all, and by way of emphasizing his misery, he had a hat of goatskin on his head.[1]

In the *Odyssey* we move among the great, and see Kings living on their domains, though the King of Ithaca is indeed more like a Lord of the Manor than a King. He employs free labour and slaves, but is not above working on the land himself; for Laertes knows how to dig round a vine, and Odysseus himself boasts that he can drive a furrow as straight as any man. It is in Hesiod that we meet the small farmer, working the ground himself, with his sons, with a slave if he can afford one, and with occasional hired labour. In each case, be it large or small, the estate is practically self-supporting: 'household economy' is the rule. We saw Arêtê, the Phaeacian Queen, weaving by the light of the fire, while Penelope of Ithaca is perhaps the most famous of all weavers, with the big winding-sheet from which she unravelled each night what she had woven by day.

The house of the lordly Alcinous 'keeps fifty maids employed. Some grind the apple-golden corn in the handmill, some weave at the loom, or sit and twist the yarn, their hands fluttering like the tall poplar's leaves, while the soft olive-oil drips from the close-woven fabrics they have finished.'[2]

In humbler life all the garments worn and all the stuffs used in the house are made by the women of the family, with perhaps the help of a slave-girl if the family is fairly prosperous, while most of the farm-gear is made on the place.

Of specialized trades we hear of only two, the trades of the smith and of the potter. These were 'demiourgoi', 'men who work for the populace', not themselves consuming the product of their own toil. The demiourgos is the craftsman: in Plato, the Creator: hence Demiurge in Shelley's *Prometheus Unbound*. It is interesting to notice that these two are the only crafts which, in Greek, have divine exponents. Hephaestus (Vulcan) the smith, and Prometheus, also a fire-god, but in Attic cult the god of the potters. There is no god of shoemaking or farming

1. *Odyssey*, XXIV, transl. E. V. Rieu.
2. *Odyssey*, VII, transl. E. V. Rieu.

or building. Obviously, these things everybody knows how to do, but it is very different with elaborate metal-work, or the making of an elegant piece of pottery. 'How on earth is it done?' – 'Some god must have invented it.' Hence Hephaestus, who, in the delightfully scandalous tale of Ares and Aphrodite which Homer tells in the eighth book of the *Odyssey*, forged an iron net, light as gossamer and so fine that it was invisible even to the blessed gods; and he pretended that he was going away to Lemnos; and Ares said, 'Come, my beloved: your husband has gone to Lemnos, to visit his barbarous Sintian friends'; and Aphrodite came; but the net descended and held them so fast as they lay that neither could move a limb, and Hephaestus called out in his rage to the other gods, who came to see the wrong done to him; and when they saw Hephaestus' clever device, unquenchable laughter came over them. Apollo, son of Zeus, turned to Hermes and said, 'Hermes, son of Zeus, was it worth it?' And the giant-slayer said (in effect), 'Yes, I would change places with him at this very moment.' – But all this is perhaps a little remote from primitive Greek economy.

In these early days the Greeks were no traders. The articles of luxury which we meet in abundance in the homes of the wealthy came from the East, in Phoenician ships, which also brought slaves. Eumaeus, the faithful swine-herd of Odysseus, was one of them. His father was king in Syrie, out beyond Sicily, and the King had a slave-girl from Sidon, whom he had bought from the villainous Taphian pirates who had abducted her. One day there came to Syrie a Phoenician ship with a cargo of trumpery, and one of the crew made love to this Sidonian girl. He heard her tale, and suggested that she should go back with them, for he knew that her parents were alive, and were wealthy people. The girl of course agreed, and improved on the scheme by suggesting that she should carry off with her the King's son, a bright little boy, who was in her charge: he would fetch a good price. The Phoenician approved of this. For a whole year the ship stayed at Syrie, while they sold off their elegancies and loaded up with other goods – cattle, skins, raw metal and wine were the common exports.

When they were ready to sail, the wicked Phoenician came to the King's house with an amber necklace to sell, and while the Queen and the other women were examining it and bargaining, the Sidonian slave-girl slipped down through the dark streets, with the child, and they were at sea before the thing was known. Justice was done to the Sidonian, for she fell into the hold, was picked up dead, and was flung overboard. The ship was carried to Ithaca, and there the child was sold to Odysseus' father, Laertes, and brought up by him and Anticleia almost as their own child, until he grew up, was given a tunic and a fine mantle, and made bailiff of the farm. Such was one side of Mediterranean trade, not only in this Dark Age, but in every other age too in which there has been no government strong enough to police the coasts and control the seas.

International trade, then, was in Phoenician hands, and in certain parts of the Mediterranean it continued to be a Phoenician preserve until the end of the third century B.C.: for Carthage was a Phoenician colony – hence the name 'Punic Wars' – and the Carthaginians managed to keep Greek traders out of the triangle formed by the western end of Sicily, the Straits of Gibraltar, and the eastern end of the Pyrenees. But – to return to the early period – the Greeks were already engaging in coast-wise traffic. Hesiod gives instructions (in his *Works and Days*) on the seasons of the year when you may start sailing and when you must stop, if you are fool enough – or greedy enough – to take to the sea: for of sailing and making wealth by trade Hesiod thought ''taint natural'. Hesiod was a farmer, accustomed to the regular rhythm and slow ways of nature, with the solid wealth that can be wrung out of nature. Wealth made out of trading was a doubtful business, and fittingly attended by dangers of all kinds. Keep away from the bitter sea: such was Hesiod's advice. Yet in the *Odyssey*, presumably an earlier poem, we have a picture of a city, obviously Greek, which is a trim port:

Our city is surrounded by high battlements: it has an excellent harbour on each side, and is approached by a narrow causeway, where the curved ships are drawn up to the road, and each owner has his separate slip. Here is the people's meeting-place, built up on either side of the fine temple of Poseidon with blocks of quarried stone bedded deeply in the ground. It is here too that the sailors attend to the rigging of the black ships, to their cables, and their sails, and the smoothing of their oars. For the Phaeacians have no use for the bow and quiver, but spend their energy on masts and oars and on the graceful craft they love to sail across the foam-flecked seas.[1]

Evidently Homer had seen such a Greek city: but we may infer that there were not many such, or he would not have thought it worth while to describe this one so minutely, nor could the art of sailing – as practised at least by the Phaeacians – have been invested with such magic: for while in one passage we read that 'they pin their faith on the clippers that carry them across the far-flung seas, for Poseidon has made them a sailor folk, and these ships of theirs are as swift as a bird or as thought itself', in another their King says, 'For the Phaeacians have no steersmen, nor steering-oars such as other craft possess. Our ships know by instinct what their crews are thinking and propose to do. They know every city, every fertile land, and hidden in mist and cloud they make their swift passage over the sea's immensities with no fear of damage and no thought of wreck.'

Homer was an Ionian Greek. Is it too prosaic to suppose that one Ionian city, daring beyond the others, had jumped far ahead of them in the art of shipbuilding, sailing and navigation, and had left them wondering? The *Odyssey* is full of the sea, and the great age of Greek colonization is at hand: but there is still to come Hesiod, the hard-bitten farmer, with his calendar of the year's work and his advice, 'Go to sea if you must, but only from mid-June to September – and even then you will be a fool', to remind us that there are more kinds of Greek than one, and that generalizing about them is dangerous.

1. Nausicaa speaking; *Odyssey*, VI, tranls. E. V. Rieu.

IV

HOMER

THE first and the greatest of European poets surely deserves a chapter to himself, both for his own sake – for in Homer we can see all the qualities which characterize Greek art – and because of the influence which his poems had on many generations of Greeks.

On the famous Homeric Question, who Homer was and how much of the *Iliad* and the *Odyssey* he wrote, I propose to say as little as possible. We can see how vague the Greek tradition was from the fact that one early Ionian writer, Hellanicus, placed him in the twelfth century, and Herodotus in the ninth – 'four hundred years before my time and not more'. There is no doubt that Herodotus is substantially correct: Hellanicus had assumed without question that a poet who so vividly described the fighting at Troy had himself seen it. But the important question is not who Homer was, but *what* he was. The *Iliad* and the *Odyssey* have been called the Bible of the Greeks. For centuries these two poems were the basis of Greek education, both of formal school education and of the cultural life of the ordinary citizen. Recitals from Homer accompanied by exposition were given by professionals who went from city to city. Plato draws a vivid, and rather malicious, portrait of one of these in his *Ion*: 'It must be marvellous, Ion, to go about, as you do, from place to place, to draw a great crowd wherever you go, and have them hanging on your lips – and you wearing your very best clothes'. Until this Bible was replaced by another, a citation from Homer was the natural way of settling a question of morals or behaviour. Homer could be quoted in diplomatic exchanges, like a Domesday book, to support a territorial claim. A kind of Fundamentalism grew up: Homer enshrined all wisdom and all knowledge. Plato laughs at this when he makes his Ion claim that, being an expert in Homer, he is an expert in all things; a city might well make him its general, because naturally he knows the art of generalship from Homer. More seriously, Homer held and nourished the minds and the imaginations of Greeks for generation after generation

– of artists, thinkers and ordinary simple men alike. Painters and poets turned to Homer for their inspiration and for their actual subjects: Aeschylus was said to have described his own work, modestly, as 'slices from Homer's banquet' – and European drama knows no greater figure than Aeschylus. Finally, next to the Greek language itself it was their common heritage of Homer which most gave to the Greeks this conviction that, in spite of the differences and hatreds which divided them, they were one people. Clearly, we must know something about Homer, that first articulate European, who suddenly blazes out, as we have said, like a great fire in the middle of this age of darkness.

The beginning of the *Iliad* is no bad introduction to Homer. Here, then, is a plain prose transcription of the tremendous scene with which the *Iliad* begins: a passage which the average Greek must have known almost, if not indeed perfectly, by heart. This is the sort of thing which men of action like Pericles and Alexander; poets, sculptors, painters, philosophers and scientists; politicians, traders; country gentlemen and artizans, had built into their minds from boyhood:

Divine Muse, sing of the ruinous wrath of Achilles, Peleus' son, which brought ten thousand sorrows to the Greeks, sent the souls of many brave heroes down to the world of the dead, and left their bodies to be eaten by dogs and birds: and the will of Zeus was fulfilled. Begin where they first quarrelled, Agamemnon the King of Men, and great Achilles.

Which god was it who made them enemies? Apollo, son of Zeus and Leto. He was enraged with the King, and sent an evil pestilence on the host, and men began to die, because his priest had been treated with scorn by Atreus' son Agamemnon. He had come to the swift ships of the Achaeans to ransom his daughter; he had brought untold money to buy her back. In his hands, on his golden staff, he carried Apollo's garland: and he besought all the Achaeans, and above all their commanders, the two sons of Atreus:

'Sons of Atreus, and you other well-armed Achaeans, may the gods who live in Olympus grant it to you to sack Priam's city and to return home in triumph: only release for me my own daughter. Take this as the price, and show your respect for the son of Zeus, Apollo the far-shooter.'

Then all the Achaeans cried, 'Yes: respect the priest, and accept his splendid gifts'. – But not Agamemnon: this did not please him, but he sent Chryses away with contempt, and said roughly: 'Sir, let me not find you loitering by our hollow ships, now or at any other time, or no protection will you find in your holy sceptre and garland. I will not set free your daughter. Sooner than that, old age shall come upon her, in my house in Argos, a long way from her own country: she shall walk to and fro at the loom, and she shall come to my bed. Begone! and do not answer back, or you will not go safe and sound.'

So he spoke: and the old man was frightened, and obeyed. He walked away in grief along the shore of the splashing sea.

This is the way in which the earliest work of European literature opens. We will venture a little further into it presently; meanwhile, let us interrupt the translation in order to make one capital point.

It has always been a commonplace of Homeric criticism that Homer plunges straight into his subject: *in medias res*, as Horace said. This is commonly taken to be a sign of Homer's literary genius – as of course it is: but perhaps we can go a little further. There is much more involved than the fact, already an important one, that Homer does not compose a long rambling epic on the Trojan War, the whole ten years of it, but contents himself with one phase: that his sense of form so disciplines his art that he can end his poem, and his subject, without even touching on the capture of Troy. This instinctive control of form is indeed notable, but the origin of it is even more so. For this is no happy inspiration, no mere 'artistic' merit: its origin lies deeper, in a certain habit of mind, and one which is Hellenic, not Homeric only. For evidently Homer could have limited his subject in this way, and still have treated it in a quasi-historical fashion, composing a poem which was as brilliant, as swift, as well-shaped as you will, but yet in essence a piece of reporting, a representation. Homer has not done this: none of the Classical Greek poets did this either.[1] The *Iliad* does not

---

1. I use this formula to save time. There is no doubt that there was plenty of bad Greek poetry. Aristophanes, for one, was always laughing at it. But what we now have is of the best, carefully selected by very competent critics of Alexandrine times and later.

describe an episode in the war, colouring the description with passing reflections about this or that aspect of life; rather, the poet has taken his 'subject', this phase of the war, as so much raw material, to be built into an entirely new structure of his own devising. He is not going to write about the war, not even about part of it, but about the theme which he states so clearly in the first five verses. What shapes the poem is nothing external, like the war, but the tragic conception that a quarrel between two men should bring suffering, death and dishonour to so many others.[1] So 'the plan of Zeus was fulfilled'. And what does this mean? That all this was specially designed by Zeus for inscrutable reasons of his own? Rather the opposite, that it is part of a universal Plan: not an isolated event – something which, as it happened, so fell out on this occasion – but something that came from very nature of things: not a particular, but a universal. It is not for us to say whether it was from pondering on this episode of the war that Homer was led to this conception, or whether his experience of life led him to this conception, which he then saw could be expressed through the Achilles-story: the important thing is that this is his subject, that such a cause has such an effect: and that it is out of this clearly conceived subject, and not merely from literary contrivance, that the *Iliad* derives the essential unity which informs it, in spite of its epic expansiveness and of later accretions.[2] Therefore, if we may be pedantic for a moment, it is not strictly true to say that Homer, in disregarding the first nine years of the war, plunges immediately into the middle of his subject. On the contrary, he begins at the beginning of his subject – and he says so, quite plainly.

So many thousands of brave men slain and dishonoured because of a quarrel: the reader will have a very incomplete idea of Homer's conception unless we see what caused the quarrel. We left Chryses the priest making his way in grief

1. See below, p. 184, on the similar composition of the *Agamemnon*.

2. The unity of the *Odyssey* is much more obvious, and is of exactly the same nature: it is not in the least simply that the material is cleverly arranged – though in fact the design of the plot is superb: the real point is that the plot was contrived like this in order to enforce an idea, that lawlessness is contrary to the will of the gods, and is punished.

along the seashore. Chryses now prays to Apollo to avenge him:

So he prayed, and Phoebus Apollo heard him. He came down from the summits of Olympus, angry at heart, with his bow hung from his shoulder, and with his close-covered quiver: and as he moved, the arrows rattled at his shoulder, so angry was he. He came like night. Then he sat, far from the ships, and let fly an arrow, and terrible was the noise that came from his silver bow. First he assailed the pack animals and the swift dogs; then he aimed his painful darts against the men themselves, and he kept on shooting. Many a pyre was lit to burn the dead.

For nine days the god's shafts fell upon the army. On the tenth, great Achilles summoned the people to council; the white-armed goddess Hera had put it into his mind, for she was anxious for the Greeks, as she saw them dying.

When they were assembled there and were all together, swift-footed Achilles arose and spoke to them. 'Son of Atreus, now I think we shall be driven – if we escape death – to return home again, since we Achaeans are beset at the same time both by war and by pestilence. Come, let us ask some seer, or priest, or maybe a reader of dreams – for it is Zeus who sends dreams – who may tell us why Phoebus Apollo is so angry: whether he sees fault in us for some vow or sacrifice neglected. Perhaps in return for the smoke of lambs and sacrificial goats, he will save us from the pestilence.'

So Achilles spoke, and sat down. From among them Calchas arose, most excellent of seers, who knew what was, what would be, and what had been before. By the secret knowledge that Phoebus Apollo had given him he had guided the Achaean ships to Ilion. He then, with good intent, spoke, and said to them:

'Achilles, beloved of Zeus, you bid me expound the wrath of Lord Apollo who shoots from afar; therefore I tell you. But you must make a compact: you must swear on oath that you will be quick to help me in word and deed; for I think that someone will be angry, someone who has great sway over all the Argives, and the Achaeans obey him too: for when a King is angry with a poor man, he is too strong for him. Even if he does swallow his rage for that day, yet he keeps his resentment in his heart, to satisfy it another time. Tell me if you will protect me.'

Achilles promises that he will protect Calchas, even if the prince he refers to is Agamemnon himself. Thereupon Calchas declares that Apollo is angry for the treatment given to his priest by Agamemnon; nor will the pestilence cease until the girl is sent back, not for any ransom, but with a herd of cattle for sacrifice.

So he spoke: and he sat down. And there arose among them the heroic son of Atreus, Agamemnon whose sway was wide. He was angry; his black heart was filled with a great rage, and his eyes were like a blazing fire. First he spoke to Calchas, and gave him a malignant look: 'Seer of evil: never yet have you told me anything favourable. You delight, always, in prophesying evil; never have you either said or done anything good. So now, you speak to the Greeks of the god's mind – as if the Far-shooter is bringing these evils upon them for this, that I would not take a glittering price for Chryses' daughter, because I would rather have the girl herself in my house. For I find her better than Clytemnestra my wedded wife.

Clytemnestra is not so good as she is, neither in face nor in figure, neither in wit nor in handiwork. But even so, I will give her back, if this is better. I would rather the army lived than died. But get me some other prize of valour, that I may not be the only Argive without his prize; for this is not decent. You all see that my prize is now lost.'

Then great Achilles, the swift runner, answered him: 'Renowned son of Atreus, most covetous of all men, how indeed can the brave-hearted Achaeans give you a prize? We know that there is no common store of wealth at hand; what plunder we took from the towns has been shared between us, and it is not decent to take this back again from the army. But you should give up this girl for the god's sake, and we Achaeans will repay you three and four times over, if ever Zeus gives it us to sack the strong city of Troy.'

In answer to him mighty Agamemnon said: 'Godlike Achilles, great warrior though you are, do not try to trick me like this. You will not get the better of me, nor win my consent. That you may keep your prize, would you have me sit here robbed of mine? Do you bid me give back this girl? Then let the stout-hearted Achaeans give me a prize pleasing to my heart, a worthy recompense for this. Or if they will not give it, then I will take it myself – yours, or the prize Ajax has, or Odysseus: I will go and take it. And the man I go to can be angry if he likes. But this we can think of another time. Now, we will launch a black ship upon the great sea; we will summon rowers to it; we will put the oxen into it, and we will put on board beautiful Chryseis. And let some man of authority take command – Ajax or Idomeneus or great Odysseus or you, son of Peleus, most formidable of all men, that you may perform the sacrifice and placate for us the Far-shooter.'

Swift-footed Achilles scowled, and said to him: 'Greedy and shameless, through and through! How can Achaeans with a good heart obey orders of yours to go on a march or to fight with men in battle? It was not because of Trojans that I came here to fight. I had no quarrel with them: they had never driven off cows of mine, nor horses, nor ever had they ravaged crops in my nourishing and rich fields of Phthia, for between us there lie many shadowy mountains and a wide, roaring sea. No, we followed you, unscrupulous man, to win from the Trojans glory for Menelaus and you – hound! You do not give this a second thought. And now you threaten to come and take away my prize! I worked bitterly for that, and the sons of the Achaeans awarded it me. When the Achaeans sack some stoutly-defended town here the prize I get is not equal to yours. No: in the turmoil of war my right arm does more than yours, but when the sharing-out comes, yours is the greatest prize, and I go to my ships, weary from battle, with little for my own. But I will go off to Phthia. How much better, to go home on my sharp-prowed ships! I have little mind to pile up booty and wealth for you, and then to be spurned.'

In answer to him said Agamemnon, King of men: 'Run away and welcome, if your heart is set on it. I will not beg you to stay for my sake; there are others here who will pay my honour; above all, Zeus who plans all things. I loathe you above all the Kings whom Zeus nurtures. Your heart is ever set on strife and battle and war. Though you are a man of strength, that strength, I suppose, is a gift from god? Get you home, with your ships and your men. Lord it among your Myrmidons. You are nothing to me: your rage I despise. But I can tell you this: Phoebus Apollo is taking Chryseis from me. I am giving her passage in my ship, with my men. But I will go to your tent myself and take your prize, lovely Briseis. So shall you learn how high above you I stand, and no one else shall dare to think himself on a level with me.'

So spoke Agamemnon: but to Achilles it was past bearing. His heart within his shaggy breast was torn, whether he should draw his sharp sword from his side, send away all others, and slay Atreus' son, or put an end to his wrath and quieten his heart. While he was thinking on this in his mind he began to draw his great sword from its sheath. But Athena came down from heaven: the white-armed goddess Hera had sent her, both of them out of the love and care they bore for him. She stood behind him, and caught Peleus' son by his brown hair, appearing to him alone; no other saw her. Achilles marvelled, and his eyes were blazing terribly. He addressed her in these winged words: 'Why have you come, daughter of Aegis-bearing Zeus? Is it to witness the wicked arrogance of Agamemnon, Atreus' son? But I say outright – and this I fancy will come to pass – some day his overweening pride shall cost him his life.'

Athena tells him – to cut the translating short – that she has come to tell him to quell his anger: some day, for this insult, they will offer Achilles three and four times as much as what Agamemnon is now taking from him.

Achilles of course obeys, for, as he briefly observes, 'It is better so'. Athena returns to Olympus, and Achilles blazes out at Agamemnon – and his speech begins 'Drunkard! with the face of a dog and the heart of a deer ...'

I have translated so much for several reasons. One, that we may have a text for future reference; another, that the reader might perhaps be given some impression of the vividness of it all. We have spoken, and shall speak again, of the intellectual quality of Greek art; it was well, therefore, to show the reader very forcibly that this does not in the least imply abstraction or aridity. This quarrel is seen so vividly that it is no wonder Hellanicus thought that Homer was contemporary with the Trojan War. And it is not only externals that are seen with this vividness. The artistic function of this passage, as Homer himself tells us, is to describe that event – the quarrel – from which came so much suffering to the Greeks, in accordance with what Homer calls 'the plan of Zeus', and we should call the inevitable working-out of events. The cause is the 'wicked arrogance' of Agamemnon, and the 'ruinous wrath' of Achilles; this is quite plain.

But what Homer gives us is not two abstract qualities in conflict; we see two men quarrelling violently. Nothing could be more 'real', less abstract. As in life, there is something to be said on each side, only both men go too far. The quarrel flares up because each man happens to be the sort of man that he is. It is an affair of a moment – but 'it sent the souls of many brave heroes down to the world of the dead, and left their bodies to be eaten by dogs and birds. And the plan of Zeus was fulfilled.'

This is, not of course exclusively, but characteristically, Greek, this power of seeing the immediate event so sharply, and at the same time of apprehending the universal law which it exemplifies. We are shown something of the framework of the whole universe in one event, yet the treatment of this event has all the sharpness of the most brilliant reporting. Homer does not need to blur the sharpness of his picture by generalizing comments; all his generalizing has been done already, in the ground-plan of the whole edifice.

One thing more. In this passage, as in all Classical Greek art, there is a notable absence of natural background. We see neither the towering walls of Troy nor the Scamander shimmering in the distance; we do not know where this Assembly of the Greeks is held, whether in a tent, or on a hill-side, or on the shore beside the hollow ships. As in Greek vase-painting, all our attention is concentrated on the human figures. So in Greek tragedy. The Shakespearian sunlight and thunderstorms are completely absent; if a character speaks of the scenery around him, it is to emphasize that he is cut off from his fellow-men. It would be easy and comforting if we could say that the Greek was insensitive to nature and leave it at that. But we cannot. To confine ourselves to Homer: no man insensitive to nature could have used such a wealth of natural similes, all so exact in detail – similes drawn from animals, birds, sea, sky and storms, little illustrative pictures that distantly recall the illuminations in medieval manuscripts. There is no question whatever that the Greek was aware of the beauty and the variety of nature. Besides, it is not only the background of nature which is, in general, absent. As we have seen, the *Iliad* begins without the slightest hint of where the action is taking place: we must be somewhere on Trojan territory, but where? Homer is not sufficiently interested to tell us. Nor does he give us that background which a modern writer could hardly omit – the others, the more passive actors in the scene: the other Greek leaders, and the army. Nothing is described but the essential figures.

But the modern reader not only misses the background that he expects, he also finds a background which, at first, he cannot understand – namely, the background of divine action. We do not see the walls of Troy, but we do see councils taking place in Olympus, and individual gods interfering in battle or – as in our passage – in debate. It is not surprising if this gives the impression that the human characters in the action are nothing but pawns pushed about on a chessboard by a set of capricious and irresponsible deities – yet this is difficult to reconcile with the picture of autonomous, responsible human agents, which Homer takes such pains to draw for us. This Agamemnon and this Achilles are real grown-up men, treated in a grown-up way: in fact, considering the primitive savagery which we meet so frequently in the Homeric picture of life, this mature grown-up-ness is at times almost disconcerting. Yet it all goes with a divine machinery which seems almost child-like, as when, in our passage, Athena comes down from Olympus, plucks Achilles' hair, and gives him a piece of good advice. So in the later tragedy – though in a much less picturesque way – the gods, through oracles, dreams and the rest, seem to control and direct the actions of men, even when these men are presented as completely independent and responsible agents.

This question of background, is, then, puzzling, and although this is not the place for a disquisition on Greek religion, some interim explanation is due to the reader. Homer has of course no systematic theology: indeed, the very idea of systematic thought has not yet come into existence. Moreover, he is working in a traditional form – for there must have been many writers of epic lays before Homer; so that the traditional and the new may be found side by side. In one place Zeus decides that the Greeks must be punished; therefore the Trojans are able to drive them back to their ships. In another, a god or goddess descends into the middle of the fray to save a favourite

who is in grave danger – and this, it may be, is done contrary
to the wish of Zeus. Then in contrast we meet a passage like
the one at the beginning of the *Odyssey*, in which Zeus is made
to say, 'How foolish men are! How unjustly they blame the
gods! It is their lot to suffer, but because of their own folly
they bring upon themselves sufferings over and above what is
fated for them. And then they blame the gods.' In modern
terms: life is in any case hard, but it is our own sins and errors
which make it harder than it need be. The grave philosophic
wisdom of this is not easy to reconcile with the divine caprice
that we find in the other passages: still less with the joyous
irreverence that we met in the story about Ares and Aphrodite.

It all seems rather bewildering. The unsystematized blending
of old and new explains something; and, for the rest, it may
help the reader if he thinks of the gods being an early attempt
to explain why things happen, especially things which seem to
be out of the ordinary. As we saw in the last chapter, the skill
of the metal-worker was something beyond the skill of the
ordinary man. As it was out of the ordinary, it was of divine
origin: then there must be a fire-god. In our passage from the
Iliad we learn that Achilles has strength beyond the ordinary:
this, says Agamemnon, is the gift of some god: and the explanation carries with it a very philosophic inference; it is
nothing to presume on; what a god gives, a god may take
away. Again, two forces contend in Achilles' mind, blind rage
and wise restraint. We might say, 'By a superhuman effort of
self-control ...', the Greeks said, 'By the help of some god ...';
and the Greek poet or vase-painter would portray Athena, in
bodily presence, counselling Achilles. The difference is not
great; and the fact that Achilles has his strength from a god or
makes a wise decision with the help of Athena, does not in the
least detract from the greatness of Achilles: the gods do not so
favour ordinary men, and he whom they do favour is not ordinary. We are not to think that the gods suddenly took up any
weakling and gave him strength: they did not behave like this.

Such then is the background against which we see the men
and the events not only of the Greek epic but also of most other
classical Greek art. It did, of course, degenerate into mytho-

logical prettiness: this was a post-classical development, but it captivated Rome, and it delighted the eighteenth century, with the result that the modern reader, before he can get a direct view of Homer or the later Greek classics, has first to clear away a certain amount of wedgwood ware and similar elegancies. But to the Greeks this background was not decoration: it was rather a kind of perspective – not in space, but in meaning. It makes us see the particular action that we are watching not as an isolated, a casual, a unique event; we see it rather in its relation to the moral and philosophical framework of the universe. This framework, I must repeat, is not one which Homer consciously expounds: he had no complete philosophical system. Nevertheless, he sees that there is a unity in things, that events have their causes and their results, that certain moral laws exist. This is the framework into which the particular action is seen to fit. The divine background of the epic means ultimately that particular actions are at the same time unique and universal.

The Greeks then, who for a thousand years turned to Homer for the education of their young and for the delight and instruction of the mature, were not turning to mere venerable relics or patriotic historical sagas or charming fairy-stories, but to poems which already possessed all those qualities which made the Greek civilization what it was. We have considered one passage in some detail: we have seen something, perhaps, of that instinctive intellectual power which so firmly organizes the whole poem; something, perhaps, of the essential seriousness that penetrates it; something of the sharpness with which Homer sees his object and of the vividness and economy with which he makes us see it too. But Homer, and all his great successors, have another quality which we have not yet spoken of, a quality which we must not allow to be obscured by all this talk of intellectuality and moral seriousness. That is his humanity. Let Homer himself illustrate this: he is a better writer than I am.

The battle is raging in the plain below Troy, and the Greek hero Diomedes is causing great havoc among the Trojans: so much so that Hector leaves the battlefield in order to ask the women in the city to pray to Athena for her help against this formidable man. Hector, entering the Scaean gate, is at once surrounded by wives and daughters anxious for news of their men in the field: 'but he bade all of them pray to the gods; and to many he gave sorrow'. He makes his way to the palace of his father, King Priam. Hecuba the Queen sees him and asks him, in truly heroic style, 'My son, why have you left the fierce battle and come here? The ill-omened Achaeans are pressing us very hard. Perhaps you are minded to pray to Zeus. Wait a while: I will fetch sweet wine, that you may first pour a libation to Zeus, then drink some yourself: for wine strengthens a weary man, and you are weary from defending your kinsmen.'

But Hector refuses: 'Wine may cause me to forget my duty, and I may not pour a sacred libation with blood on my hands'. He tells his mother to offer to Athena the most beautiful robe the Palace possesses – which she does: and Homer tells us where she got it. It was bought of Phoenician traders from Sidon. Hector sees Paris and sternly sends him back to the battle. Paris had been wounded and since then has been spending his time pleasantly with Helen: 'may the earth swallow him', says Hector. He sees Helen: she reproaches herself bitterly, and says, 'Come, sit awhile with me; for on your shoulders more than any lies the burden of my shamelessness and the wild folly of Paris'. But Hector will not stay: his companions in the battle need him and are longing for his return. 'And', he says, 'I must go to my own house, and see my servants and my dear wife and my infant son: for I know not if I shall ever come back to them again, or if the gods will even now lay me low beneath the hands of the Achaeans.'

But Andromache is not there. She had heard that the Trojans were being driven back, and she ran out, like a mad woman, distracted with anxiety, to the city-walls, to watch; and the nurse followed with the child. There Hector found her. Andromache grasped his hand, and said:

O Hector! your strength will be your destruction; and you have no pity either for your infant son or for your unhappy wife who will soon be your widow. For soon all the Achaeans will set upon you and kill you; and if I lose you it would be better for me to die. I shall have no other comfort, but my sorrow. I have no father and no mother: for my father Eetion was slain by Achilles; but yet (a touch of pride here) Achilles forbore to take his weapons: they were buried with his body. And I had seven brothers in my home, and all of them swift-footed Achilles slew; and my mother, who was Queen at Placos, died in my father's house. Hector *you* are father and mother and brother to me, and you are my proud husband. Come, take pity on me now! Stay on these walls, and do not leave your son an orphan and me a widow. And', she says, for she is a woman of intelligence, and has been observing things through her tears, 'post men by that fig-tree, where the Greeks have been attacking.' To her in reply said Hector of the flashing helmet, 'Lady, this will I see to. But I should feel great shame before the Trojans and the Trojan women of long robes if like a coward I should linger away from battle. Nor do I find that in my heart, for I have been taught to be brave always, and to fight in the forefront among the Trojans, winning great glory for my father and myself. For well do I know this, and I am sure of it: that day is coming when the holy city of Troy will perish, and Priam and the people of wealthy Priam. But my grief is not so much for the Trojans, nor for Hecuba herself, nor for Priam the King, nor for my many noble brothers, who will be slain by the foe and will lie in the dust, as for you, when one of the bronze-clad Achaeans will carry you away in tears, and end your days of freedom. Then you may live in Argos, and work at the loom in another woman's house, or perhaps carry water for a woman of Messene or Hyperia, sore against your will: but hard compulsion will lie upon you. And then a man will say, as he sees you weeping, "This was the wife of Hector, who was the noblest in battle of the horse-taming Trojans, when they were fighting around Ilion." This is what they will say: and it will be fresh grief for you, to fight against slavery, bereft of a husband like that. But may I be dead, may the earth be heaped over my grave before I hear your cries, and of the violence done to you.'

So spake shining Hector, and held out his arms to his son. But the child screamed and shrank back into the bosom of the well-girdled nurse, for he took fright at the sight of his dear father – at the bronze, and the crest of horsehair which he saw swaying terribly from the top of the helmet. His father laughed aloud, and his lady mother too. At once shining Hector took the helmet off his head and laid it on the ground, and when he had kissed his dear son and dandled him in his arms, he prayed to Zeus and to the other gods: 'Zeus and ye other gods, grant that this my son may be, as I am, most glorious among the Trojans and a man of might, and greatly rule in Ilion. And may they say, as he returns from war, "He is far better than his father." And may he slay the foeman and carry off his weapons, and may his mother have delight in him.'

This passage gives us a glimpse into the very soul of the Homeric hero. What moves him to deeds of heroism is not a sense of duty as we understand it – duty towards others: it is rather duty towards himself. He strives after that which we translate 'virtue', but is in Greek *aretê*, 'excellence'. And what Agamemnon and Achilles quarrel about is not simply a girl: it is the 'prize' which is the public recognition of his *aretê*. We shall have much to say about *aretê*: it runs through Greek life.

This scene – at any rate, in Greek – is such that the scholar who knows it by heart first expounds the variants in the MSS., the exact shades of meaning in the words, the grammatical complexities – and then cannot trust his voice to translate it steadily; nor is it by any means the only one of that kind in the *Iliad*. Nor is this timeless humanity confined to the great scenes, as one or two casual touches will show. Consider this short passage:[1]

Diomedes left them lying dead: and he went in pursuit of Abas and Polyidos, the sons of Eurydamas, the old man who could interpret dreams. And mightily did Diomedes slay them. And he went after Xanthus and Thoon, sons of Phaenops; and Phaenops lived through a sad old age, for he got him no other sons to leave his possessions to; for Diomedes slew them both and took sweet life from them. They did not return to him alive from the battle, and strangers divided their inheritance.

Consider one verse given to Diomedes a little later.[2] The young hero Glaucus sees the havoc that Diomedes is working among the Trojans, and decides to do battle with him. Diomedes – such is the knightly code – asks him who he is, 'for I

have not set eyes on you before in battle that ennobles men ...
And you surpass them all in courage, that you can stand there,
waiting for my long spear.' – Now comes the significant
detail. Diomedes might so naturally have said, 'Ill-fated are
those men who oppose my strength'; but he says instead, 'Ill-
fated are they whose sons oppose my strength'. Scenes of
battle are described with what looks like gusto; the hero of the
moment storms his way along and leaves a list of the slain
behind him; we are told precisely where the deadly spear
entered the body of the defeated warrior, and very often where
it came out again; the conqueror lays up for himself a glory
that will live after him. But Homer has a thought for the
wider life of men: he does not forget – nor yet does he obtrude
– those to whom another man's glory brings sorrow.

It would be a mistake to describe the *Iliad* as a tragedy,
because (like most things Greek) it is precisely what it pur-
ports to be, an epic poem, with all the leisureliness and expansiveness of an epic poem. Nevertheless, it is intensely tragic,
being in this too thoroughly Greek: the tragic turn of thought
was habitual with the Greeks. Before we try to explain this,
still using as our illustration the all-embracing Homer, it might
be well to make one or two negative points. In the first place,
the reason for this tragic vein is not that the Greek thought life
a poor thing. We have just mentioned the apparent gusto with
which Homer describes scenes of fighting: everything else is
described with the same exact enthusiasm. He *saw* everything
with intense interest, whether it was Odysseus building his
boat, or heroes preparing and eating their very satisfying
suppers in camp, and as likely as not, following the meal with
song. That life was a vale of tears, in which nothing could
matter very much, was an idea that very few Greeks entertained. They had the keenest appetite for activity of all kinds –
physical, mental, emotional; a never-ending delight in doing
things, and in seeing how they were done. Almost any page of
Homer will bear testimony to this. The undercurrent of
tragedy is assuredly not due to any feeling that life is not worth
while; it was a feeling of tragedy, not of melancholy.

Nor again must we imagine that an inclination to the tragic

meant a dislike of the comic. To be sure, there is little comedy in the *Iliad*, just as there is very little comic relief in the tragedies of the later Attic stage: but we have already made acquaintance of a notably comic story in the *Odyssey*; and we should not forget that, just as the Attic stage had its Aristophanes as well as its Aeschylus – and Aeschylus himself had a great reputation in antiquity as a writer of the farcical satyr-drama – so epic had its counterpart in the burlesque epic, of which the *Battle of Frogs and Mice* survives. This strain of tragedy which haunts Greek thought had nothing to do with gloom: the Greek loved laughter, just as he loved life. It was, I think, the product of those two great qualities which we have been contemplating in Homer, intellectualism and humanity. The former enabled the Greek, as I have tried to show, to see more clearly than some the great framework in which human life must be lived, the framework which Homer expressed partly as the will and the activities of the gods, partly as a shadowy Necessity to which even the gods must bow. Actions must have their consequences; ill-judged actions must have uncomfortable results. The Gods, to the Greek, are not necessarily benevolent. If they are offended they hit out implacably: as Achilles says to the broken Priam, they give two sorrows for every blessing. Nor is this clear appreciation of the human scene relieved either by bright hopes of a better world hereafter or by any belief in progress. As to the former, the Greek in Homer could look forward to a dim shadowy life in Hades; and as Achilles said, 'I would rather be a slave on earth than a King in Hades'. The only real hope of immortality was that one's fame might live on in song. As to the latter, it was impossible; for the nature of the gods cannot change, and that the nature of men should change was an idea that occurred to nobody for a long time yet; and even if it did, the gods would still give the two sorrows for every blessing. Life would still remain what it is, in all its essentials.

One can imagine such an outlook, so remarkably free from illusions, developing into an arid religion and breeding a resigned and hopeless fatalism; but it was combined with this almost fierce joy in life, the exultation in human achievement

and in human personality. So far was the Greek from thinking
that Man was a mere nothing in the sight of the gods that he
had always to be reminding himself that Man is not God, and
that it is impious to think it. Never again, until the Greek
spirit intoxicated Italy at the Renaissance, do we find such
superb self-confidence in humanity – a self-confidence which,
in Renaissance Italy, was not restrained by the modesty imposed on the Greek by his instinctive religious outlook.

The tragic note which we hear in the *Iliad* and in most of
Greek literature was produced by the tension between these
two forces, passionate delight in life, and clear apprehension of
its unalterable framework:

As is the life of the leaves, so is that of men. The wind scatters the
leaves to the ground: the vigorous forest puts forth others, and they
grow in the spring-season. Soon one generation of men comes and
another ceases.

Neither the thought nor the image is peculiar to Homer: the
peculiar poignancy is, and it comes from the context. We do not
find it in the magnificent Hebrew parallel:

As for man, his days are as grass. As a flower of the field, so he
flourisheth. For the wind passeth over it, and it is gone, and the place
thereof shall know it no more.

The note here is one of humility and resignation: Man *is* no
more than grass, in comparison with God. But the Homeric
image takes a very different colour from its context of heroic
striving and achievement. Man is unique; yet for all his high
quality and his brilliant variety he must obey the same laws as
the innumerable and indistinguishable leaves. There can be no
romantic protest – for how can we protest against the first law
of our being? – nor resigned acceptance – such as we find, for
example, among the Chinese, to whom the individual is only
an ancestor in the making, one crop of leaves on one tree in
the forest. There is instead this passionate tension which is a
spirit of tragedy.

Many more examples could be cited from Homer, particularly from the *Iliad*. One must suffice; it will illustrate it from a

different point of view. Typical of the limitations, even the contradictions of life, is the fact that what is most worth having can often be had only at the peril of life itself. The hero proves his courage and wins his glory only, it may be, in his death – to the sorrow of his kinsmen. Beauty has danger and death as its neighbour. Here is an interlude in Homer's description of fierce fighting around the walls of Troy, watched from the walls by Priam and others of the old men:

So did the Trojan princes sit on the tower. And they saw Helen coming to the Tower, and said to each other softly, in winged words: 'Small blame to the Trojans and the well-armed Achaeans that they suffer so long, and so bitterly, for one like *that*, lovely as a goddess. Yet even so, beautiful though she is, let her go home in a ship, and not leave sorrows to us and our children.' So they spoke: but Priam called out to Helen, 'Come, dear child, come and sit by me, and look upon him who was your husband, and upon your other kinsmen and friends. I cannot blame you: it was the gods who caused it, and brought war and tears upon us.'

'It was the gods': not a sententious shuffling-off of responsibility, but the recognition that such things as these are part of the human lot. Beauty, like glory, must be sought, though the price be tears and destruction. Is not this thought at the very centre of the whole legend of the Trojan War? For its hero Achilles, the very perfection of Greek chivalry, was given precisely this choice by the gods. They offered him a long life with mediocrity, or glory with an early death. Whoever first made this myth expressed in it the essence not only of Greek thought but also of Greek history.

I have written so much about the *Iliad*, partly because it contains so much of the essential Greek spirit, partly in order to show the reader the sort of thing on which the Greeks were educated for centuries. The *Odyssey* must be sacrificed, though equally a part of this education, and in many ways the necessary complement of the *Iliad*: a poem, as Longinus said, of character rather than of passion; a poem full of the Greek love of adventure and strange tales; and, like the *Iliad*, a poem which might have been only a sackful of old stories, but has instead an intelligent and artistic unity which comes inevitably from one central idea – in this case, a belief in an ultimate justice. Did one poet write both poems? Did one poet, indeed, compose either? And when did he, or they, live? This is the famous Homeric Question which scholars have debated for a century and a half: the reader will not expect it to be settled here. The later Greeks themselves possessed a whole cycle of epics on the Trojan war. Two of these were of surpassing excellence, and were attributed to Homer. This attribution was accepted quite wholeheartedly until modern times, when closer investigation showed all sorts of discrepancies of fact, style and language both between the two epics and between various parts of each. The immediate result of this was the minute and confident division of the two poems, but especially of the *Iliad*, into separate lays of different periods, appropriately called 'strata' by critics who sometimes imperfectly distinguished between artistic and geological composition. The study of the epic poetry of other races, and of the methods used by poets working in this traditional medium, has done a great deal to restore confidence in the substantial unity of each poem: that is to say, that what we have in each case is not a short poem by one original 'Homer' to which later poets have added more or less indiscriminately, but a poem conceived as a unity by a relatively late 'Homer' who worked over and incorporated much traditional material – though the present *Iliad* certainly contains some passages which were not parts of 'Homer's' design. Whether the same poet wrote both poems is a point on which opinions differ and probably always will. The difference in tone and in treatment is great. Longinus, the finest critic of antiquity, observed this, and remarked, 'Homer in the *Odyssey* is like the setting sun; the grandeur remains, but not the intensity'. It may be the same sun. But a man has a right to an opinion who has immersed himself in Homer to the extent of translating one of the poems. Accordingly, it is interesting to observe that of the two recent English translators, T. E. Lawrence is so certain that the two poets are not the same that he does not even consider the possibility: while Mr E. V. Rieu says, 'His readers may feel as sure that they are in one man's hands as they do when they turn to *As You Like It* after reading *King John*'.

We will leave it at that, for the Homeric question, fascinating though it is to scholars, must not be allowed to obscure Homer from us. It is an interesting, though idle, speculation, what would be the effect on us if all our reformers, revolutionaries, planners, politicians and life-arrangers in general were soaked in Homer from their youth up, like the Greeks. They might realize that on the happy day when there is a refrigerator in every home, and two in none, when we all have the opportunity of working for the common good (whatever that is), when Common Man (whoever he is) is triumphant, though not improved – that men will still come and go like the generations of leaves in the forest; that he will still be weak, and the gods strong and incalculable; that the quality of a man matters more than his achievement; that violence and reck-lessness will still lead to disaster, and that this will fall on the innocent as well as on the guilty. The Greeks were fortunate in possessing Homer, and wise in using him as they did.

v

THE POLIS

'POLIS' is the Greek word which we translate 'city-state'. It is a bad translation, because the normal polis was not much like a city, and was very much more than a state. But translation, like politics, is the art of the possible; since we have not got the thing which the Greeks called 'the polis', we do not possess an equivalent word. From now on, we will avoid the misleading term 'city-state', and use the Greek word instead. In this chapter we will first enquire how this political system arose, then we will try to reconstitute the word 'polis' and recover its real meaning by watching it in action. It may be a long task, but all the time we shall be improving our acquaintance with the Greeks. Without a clear conception what the polis was, and what it meant to the Greeks, it is quite impossible to understand properly Greek history, the Greek mind, or the Greek achievement.

First then, what was the polis? In the *Iliad* we discern a political structure that seems not unfamiliar – a structure that can be called an advanced or a degenerate form of tribalism, according to taste. There are kings, like Achilles, who rule their people, and there is the great king, Agamemnon, King of Men, who is something like a feudal overlord. He is under obligation, whether of right or of custom, to consult the other kings or chieftains in matters of common interest. They form a regular council, and in its debates the sceptre, symbol of authority, is held by the speaker for the time being. This is recognizably European, not Oriental; Agamemnon is no despot, ruling with the unquestioned authority of a god. There are also signs of a shadowy Assembly of the People, to be consulted on important occasions: though Homer, a courtly poet, and in any case not a constitutional historian, says little about it.

Such, in outline, is the tradition about pre-conquest Greece. When the curtain goes up again after the Dark Age we see a very different picture. No longer is there a 'wide-ruling Agamemnon' lording it in Mycenae. In Crete, where Idomeneus had been ruling as sole king, we find over fifty quite independent poleis, fifty small 'states' in the place of one. It is a small matter that the kings have disappeared; the important thing is that the kingdoms have gone too. What is true of Crete is true of Greece in general, or at least of those parts which play any considerable part in Greek history – Ionia, the islands, the Peloponnesus except Arcadia, Central Greece except the western parts, and South Italy and Sicily when they became Greek. All these were divided into an enormous number of quite independent and autonomous political units.

It is important to realize their size. The modern reader picks up a translation of Plato's *Republic* or Aristotle's *Politics*; he finds Plato ordaining that his ideal city shall have 5,000 citizens, and Aristotle that each citizen should be able to know all the others by sight; and he smiles, perhaps, at such

C

philosophic fantasies. But Plato and Aristotle are not fantasts. Plato is imagining a polis on the normal Hellenic scale; indeed he implies that many existing Greek poleis are too small – for many had less than 5,000 citizens. Aristotle says, in his amusing way – Aristotle sometimes sounds very like a don – that a polis of ten citizens would be impossible, because it could not be self-sufficient, and that a polis of a hundred thousand would be absurd, because it could not govern itself properly. And we are not to think of these 'citizens' as a 'master-class' owning and dominating thousands of slaves. The ordinary Greek in these early centuries was a farmer, and if he owned a slave he was doing pretty well. Aristotle speaks of a hundred thousand citizens; if we allow each to have a wife and four children, and then add a liberal number of slaves and resident aliens, we shall arrive at something like a million – the population of Birmingham; and to Aristotle an independent 'state' as populous as Birmingham is a lecture-room joke. Or we may turn from the philosophers to a practical man, Hippodamas, who laid out the Piraeus in the most up-to-date American style; he said that the ideal number of citizens was ten thousand, which would imply a total population of about 100,000.

In fact, only three poleis had more than 20,000 citizens – Syracuse and Acragas (Girgenti) in Sicily, and Athens. At the outbreak of the Peloponnesian War the population of Attica was probably about 350,000, half Athenian (men, women and children), about a tenth resident aliens, and the rest slaves. Sparta, or Lacedaemon, had a much smaller citizen-body, though it was larger in area. The Spartans had conquered and annexed Messenia, and possessed 3,200 square miles of territory. By Greek standards this was an enormous area: it would take a good walker two days to cross it. The important commercial city of Corinth had a territory of 330 square miles – about the size of Huntingdonshire. The island of Ceos, which is about as big as Bute, was divided into four poleis. It had therefore four armies, four governments, possibly four different calendars, and, it may be, four different currencies and systems of measures – though this is less likely. Mycenae was in historical times a shrunken relic of Agamemnon's capital, but still independent.

She sent an army to help the Greek cause against Persia at the battle of Plataea; the army consisted of eighty men. Even by Greek standards this was small, but we do not hear that any jokes were made about an army sharing a cab.

To think on this scale is difficult for us, who regard a state of ten million as small, and are accustomed to states which, like the U.S.A. and the U.S.S.R., are so big that they have to be referred to by their initials; but when the adjustable reader has become accustomed to the scale, he will not commit the vulgar error of confusing size with significance. The modern writer is sometimes heard to speak with splendid scorn of 'those petty Greek states, with their interminable quarrels'. Quite so; Plataea, Sicyon, Aegina and the rest are petty, compared with modern states. The Earth itself is petty, compared with Jupiter – but then, the atmosphere of Jupiter is mainly ammonia, and that makes a difference. We do not like breathing ammonia – and the Greeks would not much have liked breathing the atmosphere of the vast modern State. They knew of one such, the Persian Empire – and thought it very suitable, for barbarians. Difference of scale, when it is great enough, amounts to difference of kind.

But before we deal with the nature of the polis, the reader might like to know how it happened that the relatively spacious pattern of pre-Dorian Greece became such a mosaic of small fragments. The Classical scholar too would like to know; there are no records, so that all we can do is to suggest plausible reasons. There are historical, geographical and economic reasons; and when these have been duly set forth, we may conclude perhaps that the most important reason of all is simply that this is the way in which the Greeks preferred to live.

The coming of the Dorians was not an attack made by one organized nation upon another. The invaded indeed had their organization, loose though it was; some of the invaders – the main body that conquered Lacedaemon – must have been a coherent force; but others must have been small groups of raiders, profiting from the general turmoil and seizing good land where they could find it. A sign of this is that we find members of the same clan in different states. Pindar, for example, was a citizen of Thebes and a member of the ancient family of the Aegidae. But there were Aegidae too in Aegina and Sparta, quite independent poleis, and Pindar addresses them as kinsmen. This particular clan therefore was split up in the invasions. In a country like Greece this would be very natural.

In a period so unsettled the inhabitants of any valley or island might at a moment's notice be compelled to fight for their fields. Therefore a local strong-point was necessary, normally a defensible hill-top somewhere in the plain. This, the 'acropolis' ('high-town'), would be fortified, and here would be the residence of the king. It would also be the natural place of assembly, and the religious centre.

This is the beginning of the town. What we have to do is to give reasons why the town grew, and why such a small pocket of people remained an independent political unit. The former task is simple. To begin with, natural economic growth made a central market necessary. We saw that the economic system implied by Hesiod and Homer was 'close household economy'; the estate, large or small, produced nearly everything that it needed, and what it could not produce it did without. As things became more stable a rather more specialized economy became possible: more goods were produced for sale. Hence the growth of a market.

At this point we may invoke the very sociable habits of the Greeks, ancient or modern. The English farmer likes to build his house on his land, and to come into town when he has to. What little leisure he has he likes to spend on the very satisfying occupation of looking over a gate. The Greek prefers to live in the town or village, to walk out to his work, and to spend his rather ampler leisure talking in the town or village square. Therefore the market becomes a market-town, naturally beneath the Acropolis. This became the centre of the communal life of the people – and we shall see presently how important that was.

But why did not such towns form larger units? This is the important question.

There is an economic point. The physical barriers which Greece has so abundantly made the transport of goods difficult, except by sea, and the sea was not yet used with any confidence. Moreover, the variety of which we spoke earlier enabled quite a small area to be reasonably self-sufficient for a people who made such small material demands on life as the Greek. Both of these facts tend in the same direction; there was in Greece no great economic interdependence, no reciprocal pull between the different parts of the country, strong enough to counteract the desire of the Greek to live in small communities.

There is a geographical point. It is sometimes asserted that this system of independent poleis was imposed on Greece by the physical character of the country. The theory is attractive, especially to those who like to have one majestic explanation of any phenomenon, but it does not seem to be true. It is of course obvious that the physical subdivision of the country helped; the system could not have existed, for example, in Egypt, a country which depends entirely on the proper management of the Nile flood, and therefore must have a central government. But there are countries cut up quite as much as Greece – Scotland, for instance – which have never developed the polis-system; and conversely there were in Greece many neighbouring poleis, such as Corinth and Sicyon, which remained independent of each other although between them there was no physical barrier that would seriously incommode a modern cyclist. Moreover, it was precisely the most mountainous parts of Greece that never developed poleis, or not until later days – Arcadia and Aetolia, for example, which had something like a canton-system. The polis flourished in those parts where communications were relatively easy. So that we are still looking for our explanation.

Economics and geography helped, but the real explanation is the character of the Greeks – which those determinists may explain who have the necessary faith in their omniscience. As it will take some time to deal with this, we may first clear out of the way an important historical point. How did it come about that so preposterous a system was able to last for more than twenty minutes?

The ironies of history are many and bitter, but at least this must be put to the credit of the gods, that they arranged for the Greeks to have the Eastern Mediterranean almost to themselves long enough to work out what was almost a laboratory-experiment to test how far, and in what conditions, human nature is capable of creating and sustaining a civilization. In Asia, the Hittite Empire had collapsed, the Lydian kingdom was not aggressive, and the Persian power, which eventually overthrew Lydia, was still embryonic in the mountainous recesses of the continent; Egypt was in decay; Macedon, destined to make nonsense of the polis-system, was and long remained in a state of ineffective semi-barbarism; Rome had not yet been heard of, nor any other power in Italy. There were indeed the Phoenicians, and their western colony, Carthage, but these were traders first and last. Therefore this lively and intelligent Greek people was for some centuries allowed to live under the apparently absurd system which suited and developed its genius instead of becoming absorbed in the dull mass of a large empire, which would have smothered its spiritual growth, and made it what it afterwards became, a race of brilliant individuals and opportunists. Obviously some day somebody would create a strong centralized power in the Eastern Mediterranean – a successor to the ancient sea-power of King Minos. Would it be Greek, Oriental, or something else? This question must be the theme of a later chapter, but no history of Greece can be intelligible until one has understood what the polis meant to the Greek; and when we have understood that, we shall also understand why the Greeks developed it, and so obstinately tried to maintain it. Let us then examine the word in action.

It meant at first that which was later called the Acropolis, the stronghold of the whole community and the centre of its public life. The town which nearly always grew up around this was designated by another word, 'asty'. But 'polis' very soon meant either the citadel or the whole people which, as it were, 'used' this citadel. So we read in Thucydides, 'Epidamnus is a polis on the right as you sail into the Ionian gulf'. This is not like saying 'Bristol is a city on the right as you sail up the

Bristol Channel', for Bristol is not an independent state which might be at war with Gloucester, but only an urban area with a purely local administration. Thucydides' words imply that there is a town – though possibly a very small one – called Epidamnus, which is the political centre of the Epidamnians, who live in the territory of which the town is the centre – not the 'capital' – and are Epidamnians whether they live in the town or in one of the villages in this territory.

Sometimes the territory and the town have different names. Thus, Attica is the territory occupied by the Athenian people; it comprised Athens – the 'polis' in the narrower sense – the Piraeus, and many villages; but the people collectively were Athenians, not Attics, and a citizen was an Athenian in whatever part of Attica he might live.

In this sense 'polis' is our 'state'. In Sophocles' *Antigone* Creon comes forward to make his first proclamation as king. He begins, 'Gentlemen, as for the polis, the gods have brought it safely through the storm, on even keel'. It is the familiar image of the Ship of State, and we think we know where we are. But later in the play he says what we should naturally translate, 'Public proclamation has been made ...' He says in fact, 'It has been proclaimed to the polis ...' – not to the 'state', but to the 'people'. Later in the play he quarrels violently with his son; 'What?' he cries, 'is anyone but me to rule in this land?' Haemon answers, 'It is no polis that is ruled by one man only'. The answer brings out another important part of the whole conception of a polis, namely that it is a community, and that its affairs are the affairs of all. The actual business of governing might be entrusted to a monarch, acting in the name of all according to traditional usages, or to the heads of certain noble families, or to a council of citizens owning so much property, or to all the citizens. All these, and many modifications of them, were natural forms of 'polity'; all were sharply distinguished by the Greek from Oriental monarchy, in which the monarch is irresponsible, not holding his powers in trust by the grace of god, but being himself a god. If there was irresponsible government there was no polis.

Haemon is accusing his father of talking like a 'tyrannos'[1] and thereby destroying the polis – but not 'the State'.

To continue our exposition of the word. The chorus in Aristophanes' *Acharnians*, admiring the conduct of the hero, turns to the audience with an appeal which I render literally, 'Dost thou see, O whole polis?' The last words are sometimes translated 'thou thronging city', which sounds better, but obscures an essential point, namely that the size of the polis made it possible for a member to appeal to all his fellow-citizens in person, and this he naturally did if he thought that another member of the polis had injured him. It was the common assumption of the Greeks that the polis took its origin in the desire for Justice. Individuals are lawless, but the polis will see to it that wrongs are redressed. But not by an elaborate machinery of state-justice, for such a machine could not be operated except by individuals, who may be as unjust as the original wrongdoer. The injured party will be sure of obtaining justice only if he can declare his wrongs to the whole polis. The word therefore now means 'people' in actual distinction from 'state'.

Iocasta, the tragic Queen in the *Oedipus*, will show us a little more of the range of the word. It becomes a question if Oedipus her husband is not after all the accursed man who had killed the previous king Laius. 'No, no,' cries Iocasta, 'it cannot be! The slave said it was "brigands" who had attacked them, not "a brigand". He cannot go back on his word now. The polis heard him, not I alone.' Here the word is used without any 'political' association at all; it is, as it were, off duty, and signifies 'the whole people'. This is a shade of meaning which is not always so prominent, but is never entirely absent.

Then Demosthenes the orator talks of a man who, literally, 'avoids the city' – a translation which might lead the unwary to suppose that he lived in something corresponding to the Lake District, or Purley. But the phrase 'avoids the polis' tells us nothing about his domicile; it means that he took no part in

---

1. I prefer to use the Greek form of this (apparently) Oriental word. It is the Greek equivalent of 'dictator', but does not necessarily have the colour of our word 'tyrant'.

public life – and was therefore something of an oddity. The affairs of the community did not interest him.

We have now learned enough about the word polis to realize that there is no possible English rendering of such a common phrase as, 'It is everyone's duty to help the polis'. We cannot say 'help the state', for that arouses no enthusiasm; it is 'the state' that takes half our incomes from us. Not 'the community', for with us 'the community' is too big and too various to be grasped except theoretically. One's village, one's trade union, one's class, are entities that mean something to us at once, but 'work for the community', though an admirable sentiment, is to most of us vague and flabby. In the years before the war, what did most parts of Great Britain know about the depressed areas? How much do bankers, miners and farm-workers understand each other? But the 'polis' every Greek knew; there it was, complete, before his eyes. He could see the fields which gave it its sustenance – or did not, if the crops failed; he could see how agriculture, trade and industry dove-tailed into one another; he knew the frontiers, where they were strong and where weak; if any malcontents were planning a *coup*, it was difficult for them to conceal the fact. The entire life of the polis, and the relation between its parts, were much easier to grasp, because of the small scale of things. Therefore to say 'It is everyone's duty to help the polis' was not to express a fine sentiment but to speak the plainest and most urgent common sense.[1] Public affairs had an immediacy and a con-creteness which they cannot possibly have for us.

One specific example will help. The Athenian democracy taxed the rich with as much disinterested enthusiasm as the British, but this could be done in a much more gracious way, simply because the State was so small and intimate. Among us, the payer of super-tax (presumably) pays much as the income-tax payer does: he writes his cheque and thinks, 'There! *That's* gone down the drain!' In Athens, the man whose wealth ex-ceeded a certain sum had, in a yearly rota, to perform certain 'liturgies' – literally, 'folk-works'. He had to keep a warship

1. It did not, of course, follow that the Greek obeyed common sense any oftener than we do.

in commission for one year (with the privilege of commanding it, if he chose), or finance the production of plays at the Festival, or equip a religious procession. It was a heavy burden, and no doubt unwelcome, but at least some fun could be got out of it and some pride taken in it. There was satisfaction and honour to be gained from producing a trilogy worthily before one's fellow-citizens. So, in countless other ways, the size of the polis made vivid and immediate, things which to us are only abstractions or wearisome duties. Naturally this cut both ways. For example, an incompetent or unlucky commander was the object not of a diffused and harmless popular indignation, but of direct accusation; he might be tried for his life before an Assembly, many of whose past members he had led to death.

Pericles' Funeral Speech, recorded or recreated by Thucydides, will illustrate this immediacy, and will also take our conception of the polis a little further. Each year, Thucydides tells us, if citizens had died in war – and they had, more often than not – a funeral oration was delivered by 'a man chosen by the polis'. To-day, that would be someone nominated by the Prime Minister, or the British Academy, or the B.B.C. In Athens it meant that someone was chosen by the Assembly who had often spoken to that Assembly; and on this occasion Pericles spoke from a specially high platform, that his voice might reach as many as possible. Let us consider two phrases that Pericles used in that speech.

He is comparing the Athenian polis with the Spartan, and makes the point that the Spartans admit foreign visitors only grudgingly, and from time to time expel all strangers, 'while we make our polis common to all'. 'Polis' here is not the political unit; there is no question of naturalizing foreigners – which the Greeks did rarely, simply because the polis was so intimate a union. Pericles means here: 'We throw open to all our common cultural life', as is shown by the words that follow, difficult though they are to translate: 'nor do we deny them any instruction or spectacle' – words that are almost meaningless until we realize that the drama, tragic and comic, the performance of choral hymns, public recitals of Homer, games, were all necessary and normal parts of 'political' life.

This is the sort of thing Pericles has in mind when he speaks of 'instruction and spectacle', and of 'making the polis open to all'.

But we must go further than this. A perusal of the speech will show that in praising the Athenian polis Pericles is praising more than a state, a nation, or a people: he is praising a way of life; he means no less when, a little later, he calls Athens the 'school of Hellas'. – And what of that? Do not we praise 'the English way of life'? The difference is this; we expect our State to be quite indifferent to 'the English way of life' – indeed, the idea that the State should actively try to promote it would fill most of us with alarm. The Greeks thought of the polis as an active, formative thing, training the minds and characters of the citizens; we think of it as a piece of machinery for the production of safety and convenience. The training in virtue, which the medieval state left to the Church, and the polis made its own concern, the modern state leaves to God knows what.

'Polis', then, originally 'citadel', may mean as much as 'the whole communal life of the people, political, cultural, moral' – even 'economic', for how else are we to understand another phrase in this same speech, 'the produce of the whole world comes to us, because of the magnitude of our polis'? This must mean 'our national wealth'.

Religion too was bound up with the polis – though not every form of religion.[1] The Olympian gods were indeed worshipped by Greeks everywhere, but each polis had, if not its own gods, at least its own particular cults of these gods. Thus, Athena of the Brazen House was worshipped at Sparta, but to the Spartans Athena was never what she was to the Athenians, 'Athena Polias', Athena guardian of the City. So Hera, in Athens, was a goddess worshipped particularly by women, as the goddess of hearth and home, but in Argos 'Argive Hera' was the supreme deity of the people. We have in these gods tribal deities, like Jehovah, who exist as it were on two levels at once, as gods of the individual polis, and gods of the whole Greek race. But beyond these Olympians, each polis

1. Not the mystery-religions. (See p. 19 f.)

had its minor local deities, 'heroes' and nymphs, each wor-shipped with his immemorial rite, and scarcely imagined to exist outside the particular locality where the rite was per-formed. So that in spite of the panhellenic Olympian system, and in spite of the philosophic spirit which made merely tribal gods impossible for the Greek, there is a sense in which it is true to say that the polis is an independent religious, as well as political, unit. The tragic poets at least could make use of the old belief that the gods desert a city which is about to be captured. The gods are the unseen partners in the city's welfare.

How intimately religious and 'political' thinking were con-nected we can best see from the *Oresteia* of Aeschylus. This trilogy is built around the idea of Justice. It moves from chaos to order, from conflict to reconciliation; and it moves on two planes at once, the human and the divine. In the *Agamemnon* we see one of the moral Laws of the universe, that punishment must follow crime, fulfilled in the crudest possible way; one crime evokes another crime to avenge it, in apparently endless succession – but always with the sanction of Zeus. In the *Choephori* this series of crimes reaches its climax when Orestes avenges his father by killing his mother. He does this with repugnance, but he is commanded to do it by Apollo, the son and the mouthpiece of Zeus – Why? Because in murdering Agamemnon the King and her husband, Clytemnestra has committed a crime which, unpunished, would shatter the very fabric of society. It is the concern of the Olympian gods to defend Order; they are particularly the gods of the Polis. But Orestes' matricide outrages the deepest human instincts; he is therefore implacably pursued by other deities, the Furies. The Furies have no interest in social order, but they cannot permit this outrage on the sacredness of the blood-tie, which it is their office to protect. In the *Eumenides* there is a terrific con-flict between the ancient Furies and the younger Olympians over the unhappy Orestes. The solution is that Athena comes with a new dispensation from Zeus. A jury of Athenian citizens is empanelled to try Orestes on the Acropolis where he has fled for protection – this being the first meeting of the Council of the Areopagus. The votes on either side are equal; therefore, as an act of mercy, Orestes is acquitted. The Furies, cheated of their legitimate prey, threaten Attica with destruction, but Athena persuades them to make their home in Athens, with their ancient office not abrogated (as at first they think) but enhanced, since henceforth they will punish violence within the polis, not only within the family.

So, to Aeschylus the mature polis becomes the means by which the Law is satisfied without producing chaos, since public justice supersedes private vengeance; and the claims of authority are reconciled with the instincts of humanity. The trilogy ends with an impressive piece of pageantry. The awful Furies exchange their black robes for red ones, no longer Furies, but 'Kindly Ones' (Eumenides); no longer enemies of Zeus, but his willing and honoured agents, defenders of his now perfected social order against intestine violence. Before the eyes of the Athenian citizens assembled in the theatre just under the Acropolis – and indeed guided by citizen-marshals – they pass out of the theatre to their new home on the other side of the Acropolis. Some of the most acute of man's moral and social problems have been solved, and the means of the reconciliation is the Polis.

A few minutes later, on that early spring day of 458 B.C., the citizens too would leave the theatre, and by the same exits as the Eumenides. In what mood? Surely no audience has had such an experience since. At the time, the Athenian polis was confidently riding the crest of the wave. In this trilogy there was exaltation, for they had seen their polis emerge as the pattern of Justice, of Order, of what the Greeks called Cosmos; the polis, they saw, was – or could be – the very crown and summit of things. They had seen their goddess herself acting as President of the first judicial tribunal – a steadying and sobering thought. But there was more than this. The rising democracy had recently curtailed the powers of the ancient Court of the Areopagus, and the reforming statesman had been assassinated by his political enemies. What of the Eumenides, the awful inhabitants of the land, the transformed Furies, whose function it was to avenge the shedding of a kinsman's blood?

There was warning here, as well as exaltation, in the thought that the polis had its divine as well as its human members. There was Athena, one of those Olympians who had presided over the formation of ordered society, and there were the more primitive deities who had been persuaded by Athena to accept this pattern of civilized life, and were swift to punish any who, by violence from within, threatened its stability.

To such an extent was the religious thought of Aeschylus intertwined with the idea of the polis; and not of Aeschylus alone, but of many other Greek thinkers too – notably of Socrates, Plato, and Aristotle. Aristotle made a remark which we most inadequately translate 'Man is a political animal'. What Aristotle really said is 'Man is a creature who lives in a polis'; and what he goes on to demonstrate, in his *Politics*, is that the polis is the only framework within which man can fully realize his spiritual, moral and intellectual capacities.

Such are some of the implications of this word: we shall meet more later, for I have deliberately said little about its purely 'political' side – to emphasize the fact that it is so much more than a form of political organization. The polis was a living community, based on kinship, real or assumed – a kind of extended family, turning as much as possible of life into family life, and of course having its family quarrels, which were the more bitter because they were family quarrels.

This it is that explains not only the polis but also much of what the Greek made and thought, that he was essentially social. In the winning of his livelihood he was essentially individualist: in the filling of his life he was essentially 'communist'. Religion, art, games, the discussion of things – all these were needs of life that could be fully satisfied only through the polis – not, as with us, through voluntary associations of like-minded people, or through *entrepreneurs* appealing to individuals. (This partly explains the difference between Greek drama and the modern cinema.) Moreover, he wanted to play his own part in running the affairs of the community. When we realize how many of the necessary, interesting and exciting activities of life the Greek enjoyed through the polis, all of them in the open air, within sight of the same acropolis, with the same ring of mountains or of sea visibly enclosing the life of every member of the state – then it becomes possible to understand Greek history, to understand that in spite of the promptings of commonsense the Greek could not bring himself to sacrifice the polis, with its vivid and comprehensive life, to a wider but less interesting unity. We may perhaps record an Imaginary Conversation between an Ancient Greek and a member of the Athenæum. The member regrets the lack of political sense shown by the Greeks. The Greek replies, 'How many clubs are there in London?' The member, at a guess, says about five hundred. The Greek then says, 'Now, if all these combined, what splendid premises they could build. They could have a club-house as big as Hyde Park.' 'But,' says the member, 'that would no longer be a club.' 'Precisely,' says the Greek, 'and a polis as big as yours is no longer a polis.'

After all, modern Europe, in spite of its common culture, common interests, and ease of communication, finds it difficult to accept the idea of limiting national sovereignty, though this would increase the security of life without notably adding to its dullness; the Greek had possibly more to gain by watering down the polis – but how much more to lose. It was not commonsense that made Achilles great, but certain other qualities.

VI

CLASSICAL GREECE: THE EARLY PERIOD

THE modern map of the Mediterranean and adjacent waters is full of Greek names. Sebastopol, Alexandria, Benghazi – and of course the neighbouring Apollonia, which our newspapers never know how to spell, the worship of Apollo not being very vigorous in Fleet Street – Syracuse, Naples, Monaco: all these names, and hundreds of others, are Greek by origin, though many of them have become very much battered by being used for centuries on foreign tongues. Not all of them go back to early classical days. Alexandria commemorates its founder, Alexander the Great, with whom this volume will end. Sebastopol is the Greek for 'city of Augustus', a foundation therefore of Roman Imperial times; Benghazi is Berenike (Macedonian Greek for Pherenike, 'bringer of victory'), the name of one of the queens of the Macedonian line of Ptolemies who ruled Egypt from the time of Alexander (320 B.C.) down to the Cleopatra who fascinated Caesar, Shakespeare and Shaw. Nevertheless, a very large number of these names go back to the period with which we are now concerned, the eighth, seventh and sixth centuries. Marseilles started life as Massilia, and Massilia was founded, by the Greeks, at about 600. This coast in fact is a museum of Greek names. Monaco got its name from a shrine of Heracles Monoikos. 'Heracles who dwells alone': Nice was Nikaia, 'Victoria', Antibes is Antipolis, 'the city opposite'; Agde is Agathê, 'the good place'. South-west Italy too is full of Greek names: Naples for example is Neapolis, 'New town', and Reggio is Rhegion, 'the Rent' – so named from the narrow strait.

The Ionian poet Homer obviously knew next to nothing of the Western Mediterranean or of the Black Sea: these were regions vaguely known and filled with marvels. Ithaca, off the west coast of Greece, is the boundary of his knowledge towards the west – and he does not seem to be so very certain even about Ithaca. Yet within three hundred years at the most we find Greek cities firmly planted not only all around the Aegean, but also in the more reasonable parts of the Black Sea (including the Crimea), along the Libyan coast, in south and west Italy, in Sicily, on the south coast of France and the east coast of Spain. Indeed Sicily and the neighbouring parts of Italy became known as 'Greater Greece'; it was from here, and not from the Greek motherland, that Rome first imbibed Greek civilization.

This was not the first great expansion of Greece, nor was it the last. We have seen how the Ionians (and others) had swarmed eastwards across the Aegean when the Dorians came: and centuries later Greeks settled all over Alexander's new dominions – as indeed in the last century Greeks settled in America in such numbers that the money they sent home was an important item in the national economy. The Greeks have usually been a fertile race, and the nature of the country imposes a very definite limit on the population – which is true indeed of Mediterranean lands even today.

We are extremely ill-informed about the causes and the course of the great colonizing movement which began at about 750 and continued for some two hundred years. That over-population was the chief cause seems tolerably certain, though other factors no doubt played their part: political unrest, for example, and disasters from without. For example, when Cyrus the Great conquered Ionia in 545, the inhabitants of two cities, Tenos and Phocaea, resolved to emigrate in a body rather than live as subjects of Persia. The Teians established themselves on the coast of Thrace, and founded Abdera, but the Phocaeans went further afield. They resolved to go to Corsica. They sank a large lump of iron in their harbour (according to the charming story in Herodotus), and swore that they would not return until the iron floated. But not long after they had started, many of them, overcome by a longing for their own city, turned back. The rest went on, and joined their own existing colony of Alalia in Corsica (later Aleria, and still existing under that name as a hamlet).

One thing seems quite certain about the earlier colonies at least, they were not founded for reasons of trade; they were not 'factories'. All that we know of them suggests that land was what the colonists were looking for. The Greek farmer, working on a very little margin, lived a precarious existence. The subdivision of a family plot soon reaches the point where efficient farming is impossible, and – as we shall see presently in discussing Athens – big estates have an unconscionable habit of swallowing small ones. The cry for a redistribution of land was often heard in Greece, and colonization was a safety-valve. The impoverished peasant would give up his shrunken and mortgaged bit of land in the home-country for a share in the vacant land overseas – and the struggle could begin afresh: either he and his descendants would prosper and become the landed nobility of the new polis, or they would fail and be ready once more for colonization or revolution.

But though land and not trade was the first object, colonization did greatly stimulate both trade and industry, to such an extent that some later colonies were founded with an eye to trade rather than agriculture. The new lands could sometimes grow crops different from those of the old ones, and the colonies brought the Greeks into close contact with 'barbarian' peoples who had interesting things to sell. Of the old trade-routes, for example the amber-route from the Baltic, some could now be tapped nearer their source. So the exchange of goods became brisker, and new contacts brought new ideas and new techniques. Gradually, in no spectacular way, the standard of material civilization rose, much more in some places than in others. Corinth, for example, a city so favourably situated for trade, was busy building ships, making things in bronze, and developing, on its pottery, a naturalistic style of painting such as Greece had not seen for centuries, while Arcadian villages not thirty miles away remained entirely unaffected by these new things. Other cities which participated in this growth of trade and industry were Aegina, Chalcis in Euboea, and Miletus in Ionia. Chalcis was concerned in the first Greek war of historical times, a war with her neighbour Eretria for the possession of the neighbouring Lelantine plain. Many other states came in on either side, having no apparent interest in the disputed territory: it is likely therefore that commercial rivalries were already playing their part.

A word on the political aspect of colonization. The word 'colony' is misleading, but as usual, it is the best we can do. The Greek *apoikia* means, literally, 'an away-home'. The apoikia was in no sense an extension or dependency of the parent-city; it was a new and independent foundation. The mother-city organized the swarm; frequently members of other poleis were invited to join. The mother-city would choose from its own members an official leader: he would supervise the apportioning of the new lands among the colonists, and would be honoured in perpetuity as the Founder. It was usual to consult the oracle at Delphi before trying to establish a new colony. This was not simply a religious fortification against unknown dangers. Delphi had now attained preeminence among all the Greek holy sites, and as the oracle was constantly being consulted by enquirers from every part of the Greek world – and indeed sometimes by 'barbarians' too – the Delphic priests acquired a great deal of information about this and that (not to mention considerable political influence). In going to Delphi, therefore, the Greek hoped to receive, as it were, not only the blessing of the bishops but also expert advice from the Colonial Research Bureau.

When the colony was founded, the ties between it and the mother-city were purely religious and sentimental. The fire which blazed on its public hearth had been kindled by fire brought from the mother-city; citizens of the latter were normally given certain complimentary privileges if they visited the colony: if the colony gave birth to another, it was proper to invite the original city to nominate a founder. Of strictly political connexion there was none whatever; war between a city and her colony (as between Corinth and Corcyra, in the first book of Thucydides) could be represented as unnatural and indecent, but it was not rebellion or secession; therefore this outpouring of Greeks from metropolitan Greece and Ionia, though it carried Greek influence to every part of the Mediterranean, except where Carthage or the Etruscans barred the way, did nothing towards creating a Greek Empire or state. It meant only that the number of independent Greek poleis was enormously increased – and that the sympathies and feuds of the homelands were repeated further afield.

The reader may be uneasily wondering if he is going to be asked to follow the history of several hundreds of independent states simultaneously. No. In the first place, political history must be kept in its place when one is writing about a people: it is a framework perhaps, it is one expression of a people's character, and it is, for good or ill, one of the people's achievements: it is not the whole story. In the second place, about most of these states we know nothing whatever. Nowadays, we are, in the interests of History, recording facts with such conscientious passion that we are making the writing of history impossible.

Greece lays her historian under the opposite disadvantage. The idea of recording contemporary events, other than mere lists of magistrates or priests, hardly dawned before the fifth century – and when it did dawn we have, almost at once, not merely a record, but also an interpretation of events. But even for the fifth century our records are very scanty. For the earlier period it seems most reasonable for us to look in turn, and in a very general way, in three directions: first to Ionia, then to Sparta, then to Athens. The later periods will inevitably concentrate our attention more and more upon Athens.

IONIA

It was long thought that it was among the Ionian Greeks that Greek civilization first began to recover from the Dark Age; that it was Ionians who first began to explore the seas, to found colonies, to develop the arts, to live that full and free life which became characteristically Greek. In Ionia the old Minoan culture lingered, and in Ionia there was more direct contact with the older civilizations of the East. That view is now seriously challenged (notably by R. M. Cook, *Journal of Hellenic Studies*, 1946). The evidence is admittedly scanty and uncertain, but it seems fairly clear that European Greece took the lead in colonizing, and that eastern influence worked upon the Greeks of the mainland at least as early as upon the Ionians. Homer, the first great poet, was an Ionian – but it was in Attica that vase-painting first revived.

Nevertheless, what we know of Ionia in this early period does suggest to our minds something more 'modern' than what we know of the culture of the mainland, and it is unquestionable that the great intellectual movement which we shall discuss later began in Ionia. This feeling of 'modernity' may well be an effect of the Ionian character and temperament rather than a more advanced state of civilization, for the Ionian was much more of an individualist than the European Greek. For example, there is a pleasant story about the Ionians in Herodotus. It is not necessarily true, for Herodotus, being a native of Carian Halicarnassus, was a neighbour of the Ionians, and therefore, by the almost universal Law of Neighbours, prejudiced against them. Nevertheless, it is clearly a tale which he expected to win credence among the other Greeks. It befell the Ionians to be conquered by Cyrus the Great of Persia at about 550, and to rise in revolt soon after 500. An Ionian fleet was assembled at the small island of Lade, and the commander of the detachment from Phocaea (according to Herodotus) made a typically Hellenic speech, in which diffidence is not prominent. 'Things have come to a crisis, gentlemen. Either we shall be free men, or slaves – and runaway slaves at that. Now, if you are willing to accept hardships for a time, you can defeat the enemy and win your freedom, but if you persist in laziness and indiscipline I am afraid you will pay heavily for your revolt. Listen to me, and entrust yourselves to me, for I undertake that if the gods do not favour the enemy we shall have the better of them.' 'Hearing this,' says Herodotus, 'the Ionians entrusted themselves to Dionysius.' He put the ships to sea by day, exercising the oarsmen in manoeuvres, and keeping the marines in their heavy armour – and the Greek sun is hot. The Ionians, not accustomed to this, put up with it for seven days, but then they said to each other, 'What god have we offended that we are visited with this punishment? Have we gone clean out of our minds, that we have handed ourselves over to a vainglorious fool from Phocaea – a place which can contribute only three ships? And he takes us and tortures us unbearably. Half of us are already sick, and the rest expect to be, soon. No slavery can be worse than this. Come, let us put up with it no longer.' Nor did they (says Herodotus), but instead of labouring on shipboard they passed the days more pleasantly on shore, in their tents – with the inevitable result.

A malicious story, but malicious exaggeration must have something to work on: and the Ionians did strike the other Greeks as somewhat lacking in seriousness and discipline. They did in fact make a brave show against Persia, and although their separate cities did not maintain the political cohesion that would have saved them, not many Greeks could safely make this a matter of reproach to them.

A passage in the 'Homeric' Hymn to Apollo gives an Ionian impression of Ionia:

But it is in Delos that thou, Apollo, takest most delight, the holy island in which the Ionians in their trailing robes gather together with their children and their modest wives: and they give thee pleasure as they busy themselves with boxing, dancing and song when the day of the festival comes.

And if a man came upon the Ionians as they were gathered together, he would say that they were exempt from old age and death, such grace would he see in all; and he would rejoice when he looked upon the men and the women in their lovely clothes, and upon their swift ships and their great possessions.

Grace and charm are the marks of Ionian art, as strength and beauty are of the Dorian. To appreciate this, one has only to compare Ionian architecture with Dorian: the general lightness of the Ionic style, set off by the charming volutes of the Ionic capital, makes a striking contrast. In sculpture, while Dorians and Ionians alike were striving to express the ideal Athlete, the Ionians were delighting also in the problems set by the carving of robed figures, trying, very successfully, to represent in stone the different textures of flesh, wool and linen. There is a delicate sensuousness in Ionian work which Dorian does not show. Their festivals too were less austere: music and poetry were more prominent in them. In general, Ionia makes a very lively and a very gay impression, with a suggestion – no more – of an Oriental or at least a southern softness. It is no surprise to find Plato, in the fourth century, rejecting the Ionian modes in music and rhythm as voluptuous and enervating – though we must remember that Plato rejected much that is good.

The sixth century was the great age of lyric poetry, and the personal lyric came almost exclusively from Ionia – if we may use the name, for once, in a loose geographical sense, to include the poets of Aeolian Lesbos, of whom Sappho is the great glory. Of all this lyric poetry we have only miserable remnants. We have enough of Sappho (some quoted by later writers, some discovered recently in the sand of Egypt) to see for ourselves what a passionate and breath-taking poetess she was, but not enough of Archilochus (an Ionian) to understand why the ancients put him next to Homer.

> I was in love with you once, Atthis, long ago –

This verse, beautiful in Sappho's Aeolic Greek, has survived because in the second century A.D. it was quoted by Hephaestion, a metrician – and a singularly stupid one too.

> When you are dead you will lie in your grave, forgotten for ever
> Because you despise the flowers of the Muse; in Hades – as here –
> Dimly your shadow will flit with the rest, unnoticed, obscure.

These savage lines are quoted in a moral essay by Plutarch, and he adds that Sappho wrote them 'against a certain rich lady'. Something similar seems to have been the context of another contemptuous fragment (this one cited in a commentary on Pindar): 'In these women the spirit has grown cold: their wings have failed.'

Sappho's most famous ode is the passionate love-poem very successfully turned into Latin by Catullus – the only Latin poet who could have done it at all: but love and hate are not her only themes:

> The stars around the lovely moon
> Veil again their shining beauty
> When the moon grows full and blazes
> Down on all the earth.

The true Ionian poets, so far as we know them, do not write with the intensity of Aeolic Sappho, but they resemble her, and are unlike their contemporaries in Sparta and Athens, in writing on themes which interest them as individuals. Their poetry is rarely 'political', like the poetry of Tyrtaeus and Solon. Archilochus was renowned for his biting personal satire; Anacreon sang gaily of love and wine, or sadly about the coming of old age. The Ionian poet Pythermus survives in one verse only:

> There's nothing else that matters – only money –

so like Belloc's verse:

> But money gives me pleasure all the time.

Another typical fragment is:

> I hate a woman thick about the ankles.

The tale is well-known of the Spartan who said to her son as
he was going out to battle, 'Come back with your shield – or
on it': for to throw away one's shield was the ultimate disgrace.
But Archilochus could write, cheerfully – setting a literary
fashion which Horace followed more than five hundred years
later:

> Some lucky Thracian has my noble shield:
> I had to run; I dropped it in a wood.
> But I got clear away, thank God! So hang
> The shield! I'll get another, just as good.

There is something very attractive about Ionian life.

SPARTA

If a scholar found, in a fragment purporting to be of some
Dorian poet, the verse 'I hate a woman thick about the
ankles', he would at once assume that something was wrong.
No doubt the Spartan had his opinions about women's ankles,
but they did not write like this in the Peloponnese: the Dorians
were both more grave and less individualist. While the Ionian
and the Aeolian poets were freely writing about their own
loves and hates, Tyrtaeus in Sparta was passionately urging his
fellow-citizens to rise to the very heights of heroism against
their foes in Messenia, and Alcman was composing grave
though charming choral hymns to be performed by the Spartan girls at their festivals. While Ionian philosophers were
finding new and exciting paths of thought, guided only by
their own individual command of reason, the Dorians remained massively traditional in their ideas and their outlook.
While the architects and sculptors of Ionia were seeking elegance and variety, those of the Peloponnese were striving for
perfection within the narrow range of a few severe types.
Ionian and Dorian represent in a very pure form two opposing
conceptions of life – the dynamic and the static, the individualist

and the communal, the centrifugal and the centripetal – which we can see today by looking West and then East. In Athens, for a time, these opposites were to find the reconciliation which they needed; hence the perfection of Attic culture in the age of Pericles.

As Attic sculpture and architecture combined Dorian austerity with Ionian grace, as Athenian drama made a harmonious and organic combination of the communal choral hymn and the art of the actor, so for a short time Athenian life was able to combine Ionian liberty and individual brilliance with a Dorian sense of discipline and cohesion. But in the early classical period this reconciliation was still distant.

The culture and the political history of the Peloponnese – the chief though not the only home of the Dorians – were both dominated by Sparta, and Sparta is not easy to appraise. Sparta is a city of strange contradictions, not easily to be grasped by the modern mind: and her early history is obscure, richer in legends than in facts, and of the apparent facts many are due to the hypothetical reconstructions of later philosophers: for it is one of the many paradoxes of Sparta that this city, which proved among Greek cities conspicuously barren in things of the mind, had a perpetual fascination for Greek philosophers.

We have seen how the invading Dorians took possession of most of the Peloponnese, and how the Spartans firmly planted themselves, a dominant and an aloof minority, in one of the two most southerly and fertile valleys of the mainland of Europe. It would be very gratifying if we could now write, 'In the course of a few centuries this hardy mountain-race, overcome by heat and luxury, sank into an almost Oriental lethargy' – but this did not happen; quite the contrary. When Sparta dwindled and fell it was not from lack of energy but from lack of citizens and of ideas, and for this she herself was responsible.

The critical events in Spartan history were two: of neither do we know very much. The first was the resolve to hold aloof from the conquered population, and of that we know nothing beyond the bare fact, though we can see that it was a natural consequence of what we can see in all their history, their acute feeling that they were a closely-knit community. It must have been as a highly-organized and self-conscious group that they conquered the valley of the swift Eurotas: such they remained: they were not individuals willing to accommodate themselves to an existing pattern of life, but a community bringing their own pattern with them and determined to preserve it. Society in Lacedaemon therefore became stratified in an uncommon way (though there was a parallel in Thessaly): there were the 'Spartiates', the only true Spartans, on the top; the Perioikoi ('Neighbours') below them – a class that was free, but with no political rights; and at the bottom the *Helots*, not personal slaves of the Spartans, but serfs of the Spartan community, most of them working on the land, and contributing half its produce to the citizens to whom they were severally assigned.

Of the second critical event we know a little more, but not very much. As we have seen, the normal relief of over-population was the sending out of a colony. Sparta too sent out colonies – Tarentum was one – but not very many. Her remedy for land-hunger was much more drastic: she conquered her western neighbour Messenia, annexed the territory, and reduced the inhabitants to serfdom. Such annexation was extremely rare in Greece, for the obvious reason that it was impossible to exploit a neighbour's territory without a standing army to hold it, and Sparta was the only state which had a standing army – its citizen-class supported by the labour of the Helots. The task of holding Messenia was almost too much for Sparta. A generation or two after the conquest, that is to say towards the end of the eighth century, the Messenians revolted and the revolt was obviously a desperate affair; it was apparently something like twenty years before it was finally stamped out, and the exhortations of Tyrtaeus show what efforts Sparta had to make.

This enslavement of Messenia made the Spartiates more than ever a minority in their own country, and a threatened minority at that. It may have been the Messenian revolt that induced the Spartans to adopt the famous institutions of Lycurgus.

About Lycurgus nothing is known, not even whether he was fact or fiction (J. B. Bury, a determined 'rationalist', remarked about him, characteristically, 'He was not a man: only a god'). Many of these Institutions were demonstrably much older, but at least we can see that a considerable change came over Spartan life at about this time. It is now, at the end of the seventh century, that all the grace and charm disappears from Spartan life, and the city begins to present its familiar barrack-like appearance. 'Lycurgus' met the situation with an impeccable logic: the citizen-body was organized for what it was, a dominant minority holding down and exploiting a vastly more numerous population of active and dangerous serfs.

The Spartiate was forbidden to engage in agriculture, trade or professional work: he must be a professional soldier. He had his farm, worked for him by helots, he dined in public 'messes', to which he contributed his share from his farm: if he failed to contribute, he ceased for the time being to be a full citizen. Family life was severely limited. Babies adjudged weak were done away with; boys lived with their mothers until they were 7; from 7 to 30 they received the appropriate kind of public military instruction and exercise. Girls too were given a careful physical training.

They had games, the girls wearing so little that even Greeks were shocked. Of formal intellectual education there was none, though great stress was laid on modesty of demeanour, as well, naturally, as on the virtue of obedience and courage. The helots were kept down ruthlessly: a secret police was charged with the task of killing any who threatened to become dangerous – so Plutarch says, but he may have misunderstood it.

But 'Lycurgus' did not aim only at making the citizen-body an efficient fighting-machine always in readiness. He took extraordinary pains to make it self-sufficient and immobile. Trade was discouraged, foreign visitors were admitted only grudgingly, and from time to time summarily expelled: foreign ideas must at all costs be kept out. (A contemporary parallel may suggest itself to the unenlightened.) When Athens had an intelligently controlled currency, accepted everywhere, even in distant Gaul, and besides this a quite serviceable banking system, Sparta was still, of set purpose, using an ancient and clumsy iron currency – though the compulsory use of iron at home did not blind Spartans abroad to the superior attractions of gold.

The political constitution too sounds just as preposterous. There were two kings – reminiscent of the two equal consuls of the Roman Republic. The origin was probably different, but the desired effect was the same: in each case the duality was a check on autocracy. At home the kings were overshadowed by the Ephors ('Overseers'), five annual magistrates chosen more or less by ballot: but a Spartan army abroad was always commanded by one of the kings, who then had absolute powers. There was also a Senate, and there was an Assembly of all Spartans, but the Assembly could not debate, and it expressed its decisions – to the amusement of other Greeks – not by voting but by shouting: the loudest shout carried the day. It was a constitution which baffled the later Greek theorists, accustomed as they were to classify everything in heaven and earth: they did not know whether to call it a monarchy, an aristocracy, an oligarchy or a democracy. It was a constitution arrived at by abolishing nothing old (the kings, for instance), and developing nothing new to its logical conclusion.

The historian is only doing his duty when he points out that this bleak and negative way of life was forced on the Spartans by their resolve to live on the labour of the helots; that its rigidity proved in the end morally, intellectually and economically ruinous; and that the life to which it condemned the helots must have been dismal – even though we may suspect that history, as usual, has diligently recorded the dismal and forgotten the rest. But if the historian stops there he has not done all his duty. In spite of the helots, and in spite of this rigidity and barrenness, Sparta, at least down to the Peloponnesian War, is singularly impressive, and there were Greeks in plenty who, while seeing Sparta's faults clearly enough, yet had a great, even an envious, admiration at least of the Spartan ideal.

For it is important to realize that this life was, to the Spartan, an ideal. I have spoken (in order to be up to date) of the 'exploitation' of the helots. If the modern term had its modern connotation, it would mean that the Spartan citizens lived in some degree of comfort on the produce of helot labour: in fact, their life was so austere that a modern, given the choice, might well prefer to live as a helot rather than as a citizen. Stories about Sparta and Spartans were innumerable, many of them, admittedly, recorded by philo-Spartan writers, but those that deal with the Spartan way of life all point in one direction. A Sybarite, entertained at the public mess at Sparta, remarked 'Now I understand why Spartans do not fear death!' Another visitor, faced with a Spartan black broth, said, 'You need a swim in the Eurotas before you can eat this'. King Agesilaus, asked what was the greatest benefit conferred on the Spartans by Lycurgus' laws, replied, 'Contempt of pleasure'. Diogenes the Cynic, being at Olympia, saw some young men from Rhodes wearing very fine clothes, and ejaculated 'Affectation!' Then he saw some Spartans dressed shabbily, and said, 'More affectation!'

That many an individual Spartan did not live up to his city's ideal is a phenomenon that we can understand readily enough, but Sparta did have an ideal, and a very exacting one: one which gave a meaning to his life, and could make him proud of being a Spartan. The personal heroism of Spartan soldiers, and Spartan women too, is both legend and fact. We can be less certain of Spartan behaviour in ordinary life, because so few other Greeks knew Sparta well enough to report on it, but the following story from Plutarch is typical. An old man wandered about at the Olympic games looking for a seat, and was jeered at by the crowd. But when he came to the place where the Spartans were sitting, every young man and many of the older ones got up to offer him a place. The crowd applauded the Spartans, whereupon the old man said with a sigh, 'All Greeks *know* what is right, but only the Spartans *do* it'.

In fact, what impressed the Greeks, even those who disliked the Spartan state, was the fact that they had imposed on their lives a certain form, or pattern, and renounced so much for it. That this pattern was to a great extent imposed on them from without, by the Helot danger, is true, but it is also true that they converted the involuntary into a voluntary compulsion. In history one must be on one's guard against seeing the obvious and missing the significant, and the significant thing here is that the Laws of Lycurgus aimed not merely at the subjection of the helots to the Spartan state but at the creation of the ideal citizen. It was a narrow ideal, but for all that it was an ideal.

The Greeks admired this: the laws of Sparta did so thoroughly what the Greek thought was the highest function of law. Our own conception of Law is so completely Roman that we find it hard to think of Law as a creative, formative agent, but this was the normal Greek conception. The Romans thought of law at first in a purely practical way: it regulated relations between people and their affairs, and was itself a codification of practice. Not until Roman lawyers came under Greek influence did they begin to deduce from their laws general principles of Law, and to extend these in the light of philosophical principles. But the Greek thought of the collective laws, the *nomoi,* of his polis as a moral and creative power. They were designed not only to secure justice in the individual case, but also to inculcate Justice: this is one reason why the young Athenian, during his two years with the colours, was instructed in the *nomoi* – which are the basic laws of the state, to be distinguished from specific enactments regulating such things as putting lights on motor-cars: these were only psephismata or 'things voted'. The Greeks had no doctrinal religion or church; they did not even have what we think is a satisfactory substitute, a Minister of Education; the polis instructed the citizens in their moral and social duties through the Laws.

Therefore Sparta was admired for her *Eunomia,* her 'state of being well-lawed', because – whether you liked her ideal or not – she did through her laws and institutions train her citizens in this ideal with unusual completeness: she did train citizens selflessly devoted to the common good: and if in conspicuous instances she failed, the fault lay perhaps in the imperfections of human nature rather than of the laws. She was praised because she had not changed her laws for centuries – or was supposed not to have changed them. This, to us, seems childish – but if anything Greek seems childish, we should do well to look again. We think it axiomatic that laws should change with changing circumstances: the Greek perhaps was not quite so humble as we are in the face of circumstances – he had less reason to be, in his more static world. He had, in varying degrees, the idea of imposing a pattern on life rather than of accommodating himself to the pattern of life. Sparta did that – so it was believed – when it accepted the Laws of Lycurgus, which Delphi had approved. Why then change the pattern? We do not smile when we hear that the dogmas of the Church have not changed for centuries. The Laws of Lycurgus were, to the Spartans, a pattern of 'Virtue', that is to say of aretê, of human excellence regarded strictly from within the citizen-body. It was a narrower conception of 'virtue' than the Athenian, and it offends modern humanitarians almost as much as its demands would scare them, but though cruel in some aspects and brutal in others, it has a heroic quality. No one can say that Sparta was vulgar. Nor would a Spartan have admitted that Sparta was artistically barren. Art, *poiesis*, is creation, and Sparta created not things in words or stone, but men.

ATHENS

The Athenians occupied a territory, Attica, which is slightly smaller than Gloucestershire, and in their greatest period were about as numerous as the inhabitants of Bristol – perhaps rather less. Such was the size of the state which, within two centuries and a half, gave birth to Solon, Pisistratus, Themistocles, Aristeides and Pericles among statesmen, to Aeschylus, Sophocles, Euripides, Aristophanes and Menander among dramatists, to Thucydides, the most impressive of all historians, and to Demosthenes, the most impressive of orators, to Mnesicles and Ictinus, architects of the Acropolis, and to Phidias and Praxiteles the sculptors, to Phormio, one of the most brilliant of naval commanders, to Socrates and to Plato – and this list takes no account of mere men of talent. During the same period she beat off Persia, with the sole aid of 1,000

Plataeans, at Marathon; did more than the rest of Greece together to win the still more critical victory of Salamis; and built up the only truly Greek empire that ever existed. For a considerable part of this period the exquisitely designed and painted Athenian vases were sought and prized all over the Mediterranean and in Central Europe, and – perhaps the most remarkable thing of all – the popular entertainment, that which corresponds to our cinema, was the loftiest and most uncompromising drama which has ever existed. This fact is one quite outside our own experience, so much so that even a modern historian of Greece has opined that the ordinary Athenian would have welcomed something worse had it been available. But this is quite inadmissible. We do not hear that the ordinary citizen came to the theatre late in the day, when the tragedies were over and the farcical satyric play was about to begin. On the contrary, the comedies of Aristophanes always assume that a close parody of Euripides or Aeschylus will set the theatre in a roar of laughter. If the ordinary Athenian had wanted something more 'popular', he could have had it: he was in complete and direct control. In short, the contribution made to Greek and European culture by this one city is quite astonishing, and, unless our standards of civilization are comfort and contraptions, Athens from (say) 480 to 380 was clearly the most civilized society that has yet existed.

Achievement of this quality and this range obviously betokens a people unusually rich in natural genius, but it implies something else just as important, namely those conditions of life which enabled this natural genius to develop and fully to express itself. Therefore in this and the next two chapters we shall trace in some detail the development of the Athenian polis. The flowering of Athenian culture in the fifth century is often called a 'miracle'. Similarly, certain diseases were called 'miraculous' or 'god-sent' – in common Greek parlance – but one of the Greek medical writers very sensibly declares that no disease is exceptional, all being equally natural and equally 'god-sent'. It shall be our aim to imitate this eminently scientific doctor, and to show, if we can, that the achievement of Periclean Athens is just as miraculous, and just as natural, as that of any other time and place. In this chapter our task will be to watch the development of Athens during the early classical period.

We have seen that Athenian legend asserted that the Athenian people was indigenous to Attica, and the traditional list of Athenian kings – for what it is worth, which is something, at least – would take us back to perhaps the fourteenth century. That there was a Mycenean town at Athens is now known, but Athens has no prominent place in the *Iliad*: it was the later political union of the dozen small poleis in Attica which led the way to Athenian greatness. It is interesting to note that when pottery begins to revive from the degeneracy of the latest Mycenean times and the feeble provincialism of the Dark Age, it is in Athens that the revival begins, at about 900. The 'Dipylon' vases (so called from the Dipylon gate, near which they were found) are decorated in the geometric style of the Mycenean period, but suddenly power has returned: the meaningless ornamentation of the decadence is abandoned. It seems that Attica, less disturbed than other places by the Dorian commotion, first resumed contact with the ancient culture.

From say 900 to 600, when Sparta was asserting her primacy in the Peloponnese, and becoming the acknowledged leader of the Hellenic race, Athens was a second- or even third-class power. It must have been during this period that some statesman of genius proposed and carried through the union of Attica – the first of the major political achievements of this people. For the Athenians undoubtedly had a genius for statesmanship. To compare the Romans with the Athenians in this respect is quite absurd. The Romans had many gifts, but statesmanship was not one of them. No major reform was ever carried through in Rome without civil war: the achievement of the Republic was to fill Rome with a pauperized rabble, to ruin Italy and provoke slave-revolts, and to govern the empire – or at least its richer parts – with an open personal rapacity that an Oriental monarch would not have tolerated: while the achievement of the Empire was to accept the fact that political life was impossible, and to create, in its place, a machine. I know that the Athenian Empire lasted for fifty years and the Roman for five hundred, but the possession of an Empire is not necessarily a sign of political success, and in any case I am speaking of genius, not success. In the intervals of creating sheer chaos, the Roman state did much to organize and protect the lives of its members: we must not forget that in the first century A.D. the European-Mediterranean world was more peaceful and conveniently organized than at any other time, ancient or modern. But never did the Roman state, as such, transfigure the life of its members as the Athenian polis did during the sixth, fifth and fourth centuries, and even later. If a political system can do this, one is surely entitled to attribute political genius to the people who invented it – though one should be careful not to pretend that the system was ideal; and the most important manifestation of that genius was, I think, the general disposition of the Athenians to deal with social troubles as reasonable people, acting together, not, like children or fanatics, by violence. Time after time we see them doing this: the privileged class is open to argument, and – on the whole – loyally accepts the verdict. There was, in the Athenian life, a pervading sense of the common interest, *To koinon*, which was as rare in ancient Greece as it is in modern Greece and indeed modern Europe.

It is reasonable to cite the Union of Attica as the first manifestation of this. Thucydides gives the traditional account of it, certainly inaccurate in one important particular: he is describing how, on the outbreak of the war, the people of Attica had to take refuge within the Athens-Piraeus fortifications:

They proceeded to bring in from the country their wives and children, and all the furniture they had, pulling down even the woodwork of their houses. The cattle and sheep they sent over to Euboea and the adjacent islands. But they made this removal with reluctance, because the greater part had always been accustomed to live in the country. This had always been the case with the Athenians more than with others. Under Cecrops and the first Kings down to Theseus, Attica had always been inhabited in independent communities, each with its Town hall and magistrates. Except in times of danger they did not consult with the King, but each community conducted its own affairs, and occasionally even made war on the King. But when Theseus became King, a man both powerful and wise, he reorganized Attica in various ways: and one of his acts was to abolish the councils and magistracies of the other cities, and to unite them all with Athens, assigning to them one town hall and one council-chamber. While they all enjoyed their property as before, they became members of this one city only. ... And from that time even to this the Athenians celebrate, at the public expense, a festival to the goddess Synoecia.[1]

Thucydides' error is of course the date: the ascription to Theseus would put this event before the Trojan War. Otherwise the tradition is credible enough. We find the monarchy in dissolution, quite helpless against the powerful heads of noble families (or clans), who have split an old monarchy of the Achaean life into small poleis, each polis comprising several 'clans'. (These local clan-groups continued to be a nuisance until they were ended by Cleisthenes at about 500 B.C.) In Attica, and almost only in Attica, there was enough common-sense to see that this was a foolish system, agreeable though it was to the Greek. It must have been ended by a combined effort of statesmanship, not by wise and powerful Theseus, for by now the monarchy existed only in name – as indeed the tradition itself makes quite clear.

The next thing that we hear of is that the code of Law was published, in 621 B.C., by a certain Draco. Law had been an affair of tradition and custom, and the noble class which had succeeded the monarchy were both the guardians and the administrators of this traditional law. Hesiod had already written savagely of 'princes who devour bribes and give crooked decisions', and in Attica things were obviously coming to a head. Patriarchal chiefs in Scotland became grasping landlords: something similar was happening in Attica, and the victims protested. No doubt the union of Attica made them more conscious both of their power and of their wrongs: at all events, the traditional law was published, in all its harshness. This at least gave some protection against arbitrary oppression.

1. The goddess Synoecia ('Union of Houses') was invented for the occasion - or inferred from the occasion. The festival would be more than an annual beano; it was a solemn recognition and acceptance by all of the act of union.

But it was not enough. Many a small farmer, failing to pay his way, had first of all mortgaged his land to the wealthy noble, then, being unable to meet his dues, had been enslaved by him, and even sold abroad. There was a general demand for the cancellation of debts, the freeing of the enslaved, and the redistribution of the land. The discontents of the time made a great impression on one Athenian, a merchant, a man who had travelled, was something of a philosopher, something of a statesman and a considerable poet. This was Solon. Solon, though he has been called the greatest economist of antiquity, did not really know much about Political Economy, for to his simple mind it seemed that the source of the trouble was not the System, but Greed and Injustice. He said so, very eloquently, in his poems. The result was remarkable. In the simple and direct fashion which these small states could use, the opposing factions agreed to give Solon the powers of a dictator for the time necessary to settle the present discontents.

Many Greek states, when they got to this point, did nothing, until the dissatisfied class revenged itself with revolution and confiscation, with the natural result that revolution and counter-revolution were their lot until the end. Solon would have nothing to do with this. He put an end, once and for all, to enslavement for debt: he reduced debts, put a limit on the size of estates, restored lands that had been lost by the debtors, and restored to Attica those who had been sold abroad. But his great service to the economy of Attica was to put her agriculture on a new foundation. Part of the trouble had been purely economic, a result of the introduction of coinage, but the major cause was that Attica was not by nature self-sufficient: most of her soil was too thin to bear corn. On the other hand, it was well suited to the olive and the vine. Solon therefore encouraged specialization: he promoted the production and export of olive-oil, and encouraged industry; foreign craftsmen were encouraged by the promise of Athenian citizenship to settle in Attica, and he ordained that every father must teach his son a trade – a point to be remembered by those who have been persuaded that the Greek was a natural aristocrat who despised work. An immediate result of this was the growth of the craft and art of the Athenian potter, whose skill and taste very soon gave them a monopoly of those magnificent Greek vases which went all over the Mediterranean world and even into Central Europe.

With the economic problem went, naturally, a political one. Athens was governed by annual archons ('rulers'), elected from among certain noble families by the Assembly of all citizens who had a certain property-qualification, and these archons, after their year of office, became members of the ancient Council of the Areopagus ('Mars' Hill'). These aristocratic archons were, from a historical point of view, the ancient monarchy put into commission, and the Council which they joined became like the very similar Roman Senate, a close and powerful corporation. With the old Council Solon did not tamper, but he abolished the birth-qualification and substituted a property-qualification. Thus the new trading-class could aspire to the highest offices, and in time the character of the Council would change. All citizens were admitted to the Assembly, and its powers were increased in ways not very clear, but at least the Assembly was now significant enough to be given an elective council of 400 – a sort of executive committee – to prepare its business.

Having done all this, Solon laid down his extraordinary office, and tactfully went on his travels.

It would be eminently satisfactory if one could now say 'Solon was scarcely out of the country before the full fury of the storm broke. The poor were enraged that they had been given so little, the nobles because they had been forced to concede so much. The two factions had in common only a fierce hatred of Solon, but this was not enough to prevent insurrections from breaking out all over Attica.' We should be on familiar ground, and should have the comfortable feeling that these Athenians were, after all, exactly like everybody else. But this did not happen. The Marxian Laws, for one thing, had not yet been passed; and for another thing, the Athenians had some idea that the common good was more important than party advantage – being perhaps in this respect, if in no other, something like the British race.

On the other hand, Attic history is no fairy-tale, and Solon had not waved any magic wand. Political unrest did break out again, and this time it produced in Athens what it produced in many other Greek cities at about this time – a tyrant.

Pisistratus was a tyrant of the normal type. The technique and the policy of the Greek tyrant was very similar to those of our own time. The personal bodyguard, the Reichstag fire, the Berlin Olympic Games, the draining of the Pontine Marsh, the clearing-up of the Forum – all these things have their close parallels in the story of Pisistratus and of other Greek tyrants. But there is a very important difference. The Greek tyrants were almost always aristocrats and civilized men. So far were they from being the rabid anti-intellectual vulgarians whom we have known, that several of them found a place in the later canon of the Seven Wise Men. Pisistratus was a good example of the tyrant.

Herodotus (who wrote rather more than a century later) describes his advent in this way. Hippocrates, an Athenian noble, who was at the Olympic games as a spectator, had prepared a sacrifice. He put the flesh into a cauldron of water, which immediately boiled over, though he had not yet put it on the fire. Chilon of Sparta – one of the Seven Wise Men – interpreting the prodigy advised Hippocrates never to have a son: but Hippocrates did beget a son – and he was Pisistratus. Now, a quarrel took place in Attica between those who lived on the coast, led by Megacles, and those of the city, led by a certain Lycurgus. (Other authorities speak of the parties of the Coast and the Plain. This may imply some clash of interests between commercialists and landowners; but it is possible to rationalize Greek politics too far: purely local and personal quarrels have always been pursued with great zeal by the Greeks.) Pisistratus, aiming at supreme power, formed a third party. Assembling his partisans under pretext of protecting the men of the hills (who would be the poorer rural class) he contrived this device. He inflicted wounds on himself and his mules, drove his chariot into the Square as if escaping from enemies without, and asked for a bodyguard. As he was an illustrious citizen, having among other things captured Nisaea from the Megarians, the Athenians allowed him to select certain citizens, to be armed not with spears but with clubs. With these he seized the Acropolis and the government, interfering, however, neither with the existing magistrates nor with the laws, and administering the city well.

This brought to their senses those noble rivals Megacles and Lycurgus. They came to terms, and drove Pisistratus out. Having done this they started quarrelling again, until Megacles offered Pisistratus (now in exile) his support if Pisistratus would marry his daughter. The bargain was struck, but the difficulty was to do the trick a second time. Herodotus thus relates the second stratagem – with some asperity.

They contrived the most ridiculous scheme that, I imagine, was ever thought of, especially considering, first, that the Greeks have always been distinguished from the barbarians by their shrewdness and freedom from simple-minded folly: second, that this trick was played on the Athenians, who are held to be the most intelligent of the Greeks. There was a woman called Phye,[1] six feet high, all but two inches, and very beautiful too. They dressed her in a complete suit of armour, rehearsed her in the part she was to play, put her in a chariot, and drove into the city, where heralds (already sent there) proclaimed, 'Men of Athens: give kind welcome to Pisistratus, whom Athena herself honours above all other men and is now conducting to her own citadel'. They spread this about the city, and the people, believing this woman to be the goddess, received Pisistratus – and also paid worship to a human being.

The story may be true: let us not forget how seriously some of our newspapers treated the Angels of Mons. If this trick was played, we may be certain that Megacles and Pisistratus got much more amusement out of it than Herodotus did.

This ingenious nobleman had to engineer yet another return – for he quarrelled with Megacles – before he was safely in the saddle: this time he used straightforward military methods, being helped by the negligence of his opponents and the acquiescence of the citizens. Nor did he stand any more nonsense from his fellow-nobles – though there was no blood-letting.

1. Very suitably, since Phye is the Greek for 'growth' or 'stature'.

Many fled: from others he took sons as hostages, and deposited them in one of the islands of which he had control. This done, he settled down to twenty years of beneficent administration (546–527). He helped the poorer farmers in various ways, distributed land from confiscated estates, built an aqueduct to give Athens a much-needed water supply, and in general contributed both to the well-being of Attica and to the stability of his regime. But he was concerned also to increase the international reputation of Athens. Other tyrants had brilliant courts; Pisistratus would have one too. Enough remains of the sculpture and vase-painting of his time to show that these arts flourished with an extreme elegance and gaiety, and we know that he attracted the Ionian poets Simonides and Anacreon to his court, even as Hiero, tyrant of Syracuse, later attracted to his Simonides, Bacchylides, the grave Pindar and Aeschylus himself. He also built, as all tyrants do. His most majestic project was a temple to Zeus Olympios; but the completion of this had to wait for an even more powerful ruler, the Emperor Hadrian, the ruins of whose temple are still one of the impressive sights of Athens.

So Pisistratus was raising Athens from a small country-town to a city of international importance: but another side of his cultural policy was more significant still. He reorganized some of the national festivals on a great scale. One was a festival of Dionysus, a nature-god (not by any means only the god of wine). In enlarging this festival, Pisistratus for the first time gave public status to a new art – tragic drama. Various forms of drama were endemic in Greece: there were dramatic dances, ritual performances in honour of Dionysus that were mimetic, character-mimes: in particular, the dithyrambic hymn and dance to Dionysus was becoming dramatic (so at least Aristotle says), with the Leader of the Chorus detaching himself and carrying on lyrical dialogue with the rest of the chorus. In Attica such a rudimentary drama had taken artistic shape, thanks very largely to one man, Thespis (of whom we know next to nothing); and Pisistratus gave it dignity by incorporating it in his new festival. The first tragic contest took place in 534, and the prize was awarded to Thespis. Nothing better expressed, or more ennobled, the spirit of the new Athens than this public drama – which we shall have occasion to speak of later.

But Epic poetry as well as the new tragic drama was given public status by this enlightened ruler: recitals of Homer were incorporated in the great Panathenaic Festival, the 'Festival of United Athens'. There is indeed a story, not traceable earlier than Cicero (five hundred years after Pisistratus), that he produced the first definite text of Homer. This is exceedingly improbable, but at least it reflects the impression that Pisistratus made on Greek cultural history.

'All this was something more than the mere gratification of a tyrant's own aesthetic instincts. It was part of a policy which only a man of real vision could have conceived. Hitherto the appreciation of art and literature had been confined to a very narrow circle. The Athenian gentry were, in fact, the cultural heirs of the long-past Heroic age when the "sweet-voiced minstrels" of Homer's poems were attached to the palaces and sang at the feasts of the great. Pisistratus' aim was to make available to the many what till now had been the privilege of the few.'[1]

The word 'tyrant' – not a Greek word, but a borrowing from Lydia – originally had none of the odious associations which it acquired and has kept, and the Greeks gratefully remembered what they owed to the Tyrants. Nevertheless, it was hard for the Greek not to be allowed to manage his own public affairs himself, and of course tyrannies degenerate. Dionysius of Syracuse once rebuked one of his sons for insolent behaviour towards a citizen: '*I* never behave like that.' 'Ah but you didn't have a tyrant for a father.' 'No, and if you behave like that, you won't have a tyrant for a son!' Few tyrannies survived the third generation: this one ended in the second. The one son, Hipparchus, was murdered in a private quarrel: the other, Hippias, suspected political motives – not unreasonably. His rule thereupon became more and more oppressive, until he was driven out by an exiled noble family, the Alcmaeonidae, with the help of Sparta and the general support of the Athenians.

1. C. E. Robinson, *Zito Hellas*, p. 51.

The tyranny, though its end was welcome, had done much for Athens. As Pisistratus had carefully preserved the forms of Solon's moderately democratic constitution, the Athenian people were for a generation given a training, under wise tutelage, in managing their own affairs. And as it happened, after the fall of the tyranny things continued to go well for Athens. An aristocratic reaction might have been expected: indeed, a certain Isagoras tried to bring it about, with armed help from Sparta. But there was another aristocratic group led by the third outstanding Athenian statesman of this century, Cleisthenes. He took the popular side, and the reaction failed.

But Cleisthenes did much more than this. He carried through a complete reform of the constitution. The power of the noble families within the nominally centralized polis had come from the fact that for the election of archons the polis was divided into 'tribes', or groups of families, so that the acknowledged leader of any group was sure of election. The groups were proving themselves too strong for the safety of the polis. Cleisthenes dealt with this danger by inventing a preposterous paper-constitution which in fact worked perfectly. He created ten brand-new 'tribes' – all provided with ancestors – each composed of a roughly equal number of 'demes' (or 'parishes'), but not contiguous: that was the whole point. Cleisthenes divided Attica roughly into three areas: city, inland, coast: each of these new 'tribes' contained 'parishes' from each of these three divisions: each therefore was a cross section of the whole population, and when it met to conduct its business its natural meeting-place was Athens – which of itself helped to unite the polis. Then since each tribe would contain farmers and hill-men, artisans and traders from Athens and the Piraeus, and men who lived in boats, local and family loyalties could do little in the election of archons: they could find expression only in the open Assembly, where they could be recognized for what they were.

The fact that so artificial a system worked requires some explanation: it seems so childish, and the Athenians were so much the opposite. Among us such a system would be damned from the start by the fact that it was so artificial, so 'made-up'.

But the Greek had no objection to something new: the fact that it was a deliberate and logical creation of a human mind would be indeed a recommendation: we saw a few pages back that this was one of the reasons which made the Greeks admire the Spartan constitution. Then we must remember how the Greek, individualist though he was, liked to work in groups, partly because he wanted to take part in what was going on, partly because he loved rivalry.

All these instincts were satisfied by Cleisthenes' system. It was so obviously and so cleverly created to serve an immediate need, the integration of the polis. It left the Athenian his deme for the transaction of local affairs – one of the most important of these being the admission of new citizens, for the new-born child had to be accepted as legitimate by the members of the deme. Also, it gave him a wider loyalty within the polis: not only did the citizen vote by 'tribes', but he fought too by 'tribes', so that this new creation was also his Regiment: and as the dramatic contests too went by tribes, it directed to a purposeful, creative end his passion for rivalry.

But this alteration of the political foundations went with an alteration in the superstructure too. Solon's reforms gave every citizen some part to play in the state, though to the poorer classes a very restricted one. The aristocratic Cleisthenes continued and nearly completed what Solon had begun. The powers of the Council of the Areopagus were greatly reduced. The Assembly of all citizens was made the sole and the final legislative body, and the magistrates were made responsible to it or to panels of the Assembly sitting as judicial bodies. It remained only for the next generation to abolish the last of the property qualifications, and to take the final and apparently preposterous step of choosing archons by lot: then the Athenian polity was as democratic as the ingenuity of man could make it.

Such, in very brief outline, were the events which transformed Athens, in less than a century, from a second-rate polis, torn with economic and political strife, into a flourishing city with a new unity, a new purpose and a new confidence. Sparta had found one ideal, Athens another.

I have said so much about sixth-century Athens because it

alone makes fifth-century Athens intelligible. A high culture
must, historically speaking, originate with an aristocratic class,
because this alone has the time and energy to create it. If it
remains for too long the preserve of the aristocrat, it becomes
first elaborate and then silly, just as, in political history, aristocracy becomes an evil if it persists in outliving its social
function. In the political sphere, the prevailing common sense
of Athens, rising to genius in Solon, Pisistratus and Cleisthenes,
brought it about that the Athenian nobility – on the whole –
came wholeheartedly into the democratic polity while its
aretê was still vigorous: of the great Athenian statesmen of the
next two generations the majority came from the highest
families – Pericles being the outstanding example. Contrast
modern France; the aristocracy, long outliving its usefulness,
had to be guillotined out of existence, with the result that the
remnants, whether or not they had anything to contribute to
republican France, have held disdainfully aloof. In the cultural
sphere, the Athenian populace was brought in to the aristocratic culture while it was still fresh and creative. Compare
England: one of the reasons why the eighteenth century was so
essentially civilized was that we have never had a sharp division
between the upper middle-class and the aristocracy, so that the
culture of the latter was absorbed by the former, and kept sane
by it. Hence the good manners and good sense of the architecture and minor arts of the period – contrasted with the
foolish excesses, in Europe, of the later Baroque, which in
themselves almost justify the French Revolution. The bourgeois society that succeeded aristocracy in Europe could learn
nothing of value to itself from baroque. In England the rising
middle-class of the nineteenth century might peacefully have
absorbed and carried on the culture of the eighteenth – but for
the catastrophe of the Industrial Revolution, which too
quickly threw up a new class too numerous and too self-
confident to be absorbed. Hence both in England and in
Europe (the Scandinavian countries excepted) the democratic
societies of the present are for different reasons without real
contact with the best of their own native traditions. From this
Athens was saved, partly by the political wisdom of the sixth

century, partly by the cultural policy of Pisistratus. The result is that Athenian culture of the fifth century had the seriousness and solidity of the good bourgeois society with all the elegance, fineness and disinterestedness of an aristocracy.

VII

CLASSICAL GREECE: THE FIFTH CENTURY

DURING the sixth century there took place in Asia events that were to affect the Greeks intimately. In 560 the kingdom of Lydia, in the western half of Asia Minor, received a monarch whose name is still familiar, the fabled Croesus. He succeeded in subduing the Greek cities of Ionia; but Croesus was a civilized man, and something of a phil-hellene, and conquest by him was no utter calamity. He was content to rule the cities through Greek 'tyrannoi' friendly to himself.

At about the same time a Persian ascended the throne of the kingdom of Media, further east. This was Cyrus the Great. He, ruling in the north of Mesopotamia, overthrew Babylonia, which was then ruled by the son of another familiar figure, 'Nebuchadnezzar the King of the Jews'. But first he dealt with his western neighbour, Lydia. These two powers had already been at war under the predecessors of Cyrus and Croesus, a war which had been ended by a total eclipse of the sun; the armies, we are told, were so much moved by it that they refused to continue the battle. This was the eclipse foretold by Thales of Miletus.[1] The second war was begun by Croesus. He consulted the oracle at Delphi, for which he had the greatest respect (so the Greeks said), and was told that if he crossed the River Halys, the frontier between him and Cyrus, he would destroy a mighty empire. He crossed the Halys, and he did destroy a mighty empire. Unfortunately, it was his own. The foolish man had forgotten to ask which

---

1. See below, p. 177 ff.

empire he would destroy.[1] This brought Persian power down to the Aegean, by 548 B.C.

Herodotus' narrative of these events is one of the most interesting parts of his interesting book. It is typical that the first history of Mesopotamia should have been composed by a Greek. This history is packed with excellent stories. There is the story – far too long to be told here – of the birth of Cyrus. In brief, it is the common tale of the wonderful child that is to be born, who will do this and that. Someone tries to prevent the birth or to kill the child. The attempt fails, and the prophecy is startlingly fulfilled. A Greek form of the story is the Oedipus-myth, and it is interesting to compare the Cyrus-story told by Herodotus with the *Oedipus Rex* composed by his friend Sophocles – essentially the same story, but in Sophocles charged with infinitely more significance.

Then there is the tale of the meeting between Croesus and Solon – and for this we must find room, as it throws such light on the Greek mind. Solon, on his travels, was royally entertained by Croesus, and shown the immense wealth of his treasuries. (If the story is historically accurate, Solon had by now been dead for some time.) Then Croesus said, 'Solon, I know of your fame as a philosopher, and I know you have travelled far and seen much. Tell me; who is the happiest[2] man you have ever met?' He asked this, says Herodotus, thinking that he was the 'happiest' of men. But Solon, with no hesitation, said Tellus of Athens; for Tellus lived in a well-governed polis, had sons who were brave and good, saw the birth of healthy grandsons, then, after a life as happy as the nature of man allows, died fighting gloriously for Athens against Eleusis, was buried with signal honour, and is remembered with gratitude.

Croesus then asked who came next in happiness – hoping to be mentioned in the second place. 'Cleobis and Biton of Argos',

1. It is conjectured that the policy of the oracle was to involve Croesus and Cyrus in a long war, to the advantage of Greece.

2. 'Happy' is a poor word here, but it seems the best we can do. If we had the expression 'well-starred' as the opposite of 'ill-starred' it would translate the Greek much better.

said Solon. These two were young men of sufficient wealth; both had won victories in the Games; and their death was notable. Their mother had to be driven to the temple of Hera, five miles distant, for a festival. Since the oxen did not come in from the fields soon enough, they drew the cart themselves. At the festival all acclaimed the strength of the young men and congratulated their mother. She, in a transport of happiness, prayed the goddess to grant her sons the greatest blessing that a man can have – and the prayer was answered; for after the sacrifice and the feast the two young men fell asleep in the very temple, and never awoke again.

Croesus was annoyed at being thought less 'happy' than private citizens, but Solon pointed out that a man lives many days, and every day brings something different; therefore, call no man 'happy' until he is dead. You never can tell.

But the tale does not end here; for years later Croesus, to the astonishment of all, was defeated by Cyrus and taken prisoner. Cyrus bound him and put him on a pyre to be burned alive, whether (says Herodotus) in fulfilment of a vow, or as a sacrifice for victory, or to see if a god would save so religious a man as Croesus. The pyre was lit, and Croesus, remembering Solon's words, groaned aloud and called his name three times. They asked him why, and Croesus told them. Then Cyrus relented – and it is interesting to see why this purely Greek story makes him relent. Not from any specifically moral scruple; he does not realize that he is being abominably cruel. He reflects that he, being himself a man, is about to burn an-other man alive, one who had been as prosperous as himself. In fact, he follows the Greek maxim 'Know thyself', which means, remember what you are – a man, and subject to the conditions and limitations of mortality. Therefore, says Hero-dotus, fearing retribution, and reflecting that nothing human is constant, he ordered the fire to be put out. But by now this was impossible. Therefore Croesus called upon Apollo to save him, if his rich offerings had gained him any favour with the god. Whereupon clouds gathered in the clear sky, a torrent of rain fell, and the fire was put out. After which, Croesus and Cyrus became friends – and Croesus gave Cyrus some very shrewd advice on how to manage the Lydians. – This is the way in which Herodotus thought history should be written.

In 499 an event occurred which determined the pattern of the new century: the Ionian cities revolted against the Persian king, Darius. Herodotus again rises to the occasion. He tells how Aristagoras, tyrannus of Miletus, went to Cleomenes, the king of Sparta, to ask for help. Aristagoras described in detail the races of Asia subject to Persia, all incredibly wealthy, most unwarlike, and an easy prey for the Spartans. To illustrate his argument 'he brought with him, so the Spartans say, a tablet of bronze on which was inscribed the circumference of the whole earth, the whole sea, and all the rivers' – in fact, the first map of which we have any record. In conclusion, he compared the poverty of life in Greece with the ease of Asia. Cleomenes promised him an answer on the third day. On the third day Cleomenes asked him how far it was from the sea-coast of the Ionians to the city of the King. But Aristagoras, though he had been cunning in everything else, and had deceived him very cleverly, made a slip here, for he should not have told him the truth if he wanted to bring the Spartans into Asia, but he told him plainly that it was three months' journey. Whereupon Cleomenes, cutting him short in his description of the journey, said, 'Milesian guest, leave Sparta before sunset, for you say things disagreeable to the Spartans, trying to lead them a three-months journey from the sea.'

But the Ionian played another card. He made himself a suppliant, and came back, finding Cleomenes with his little daughter, whose name was Gorgo. He asked Cleomenes to send the child away and listen to him again. Cleomenes agreed to listen, but without sending away the child. So Aristagoras promised him ten talents if he would give Spartan help, then more, until at last he offered fifty. Then Gorgo cried out, 'Father, unless you go away this stranger will corrupt you.' So Cleomenes went away, and Ionia got no help from Sparta.

They got some ships, however, from Athens, and some from Eretria in Euboea, and these forces were concerned in the sack of Croesus' old capital, Sardis. But the revolt failed, having made it plain to Persia that she could not hope to hold Ionia in peace without at least making a demonstration of her power across the Aegean. Accordingly in 490 an expedition was sent against the two offending cities. Eretria was sacked, and a Persian force was landed on the east coast of Attica, at Marathon. The Persians had with them the embittered son of Pisistratus, Hippias, who had been driven out of Athens twenty years before. He was to be installed as tyrant, under Persian protection.

But for a small force of 1,000 men from Plataea, the Athenians were left to face the Persians alone. They won, at the cost of 192 men. Aeschylus was in this fight, and his brother. The brother was killed, but Aeschylus came back home – and we may be glad of it, for he had not yet written the *Persians*, the *Seven against Thebes*, the *Prometheus*, or the Orestes-trilogy.

It was obvious that Persia would try again, but fortunately a revolt in Egypt and the death of Darius kept them busy for ten years. These ten years decided the future of Athens. It happened that in the mining area of Sunium a very rich vein of silver was struck. These small Greek cities had very simple and direct ideas about public finances, as they had about public morality and most other things: it was proposed that the money should be distributed like a dividend, among the citizens. But Themistocles saw further than this. It happened that Athens had for some time been carrying on a struggle with the near-by island of Aegina, an important commercial city, and had been hampered by the lack of ships. Themistocles therefore persuaded the Athenians to spend their windfall on a fleet: Aegina was the immediate object, but he had in mind the Persian danger, and could foresee, no doubt, that Athens had a future as a commercial and naval power.

The fleet was built, just in time. The second Persian attack came in 480, this one not a mere punitive expedition, but a full-scale invasion, by land. This time some sort of Greek unity was achieved, though in the Peloponnese Argos held aloof, because the hated Spartans did not. The story of the two-year war cannot be told here: it is most brilliantly recounted in Herodotus, even though this most humane of historians never really understood the strategy of it. The northern defences went down one by one. Thermopylae was a glorious episode, but a naval action in the neighbouring waters off Cape Artemisium was not discouraging, for it showed that the heavier and slower Greek ships – nearly two-thirds of them Athenian – could fight with some hope against the enemy fleet (mainly Phoenician and Ionian) in narrow waters where the enemy could not manoeuvre. But the time came when the Athenians had to abandon Attica and transport their non-combatants and what property they could to the island of Salamis, whence they could see the Persians burning their houses and destroying the temples on the Acropolis.

Now came one of the most momentous debates in history. Herodotus may have been a little confused about the details, and he may have accepted as fact what was only post-war recrimination, but it is a picture of a Greek event drawn by a Greek, and is, essentially, true to Greece. The northern Greeks had all submitted and were fighting now with Persia: no one was left but the Peloponnesians, a few islands, and Athens – and Attica was lost. The Peloponnesian land forces were at the Isthmus, busy fortifying it, and, of their sea-captains, most were in favour of moving the allied fleet back there from Salamis, afraid that they might be blockaded there by the Persians. Themistocles saw that the narrow waters inside Salamis would give the Greek fleet a chance of victory, while at the Isthmus they would certainly be defeated – even if the fleet held together, which was unlikely. Themistocles urgently persuaded Eurybiades, the Spartan commander-in-chief, to reopen the debate (so Herodotus reports). He agreed, and Themistocles began to speak before Eurybiades had formally put the question to the meeting. 'Themistocles,' said the Corinthian commander, 'in the games those who start too soon are whipped.' 'And those who start too late', was the retort, 'win no prizes.' He stated his case, but Adeimantos the Corinthian said he had no right to speak at all, since he no longer represented a city. Themistocles then, says Herodotus, spoke with great severity both of Adeimantos and of Corinth, and said the Athenians even now had a bigger polis and more territory than Corinth for so long as they had two hundred ships fully manned they could conquer anybody's territory. Then he turned to Eurybiades, and told this unhappy man that unless he agreed to stay and fight at Salamis the Athenians would sail away and refound their polis in Italy. Faced with this, Eurybiades had to agree.

The next thing was to induce Xerxes to fight in the narrows. This was perfectly simple – to Themistocles. He sent a personal slave in a boat to the Persian camp to say that he came from Themistocles, who was secretly on the Persians' side – which indeed was plausible enough. The Greeks were going to retreat during the night, by the western exit from the Bay of Salamis: let the Persians then block up the western strait: they would have the Greeks caught in a trap. The Persians were thoroughly deceived. One detachment was sent to block the western exit: the rest crowded into the narrow waters – 'And when the sun set, where were they?'

It was a shattering victory, and Athens had most of the glory. The next summer it was the turn of the Spartans. At Plataea, thanks not to Spartan generalship, which was poor, but to the magnificent steadiness of the Spartan troops, the Persian army was routed (the Thebans fighting bravely, on the wrong side) and the grand invasion was over. All that remained was to liberate Ionia, and to ensure that never again should the Persian King dare to interfere with free Greeks. But alas! a hundred years later the King was able to impose a Peace of his own design on the warring Greek states, without fighting a single battle.

But meanwhile the effects of the victory on Greece were profound. The Greeks had always thought fairly well of themselves, in comparison with 'barbarians': that impression was confirmed. They had always thought that their free institutions were better than Oriental despotism: events proved that they were right. The Asiatic master compelled obedience by torture and the lash: the Greeks took their decisions by debating and persuading – and then acted like one man: and they conquered. No wonder that the next generation filled its temple-pediments with sculptured representations of the old mythical battle between the earth-born Giants and the

Olympian Gods. The Greek Gods had triumphed again, freedom and reason had defeated despotism and fear.

Athens had especial reason to feel exalted. Men in Athens saw this victory who had heard from their own fathers how Solon had freed the very soil of Attica from enslavement to the wealthy, and had laid the foundations of democracy: they themselves had seen Pisistratus lending seed-corn to the poor, and gradually making of quiet Athens a city of which other Greeks took some notice: in middle age they had seen the tyranny ended, and a new liberal constitution framed by Cleisthenes: there had been bitter conflicts, and party feeling still ran very high – dramatized in the story which someone told Herodotus, of how the great Aristeides, an ostracized party-leader,[1] crossed by night from his temporary home in Aegina to Salamis just before the battle: he called Themistocles out of that war-council, and said 'You and I have been the bitterest enemies: now our rivalry is, which of us can do Athens the greatest service. I have slipped between the Persian lines to tell you this: we are surrounded by the Persian fleet. Go in and tell them.' 'Thank God!' said Themistocles: 'but you go in and tell them. They will believe *you*.' – Our Athenian had seen the young democracy weathering party conflicts like these: he had seen the Athenian army triumphant at Marathon: then he had seen his city at one plunge taking to the sea, and risking everything at sea. Now he saw the towns and villages of Attica burnt, and the immemorial Acropolis, home of Cecrops, of Erechtheus, of Theseus, of Athena herself, laid in hopeless ruin: but the polis was triumphant, and, more than any other, had saved Greece. Greece now had not one leader, but two: the quiet country town of his boyhood now stood, admired of all, alongside the heroic city of Sparta. Success like this, won not by good fortune but by good sense, and by self-restraint

1. 'Ostracism' was a device invented by Cleisthenes, as a check to the excessive personal animosities of public life in Athens. Any year the Assembly could decide to have an 'ostracism', with no names mentioned. If it did so, each citizen could write on a potsherd ('ostracon') the name of any citizen whom he would like to see honourably removed from the city for ten years. If 6000 votes, or more, were cast against any one man, he had to go – with no further penalty. It was a means of removing the leader of a dangerous faction.

more than self-assertion, was naturally a spur to further effort. By the time of the Persian War Athens had only just found herself: what more might she not do? There is some parallel between Athens of 480 and England of 1588: in whatever direction men looked they saw exciting possibilities – but the Athenian saw even more than the Englishman. Politically, there was the possibility of becoming the leader of a sea-alliance comparable with Sparta's Peloponnesian League: and men could take pride in the fact that what the city did would be done, not by powerful magistrates acting in their name, but by the ordinary Athenians themselves, in their sovereign Assembly. Intellectually, the whole world of thought and knowledge was opening up, thanks very much to their own kinsmen of Ionia. In trade and industry, Athens was rapidly overhauling those other Greek cities who had had such a long start of her: the combination of Attic taste and intelligence with her central position, her excellent harbours, and her now overwhelming sea-power, was formidable indeed; and besides this, Athens, like London, enjoyed certain imponderable advantages derived from her probity and common-sense methods. Artistically, too, a new world was opening up. The long struggle with bronze and marble had brought architecture and sculpture to the verge of classical perfection, and it was to be the task of the Athenian artists, working nearly always for the polis, to combine Ionian elegance with Dorian strength. The Athenian potters and painters were approaching their greatest triumphs: the most Athenian art of all, tragic drama, was growing more assured and more exciting every year, and very interesting possibilities were being explored in a hilarious rustic rough-and-tumble which, in fact, very soon gave birth to the brilliant and sophisticated comedy of Aristophanes and his rivals. Such was the spirit of the dawning Periclean Age – if we remember too that it was steeped in the perennial Homer, who taught that habit of mind – essentially aristocratic, in whatever class of society it may be found – which puts quality before quantity, noble struggle before mere achievement, and honour before opulence.

Political history I must treat in a very summary fashion.

The Greek Alliance had done its immediate task in driving the Persian out of Europe, but it remained to liberate Ionia and to break Persian sea-power. In this, Sparta showed little interest. Sparta was essentially a land-power, with an agricultural economy; she was satisfied if no other Greek state or combination of states was strong enough to threaten her in the Peloponnese or to raise the ever-present bogey of a revolt of the Helots. Moreover, the liberation of Ionia and the defence of the Aegean was a matter for ships – for Athens therefore. And Athens was ready enough for the task, which (she could remind herself) befitted her, as the original home of the Ionian race.

Athens therefore organized a naval confederacy, whose headquarters were the sacred and central island of Delos. Those who joined it – and these were practically all the maritime cities of the Aegean – contributed a fixed number of ships and men: or, if they preferred it, the equivalent in money. The assessments were fixed by Aristeides of Athens, 'Aristeides the Just'; and his justice is shown by the fact that no assessment of his was ever challenged. The central fact was the enormous preponderance of Athens: she had a fleet of 200 ships, and many of the members were assessed at one ship. Of the small allies, a large number preferred to pay the money-contribution and be done with it.

Operations against Persia continued for some years. Then arose the insoluble problem of the right of secession. The important island of Naxos refused to be a member of the League any longer: the threat from Persia was now at an end; why then should Naxos contribute forces to a League which was only Athens in disguise? To which Athens could reasonably reply that if there was no League the Persian menace would very soon revive. She treated this secession as a revolt, crushed it, and imposed a money-payment on the Naxians. Other such 'revolts' were treated in the same way. Then Aegean states which had held aloof were compelled to join – again, with some reason, for why should any Aegean state enjoy the security which others provided, without contributing to it?

Two other things were done, both sensible, but both helping to transform the League into an Empire. The headquarters of the League were moved from Delos to Athens – from a small island to which people went mainly for religious purposes to the city to which people were glad to go for any purpose. That suspicious thing 'administrative convenience' could be cited, and it could be represented that the League's treasury was safer in Athens – as indeed it was, for Athens had just lost two fleets in an Egyptian adventure: but for all that, it strengthened the impression, in Athens and out of it, that what was in name a League was in fact an Empire. Then commercial disputes between members were made referable to Athenian courts. This was in fact a great simplification of procedure. In the absence of any system of international law, legal processes between members of different cities were possible only if the two cities had a treaty expressly providing for them; if not, direct reprisal – a sort of official piracy – was the only way of ensuring that complaints should be listened to. The Athenian courts were reasonably honest, and they were disinterested. Great care was taken to ensure that no advantage was enjoyed by an Athenian in litigation with a member of an allied city. Nevertheless, it looked bad.

The general efficiency and honesty with which Athens managed the League are shown by the fact that cities continued to join it voluntarily, and that when the war with Sparta came the members on the whole remained surprisingly loyal to Athens, even though they were called subjects of an imperial city.

But it was inevitable that the Athenian citizen should begin to think imperially when he saw members of the League coming to Athens for judgment, and knew that the treasure of the League was kept in his own Acropolis, that the policy of the League must in fact be a policy agreeable to Athens, and that the military force of the League was largely made up of Athenian ships and men. It was all very flattering to Athenian pride, and profitable too, for citizen-jurors were paid, and of the money-contribution which more and more of the allies rendered in lieu of ships and men quite a lot went, legitimately, into Athenian pockets in the form of service-pay.

A great deal more found its way there, perhaps more questionably, through Pericles' rebuilding policy. The funds of the League were piling up, and the temples which the Persians had destroyed had not been set up again. Part of Pericles' policy – a continuation of the policy of Pisistratus – was to make Athens the artistic, as well as the intellectual and political, centre of Greece, and Athens had an unemployment problem. The Parthenon, the magnificent gateway to the Acropolis, picture galleries flanking it – these and other buildings were the outcome of these needs and desires. There were protests, even at home, but Pericles replied that the allies paid Athens for protection, and paid no exorbitant sum; they were protected, the Athenian fleet was highly efficient, and there was an ample reserve of money. Athens was entitled to spend the surplus on such buildings and statues as brought honour to her and to all Greece. He might have argued – perhaps he did – that Athens alone had willingly given up her city to the destroyer in order to continue the fight for Greek freedom; and he probably said now what he said later, in the Funeral Speech, 'We throw open our Polis to all'.

But why did Athens not become the capital of a unified Aegean state? Rome could give her citizenship successively to the other Latin cities, to all Italy, to the whole empire: if Rome could do this, why not Athens?

Patronizing talk of political incapacity or shortsightedness will not do. It is the inescapable fact, which we so often try to escape, that everything has to be paid for, and there are many things, desirable in themselves, for which the price is too high. If this were not so, human existence would not be tragic. We ourselves have just had an illustration. Some of our politicians had pleasant dreams of a perfectly planned and perfectly efficient national economy – an excellent thing. But the price was direction of labour, and the Englishman, with his strange addiction to personal freedom, refused to pay the price.

As an earlier chapter tried to show, the Greeks had a similar addiction to the independent polis – it was the polis, to the Greek mind, which marked the difference between the Greek and the barbarian: it was the polis which enabled him to live the full, intelligent and responsible life which he wished to live. Athens could not extend her citizenship to the allies without curtailing the political activities and responsibility of each Athenian citizen. Government must have been delegated to representatives, and then the Athenian would have felt that the polis was no longer his own. Life would have lost its savour. The Roman – under severe pressure, by the way – could include Latins in his *civitas* because the *civitas* was only a machine of government: so long as it protected him he did not much mind who worked it. The Athenian did not think that way – nor did the allies of Athens, for it is as certain as such things can be that if Athens had offered them common citizenship they would not have accepted it, for if the Greek was not within a day's walk of his political centre, then his life was something less than the life of a real man.

To the modern mind this may seem odd: no doubt it seems odd to those Russians who know anything about us that we prefer our notions of personal liberty to the triumphs, real or prospective, of their system. But this indeed was the choice that lay before the Greeks: to accept a much lower quality of life by diluting and practically losing the polis, or, eventually, to perish. If – in the spirit of Cyrus at Croesus' pyre – we reflect that we too are an imperilled political society clinging desperately to a certain conception of life, our judgment on the Greeks may become a little less complacent. Pericles' policy – that is to say, the policy which prevailed with the Athenian Assembly – was to try to make the best of both worlds, to enjoy to the full both polis and Empire. We shall perhaps be able to condemn him with better heart when we ourselves have succeeded in reconciling love of liberty with survival.

During the half-century that separated the Persian from the Peloponnesian war the policy of Athens was guided first by the aristocratic Cimon (son of Miltiades the victor of Marathon), then by Pericles. Cimon's policy was to drive back the Persian, and to keep on friendly terms with Sparta. The former was easier than the latter. The swift rise of Athens, still more the transformation of the League into hardly disguised Empire, aroused both fear and resentment: so much so that Cimon's policy became obviously impossible. Pericles, whose predominance in the Assembly was almost undisputed from 461 until his death in 429, accepted Spartan hostility as inevitable, made terms with Persia, and tried to make Athens unchallenge-able in Greece. The energy shown by the Athenians during these years is almost incredible: they aimed at, and for a short time held, an empire which comprised or controlled not only the whole Aegean, but also the Corinthian Gulf and Boeotia: and there were those who dreamed, and continued to dream, of conquering distant Sicily. Our talk of debates and theatres and law-courts and processions must not obscure the fact that the fifth-century Athenian was first and foremost a man of action. In 456 the Athenians had a whole armful of respon-sibilities close at home, but that did not deter them from send-ing two hundred ships to assist Egypt in a rebellion against Persia, and when these were destroyed they sent another force of similar size, with similar results. A war memorial of the time records the names of those of the Erechtheid tribe 'who died in battle in one year in Cyprus, Egypt, Phoenice, Halieis (in the Peloponnese), Aegina and Megara'. It cannot be said of the Athenians that they exploited an empire gained by the energies and sacrifice of others. The war which all Greece thought inevitable broke out in 431. We will say something about it in the next chapter: this one may close with a short survey of the democratic institutions under which Athens conducted it, preceded by two sketches of the Athenian character, taken from Thucydides' history of the war. The first was given by a Corinthian delegation which came to Sparta to urge Sparta to declare war.

You have no idea (say the Corinthians) what sort of people these Athenians are, how totally different from yourselves. They are always thinking of new schemes, and are quick to make their plans and to carry them out: you are content with what you have, and are re-luctant to do even what is necessary. They are bold, adventurous, sanguine: you are cautious, and trust neither to your power nor to your judgment. They love foreign adventure, you hate it: for they think they stand to gain, you that you stand to lose something. When victorious they make the most of it: when defeated, they fall back less than anyone. They give their bodies to Athens as if they were public property: they use their minds for Athens in the most individual way possible. They make a plan: if it fails, they think they have lost something; if it succeeds, this success is nothing in comparison with what they are going to do next. It is impossible for them either to enjoy peace and quiet themselves or allow anyone else to.[1]

Now Pericles himself, two years later, in his Funeral Oration. First he praises the liberality of Athens: the law is impartial, public distinction is given to merit, not to party or class: in social matters toleration reigns, and in public matters there is self-restraint and an absence of violence. Athens too is rich in the spiritual, intellectual and material things of civilization. So far Pericles is comparing Athens with Greece in general: now he turns to Sparta in particular.

We admit anyone to our city, and do not expel foreigners from fear that they should see too much, because in war we trust to our own bravery and daring rather than to stratagems and preparations. Our enemies prepare for war by a laborious training from boyhood: we live at our ease, but are no less confident in facing danger. Indeed, the Spartans have never ventured to attack us without the help of their allies. So, with a courage which comes from natural disposition rather than from laws, we have two advantages, for we avoid the preliminary labour, and are just as good as they when the test comes. We love the arts, but without lavish display, and things of the mind, but without becoming soft.

After this direct contrast with Sparta Pericles becomes more general again. In Athens, wealth gives opportunity for action, not reason for boasting, and it is idleness, not poverty, which is disgraceful. A man has time both for his private affairs and for the affairs of the city, and those engaged in business are yet quite competent to judge political matters.[2] A man who takes no part in public business some call a quiet man: we Athenians call him useless. Speech we do not regard as a hindrance to action,

1. Paraphrase of Thucydides, I, 70.
2. This is obviously a criticism of other mercantile and industrial cities, such as Corinth: and it contains the interesting implication that these cities were not governed by business men. The Conservative Central Office may be glad to have the exact reference to this passage: Thucydides, II, 40.

but as a necessary preliminary: other people are made bold by ignorance, timid by calculation; we can calculate, and still be audacious. Also, we are generous, not out of expediency, but from confidence. In fact, our polis is an education to all Greece.

This speech of Pericles gives no doubt an idealized picture of Athens, but for all that it is substantially a true picture, and in any case the ideals of a people are an important part of what they are. The essential truth of this picture is not a matter of exact demonstration, but when we have contemplated any side of the activity of Periclean Athens, we can turn to this speech, and its noble praise of the Athenian polis, and feel the conviction that the Athenians of this period must indeed have been like this, in all essentials. There is the astonishing beauty of the Parthenon – in size so modest, only 220 feet long: in impression so overwhelming; in photographs, only another Greek temple, but in reality the most thrilling building there is. There are the plays of Sophocles, composed for and crowned by this Athenian people. I myself – if a personal reference may be permitted – have given detailed lectures on them for thirty years, and find them now fresher, more exciting, more packed with thought than ever I did: nothing in them is perfunctory, nothing done for display (superb though the technique is), nothing second-rate. There are, perhaps more eloquent than anything, the simple tombstones carved by anonymous sculptors, most moving in their quiet dignity and sincerity. There are ordinary objects of domestic use, and they have the same qualities. Nowhere is one so certain as in Periclean Athens that one will never meet anything vulgar, bizarre, quaint or superficial. Most characteristic is comedy: it has roaring obscenities that could not possibly be printed today, but never anything to snigger at. The reason is that a people of fine quality were living in conditions which habituated them to high spiritual, mental and physical endeavour.

Which brings us back to the polis. Everywhere the polis gave a certain fullness and meaning to life, but most notably in Athens, where political democracy was carried to its logical extreme. There are of course those who deny that Athens was a democracy at all, since women, resident aliens and slaves had no voice in the conduct of affairs. If we define democracy as participation in the government by all the adult population of a country, then Athens was no democracy – nor is any modern state: for because of its size every modern state must delegate government to representative and professional administrators, and this is a form of oligarchy.

If we define it as participation in the government by all citizens, then Athens was a democracy – and we must remember that the normal Greek qualification for citizenship was that at least the father, if not both parents, should have been citizens – the Greek 'state' being (in theory and in sentiment) a group of kinsmen, not merely the population in a certain area.

But for our present purpose the exact definition of democracy is unimportant:[1] our concern is to see how the political institutions of Athens affected the life and the mind of the Athenian. In this chapter we will describe them: in the next we will watch them at work under the stress of a desperate war.

The Assembly was supreme, and everything possible was done to maintain its supremacy in fact as well as on paper. There was no possibility in Athens of the machine taking control – another advantage of the small scale. The Assembly consisted of every adult Athenian male who had been accepted as legitimate by his 'deme', and had not been expressly disfranchized for some grave offence. No trace of property-qualification remained except – significantly – in the army. So much was the polis the community of citizens, so little a super-human 'state', that the citizen had to find his own equipment: consequently the man rich enough to own a horse served in the cavalry – on his own horse, though while he was on service the polis paid for its keep. The moderately well-to-do served in the heavy infantry (hoplites), providing his own armour;

1. Since the meaning of the word 'democracy' is of some topical interest, a note on the Greek usage may be appended here. In ordinary parlance, 'demokratia' (literally, 'control by the people') meant political democracy as described above, but the political theorists, notably Plato and Aristotle, used it in the sense 'government by the poor', and consequently condemned it as being only an inverted form of oligarchy or tyranny, government inspired by self-interest. 'Polity' was the name given to government by general consent, without reference to class.

and the poor, who could provide nothing but themselves, served as auxiliaries, or rowed in the fleet. The resident aliens served alongside citizens, but slaves never served in either army or navy, except once in a moment of great danger, when slaves were invited to enlist on the promise (which was honoured) of freedom and full civil (not political) rights.

This Assembly, a mass-meeting of all the native male residents of Attica, was the sole legislative body, and had, in various ways, complete control of the administration and judicature. First, the administration. The old Areopagus, composed of ex-archons, did nothing now except deal with cases of homicide. The archons, once so powerful, were now chosen by annual ballot from the Assembly. Any citizen, any year, might find himself one of the nine archons: this meant, naturally, that the archonship, although it had administrative responsibility, had no real power. Power remained with the Assembly. The Assembly met once a month, unless specially convened to settle something of importance. Any citizen could speak – if he could get the Assembly to listen; anybody could propose anything, within certain strict constitutional safeguards. But so large a body needed a committee to prepare its business, and to deal with matters of urgency. This committee was the Council ('boulê') of five hundred, not elected, but chosen by ballot, fifty from each tribe. Since this Council was chosen haphazard, and was composed of entirely different people each year, it could develop no corporate feeling. That was the whole idea: nothing must overshadow the Assembly. Most of the administrative boards ('Government departments') were manned by members of the Boulê. But since five hundred men could not be in constant session, and were too many to make an efficient executive committee, there was an inner council, the 'prytany', composed, in turn, of the fifty men drawn from each of the ten tribes, which remained in session for one-tenth of the year. Of these, one was chosen by ballot to be chairman each day. If there was a meeting of the Assembly, he presided: for twenty-four hours he was titular Head of the State. (It happened, Greece being an essentially dramatic country, that Socrates held this position one day towards the end of the war when the Assembly ran amok – as sometimes happened, but not often – and quite illegally demanded to impeach the whole of the Board of Generals for failing to rescue survivors of the successful naval battle of Arginusae. Socrates defied the mob, and refused to put the irregular proposal to the vote.) As a further check on the Administration, all outgoing magistrates had to submit to the Assembly an account of their official acts, and their responsibility did not end until they had passed this 'audit'. Until they had done this they might neither leave Athens nor sell property.

One important office could not be left to the hazard of the ballot – the command of the forces, on land or afloat. The ten Stratêgoi ('generals' or 'admirals' indifferently) were elected – but annually, though re-election was permissible and indeed normal: but it was no unusual thing for an Athenian to be a general in one campaign and a private soldier in the next. This was an extreme case of the basic conception of democracy, 'to rule and to be ruled in turn'. It was as if the trade-union official of one year automatically returned to his bench the next. Being the only officials expressly elected on the grounds of special competence, and holding offices of such importance, the stratêgoi naturally wielded great influence in the city's affairs. It was through this office, and through his personal ascendency in the Assembly, that Pericles led the Athenians for so long.

The Assembly controlled not only legislation and administration, but justice as well; as there were no professional administrators, so there were no professional judges or pleaders. The principle was preserved that the aggrieved man appealed directly to his fellow-citizens for justice – in the local courts for trivial matters, in Athenian courts for important matters, criminal or civil. The jury was virtually a section of the Assembly, varying in size from 101 to 1,001, according to the importance of the case. There was no judge, only a purely formal chairman, like our 'foreman'. There were no pleaders: the parties conducted their own case, though in fact a plaintiff or defendant might get a professional 'speech-writer' to make up his speech: but then he learnt it and gave it himself. This popular jury was judge both of law and of fact, and there was no appeal. If the offence was one for which the law laid down no precise penalty, then – since a large jury could not conveniently fix the sentence – the prosecutor, if he won his case, proposed one penalty, the accused proposed an alternative, and the jury had to choose one of the two. This explains the procedure in Plato's *Apology*: when Socrates had been condemned, the prosecution demanded the death penalty, but Socrates, first suggesting the Freedom of the City as the alternative, formally proposed, not exile, which the jury would gladly have accepted, but an almost derisory fine.

This survey, brief though it is, will bring out one essential point, that public affairs in Athens were run, so far as possible, by amateurs. The professional was given as little scope as possible; indeed, the expert was usually a public slave. Every citizen was, in turn, a soldier (or sailor), a legislator, a judge, an administrator – if not as archon, then certainly as member of the Boulê. The extraordinary use made of amateurs may strike the reader as ludicrous: it was indeed severely criticized by Socrates and Plato, though not so much because it was inefficient as because it entrusted to men entirely ignorant of it the major function of 'the political art', namely, to make men better. But this is by the way.

Beneath this general aversion to the professional there was a more or less conscious theory of the polis: namely that the duty of taking part, at the appropriate season of life, in all the affairs of the polis was one that the individual owed both to the polis and to himself. It was part of that full life which only the polis could provide: the savage, living for himself alone, could not have it, nor the civilized 'barbarian' living in a vast empire ruled by a King and his personal servants. To the Athenian at least, self-rule by discussion, self-discipline, personal responsibility, direct participation in the life of the polis at all points – these things were the breath of life.

And they were incompatible with a representative government administering a large area. This is the reason why Athens could not grow as Rome did, by incorporating other poleis. To the Athenian, the responsibility of taking his own decisions, carrying them out, and accepting the consequences, was a necessary part of the life of a free man. This is one reason why the popular art of Athens was the tragedy of Aeschylus and Sophocles and the comedy of Aristophanes, while ours is the cinema. The Athenian was accustomed to deal with things of importance: an art therefore which did not handle themes of importance would have seemed to him to be childish.

This account of the Athenian constitution, necessarily a very short one, will probably suggest to the reader at least two reflections: how very amateurish it all sounds, and what an enormous amount of time the Athenians must have spent in public business, if such a system was to work at all.

To begin with the former point. It was government by amateurs in the strict sense of this word: that is to say, by people who liked government and administration. To put it in this way is perhaps misleading, because the words 'government' and 'administration' have, among us, acquired capital letters: they are things in themselves, pursuits to which some misguided persons devote their lives. To the Greeks, they were merely two sides of that many-sided thing, the life of the polis. To attend to the business of the polis was not only a duty which a man owed to the polis: it was also a duty which a man owed to himself – and it was an absorbing interest too. It was part of the complete life. This is the reason why the Athenian never employed the professional administrator or judge if he could possibly help it. The polis was a kind of super-family, and family life means taking a direct part in family affairs and family counsels. This attitude to the polis explains, too, why the Greek never, as we say, 'invented' representative government. Why should he 'invent' something which most Greeks struggled to abolish, namely being governed by someone else?

But was it amateurish in the other sense? Was it inefficient, or inconsequent? To this question, I think, we can say no, if our standard is not perfection, but government as it is normally found among men. The regime was stable, recovering quite easily from two oligarchic revolutions made possible by the stress of unsuccessful war. It won and managed an empire: it collected its taxes; it managed its economy, its finances and its

E

currency with notable firmness: it seems to have maintained a standard of public justice which certain governments of our own time have not reached. It lost a critical war, not from lack of nerve or spirit, but from serious errors of judgment, and to these any form of government is liable. Judged by all these, the ordinary standards of efficiency, this experiment in logical democracy must be pronounced not unsuccessful.

The Athenian would have accepted all these tests of efficiency as legitimate, but would have added another: did it secure for the ordinary citizen a reasonably good life? That is to say, besides doing what we today expect from our government, did it stimulate his intellect and satisfy his spirit? In answering this question there can be no hesitation whatsoever. A much more searching test was applied by philosophers like Socrates and Plato: did this form of government train men in virtue? Plato says, in the *Gorgias*, that Themistocles, Cimon and Pericles 'filled the city with fortifications and rubbish of that sort', but failed miserably in the statesman's first duty, of making the citizens more virtuous. But efficiency of this kind is what very few governments have aimed at.

In considering efficiency of the grosser sort, two points must be borne in mind. One is the small scale of the state. This Athenian district-meeting, the Assembly, like a vigorous local council today, was for the most part dealing with problems of which many of its members at least had direct personal knowledge. Further, the complexity of things was much less than it is today – not indeed the intellectual or moral complexity of things, which is always the same, but the complexity of organization. If war was declared, it was not a matter of 'mobilizing the entire resources of the nation', with endless committees and an enormous consumption of paper: it was a matter simply of every man going home for his shield, his spear and his rations, and reporting for orders. The Assembly made its worst mistakes in making decisions on matters outside its personal knowledge. Thus, in the middle of the war it made the disastrous resolution to invade Sicily, though (as Thucydides remarks) very few knew where Sicily was, nor how big it was.

Then one must remember that all the members of this Assembly, other than the youngest, had first-hand experience of administration in the various local and tribal offices and in law-courts, and that five hundred new men every year served in the Boulê, drafting laws for submission to the Assembly, receiving foreign embassies, dealing with finance, and all the rest of it. If we take 30,000 as a reasonable estimate of the normal number of citizens, it will be seen that any one citizen was more likely than not to serve his year on the Boulê. The Assembly, in fact, was for the most part composed of men who knew what they were talking about, from personal experience.

This brings us to our second consideration, how the ordinary Athenian found time for all this. He was not a super-man, and the day contained twenty-four hours then as now. This is clearly an important question. The Greeks, like all civilized peoples in antiquity and many since, were slave-owners. From this it has been inferred by many who have not read Aristophanes but have read *Uncle Tom's Cabin*, that the culture of Attica was the work of a leisured class, supported by slaves. This belief may be consoling to us, who have so much more economic power and so much less real civilization, but it is essentially false. There is very little similarity between Greek slavery in the fifth and fourth centuries and the Roman *latifundia*, large estates worked by slaves, which were created by the depopulation of the countryside.

In the first place, agricultural slavery in Greece hardly existed: the tradition was still vigorous that the citizen owned his land and slavery offered little advantage in small-scale farming like this, as the slave would have to eat almost as much as he produced. The well-to-do farmer, like his counterpart in the town, would have a few slaves, employed mostly in personal and domestic duties. The Athenian who goes out shopping has a slave – if he can afford one – to carry his purchases, and there are one or two at home, male and female, acting as 'slavey' and Nannie. These added to the amenities of life, and to some extent promoted civilization, just as the servants we used to have enabled middle-class women to play bridge in the afternoons, and professors to write books; but they were certainly not the basis of the economic life of Attica. A modern authority[1] estimates that just before the Peloponnesian War there were something like 125,000 slaves in Attica, of whom something like 65,000 were in domestic employment – rather more than half. Professor Gomme estimates that at the same period there were about 45,000 Athenian men over 18, and therefore a total Athenian population of something over 100,000. This would give about half a slave per person on the average, but it is impossible to estimate how many households had none and how many had a lot. Other slaves Professor Gomme estimates at 50,000 in industry and 10,000 in the mines. The treatment of the latter was callous in the extreme, the only serious blot on the general humanity of the Athenians. Their slaves in general had considerable freedom, and much more legal protection than for example the Negro citizens of the U.S.A. – so much so that it was a Spartan gibe that in the streets of Athens you could not distinguish between a slave and a citizen. But in the mines, slaves were often worked until they died: conditions were much worse than they were in our own factories in the grimmest times – though an Athenian apologist might legitimately point out that at least the Athenians did not pretend that these victims were citizens, with immortal souls, and that only the most loutish slaves were sent there. But it was horrible. Partly, no doubt, it was a case of 'out of sight is out of mind', partly that the mines could hardly have been worked at all without something of the sort. Most civilizations have their private horrors: we kill 4,000 citizens annually on the roads because our present way of life could not otherwise continue. To understand is not necessarily to pardon, but there is no harm in trying to understand.

As for the (estimated) 50,000 in industry, that sounds an enormous number in proportion to the whole population. If we in Great Britain had a comparable number of industrial slaves – say ten millions – we should all be living in extreme comfort – but for the laws of economics, which would assuredly

1. A. W. Gomme, *History of Greece*, vol. I, in *History of European Civilization* (Eyre). This is perhaps the best short history in existence of the civilization of Greece.

see to it that we were worse off than ever. But in trying to estimate the economic and social effect of these 50,000 slaves, we should remember that in the absence of machinery their labour did not produce a great surplus for others to live on: some, certainly, but not a lot. There was a very effective limit to the employment of industrial slaves: in slack times an idle slave was a dead loss. He had to be fed, and his capital value was less. Therefore we find that the normal 'factory' employed both slaves and citizens – the citizens could be 'turned off'. The 'factory' was invariably a very small affair indeed: if it employed as many as twenty slaves, it was a really big concern. Thanks to the recent discovery of certain inscriptions, we happen to know something of the business side of some of the Acropolis buildings. Athens, we know, was a slave-owning state: we confidently expect therefore that the Parthenon and the Erechtheum and the rest were each built by a contractor using teams of slaves. On reflection, it is perhaps rather foolish to suppose that architecture and sculpture of this quality – so grave, so humane, so intelligent – should be created by slave-owners: these buildings are so different from the Pyramids. And we find that in fact nothing of the sort was done, but something else just as incredible. These buildings were erected through thousands of separate contracts: one citizen with one slave contracts to bring ten cartloads of marble from Pentelicus; or a citizen employing two Athenians and owning three slaves contracts for the fluting of one column. There was slavery, and it helped, like an auxiliary engine: but to suggest that it was the mainstay of Athenian economy is a serious exaggeration, and to say that it set the tone of society and estranged the ordinary citizen from hard work is ludicrous. What it did do was to keep down the level of wages: for if it became more profitable, in the long run, to buy a slave, no one would employ free labour – but slave-owning was a tricky business.

In our search, then, for the origin of the spare time which Athenians seemed to have in such abundance, we must give due importance, and no more, to slavery. For the most part, this merely increased the leisure of those who were already fairly comfortable. We must give a great deal more importance,

I think, to the extremely simple standard of life on which even the wealthy Athenian lived. His house, his furniture, his dress, his food, were such that the British artisan would reject with contempt – and indeed in the British climate he could not subsist on it.

It is of course true that machinery produces for us most of the thousands of things which we have and the Greeks did not, but this cuts both ways. We are considering at the moment not comfort but leisure – which the Greek prized above everything except glory: and it is not evident that machinery has in general much increased our leisure. It has enormously increased the complications of life, so that of the time saved us by machine-production a great deal is taken away from us by the extra work which a machine-age creates.

In the third place, when the reader has calculated how much of his working time is consumed in helping him to pay for things which the Greek simply did without – things like settees, collars and ties, bedclothes, laid-on water, tobacco, tea and the Civil Service – let him reflect on the time-using occupations that we follow and he did not – reading books and newspapers, travelling daily to work, pottering about the house, mowing the lawn – grass being, in our climate, one of the bitterest enemies of social and intellectual life. Again, the daily round was ordered not by the clock but by the sun, since there was no effective artificial light. Activity began at dawn. In Plato's *Protagoras* an eager young man wants to see Socrates in a hurry, and calls on him so early that Socrates is still in bed (or rather, 'on' bed, wrapped presumably in his cloak), and the young man has to feel his way to the bed because it is not yet light. Plato obviously thinks that this call was indeed made on the early side, but it was nothing outrageous. We envy, per-haps, ordinary Athenians who seem to be able to spend a couple of hours in the afternoon at the baths or a gymnasium (a spacious athletic and cultural centre provided by the public for itself). *We* cannot afford to take time off in the middle of the day like this. No: but we get up at seven, and what with shaving, having breakfast, and putting on the complicated panoply which we wear, we are not ready for anything until

8.30. The Greek got up as soon as it was light, shook out the blanket in which he had slept, draped it elegantly around himself as a suit, had a beard and no breakfast, and was ready to face the world in five minutes. The afternoon, in fact, was not the middle of his day, but very near the end of it.

Finally, many forms of public service were paid for, including eventually attendance at the Assembly. Athens in fact found what we have found during this century, that if we want the ordinary citizen to give up time for public work we must indemnify him for the loss of his time – though we have not yet set up a public fund to enable the poor to pay for their seats in a state theatre which we do not possess. Members of the Boulê, the archons and other officials, and the jurymen who manned the courts were paid, though modestly, from public funds; and these, to some extent, were the profits of the empire. It seems clearly established that in the fourth century Athenian citizens played a smaller part, and the resident aliens a greater, in the industry and trade of Attica, and the reason is not that the Athenians were living more on slavery, but that they were living more on the state.

This experiment in democratic government is one that can never be repeated, unless once again there should arise independent states small enough to walk across in two days. The confident way in which the Athenians carried to its logical extreme their desire to participate directly and personally in every aspect of government sounds almost like a deliberate challenge to the weakness of human nature. Is it possible for a whole people to have the sustained wisdom and self-control to manage its own affairs wisely? Can a people control an empire and its own finances, without becoming corrupt? Can it run a war? What are the temptations and dangers that assail a democracy? Athens provides almost a laboratory experiment in popular government: except that it all happened so long ago, and so far away, and in a language which is so very dead, it might almost be worth our while today to pay it some attention.

VIII

THE GREEKS AT WAR

THE Greek world was now divided. On the one side was the Athenian Empire, which men openly called a 'tyranny'; on the other, Sparta, the Peloponnesian League, and a number of states (notably in Boeotia) that sympathized with Sparta: the first group strong at sea, the second strong on land; the first in the main Ionian, the second Dorian – not that this division in itself counted for much; Athens favouring, even insisting on, democratic constitutions among her allies, the other group favouring oligarchies, or, at the most, limited democracies. It is a familiar situation. There was a general sentiment that Athens was behaving intolerably in restricting the autonomy of her nominal allies: this enabled Sparta to come forward as the champion of Greek freedom. There was also trade rivalry between Athens and Corinth, and the fear in Corinth that her commerce with the Western Greeks was being threatened. In the event, it was the Corinthians who persuaded the Spartans to take up the Athenian challenge: we quoted above a character-sketch of the Athenian people given on this occasion by a Corinthian speaker at Sparta.

This war was the turning-point in the history of the Greek polis. It lasted almost continuously from 431 to 404 – twenty-seven years of it. But for brief intermissions, fighting went on in almost every part of the Greek world – all over the Aegean, in and about Chalcidice, in Boeotia, around the coasts of the Peloponnese, in north-west Greece, in Sicily, where two powerful expeditionary forces of the Athenians were destroyed with scarcely a survivor: and Attica, all but the city and the Piraeus, which were enclosed by a single line of fortifications, was left open to the Spartan armies and systematically devastated. In the second year of the war, when the country-dwellers of Attica had been forced to abandon their homes to the enemy and to take refuge within the walls, living where they could, plague broke out and raged for months. Thucydides (who caught it but recovered) gives, in his apparently calm manner, an account of it that still makes the blood run cold: he makes a particular point of the moral break-down which it caused, for in this agony obedience to law, religion, honesty and decency vanished. Something like a quarter of the polis died, including Pericles: yet Athens recovered, swept the seas, imported her corn regularly, sent out navies and armies, and on two or three occasions could have made peace on favourable terms; until, twenty-five years after the plague, she lost her last fleet in a humiliating way, and had to submit to the mercy of Sparta.

Yet all this time the life of the polis went on. Nothing of importance was decided except by the people in Assembly: generals were elected, second, third and fourth fronts opened, peace terms discussed, reports from the front considered, by this Assembly of all citizens. Only once during the war did its nerve fail, after the Sicilian catastrophe: then the Assembly was tricked into surrendering its powers to a smaller body – which was in fact only a screen for a determined group of oligarchs. These reigned in terror for a few months: then they were overthrown, and a limited democracy was introduced (highly praised by Thucydides); but soon the old Assembly was in charge again, open to all.

But not only did the political life continue: the intellectual and artistic life continued too. To those who remember the breakdown of our cultural life in the First World War – the nervous anxiety of authorities to shut down everything possible (except Business, which was to be 'as usual'), the popular frenzy which made it unpatriotic to listen to Beethoven and Wagner, the follies of censors, the degradation of the theatre – it is humiliating to contemplate Athens at war. With no less at stake, with the enemy still nearer – even camped in Attica, with no smaller a proportion of citizens killed and families bereaved, the Athenians continued their festivals, not as self-indulgence but as a part of the life which they were fighting for. In the drama produced for them, and in their name, Sophocles, without a word about the war, continued to brood on the ultimate problems of human life and human character, Euripides to expose the hollowness of victory and the ugliness of revenge, and, most astonishing of all, Aristophanes to ridicule popular leaders, generals and the sovereign people itself, to express his loathing of the war and the delights of peace in comedies compounded of wit, fantasy, buffoonery, lyrical beauty, uproarious indecency and highbrow parody.

And all this time Socrates was in Athens, discussing, arguing, criticizing – except when he was at Poteidaea, fighting heroically in the ranks – trying to convince whoever would listen that the good of the soul was the supreme good, and rigorous dialectic the only means to its attainment.

On the other hand, when we turn to the closing years of the war, we find as much to pity and condemn as before we had to admire – when we see this same people torn with faction, entrusting themselves to their brilliant and unscrupulous Alcibiades who had in turn betrayed both Athens and Sparta: snatching apparent victory out of defeat, but throwing away the victory and turning savagely on the generals who had made it for them: still capable of blazing energy, and then losing all – as it seems – through one day's carelessness. There are few episodes in history more revealing of human character in its strength and its weakness than this war; and the fact that one can feel like this about it is due almost entirely to the genius of its contemporary historian, Thucydides.

Rather than give a formal account of the war, I will translate or paraphrase a few passages of Thucydides' history, hoping that this will give the reader an impression of the man himself, of the Greeks in action, of the Athenian Assembly in action, of its influence on the lives of the citizens, and of the tragic decline of the Athenian spirit under the stress of war. Thucydides was a wealthy Athenian of good birth, an admirer of Pericles but not of his successors, a stratêgos in the early stages of the war, and a writer whose mind makes an overwhelming impression on his reader. For concentrated power and profound comprehension of things only two other Greek writers can stand with Thucydides: one is Aeschylus, and the other is the poet who wrote the *Iliad*.

We may begin with Thucydides' report of a debate in the Assembly just before the outbreak of the war. An embassy had come from Sparta making certain diplomatic demands on the

Athenians, particularly that they should rescind an embargo on trading with Megara, a member of the Peloponnesian alliance. Finally, the last ambassadors came from Sparta, namely Rhamphias, Melesippius and Agesander, and said nothing on the matters mentioned before, but only this: 'The Spartans want peace to continue, and it would, if you were to leave the Greeks independent.' The Athenians[1] called an Assembly and submitted this for discussion, and decided to debate and reply to all these demands once and for all. Many spoke on each side, some arguing that they should go to war, others that they should rescind the Megarian decree and not allow it to stand in the way of peace. Finally there came forward Pericles son of Xanthippus, the leading citizen of the time, and the most able, whether in speech or action. He advised them in these terms.

I maintain the same opinion as always, that we should make no concessions to Sparta, though I know that men who are persuaded to declare war change their minds when they are in the midst of the war, and allow their judgment to be altered by events. But it is clear to me that I must give you the same advice as before, and of those of you who are persuaded to vote for war I make this demand, that you will support our common resolution if we meet with reverses, and if we succeed, that you will make no claim to special intelligence, because if often happens that both actions and decisions have quite unexpected results, wherefore things that turn out contrary to our calculations we attribute to Chance.

With such introduction, commending constancy and modesty in judgment, Pericles proceeds to a closely-reasoned argument designed to prove that concession, even on a trifle, would be interpreted as timidity and would bring fresh demands; and that if it should come to war the Peloponnesians would not prevail, because of their lack of resources and unity. 'If we were islanders,' he said, 'who would be more impregnable? We ought then to think of ourselves as islanders; to resign our land and houses and to guard the seas and the city[2]

1. Namely, the Boulê.
2. This implies, obviously, that Pericles' audience, in the main, lives in Attica and not in Athens and the Piraeus.

and not to risk useless battles for Attica. We should lament not the houses and land, but the lives lost, for it is not these things that gain men, but men gain these. If I thought you would do it, I would urge you to go out and ravage them yourselves, to show the Peloponnesians that this will not bring them victory. I have other grounds of confidence, if you will refrain from trying to win more territory; for I am more afraid of our own mistakes than of the enemy's designs.' So, suggesting an answer that was firm without being defiant, Pericles sat down. It was for the Assembly to decide: 'and the Athenians, thinking that he gave the best advice, voted as he had recommended'. The Spartan envoys returned home, and no more came to Athens.

The War was precipitated by a sudden attack of Thebes on Plataea, which will be related later. The Spartans invaded Attica, and settled down to ravage the lands of the important village or town of Acharnae. 'When the Athenians saw the army at Acharnae, only six miles from the city, they thought it intolerable, and a great indignity, that the enemy should be ravaging their land before their eyes – a thing that the younger men had never seen, and the older men only in the Persian Wars. All of them, especially the younger men, were resolved to go out against them, and not to put up with it. They met in groups, and there was hot debate, some urging them to go out, others trying to persuade them not to. Prophets too were reciting all kinds of oracles and were eagerly listened to. The Acharnians, knowing that they composed a large part of the Athenian army, urged them to march out, since it was their land that was being ravaged. The city was excited in every possible way. They were angry with Pericles, and forgot all the advice he had given them, and reviled him because he was general, and refused to lead them out, and they held him responsible for all that was happening to them. But Pericles, seeing that they were angry and in no wise frame of mind, and being quite certain that he was correct in refusing to attack the enemy, did not call an Assembly or any other (informal) meeting, lest they should commit themselves by meeting in an angry rather than a judicial frame of mind. Therefore he concerned himself with the defence of the city, and kept it as calm as he could; but he did continually send out cavalry, to keep the enemy from the land near the city.' – Later in the year he counter-attacked by sending a fleet to ravage the coasts of the Peloponnese.

I have quoted this incident for the reason which no doubt impelled Thucydides to recount it, namely to suggest how precarious, in the Athenian way of life, were the defences against folly: practically nothing, in fact, but the combined good sense of the populace. A strong popular impulse – 'Start the Second Front now' – did not exhaust itself in remarks chalked on walls, or in newspaper agitation: it could be carried straight to the Assembly and put into action immediately. This of itself encouraged a sense of responsibility; as did the fact that any citizen demanding that (for example) 'a second front be opened now' would be expected to show how, where and with what forces it should be done. The 'State' was not a fairy godmother, administered by experts; it was himself and the men sitting round him and listening to him.

When the long war had widened the gap, not between nobles and commons, nor between rich and poor, but between the commercial and industrial class, which prospered, and the agricultural, which suffered: and when the city had as leaders not the far-sighted and independent Pericles, but men of less wisdom and meaner spirit, more disposed to foment and exploit than to restrain outbursts of popular emotion, then these defences against folly were not strong enough.

A similar moment occurred in the next year of the war, one of the blackest moments that Athens experienced; for not only were the Spartans in Attica for the second time, but also Athens had just been swept by the awful plague – the one consequence of Pericles' strategy which Pericles could not have foreseen. '... They changed their minds, and blamed Pericles, thinking that he had persuaded them to go to war, and that he was the source of their misfortunes. They were anxious to make terms with Sparta, and did send envoys, but with no success. In their despair, they were violent against Pericles. He therefore called an Assembly (since he was still general), seeing that they were enraged, and in fact were doing exactly what he expected them to do.'

Pericles' speech (too long to quote, even in Thucydides' summary) is remarkable, and so is the reception of it by this desperate people. It is remarkable to find a popular leader speaking in so lofty a tone, and relying so entirely on argument – whether good or bad argument is not to our present point. The general tenor of the speech is as follows:

I have summoned this special Assembly to remind you of certain facts, and to protest against some of your errors. Remember, it is more important for the Polis to prosper than its individual members, for if the individual members prosper and the polis is ruined, then they are ruined with her, but if a citizen is unfortunate while the city is not, he has a much better hope of mending his fortunes.

You, in your private afflictions, are angry with me that I persuaded you to declare war. Therefore you are angry also with yourselves, that you voted with me. You took me to be what I think I am, superior to most in foresight, in oratorical ability – for if a man cannot explain himself clearly, he might as well have no foresight – in patriotism, and in personal honesty. But if you voted with me because you took me to be like this, you cannot fairly charge me with doing you an injury. *I* have not changed: it is you who have changed. A calamity has befallen you, and you cannot persevere in the policy you chose when all was well: it is the weakness of your resolution that makes my advice seem to have been wrong. It is the unexpected that most breaks a man's spirit.

You have a great polis, and a great reputation; you must be worthy of them. Half the world is yours – the sea. Attica you must think of as only a small garden, surrounding a mansion. If you shrink from the labours of sovereignty, do not claim any of its honours: and do not think that you can safely lay down an empire which is in fact a tyranny. For you, the alternative to empire is slavery.

The blows of the enemy we must bear with courage: those of the gods, with resignation. You must not blame me for misfortunes which are beyond calculation, unless you are going also to give me the credit for successes which were uncalculated.

'By this speech', says Thucydides, 'Pericles tried to divert the

Athenians' wrath from himself and their thoughts from their present distress. In point of policy, they were persuaded by him, and no longer sought to make peace ... but they did not cease from their public displeasure towards him until they had fined him in a sum of money. But not long afterwards – such is the way in which a crowd behaves – they elected him general again, and committed everything to him.'

When we reflect that this plague was as awful as the Plague of London, and that the Athenians had the additional horror of being cooped up inside their fortifications by the enemy without, we must admire the greatness of the man who could talk to his fellow-citizens like this, and the greatness of the people who could not only listen to such a speech at such a time but actually be substantially persuaded by it. Athenian democracy had many faults and many failures, but a true appraisal of it will take account of its effect on the mental and moral stamina of the Athenian people. It may be held to have failed, but if this judgment is a true one it is a judgment less on a political system than on the capacities of human nature.

Pericles died a few months later, having himself barely recovered from an attack of the plague. Thucydides goes on, in his restrained manner, to pay a magnificent tribute to a very great man, contrasting him with his successors, who, disregarding Pericles' advice not to try to extend the empire during the war, 'did the very opposite: and through private ambition and for private gain they followed an evil policy in respect both of Athens and of the allies, in matters which seemed to have nothing to do with the war: which, if successful, brought honour and profit to individuals, but, if unsuccessful, harmed the polis in the prosecution of the war.'

Space must be found for one more 'parliamentary debate'. In 428 Lesbos revolted. Lesbos, a large island, with Mitylênê as its chief city, was one of the few 'independent' allies left, and the revolt was a deadly threat to Athens. The Lesbians had relied on Spartan help, which never came: the revolt was crushed, the Lesbians submitting at discretion. How were they to be treated? It was for the Assembly to decide, and a dominating figure in the Assembly now was a leather-manufacturer,

Cleon (whom Aristophanes mercilessly satirized as a violent and illiterate buffoon). He was obviously an able man, and a good speaker – though not in the Periclean tradition – since otherwise he could not have impressed himself on the Assembly, but he was a man of coarse fibre and a vulgar mind. He persuaded the Athenians that they must take the 'strong line', and that evening a ship was sent to Mitylênê with instructions to the Athenian commander that all the men were to be put to death and the women and children sold into slavery.

'The next day there was a feeling of repentance: they reflected that the decree was cruel and indiscriminate, to slay a whole polis and not the guilty only.' Envoys from Mitylênê, taking advantage of this, and with the help of some Athenians, persuaded the authorities to summon the Assembly again immediately.

After several speeches on each side (not reported by Thucydides), Cleon got up. His speech may be summarized thus:

This debate only confirms me in my belief that a democracy cannot rule an Empire. Your allies are bound to you not by their advantage but by your power, so that any pity you show now will win you no gratitude, but will be taken as a sign of weakness, and others will rebel if they see that it is possible to rebel with impunity. Of all political faults, uncertainty is the worst. It is better to have bad laws than to be continually changing them; what is once resolved must stand. The duller citizen usually manages better than the clever one: he is content to obey the laws, and judges speeches in an honest and practical way, while the other man tries to appear cleverer than the laws, and treats speeches as oratorical performances, to be criticized as such. These are the men who have reopened this debate: no doubt they will try to prove that the Mitylêneans have rendered us a service, not done us an injury. It is your fault, because you treat a deliberative assembly as if it were a theatre-show. Mitylênê has done you more injury than any single city ever has. Their revolt was wanton, lacking any excuse or justification. Let them be punished as they deserve: what they did was deliberate, and it is only what is involuntary that can be excused. And make no foolish distinction between aristocrats and commoners. The commoners joined the others against us. They would have profited by the revolt had it succeeded; as it failed, let them pay, or you will have no allies left. Pity is due to the compassionate, not to sworn enemies: moderation should be shown to those who will be well-disposed to you in the future, not to those whose hatred of you will not be lessened: and as for that third impediment to empire, delight in oratory – and oratory can be bought – let the clever speakers display their skill on things of small importance.

A clever speech, with just enough truth in it to conceal, partially, its flattery of the vulgar and its encouragement of the violent – but one wonders if Cleon would have dared to speak like this in the presence of Pericles.

He was answered by a man who is never mentioned elsewhere, but whose name deserves to live – as Thucydides has made it live: Diodotus the son of Eucrates.

Haste goes with folly, passion with coarseness and meanness of mind; both are the enemies of wise counsel. He who argues that acts are not to be expounded in speech is either stupid or dishonest; stupid if he thinks that he can express himself in any other way about what is future and uncertain, dishonest if he shrinks from advocating a discreditable cause, but instead tries to confound his opponent and his audience by calumny. Most malignant of all are those who hint that orators are bribed: the imputation of ignorance can be borne, but not that of bribery, for if the orator is nevertheless successful, he is suspected, while if he fails, he is thought incapable and dishonest too. So good men are deterred from giving the city their advice, and wise counsel, honestly given, has come to be suspected no less than bad counsel.

But I have risen not to defend the Mitylêneans, nor to accuse anyone else. The question is not their guilt but our interests, and we are deliberating not about the present, and what they may deserve, but about the future, and how they may be of best service to us. Cleon asserts that to put them to death will best serve us, by discouraging others from revolting: I explicitly contradict this.

For the death penalty has been enacted in many cities for various offences, yet men commit them, urged on by hope of success: and no city has ever rebelled except in the conviction that the rebellion would succeed. Men are naturally disposed to do wrong, in public and private matters, and increasingly severe penalties have failed to check this; but poverty inspires recklessness through necessity, and wealth inspires ambition through hybris and pride, and the other stations of life inspire their passions. The attempt is suggested by Hope; Desire assists Hope; Chance urges men on the more, by sometimes giving unexpected success, and so encouraging men to run risks beyond their resources. Moreover, each individual, when acting with others, carries his own ideas to the extremes. Let us not therefore do something foolish by trusting to the death penalty, and allowing no possibility to those who have revolted of changing their minds. At present, if a city in rebellion finds that it cannot succeed, it will come to terms while it can still pay us an indemnity: but Cleon's policy would compel every rebellious city to hold out to the uttermost, and to leave us nothing but ruins. Moreover, at present the commons in every city are well disposed to you: if the aristocrats rebel, either they do not join them, or reluctantly. In Mitylênê the common people did not assist the rebellion, and, when they got arms, surrendered the city to you: if now you kill them, you will play into the hands of the aristocrats.

No more than Cleon do I wish you to be guided only by pity and moderation, but I ask you to give sober trial to the ringleaders, and let the rest go unpunished. This is the advantageous policy and the strong policy, because the party which deliberates wisely against his enemy is more formidable than the one which acts with a violence borne of recklessness.

The voting was close, but Diodotus won.

And at once they sent another warship with all speed, that they might not find the polis already destroyed, since the first ship had the start of a day and a night. The envoys from Mitylênê provided wine and barley-cakes for the crew, and promised great rewards if they should get there first. Such zeal did the crew show that they ate and drank as they rowed, and slept in turns. And as there happened to be no head-wind, and since the first ship had not made any haste on so repugnant an errand, while the second raced forward as I have described, Paches (the Athenian commander) had read the decree and was about to execute it when the second ship came to land and prevented the massacre. So close did Mitylênê come to destruction.

This debate, its occasion and its results, suggests many reflections: on the savagery of warfare among these civilized Greeks, hardly equalled until our own civilized times: on the satisfying fullness of life in Athens, when the ordinary citizen was called on to decide matters of this magnitude and of this complexity. It is no wonder that he resented tyranny and oligarchy, which, while leaving him defenceless in other respects, took out of his life this absorbing and responsible activity. But let us consider rather Diodotus' speech. In the first place there is a complete absence of emotionalism. Appeals to pity are expressly disclaimed: Diodotus draws no pictures of rows of bodies lying on the Lesbian seashore, weeping widows and orphans being driven into captivity: he argues his case solely on grounds of expediency – that is, of common sense. It would be a grave error to argue from this that Diodotus, and the Athenians in general, were cold-blooded addicts of statecraft: the very same crowd of citizens which took part in this debate may have met, the next week, in the theatre and witnessed a play by Euripides, a play like the *Hecuba* or the *Trojan Women*, on this very theme, the cruelty and the futility of vengeance: a play officially produced, chosen by the responsible archon. We have no right to assume that Diodotus felt no emotion. The occasion, in his view, called for reason, not for emotion; he will meet Cleon not by displaying finer feelings but by using finer arguments. In this respect this speech is like Greek poetry and Greek art: the intellectual control of feeling increases the total effect.

In another respect both these speeches are typically Greek – though my condensed paraphrase has scarcely done justice to it: the passion for generalizing. Diodotus' last sentence will serve as an example. The Greek was not happy unless he could relate the particular instance to general law; it is in generality that the truth can be seen and tested.

It would be interesting to follow, in Thucydides, the conduct of the Assembly throughout the war: to see how a certain irresponsibility grew – Cleon's remarks about the theatre being already an indication of this; how it became more impatient of control, whether of prudence or of its own laws; how Cleon's doctrine of Force more and more prevailed, notably in the barbarous treatment of Melos, an innocent neutral; how the Assembly turned its fury on unsuccessful commanders, and even on successful ones, until one begins to wonder why any

general ever risked serving his country. In spite of a few outstanding instances of moderation and true nobility, it is on the
whole a melancholy record of degeneration under the stress of
war and opportunist leadership: and Thucydides' tragic history
should be read for what he intended it to be, not merely a record
of what a particular people did in these particular circumstances,
but an analysis of human behaviour in politics and war.

But since to do this properly would require a book in itself,
it cannot be done here: and since we have so far been concerned exclusively with one Greek city, we may end this chapter with two incidents that will take us further afield.

The first is in the nature of a snapshot. It will show us a little
of the fortunes of quite an ordinary Greek polis in the war, and
something of the Athenian Empire from the point of view of a
subject-ally. Sparta produced during the war only one man
who was both something of a genius and an attractive person –
Brasidas. He conducted a brilliant campaign in northern
Greece, where Athens had many maritime allies, especially the
important town of Amphipolis, which he captured. (Incidentally, Thucydides himself was the Athenian commander at the
time in this region, and for his failure to be on the spot soon
enough to save Amphipolis he was exiled from Athens, and
did not return until the war came to an end, twenty years later.
Yet he narrates this in the most severely objective way, without a word of self-defence, and does not even mention his
exile except much later, in quite a different context.)

The same summer Brasidas, with the Chalcidians, marched upon
Acanthus, a little before the vintage. On the question of admitting
him the Acanthians were divided; there were those who had joined
with the Chalcidians in inviting him, and the commons, who were
opposed to it. However, when they were urged by Brasidas to admit
him only, and to decide after hearing what he had to say, they did
admit him, through fear for their fruit which was still out. He came
before the people to speak – and he was a very competent speaker, for
a Spartan.

Brasidas presents the Spartan case, that they are liberating
Greece from the Athenian tyranny. He professes astonishment

that at the end of a dangerous march through Greece he should find the gates of Acanthus shut against him. He promises that if they come over to the Spartan alliance they shall have complete independence, and that Sparta will not interfere in any way with their internal politics. If they refuse, he will, justly but reluctantly, ravage their country.

Brasidas was an honest man, and his speech, in the circumstances, was conciliatory: moreover, Greece in general did not yet know the value of Spartan promises, which was nothing. So, 'the Acanthians, after many had spoken on both sides, gave their votes in secret: and because the promises which Brasidas made were attractive, and because they were afraid for their fruit, the majority was in favour of revolting from the Athenians. They pledged Brasidas to the oaths which the Spartan authorities swore before sending him out, that those he won over should be independent allies, and on this understanding they admitted the army. Not long after, Stagirus also joined them in revolt. Such were the events of this summer.'

Let our last picture of Greeks at war be the beginning of the tragic story of Plataea. Plataea was a small city in Boeotia, near the Attic frontier. The Boeotian cities as a whole were oligarchic, and normally were in alliance with Thebes, the most important of them. Plataea was democratic, and in friendly relations with the Athenians: it will be remembered that the Plataeans were the only Greeks who helped Athens at Marathon. This connexion between a Boeotian city and Athens was a constant irritation to Thebes, and in 431, amid all the tension that immediately preceded the war, the following event helped to precipitate it:

At the beginning of spring about 300 Thebans, in arms, entered Plataea at about the first watch of the night under the command of two of the generals of the Boeotian Confederacy. They had been invited, and were admitted into the city, by certain Plataeans, Naucleides and his associates, who wanted to destroy their opponents and to make the city over to the Thebans in order to secure power for themselves. The Thebans, for their part, saw that war was coming, and were anxious to secure Plataea before it broke out. As it was peace-time no watch was set, which made it easier for them to enter the town. They grounded arms in the marketplace. Those who had brought them in urged them to go at once to the houses of their enemies: but they resolved instead to attempt conciliation and to win over the city by agreement, thinking that this would be the best method. They made proclamation therefore that any citizen should take his weapons and join them who wished to be an ally of the Boeotians according to the traditional usages.

When the Plataeans learned that the Thebans were in the city, they were terrified. They imagined (since they could not see them in the dark) that they were much more numerous than they were, and agreed to the terms without resistance, since the Thebans were offering violence to nobody. But while they were negotiating, they saw that the Thebans were not many, and thought that they might easily overpower them, for the majority of the Plataeans had no desire to abandon the alliance with Athens. They decided to make the attempt. They began to assemble by knocking holes through the party-walls of the houses, that they might not be seen walking through the streets; they put waggons across the streets as barriers, and took other appropriate measures. When all was ready, they fell upon them before dawn, when the Thebans would be at a disadvantage in a strange town.

When the Thebans saw that they had been deceived, they closed their ranks and tried to repel the assault. Two or three times they drove them back; but the Plataeans charged them again with great uproar, and at the same time women and slaves on the roofs, yelling and screaming, kept hurling stones and tiles at them, and heavy rain had come on too during the night; so that the Thebans became panic-stricken and fled through the town. But most of them were unfamiliar with it, and did not know, in the darkness and the mud, where to turn for safety, so that many were killed. One of the Plataeans had closed the gate by which they had entered, using the spike of a javelin for a bolt, so that there was no escape that way. Some of them, to avoid the pursuers, climbed the city-wall and jumped down: most of them were killed. Some, but not many, got through an unguarded gate, for a woman gave them an axe with which they cut through the bar. The greater number, keeping together, rushed into a large building of which the doors were open, thinking that these were city-gates. The Plataeans, finding them trapped, debated whether to set fire to the building and burn them where they stood, but in the end they accepted the unconditional surrender of these and of other Thebans whom they found wandering about the city.

These unfortunates were first used as hostages to compel the advancing Theban army to leave Plataea, then they were put to death out of hand – more sensible advice from Athens coming too late. The end of the story, and the end of Plataea, may be told briefly. The city was beleaguered by the Peloponnesians: half-way through the siege part of the inhabitants daringly escaped through the enemy's lines and got safe to Athens: finally the rest surrendered, on the terms that 'they should submit to the Spartans as their judges, who would punish the guilty, but none contrary to justice'. The Spartan conception of justice was to ask each Plataean individually whether during the present war he had done anything to help Sparta and her allies. A Plataean spokesman pointed out that there was no reason why they should have done, since they had the express treaty-right to be in alliance with Athens, if they chose; he referred also to the notable services which his city rendered to Greece during both Persian Wars, and a later service rendered to Sparta: he reminded the Spartans too what infamy and odium they would incur in the eyes of Greece by destroying a city so renowned as Plataea – but all to no purpose. The Spartans repeated their question, 'Have you rendered Sparta any service in this war?' Of those who said No, the men were killed and the women were sold into slavery. 'Such then was the end of Plataea, in the ninety-third year after they became allies of the Athenians.'

Thucydides, by design, describes this horrible affair immediately after Mitylênê. The contrast is notable. In Athens the voice of humanity had at least the opportunity of being heard, both in the Assembly and in the Theatre. Sparta had no poets now. It is likely that it was the Spartan treatment of the Plataeans that moved Euripides to write his *Andromache*, a play about Hector's captive Queen, which the poet turns into a passionate attack on Spartan cruelty and duplicity. Yet so far did the Athenians too give way to the philosophy of naked force that they themselves, some ten years later, committed a worse crime, in attacking the neutral and unoffending island of

Melos and killing or enslaving the inhabitants. Thucydides, quite unhistorically, sets forth in a formal dialogue the political and moral issues involved. He makes no comment; but he passes at once to the mad folly, as he saw it, of the disastrous Athenian attack on Sicily. Thucydides, like most Greek artists, is constructional, not representational, expressing his deepest thoughts in the architectural disposition of his material.

IX

THE DECLINE OF THE POLIS

THE Peloponnesian War virtually saw the end of the city-state as a creative force fashioning and fulfilling the lives of all its members. During the fourth century Greece steadily moves towards new ways of thought and a new way of life; so much so that to those who were born at the end of the century the age of Pericles must have seemed as remote, mentally, as the Middle Ages do to us.

The political history of Greece during this century is confused, wearisome and depressing. A very brief summary will suffice. Sparta had won the war less by her own brilliance than through the mistakes of the Athenians, and because she had been more successful than Athens in getting Persian help – the price of which was the abandonment of Ionia. What Athens and Sparta together had won from Xerxes, Athens and Sparta at war gave back to Artaxerxes. The Athenian Empire was at an end, but the 'liberation' promised by Sparta was such that many Greeks would willingly have gone back to Athenian 'tyranny', for it meant the imposition of oligarchies nearly everywhere, with a Spartan governor to keep order. It is during this period that we see Sparta at her worst. The Spartan never learned to behave himself abroad. At home he was perforce obedient and frugal; abroad he could be trusted neither with authority nor with money. The 'freedom' now conferred on Greece was freedom for Sparta to bully whom she chose. The real beneficiary of the war was Persia; she had recovered

Ionia, and Greece in disunion could never take it back from her. Therefore the complete autonomy of every Greek city was desired by all – by the Greeks themselves, by Sparta, and by Persia.

Among the oligarchies set up or supported by Sparta was a cruel and bloodthirsty group in Athens, known as 'The Thirty', led by one Critias, who had been an associate of Socrates. They ruled in terror for a few months, but oligarchy could not long survive in Attica. The democracy was restored, and with a courage and a moderation which do something to atone for the folly and the occasional violence which the democracy displayed during the war. It is true that the restored democracy was persuaded, in 399 B.C., to put Socrates to death, but this was far from being an act of brutal stupidity. Let the reader remember what had been seen and endured by the jury who tried this case – their city defeated, starved and dismantled by the Spartans, the democracy overthrown, and the people harried by a savage tyranny. Let him then reflect that the man who had done Athens most harm and had rendered the most outstanding services to Sparta was the Athenian aristocrat Alcibiades, and that this Alcibiades had been a constant associate of Socrates – and that the terrible Critias had been another. Let him reflect too that although Socrates had been a most conspicuously loyal citizen, he had been also an outspoken critic of the democratic principle. It is no matter for surprise if many simple Athenians thought that the treachery of Alcibiades and the oligarchic fury of Critias and his crew were the direct result of Socrates' teaching, and if many others, not unreasonably attributing the woes of the city to the upsetting of traditional standards of behaviour and morality, fastened some of the responsibility for this upon the continuous and public questioning of all things by Socrates. In such circumstances, would Socrates be acquitted today by a Gallup poll, especially after making so uncompromising a defence? We may doubt if the figures would be more favourable to him – a majority of 60 out of 501. That the death penalty followed was of his own choosing; he deliberately refused to offer to go into exile, and, as deliberately, he refused to be smuggled out of prison. Nothing can be more sublime than the bearing of

Socrates during and after his trial, and this sublimity must not be sentimentalized by the representing of Socrates as the victim of an ignorant mob. His death was almost a Hegelian tragedy, a conflict in which both sides were right.

The domination of Sparta did not last long; her high-handed violence raised against her a coalition of other cities which fought what was known as the Corinthian War. Peace came again in 387, in the disgraceful form of a Rescript from the Persian king, by which, once more, all Greek cities were to enjoy autonomy. The three leading cities now were Athens, Sparta and Thebes, any two of which were ready to combine to prevent the third from becoming too powerful. Athens was slowly reviving, both economically and politically; she even formed a second League, so necessary for the Aegean states was some form of central authority. In 371 occurred an event which shook Greece to its foundations. Thebes defeated the Spartan army in a straight fight at Leuctra. They had at the moment what was rare in Thebes, two men of genius, Pelopidas and Epaminondas, and these men had devised a new and bold military tactic. Instead of drawing up the heavy infantry in a line eight men deep (with cavalry and skirmishers on the flanks), they thinned one wing and the centre, and drew up the other wing to the extraordinary depth of fifty men. This mass of men, acting like a rugby scrum, broke through the Spartan line by its sheer weight, and the unbelievable had happened. But Thebes had no new political idea to contribute. Epaminondas marched four times into the Peloponnesus in order to create, against Sparta, a new centralized polis of the mountaineering Arcadians. In the last campaign he won another pitched battle, at Mantinaea, but he himself was killed, and the pre-eminence of Thebes collapsed. It had given Sparta what she deserved – but this particular piece of justice Greece could ill afford, with an unsuspected menace arising in the north.

Macedonia had never counted as part of Greece. It was a wild and primitive country, barely united under a royal family that made pretensions to Hellenic descent – they claimed to have as an ancestor no less a person than Achilles – and kept a court which at least had been civilized enough to tempt

Euripides from Athens towards the end of his life. In 359 B.C. Philip II succeeded to the throne by the usual procedure, a round of family assassination. He was ambitious, energetic and astute. He had spent part of his youth in Thebes, and there had seen how weak Greece was becoming, and had learned something about the new military tactics of Pelopidas: these he adopted and improved on, devising the famous Macedonian phalanx which dominated the battlefield until the Roman legion beat it. The aim that young Philip set before himself was to control the Greek world, with Athens if possible, without her if necessary. On a superficial view it seemed impossible; Macedonia was threatened from the north-west by wild Illyrian tribes, she was a backward country, she was cut off from the Aegean by a ring of Greek cities, and the Athenian navy was once more supreme. But Philip had some great advantages. Ample man-power and a recently discovered goldmine were among them, but, besides these, he had the advantages that the autocrat always has – secrecy, speed, and dishonesty. He dealt with the Illyrians and made Macedonia secure in a very little time; he seized the Greek city of Amphipolis, which would have barred his way south. Amphipolis was the Athenian colony which Thucydides had failed to save from Brasidas; Philip, naturally, was conquering it only to save the Athenians the trouble; he would hand it over to them at once – or soon after. He turned his attention to the other Greek cities, notably Olynthus. This city had been the centre of quite a formidable confederacy – but Sparta had not liked confederacies. Her dissolution of the Olynthian League had made things easier for Philip. Now began a long and tragic duel between the two greatest figures in fourth-century politics, Philip himself, and an Athenian private citizen – a professional speech-writer, a patriot steeped in Thucydides, perhaps the greatest orator of all time – Demosthenes. He saw the danger, rather tardily, and not in its full extent at first, but at least he saw it, and in speech after speech, with ever increasing desperation, he implored the Athenians to make a stand. Athens in the 350's makes a sad contrast with Athens in the 450's: then the Athenian forces were everywhere, the citizens ready for anything;

now Demosthenes had to beg them to defend their most vital interests, to implore them to send out a force, some part of which, at least, should be composed of citizens – for the use of mercenaries had become common – and to compel the army to remain at the seat of the war, not to go off elsewhere on a more lucrative campaign. He had to beg them not to send out any more 'paper armies' – a general with a commission to employ mercenaries, who were then, as often as not, left without their pay. 'Your allies', he said, 'are frightened to death at expeditions of this kind.' But the Athenians were unwilling to see unpleasant truths, willing to believe Philip – 'positively my last territorial demand' – willing to listen to prudent Ministers of Finance, and less honest advisers, who ridiculed Demosthenes and assured the Athenians that Philip was an honest, cultured man, and their best friend. In 1937 an English newspaper put out a placard: HITLER DEAD? In 357 B.C. Demosthenes said to his fellow-citizens: 'You run around asking each other, "Is Philip dead?" – "No, he's not dead, but he's ill." – What difference does it make if he is dead or not? You would very soon call up another Philip against you, if you conduct your affairs like this.' The parallel throughout is close enough to make bitter reading of Demosthenes' political oratory. Recent history might have been very different if we had had a leading statesman who knew his Demosthenes, and a House of Commons capable of thinking that Greek history might have something to say about contemporary problems, and that what happened longer ago than the week before last is not necessarily irrelevant today.

In the end, when Athenian dilatoriness, Greek hatreds, and the downright dishonesty of some of Philip's Athenian friends had done their worst, Demosthenes prevailed. Athens made a great and praiseworthy effort; the age-long quarrel with Thebes was ended, and the combined armies marched out against Philip. But the result was

> that dishonest victory
> At Chaeronea, fatal to liberty.

At last the Greeks had to do what they were told; Philip

planted Macedonian garrisons in three strategic cities – 'the Fetters of Greece'.

Two years later he died. Had his son and successor been the usual commonplace Macedonian king, the country might well have lapsed into nonentity, and Greece might have recovered her chaotic autonomy – for a time. But Philip's successor was not commonplace – he was Alexander the Great, one of the most astonishing men of whom we know. He was a youth of 20 – and he moved like lightning. Within fifteen months he stamped out an insurrection in Thessaly, marched into Greece and frightened to death cities that were passing votes of thanks to Philip's murderers, and thinking of revolt; he had conducted a swift campaign as far as the Danube to secure his rear, and, as Persian gold persuaded Thebes to rise against its Macedonian garrison and other cities to contemplate revolt, he marched a second time into Greece, captured Thebes and destroyed it. He left one house standing.

> The House of Pindarus, when Temple and Towre
> Went to the ground.

All this took only fifteen months; both the Greeks and the northern neighbours of Macedon had learned their lesson. Next spring (334 B.C.) Alexander crossed into Asia. Eleven years later he died, at the age of 33 – but the whole of the Persian Empire was now Macedonian, and for a short time the Punjab too, which the Persians had never ruled. Nor had Alexander merely conducted a whirlwind of conquest; wherever he had gone he had consolidated his conquests by the carefully considered founding of Greek cities, some of which, notably Alexandria in Egypt, bear to this day the name he gave them.

When Philip died, states like Athens and Thebes were, to the Greek mind, large and powerful; when Alexander died, Greeks of the homeland looked out upon an empire which stretched from the Adriatic to the Indus, and from the Caspian to Upper Egypt. These thirteen years had made a considerable change. Classical Greece was at an end, and henceforth life had an entirely different shape and meaning.

Confronted with so sudden a collapse of a whole political system we naturally look for an explanation. It is not very difficult to see at least an immediate cause, that the continuous wars of a century or more had exhausted Greece, materially and spiritually. Things could not go on like this; the city-state was no longer providing a tolerable way of life. As today, in somewhat similar circumstances, Western Europe is trying to feel its way towards some larger political unit, so in the fourth century there were some who were turning away either from the polis itself or from the democratic principle. Isocrates, the 'old man eloquent' of Milton's sonnet, was well disposed to the monarchical principle; he wrote an encomium of one Evagoras, a 'tyrannos' in Cyprus, and he urged that the Greek cities, instead of fighting each other, should join, under Philip, in a grand assault upon the decaying Persian Empire. Plato had given up democracy in despair; he formulated the idea of 'the philosopher-king', and not only formulated it, but also paid two visits to Sicily in the vain hope of making such a philosopher-king out of Dionysius the young ruler of Syracuse.

But not only externally was the polis proving a failure, in not giving Greece a tolerable way of life: internally too it was losing its grip, as we can see most clearly in the case of Athens. The contrast between the age of Demosthenes and that of Pericles is startling; to Periclean Athens the idea of employing mercenaries would have seemed the denial of the Polis – as indeed it was. Fourth-century Athens gives the impression of political lethargy, almost of indifference: men were interested in other things than the polis, and not until the last fatal day did the Athenians act in a way worthy of their great name – and then it was too late.

The contrast between the two periods goes very deep. It is not merely that Athens had been exhausted by the long Peloponnesian War. From such exhaustion communities recover, and indeed fourth-century Athens was active and enterprising enough in other directions. We cannot attribute the change to mere prostration. Nor to simple reaction from the strenuousness of political life in the fifth century; for reaction, in time, spends its force. What we meet in the fourth century is a permanent change in the temper of the people: it is the emergence of a different attitude to life. In the fourth century there is more individualism. We can see it wherever we look – in art, in philosophy, in life. Sculpture for instance begins to be introspective, to concern itself with individual traits, with passing moods, instead of trying to express the ideal or universal. In fact, it begins to portray men, not Man. It is the same with drama – and drama shows that the change is no sudden one. Already in the last two decades of the fifth century tragedy had begun to turn away from important and universal themes, and to interest itself in abnormal characters (as in the *Electra* and *Orestes* of Euripides), or in romantic stories of peculiar perils and thrilling escapes (as in the *Iphigenia in Tauris* and *Helen*). In the philosophies of the time we find schools like the Cynics and the Cyrenaics. The great question was, Where lies the Good? the Good for Man? And the answer given took no account of the polis. The Cynics, of whom the famous Diogenes was the extreme example, said that Virtue and Wisdom consisted in living according to nature, and abandoning such vanities as the desire for honour and comfort. So Diogenes lived in his tub, and the polis had to do without him. The Cyrenaics, a hedonist school, held that wisdom consists in the right choice of pleasures and in the avoidance of what would disturb the even flow of life, so that they too avoided the polis. Indeed the word 'cosmopolis' was coined at this time, to express the idea that the community to which the wise man owed allegiance was nothing less than the community of man; the wise man, wherever he lived, was the fellow-citizen of every other wise man. But, quite apart from this philosophical sense, 'cosmopolitanism' was the necessary counterpart of the new individualism. The Cosmopolis was beginning to supersede the Polis.

If we turn from art and philosophy to life and politics we find what is essentially the same thing. The ordinary citizen is more interested in his private affairs than in the polis. If he is poor, he tends to regard the polis as a source of benefits. For example, Demosthenes struggled hard to persuade the people to devote to national defence revenues which they had been regularly placing to the 'theatre-fund' – not a fund for producing plays, but one for enabling the citizens, free of charge, to attend the theatre and other festivals. The maintenance of this fund can be defended, but only on the assumption that the citizen showed as much alacrity in serving the polis as he did in accepting its favours. If the citizen was rich, he was more engrossed in his own affairs; Demosthenes compares unfavourably the splendid houses built by the wealthy of his own time with the simple ones with which the rich men of the previous century had been content. Comedy shows very clearly the change of temper. Old Comedy had been political through and through; it was the life of the polis that was criticized and burlesqued on the stage. Now it finds its material in private and domestic life, and makes jokes about cooks and the price of fish, shrewish wives and incompetent doctors.

In comparing the Athens of Pericles and of Demosthenes we find other differences which are significant, though they seem to have little to do with the growth of individualism that we have been illustrating. The leading figures in the Assembly are no longer the responsible officers of state too. Still less are the responsible officers of state also commanders in the field. Certainly the separation of these functions is not absolute; nevertheless it is typical that we find professional orators like Demosthenes and Aeschines his rival prominent in the Assembly and serving on legations, but not holding office, still less holding command in the field; a statesman like Eubulus, who devoted his considerable talents to prudent administration, and was not otherwise notable; generals like Iphicrates and Chabrias who were practically professionals, served foreign powers when Athens did not want them, and indeed lived abroad. Iphicrates married a daughter of a Thracian king, and once actually assisted him against Athens; while another son-in-law of the same monarch, a certain Charidemus, was regularly employed as general by the Athenians, although he was not Athenian at all, but simply a talented commander of mercenaries.

If then we contemplate Greece at large we see that the polis-system was breaking down; when we look inside Athens, we

see that the polis was breaking up. In fact, the collapse of the
city-state appears to be much more sudden than it really was;
it was not a matter of one battle, one decade or even one
generation. What had happened? We have found some symptoms, but what was the cause? Why did the polis break down
in the fourth century and not in the fifth? Why could Greece
combine against Persia and not against Philip? Is there any
connection between this breakdown and the individualism
that we noticed? Or between that and the ominous employment of professional soldiers? If we consider once more what
the polis meant and implied, I think we shall be able to trace
an intimate connection between all these things.

The polis was made for the amateur. Its ideal was that every
citizen (more or less, according as the polis was democratic or
oligarchic) should play his part in all of its many activities – an
ideal that is recognizably descended from the generous
Homeric conception of aretê as an all-round excellence and an
all-round activity. It implies a respect for the wholeness or the
oneness of life, and a consequent dislike of specialization. It implies a contempt for efficiency – or rather a much higher idea of
efficiency; an efficiency which exists not in one department of
life, but in life itself. How far democratic Athens went in restricting the scope of the professional expert we have seen
already; a man owed it to himself, as well as to the polis, to
be everything in turn.

But this amateur conception implies also that life, besides
being a whole, is also simple. If one man in his time is to play
all the parts, these parts must not be too difficult for the ordinary man to learn. And this is where the polis broke down.
Occidental man, beginning with the Greeks, has never been
able to leave things alone. He must enquire, find out, improve,
progress; and Progress broke the Polis.

Let us look first at the international aspect. The modern
reader who turns to those very different political philosophers
Plato and Aristotle must be struck with their insistence on this,
that the polis should be economically self-sufficient. To them,
Autarkeia, self-sufficiency, is almost the first law of its existence; they would practically abolish commerce. Historically at

least they seem to have been right. They both firmly believed that the Greek system of small poleis was the only possible basis for a really civilized life – and it is a reasonable view. But such a system could work only if one of three conditions was fulfilled. The first is that the poleis should conduct their affairs with an intelligence and a restraint of which the human race has not yet shown itself capable. The second – a *pis aller* – is that one polis should be strong enough to keep order without wishing to interfere unduly in the private affairs of the others. For some time, and in a partial way, this was done by Sparta. The third is that the whole system should be so spacious that its members should not tread on each other's corns – in other words, that they should be self-sufficient. In the early days this condition was more or less satisfied, but the opening up of the Mediterranean and the growth of commerce altered things. Commercial rivalries at once led to large-scale wars. In effect, the Greek world was shrinking, and collisions became inevitable. The development of Athens carried the process further. Her whole economic framework contradicted the law of Autarkeia, since, from the time of Solon, she came to depend more and more on exporting wine and oil and manufactured goods, and on importing corn from the Black Sea and Egypt. She therefore had to control the Aegean in some form or other, and the Dardanelles in particular; but such control, as Greece roughly told her, was incompatible with the city-state system. The system in fact began to be unworkable when it contradicted this basic law of its being.

But the polis imposed simplicity in matters other than economic. Let us consider military and naval tactics – no very great jump. We all know how the Greeks fight today, from summit to summit. It is a method of fighting imposed on them by the nature of the country – yet in the same country, for centuries, city-state warfare was waged by heavily-armed infantry who could fight only on level ground. Cavalry and, more surprisingly, light-armed troops were used only as auxiliaries, to protect flanks, cover a retreat, and the like. In so enterprising a people it seems strangely unintelligent. The explanation is simple. The soldier was the citizen, and most citizens were farmers. Campaigns had to be short, for if the crops were not grown and harvested the polis starved. A quick decision therefore was always sought, and mountain-troops can rarely achieve this. Moreover, though the citizen could be expected to keep himself proficient in the use of sword and shield, and in the simple though exacting discipline of the close battle-array, he could not afford the time necessary for the mastery of the more difficult art of mountain-warfare. Sparta alone had a professional citizen-army (supported by the labour of the helots), but since in close fighting she was supreme she had no incentive to change her methods.

But it happened that during the Peloponnesian War an enterprising Athenian commander conducted, not very successfully, a campaign in the wild country of Western Greece, and found that heavily-armed infantry was at a serious disadvantage against light-armed troops who knew how to strike, run away, and strike again. The lesson was not wasted. Light-armed tactics were studied to such effect that in the next century the Athenian Iphicrates, with some light-armed troops, caught a Spartan detachment on rough ground and cut it to bits. It was an incident of no great importance in itself, but, for all that, a portent. It meant that military tactics were becoming specialized beyond the reach of the citizen-soldier and the citizen-general. The day was nearly over when a statesman like Pericles could also be a perfectly competent commander of troops. Fighting was becoming a skilled profession. We have met some professional generals already, and professional armies were easily raised from among the displaced, unemployed or merely adventurous men left behind by the long war. Xenophon's famous Ten Thousand was such a force. There was therefore some excuse for the Athenians that they came to rely too much on mercenaries, that is, professionals; it could be represented as the efficient thing to do. But the danger of doing it is obvious. As for the ultimate antagonist, Philip, he had a standing army well trained in the newest tactics ready to strike anywhere at any time, rude mountaineers unencumbered with civilization. To this instrument the polis could not oppose a similar one without ceasing to be a polis.

Naval tactics tell the same story; here too expert skill was achieved at a price which the polis ultimately could not pay. In the Persian War the Greek ships were slow and heavy – landsmen's ships, like the Roman fleet in the first Punic war. The idea was to ram hard and then fight it out on deck. But fifty years later, in the first years of the Peloponnesian War, the Athenian 'trireme' (meaning 'with three banks of oars') was a real ship, built like a racing-craft. Weight had been sacrificed to speed and mobility, and the rowers – citizens of course, not slaves – had been trained to a very high degree of precision. For example, one tactic was to row swiftly at the enemy ship as if to ram; then at the last possible moment to swerve, ship oars on the near side, sweep alongside the enemy, snapping off all his oars on that side, while archers on deck did what damage they could, then to wheel swiftly upon the disabled enemy and to ram him at leisure.

Now, tactics like these require great precision and nerve on the part of everyone concerned. The crews in fact have to be almost professional. But how can you make professional crews out of citizens who have their living to get? Since the productivity of labour was so low, how could Athens devote so much labour to her fleet? Only because she enjoyed tribute from her subject-allies. In fact, the larger political unit, the Athenian Empire, could afford this degree of specialization; the polis could not. But the larger unit was not acceptable – a point of some interest to Western Europe today. Athens in fact gained this naval *expertise* (among other things) by exploiting other poleis. But this was an outrage to Greek sentiment; it denied one of the basic laws of the whole system, and the denial brought its own punishment.

We saw, a moment ago, that economic complexity, being the denial of Autarkeia, was incompatible with the polis in its international aspect. Now that we are considering the particular case of Athens, we may observe that internally its effects were just as serious. Indeed, though Plato's law is valid externally, it was undoubtedly the domestic experience of Athens that led him to formulate it. By the middle of the fifth century the Piraeus had become by far the busiest port in the

Mediterranean. Pericles, repudiating Plato's law in advance, declared with pride, 'The products of the whole world come to us'. So indeed they did – including the Plague. The Piraeus and Athens herself throve. Enterprising foreigners settled there, industries sprang up, the twin city became the hub of the world. It was all very splendid and very exciting – but it was more than the polis could digest. The polis rested on community of interest, but the interests, and indeed the character, of the commercial and of the agricultural parts of the Athenian people began to diverge sharply. It was the former who were the ultra-democrats, the imperialists, the war-party. If they were rich, war offered opportunities of commercial expansion; if they were poor it gave employment and pay; but to the country-people it gave roofless houses and the cutting down of their slow-maturing olive-trees. After Pericles the leaders of the Assembly were drawn mostly from the Piraeus-class – successful men of trade, like Cleon: men sometimes of great ability, but opportunists; men who by nature and training took partial views, and therefore provoked antagonists who took even more partial and violent views. Moreover, the increasing complexity of the life that came of this commercial development set up a kind of centrifugal force within the polis. Men's private affairs became more interesting and exacting, so that they tended to withdraw from public affairs. The political lethargy of fourth-century Athens was a direct consequence of this.

But this disrupting Progress was not confined to the material side of life, and it would be foolish to assert that it began there. Aristophanes maintained that it all came from trying to be too clever, and for this simple view there is much to be said.

For generations Greek morality, like Greek military tactics, had remained severely traditional, based on the cardinal virtues of Justice, Courage, Self-restraint, and Wisdom. Poet after poet had preached almost identical doctrine – the beauty of Justice, the dangers of Ambition, the folly of Violence. It was a morality which was indeed no more practised by all Greeks than Christianity was practised by all Christendom; nevertheless, like Christianity, it was an accepted standard. When a man did wrong, he was known to be doing wrong. Here was the foundation, simple and strong, on which a common life could be built; here too is the source of the strength and simplicity of classical Greek art; and the only other European art which in these qualities approaches the Greek, namely the art of the thirteenth century, was built on a similar foundation.

But the fifth century changed all that. By the end of it, nobody knew where he was; the clever were turning everything upside-down, and the simple felt that they had become out of date. To speak of Virtue was to provoke the response, 'It all depends what you mean by Virtue' – and nobody knew; one reason why the poets went out of business. As within the last hundred years new ideas and discoveries in the natural sciences have profoundly altered our outlook, upsetting, for many men, a traditional religion and morality, so that the Devil has abdicated, wickedness has ceased to exist, and all human shortcomings are the Results of the System, or the Product of Environment, so, but more acutely, the bold philosophical speculations of the Ionian philosophers of the sixth and early fifth centuries had stimulated systematic enquiry in many directions, with the result that many received ideas in morality were badly shaken.

There was Socrates, surely the most noble man who has ever lived. He had been interested in the speculations of the physicists but gave them up as fruitless, and trivial too in comparison with the important question, How are we to live? The answer to this question he did not know, but he set himself to find out, by the rigorous examination of other men's ideas. This examination showed Socrates, and the eager young men who followed him about, that the traditional morality had no foundation in logic. No one in Athens could give a definition of any moral or intellectual virtue which would survive ten minutes' conversation with this formidable stonemason. The effect, on some of the young men, was disastrous; their belief in the tradition was destroyed, and they put nothing in its place. Faith in the polis too was shaken, for how could the polis train its citizens in virtue seeing that nobody knew what it was? So Socrates cried out upon the folly of democratic

Athens, which was careful to consult the expert in a trifle like the building of a wall or a dockyard, but in the infinitely more important matter of morals and conduct allowed anyone to speak his uninstructed mind.

The lofty aim of Socrates, and of Plato after him, was to put Virtue on an unassailable logical foundation; to make it not a matter of traditional unexamined opinion, but of exact knowledge which could be mastered and taught. A laudable aim – but it led straight to the *Republic*, the professional antithesis of the amateur polis; for the training of the citizens in virtue – that is, the government of the polis – must be entrusted to those who know what virtue is. Plato's insistence on Knowledge has the effect of splitting society into individuals, each of whom is expert in one pursuit only, and should be confined to that. The master art, the most important and difficult of all, is 'the political art', and he who has mastered that, when it has been discovered, must rule. So much for the polis, and its theory that the good life means taking a share in everything.

This intellectual ferment produced, besides Socrates, a crowd of lesser men, the Sophists, whose immediate impact on the polis was even more important. The term 'sophist' had no disparaging sense at all. It was Plato who gave it that, for he disliked both their methods and their aims; they were teachers, not enquirers, and their aims were practical, not philosophic. The word means 'teacher of *sophia*', and '*sophia*' is one of those difficult Greek words, meaning either 'wisdom', 'cleverness', or 'practical ability'. Perhaps 'Professor' would be a rough modern equivalent to 'Sophist'. It has a similar range – from Professors of Greek to Professors of Phrenology – and although some Professors research, all teach, and all are paid – which was a great reproach to the Sophists. Some of them were serious philosophers, educators or scholars; others only cheapjacks, who professed to teach only the sublime art of getting on. Did you Want to Improve your Memory? Did you Want to be a £1,000-a-year Man? Some sophist would teach you – for a fee. Sophists went from city to city, lecturing on their particular subject – some indeed undertaking to lecture on any subject – but always for a fee. They were immensely popular with ambitious or enquiring young men, and the effect of their teaching may be indicated under two heads.

In the first place, they, like Socrates, criticized the traditional morality. Some made serious attempts to give it a solid foundation. Others taught new and exciting doctrines – like Thrasymachus, who figures in the first book of the *Republic*. Thrasymachus is represented as a hard-boiled man impatient with all hazy ideas about Justice; let us have something clear and precise. Pressed to give his own clear and precise idea, he declares 'Justice is simply the interest of the stronger'. A much greater man than this, Protagoras, held that there was no absolute good and evil: 'Man is the measure of all things'. That is, truth and morality are relative. We, who have seen to what base uses can be put the scientific doctrine of the survival of the fittest, can imagine without much difficulty what use men of violence and ambition could make of this dictum. It could be made to give an air of scientific or philosophic respectability to any wickedness. Men can do wicked things without being taught by sophists, but it was useful to learn arguments which would make them sound fair to the simple.

But sophists who left ethics alone had just as disturbing an effect. Education had been a by-product of the life of the polis, common therefore to all. Men of native ability went further than the rest, but all were on the same ground; the polis remained one. With the advent of the sophists, education became specialized and professionalized, open only to those who could and would pay for it. Now for the first time there was a real cleavage between the enlightened and the simple, with the natural result that the educated classes in the different cities began to feel that they had more in common with each other than with the uneducated of their own city. Cosmopolis was brought nearer.

Among the practical arts which the sophists taught the most important was rhetoric. The art of Persuasion, so important to the Greek, had been analyzed, elaborated, and reduced to a system. Hitherto it had been a matter of native wit and practice; now it could be learned – at a price. It was taken up with

enthusiasm. The Athenians, who already found delight
enough in a well-argued and well turned speech, were ravished
– at least for a time – with the elaborate style and the subtle
arguments invented and taught by these professionals, becoming, as Cleon told them, connoisseurs rather than citizens;
while the plain man, worsted in debate or cast in his suit,
grumbled at the way in which justice was being perverted.
(The *Clouds* of Aristophanes illustrates this.) Unless you had
mastered this new style, you were, or might be, at a serious
disadvantage if you had to put a case to your fellow-citizens.
It is the same phenomenon that we have met before: the highly
trained expert, the specialist, finds no natural place in the polis,
and when he appears, as he did in so many departments of life
in the fifth century, the cohesion is weakened or the natural
bounds of the polis are overpassed.

x

THE GREEK MIND

Now that we have surveyed, in brief fashion, the history of the
Greeks down to the virtual end of the city-state, we may pause,
and survey the character of the Greek mind and some of its
achievements during this period.

A sense of the wholeness of things is perhaps the most typical
feature of the Greek mind. We have already met some notable
expressions of this – the way in which Homer, for all his love
of the particular detail and the individual character, yet fixes it
firmly into a universal frame; the way in which so many
Greeks are several things at once, as Solon is political and
economic reformer, man of business, and poet; the way in
which the polis itself is not a machine for governing, but
something which touches almost the whole of life. The modern
mind divides, specializes, thinks in categories; the Greek instinct was the opposite, to take the widest view, to see things as
an organic whole. The speeches of Cleon and Diodotus showed

precisely the same thing: the particular issue must be generalized.

Let us now try to illustrate this 'wholeness' a little further, beginning with that very Greek thing, the Greek language.

He who is beginning Greek is in constant difficulties with certain words which, he thinks, ought to be simple, and in fact are, but at first seem unexpectedly difficult. There is the word 'kalos' and its opposite 'aischros'. He is told that the former means 'beautiful'. He knows the Latin equivalent, 'pulcher', and is quite happy. He reads of a 'kalê polis', 'a beautiful city'; Homer calls Sparta 'kalligynaikos', 'city of beautiful women'; all is well. But then he reads that Virtue is 'beautiful', that it is a 'beautiful' thing to die for one's country, that the man of great soul 'strives to attain the beautiful'; also that a good weapon or a commodious harbour is 'beautiful'. He concludes that the Greek took an essentially aesthetic view of things; and the conclusion is confirmed when he finds that the word 'aischros', the Latin 'turpis', the English 'base' or 'disgraceful', also means 'ugly', so that a man can be 'base' not only in character but also in appearance. How charming of the Greeks to turn Virtue into Beauty and Vice into Ugliness!

But the Greek is doing nothing of the sort. It is we who are doing that, by dividing concepts into different, though perhaps parallel categories, the moral, the intellectual, the aesthetic, the practical. The Greek did not: even the philosophers were reluctant to do it. When Plato makes Socrates begin an argument by saying, 'You will agree that there is something called the Kalon', we may be sure that he is going to bamboozle the other man by sliding gently from kalon, 'beautiful', to kalon, 'honourable'. The word really means something like 'worthy of warm admiration', and may be used indifferently in any of these categories – rather like our word 'fine'. We have words like this in English: the word 'bad' can be used of conduct, poetry or fish, in each case meaning something quite different, but in Greek this refusal to specialize the meaning is habitual.

The word 'hamartia' means 'error', 'fault', 'crime' or even 'sin'; literally, it means 'missing the mark', 'a bad shot'. We exclaim, 'How intellectualist these Greeks were! Sin is just "missing the mark"; better luck next time!' Again we seem to find confirmation when we find that some of the Greek virtues seem to be as much intellectual as moral – a fact that makes them untranslatable, since our own vocabulary must distinguish. There is 'Sôphrosynê', literally 'whole-mindedness' or 'unimpaired-mindedness'. According to the context it will mean 'wisdom', 'prudence', 'temperateness', 'chastity', 'sobriety', 'modesty', or 'self-control', that is, something entirely intellectual, something entirely moral, or something intermediate. Our difficulty with the word, as with *hamartia*, is that we think more in departments. *Hamartia*, 'a bad shot', does not mean 'Better luck next time'; it means rather that a mental error is as blameworthy, and may be as deadly, as a moral one.

And then, to complete our education, we find that in regions where we should use intellectual terms, in political theory for example, Greek uses words heavily charged with a moral content. 'An aggressive policy' is likely to be *adikia*, 'injustice', even if it is not *hybris*, 'wanton wickedness'; while 'aggrandizement' or 'profiteering' is *pleonexia*, 'trying to get more than your share', which is both an intellectual and a moral error, a defiance of the laws of the universe.

Let us turn back to Homer for a moment. The poet of the *Iliad* had what some misguided people today think the most necessary qualification for the artist: he was class-conscious. He writes only of kings and princes; the ordinary soldier plays no part in the poem. Moreover, these kings and princes are portrayed sharply with all the limitations of their class and time; they are proud, fierce, vengeful, glorying in war though at the same time hating it. How could it happen then that such heroes could become exemplars and a living inspiration to the later bourgeoisie? Because, being Greeks, they could not see themselves in any context but the widest possible, namely as men. Their ideal was not a specifically knightly ideal, like Chivalry or Love: they called it *aretê* – another typically Greek word. When we meet it in Plato we translate it 'Virtue' and consequently miss all the flavour of it. 'Virtue', at least in modern English, is almost entirely a moral word; *aretê* on the other hand is used indifferently in all the categories and means simply 'excellence'. It may be limited of course by its context; the *areté* of a race-horse is speed, of a cart-horse strength. If it is used, in a general context, of a man it will connote excellence in the ways in which a man can be excellent – morally, intellectually, physically, practically. Thus the hero of the *Odyssey* is a great fighter, a wily schemer, a ready speaker, a man of stout heart and broad wisdom who knows that he must endure without too much complaining what the gods send; and he can both build and sail a boat, drive a furrow as straight as anyone, beat a young braggart at throwing the discus, challenge the Phaeacian youth at boxing, wrestling or running; flay, skin, cut up and cook an ox, and be moved to tears by a song. He is in fact an excellent all-rounder; he has surpassing *areté*. So too has the hero of the older poem, Achilles – the most formidable of fighters, the swiftest of runners, and the noblest of soul; and Homer tells us, in one notable verse, how Achilles was educated. His father entrusted the lad to old Phoenix, and told Phoenix to train him to be 'A maker of speeches and a doer of deeds'. The Greek hero tried to combine in himself the virtues which our own heroic age divided between the knight and the churchman.

That is one reason why the epic survived to be the education of a much more civilized age. The heroic ideal of *areté*, though firmly rooted in its own age and circumstances, was so deep and wide that it could become the ideal of an age that was totally different.

In the passage which I translated from the *Iliad* there is one detail that strikes me as being extremely Greek. 'His heart within his shaggy breast was torn, whether he should ... slay Atreus' son, or put away his wrath'. Tennyson, translating Virgil, writes, of a similar moment:

> This way and that dividing his swift mind.

The mind, to be sure, is not the heart, but we should be astonished if Tennyson, or Virgil, in mentioning either heart or mind, had at the same time mentioned a physical detail of the body in which this heart or mind resided. Homer finds it perfectly natural to notice that the chest is a hairy one. He sees the whole man at once.

It is not a point to emphasize, but it does introduce another aspect of this wholeness of mind, one in which the Greeks contrasted sharply with the 'barbarians' and with most modern peoples. The sharp distinction which the Christian and the Oriental world has normally drawn between the body and the soul, the physical and the spiritual, was foreign to the Greek – at least until the time of Socrates and Plato. To him there was simply the whole man. That the body is the tomb of the soul is indeed an idea which we meet in certain Greek mystery-religions, and Plato, with his doctrine of immortality, necessarily distinguished sharply between body and soul; but for all that, it is not a typical Greek idea. The Greek made physical training an important part of education, not because he said to himself, 'Look here, we mustn't forget the body', but because it could never occur to him to train anything but the whole man. It was as natural for the polis to have gymnasia as to have a theatre or warships, and they were constantly used by men of all ages, not only for physical but also for mental exercise.

But it is the Games, local and international, which most clearly illustrate this side of the Greek mind. Among us it is sometimes made a reproach that a man 'makes a religion of games'. The Greek did not do this, but he did something perhaps more surprising: he made games part of his religion. To be quite explicit, the Olympian Games, the greatest of the four international festivals, were held in honour of Zeus of Olympia, the Pythian Games in honour of Apollo, the Panathenaic Games in honour of Athena. Moreover, they were held in the sacred precinct. The feeling that prompted this was a perfectly natural one. The contest was a means of stimulating and displaying human *aretê*, and this was a worthy offering to the god. In the same way, games were held in honour of a dead hero, as to Patroclus in the *Iliad*. But since *aretê* is of the mind as well as of the body, there was not the slightest incongruity or affectation in combining musical contests with athletic; a contest in flute-playing was an original fixture in the Pythian Games – for was not Apollo himself 'Lord of the Lyre'?

It was *aretê* that the games were designed to test – the *aretê* of the whole man, not a merely specialized skill. The usual events were a sprint, of about 200 yards, the long race (1½ miles), the race in armour, throwing the discus, and the javelin, the long jump, wrestling, boxing (of a very dangerous kind), and chariot-racing. The great event was the pentathlon: a race, a jump, throwing the discus, and the javelin, and wrestling. If you won this, you were a man. Needless to say, the Marathon race was never heard of until modern times: the Greeks would have regarded it as a monstrosity. As for the skill shown by modern champions in games like golf or billiards, the Greeks would certainly have admired it intensely, and thought it an admirable thing – in a slave, supposing that one had no better use for a slave than to train him in this way. Impossible, he would say, to acquire skill like this and at the same time to live the proper life of a man and a citizen. It is this feeling that underlies Aristotle's remark that a gentleman should be able to play the flute – but not too well.

The victor in one of the great games was a Man. He was indeed almost something more, a Hero, and was treated as such by his fellow-citizens. Public honours were paid him – which might include the grant of dinner in the town-hall at the public expense for the rest of his life (something to off-set the Crown of Wild Olive), and, especially among the Dorians, the custom grew of commissioning a poet-composer to write a solemn choral hymn in his honour, for performance at a banquet or at some religious festival. So it came about that of the two most majestic and serious poets of the early fifth century, Aeschylus and Pindar, the latter is known to us entirely (but for some fragments of other poems) as a writer of victory-odes. A strange idea to us, that a serious poet should write odes to athletes. What is more surprising is to find, in such an ode, a passage like this:

> He who wins, of a sudden, some noble prize
> In the rich years of youth
> Is raised high with hope; his manhood takes wings;
> He has in his heart what is better than wealth.
> But brief is the season of man's delight.
> Soon it falls to the gound; some dire decision uproots it.
> – Thing of a day! such is man; a shadow in a dream.

Yet when god-given splendour visits him
A bright radiance plays over him, and how sweet is life!
– Aegina, dear mother, guide this city in the path of liberty
Through Zeus, and with the favour of Aeacus the Hero,
And Peleus, and stout Telamon, and Achilles.

This is grand poetry, even when uprooted from its original Greek. For a worthy parallel one has to turn to *Ecclesiastes*. It is the conclusion of an ode written to celebrate the victory in the boys' wrestling match at Delphi of a young gentleman from Aegina.

Not all of Pindar's odes are as sombre as this, by any means. When he wrote this one he was quite an old man, and the Aeginetans – a kindred Dorian people for whom he had very friendly feelings – were menaced by Athens; hence the solemn invocation of Aeginetan heroes at the close. But the seriousness of it is not in the least unusual. Pindar thinks not of the mere athletic event – which he never condescends to describe – but of the *aretê* shown by the victor; and from this it is natural enough, for a Greek poet, to pass to any form of *aretê*, whether in the individual or in the polis. The victory is seen in the widest context.

To Pindar, physical, moral and intellectual excellence – and, be it added, plain Wealth – were all parts of the one whole; one reason, perhaps, why Pindar can make a man feel, while the spell is on him, that he is the only real poet who has ever written. This high conception of the Games, transmuted though it may be, by Pindar, into something higher than the ordinary man's conception, was real enough; but it was nevertheless 'a thing of a day'. 'A bright radiance was on it, and a god-given splendour', but this complete fusion of the physical, the intellectual, the moral, the spiritual and the sensuous disintegrated. Some twenty years after Pindar's death Euripides wrote a scathing passage on Olympic victors, men of brawn and no mind, who receive the adulation of a city to which they contribute nothing; and Pindar himself wrote an ode, his only perfunctory one, for a certain Xenophon of Corinth who seems to have been a semi-professional pot-hunter and nothing more.

This instinct for seeing things as a whole is the source of the essential sanity of Greek life. The Greeks had their passions; their political records are no freer than other peoples' from paroxysms of savagery; the hungry exile would ruin his city if only he could return and rule, whether he was oligarch or democrat. But their standard, in all their activities, was a sane balance. It is difficult to think of a Greek who can be called a fanatic; the religious excesses of the East or of the Middle Ages find no place in the life of Classical Greece – nor for that matter the less interesting excesses of our own age, such as commercialism. The Greek knew mystical ecstasy, and sought it, in cults of Dionysus, but this was one part of a definite scheme of things. There is great significance in the religious legend that for three months in the year Apollo left Delphi and Dionysus took his place. Euripides draws a portrait of a fanatic – Hippolytus, the pure and virginal worshipper of the virgin goddess Artemis, who will pay no honour to the love-goddess Aphrodite. He is the kind of whom the Middle Ages might have made a saint; Euripides makes of him a tragic misfit; Man must worship both these goddesses, antagonistic though they may seem. Hippolytus is destroyed by the Aphrodite whom he slights, and his Artemis can do nothing to protect him.

Now we must turn to another feature of the Greek mind, its firm belief in Reason. There is a pleasing, though possibly libellous, story of a Chinese philosopher who was asked what the Earth rested on. 'A tortoise', said the philosopher. 'And what does the tortoise rest on?' 'A table.' 'And what does the table rest on?' 'An elephant'. 'And what does the elephant rest on?' 'Don't be inquisitive.' Whether Chinese or not, this is emphatically not Hellenic. The Greek never doubted for a moment that the universe is not capricious: it obeys Law and is therefore capable of explanation. Even in pre-philosophical Homer we find this idea, for behind the gods (though sometimes identified with them) is a shadowy power that Homer calls Ananke, Necessity, an Order of things which even the gods cannot infringe. Greek Tragedy is built on the faith that in human affairs it is Law that reigns, not chance. In Sophocles'

Oedipus Rex – to take rather a difficult example – it is pro-
phesied before Oedipus is born that he will kill his father and
marry his mother. He does these things, in complete ignorance.
But it makes nonsense of the play to interpret this as meaning
that man is the plaything of a malignant Fate. What Sophocles
means is this, that in the most complex and apparently fortuitous combination of events there is a design, though what
it means we may not know. It is because the gods can see the
whole design that Apollo could foretell what Oedipus would
do. In Aeschylus, the Law is simpler: it is moral law. Punishment follows Hybris as the night the day. It was because of
this firm faith in Law that Whitehead called the Greek tragic
poets, rather than the early Greek philosophers, the true
founders of scientific thinking.

But we can illustrate this instinctive belief in Reason most
easily from the early philosophers, brief though our account of
them must be.

Greek speculation about the origin and nature of the universe
did not by any means begin where most histories of philosophy
make it begin, with Thales of Miletus, but he was the first who
expressed his ideas in logical and not mythological terms.
Thales, being a merchant, had travelled to Egypt, and there
learned something of Egyptian mathematics and Chaldean
astronomy. The Chaldeans had built up a very respectable
knowledge of the behaviour of things in the sky – though their
motive in doing this was nothing so idle as mere curiosity.
They were practical people; they used astronomy for the
important business of regulating the calendar; moreover, like
the readers of our Sunday newspapers, they wanted to know
what was going to happen next, and supposed the stars would
tell them. (The Greeks – in the classical age – had a proper
contempt for astrology.) They had also done very well in
Commercial Arithmetic, as the Egyptians had in practical
Geometry. ('Geometry' is the Greek for 'Land-measuring'.)
The Egyptians were a highly intelligent people; they had
measured the fall of the Nile over a stretch of 700 miles with an
error of only a few inches; and they had discovered, and used,
the fact that the square on the hypotenuse of a right-angled

triangle is equal to the sum of the squares on the other sides. The Greeks had done nothing to compare with this; their thought, characteristically, had been grappling with moral, religious and social problems. What speculation had been devoted to the physical universe had centred around the useless problem of how it came into existence rather than how it worked.

What we know about Thales is very little, derived from later philosophers and historians of philosophy, but it is very significant. He had learned enough astronomy to predict that during the year 585 the sun would be totally eclipsed. The eclipse duly came off, on the day which we call May 28. What he had learned of geometry he applied to the problem of measuring the distance of a ship at sea, and he is said to have done something too for the art of navigation, and for the calendar. He was evidently a practical man; and – being a Greek – he was interested in politics, for (according to Herodotus) he made the very sensible suggestion to the distracted Ionian cities that they should form a political league with its centre in Teos. The usual story of the absent-minded Professor is told of Thales, that on a walk he was so intently looking up into the heavens that he tumbled into a well; but a story of the other kind is related by Aristotle – himself something of a philosopher and therefore not disinterested. Thales was reproved for wasting his time on idle pursuits. Therefore, noticing from certain signs that the next crop of olives would be a large one, he quietly bought an option on all the wine-presses of Lesbos, so that when the large crop came and every-one wanted to make his oil at once, they all had to go to Thales for a press. So he demonstrated that a philosopher can make money enough, if he thinks it worth doing.

But the important thing that Thales did was to ask a simple question, and give an incorrect answer. The question was, what is the world made of? The answer was, Water.

There are many interesting points here. The first is the mere asking of the question. These Greeks, practical men though they were, had a passion for asking useless questions; for example, Herodotus goes to Egypt, finds a god there who (to him) is obviously Heracles, but much more ancient; concludes that the Greeks learned of Heracles from the Egyptians, and being now thoroughly interested makes a special journey to Tyre, where he heard that there was a very ancient temple dedicated to this god, and another journey to Thasos. Such purely disinterested enquiry is entirely characteristic of the Ionians in particular. But to return to Thales. He wants to know something quite useless – his question would never have occurred to a Roman – and he assumes that it is capable of being answered. By what method did he arrive at his answer? Unfortunately we do not know, but since we do know how some of his immediate successors set to work, including the excellent Herodotus, we can to some extent guess. Water is ubiquitous; it surrounds the land, it comes down from the sky, it gushes out of the earth. Moreover, it forms deltas, as Thales knew very well. Also it is manifestly a component of many solids, and it has the property of being in turn a solid, a liquid and a gas. In view of the common belief that these early Greek speculators were purely theoretical, it is worth while to remark that Empedocles used a wine-skin to prove that air is a material substance, and a water-clock to demonstrate atmospheric pressure, and that Xenophanes based a theory of geological change on the existence of sea-shells on mountains and the imprint of seaweed and fishes in the stone quarries of Syracuse. These men were quite capable of using their eyes and their minds together, and we need not suppose that Thales' answer was based on nothing but abstract reasoning.

But most significant of all is the fact that he assumed, in spite of appearances, that the world consists not of many things but of one. Here we meet a permanent feature of Greek thought: the universe, both the physical and the moral universe, must be not only rational, and therefore knowable, but also simple; the apparent multiplicity of physical things is only superficial. We shall see presently that the Greek dramatist thinks in precisely the same way: 'Don't bother about the apparent variety and richness of life: get down to the simple truth.' Could Thales have met a nineteenth-century chemist and heard that the elements are sixty-seven (or whatever the

number is), he would have objected that this was far too many.
Could he have met a twentieth-century physicist and heard
that all these are really different combinations of one thing,
he might reply, 'That's what I always said'.

Before we leave Thales it is perhaps worth while to point
out his complete freedom from any form of religious mysticism,
such as one might reasonably expect from a thinker whose
predecessors had all expressed themselves in mythological
terms. It would not have been surprising if he had assumed
that the elements of the world were three, or seven, or some
other sacred number. Nothing of the sort is to be seen among
the Ionians, although mysticism is strong enough in a school
which we shall mention presently, the Pythagoreans.

To give even a bald summary of the course taken by the
philosophic movement begun by Thales is impossible. We
may, however, mention some of the developments; in all,
the boldness of the thinking will be obvious. It is as if the
human mind for the first time took its toes off the bottom and
began to swim, and to swim with astonishing confidence.

Anaximander was Thales' immediate successor – another
practical man. He made the first map, and he led a colony
from Miletus to Apollonia. He seems to have argued that the
ultimate physical reality cannot itself be one of the physical
substances, so that for Water he substituted an 'undefined
something', with no properties, but containing 'oppositions'
within itself, such as hot and cold, wet and dry. Through these
Oppositions, and under the influence of an eternal motion, the
objects of sense are formed out of the Undefined, and return
to it when they decay. He had too the conception of a Balance
of Forces in nature, which he expressed through a term, *dikê*,
which in a different context means 'justice'. The eternal motion
was pictured as an eddy or vortex with the earth in the centre
– an idea which enabled Anaximander to improve on Thales'
doctrine that the (flat) earth rests on water; Anaximander held
that it is freely suspended in space, being in every direction
equidistant from the periphery of the vortex.

This was a very notable advance, and the freedom of
Anaximander's thought is shown most remarkably in his

speculations on the origin of the human race, which mythology had derived indirectly from the gods and the Titans. This Ionian suggested that all living creatures arose from water as it was evaporated by the sun, and that man was originally a fish. Here we may notice, as illustrating the quality of his mind, that he was not on the one hand driven to a novel and possibly repugnant hypothesis by a mass of scientific evidence that he could not resist, for until Aristotle set to work there was no considerable body of observed and classified fact. On the other hand, his theory is not a random guess. It is based partly on pure reasoning. Other animals quickly become self-supporting; man needs a long period of suckling; he could never have survived had this always been the case; therefore – and this is the interesting point – man has developed from other animals. Logically, other conclusions are possible, but we happen to be told that Anaximander had observed the habits of the smooth shark (*Galeus levis*), a fish that has mammalian characteristics. What other arguments may have moved him we do not know, but we can see that it was a combination of pure reasoning with observation that led him to state a theory which was startling when repeated to our own grandfathers.

Even greater confidence in reason was displayed by the Eleatic school (notably Parmenides and Zeno, the inventor of the famous paradoxes). These submitted the physical theories of the Ionians to logical examination, and, by metaphysical reasoning, led to the formulation of the atomic theory. Parmenides' reasoning may be indicated thus: non-existence does not exist; that is, there is no such thing as nothing. Therefore, what is, is eternal, for if not, it must have arisen from, or must end in, nothing; and nothing does not exist. Motion is an illusion, for a thing can move only by going into empty space, i.e. nothing. Matter is uniform, for it cannot be mixed with nothing to become rarer; the Universe is a motionless, uniform, spherical *plenum*.

Nonsense, of course – but the modern researcher does not despise the negative result. Investigation into the laws of logic was one result of Parmenides' thought: another was the theory of Leucippus and Democritus, who accepted Parmenides' conception of the universe, but postulated an infinite number of them, also empty space in which they could move. These were the atoms that constitute everything that is, being brought together and separated again by a natural motion.

Another problem that was debated was the nature, and indeed the possibility, of knowledge. It had been universally assumed that Reality was something stable, but Heraclitus, an obscure and oracular writer, preached the alarming doctrine that the contrary is true: the essence of the universe is Change; everything is in a state of flux. You cannot step into the same river twice, for the second time it is not the same river – a statement which a successor wittily emended to read 'You cannot step into the same river once', since it is changing while you step. Can you say then that a thing *is*, when it is always becoming something different? Can you in fact make any firm statement about anything? This Heraclitan philosophy had a profound influence on Plato, for the distinction between the changing, imperfect and ultimately unknowable world of sense, and the unchanging, perfect and knowable world of Reality is of course fundamental to Platonism.

It is not only the philosophers who have this mental habit of disregarding what is on the surface – the transitory appearances of things, their multiplicity and variety – and trying to reach the inner, the simplifying, reality. Do we not find something very similar in Greek sculpture, which, until the beginning of the fourth century at least, made not the slightest attempt at portraying the individual, but strove always to perfect its representation of The Athlete, or The God? We certainly find something similar in Greek Tragedy. Between the Greek and our own classical drama there is the same sort of difference as there is between Greek and Gothic architecture, and the differences illustrate this habit of mind that we are discussing. As Gothic architecture delights in multiplicity of parts, in the utmost contrast of light and shade, and in ornamentation that draws upon the whole realm of nature – on birds, beasts and flowers, on figures of kings, saints and angels, and on grotesques too – so does Elizabethan tragedy, on its crowded and various stage, present the whole complexity and richness of life – kings and citizens, counsellors and soldiers, lovers, comics, children, fairies. Everything is there. It has been said that a Gothic cathedral is never finished, and conversely Shakespeare has often been cut – but who could add anything to a Greek temple that would not be an obvious excrescence, or cut a scene from a Greek play without making it unintelligible?

The reason for these differences is not that the Greeks had a superior sense of form, or an inferior imagination or joy in life, but that they thought differently. Perhaps an illustration will make this clear. With the historical plays of Shakespeare in mind, let the reader contemplate the only extant Greek play on a historical subject, the *Persians* of Aeschylus, a play written less than ten years after the event which it deals with, and performed before the Athenian people who had played so notable a part in the struggle – incidentally, immediately below the Acropolis which the Persians had sacked and defiled. Any Elizabethan dramatist would have given us a panorama of the whole war, its moments of despair, hope and triumph; we should see on the stage the leaders who planned and some of the soldiers who won the victory. In the *Persians* we see nothing of the sort. The scene is laid in the Persian capital, one action is seen only through Persian eyes, the course of the war is simplified so much that the naval battle of Artemisium is not mentioned, nor even the heroic defence of Thermopylae, and not a single Greek is mentioned by name. The contrast could hardly be more complete.

To say that the Athenian stage and the Greek dramatic form did not permit a realistic treatment of the war is true, but not true enough. The real point here is that both the stage and the dramatic form are what they are because the dramatists had no desire to be realistic. It is the dramatists who make the theatre and the dramatic form, not the theatre and the form which dictate to the dramatists. But every detail in the play is seen to be not only natural but also necessary when we realize that Aeschylus had no intention of writing a 'historical' play, but a play rather on the idea that Hybris (in this case, the wanton defiance of the will of Heaven shown by Xerxes) is inevitably punished by Heaven. In the play, Xerxes is overthrown by Zeus, the Greeks being only his intermediaries, and the very soul of Greece too. It is not the event, but its inner meaning, that Aeschylus is dramatizing; and if the historical events, in any particular, do not express the inner meaning clearly enough, Aeschylus alters them, thus illustrating in advance the dictum of Aristotle that poetry is more philosophical than history.

Now we begin to see the connexion between a good many of the qualities of the Greek – between his confidence in Reason, his strong sense of form, his love of symmetry, his creative, or constructive, bent, his tendency to rely on *a priori* reasoning. No doubt there are several paths through this jungle of notions, but as we have made our way from Thales to Aeschylus, let us go on from that point.

I have suggested that the instinct which sent the first philosophers straight through the external aspect of nature to an assumed reality and unity underneath is the same instinct that is shown by the tragic poet who does not dramatize the course of the war, but uses the events of the war – some of them – in order to present what he thinks to be its real significance. It is because the Greek artist is always doing this that he is, in a special sense, always constructing or creating. It is perfectly true that all artists do this, but not all do it in the same way. There is all the difference in the world between giving a picture of life by building up a synthesis, through significant selection, combination and contrast, and interpreting it in the Greek fashion. The one leads to variety and expansiveness, the other to simplicity and intensity. As the Greek is trying not to give a representative picture of life, but to express one conception, as forcibly and as clearly as he can, the form that he achieves is much more logical and taut. Perhaps another example will help, a comparison between two plays which have in common that they use an enormous amount of story-material: *Antony and Cleopatra*, and the *Agamemnon*. Shakespeare bases his plot on Plutarch, and, roughly speaking, puts into it what he finds in Plutarch. Plutarch, as historian, records in the course of his narrative that one of Pompey's captains suggested to him the ingenious plan of sailing out to sea with the Triumvirs and throwing them overboard. Shakespeare reads this, realizes that it would make a good scene, and puts it all into his play. What it has to do with the tragic love of Antony and Cleopatra (which is, I suppose, what the play is about) is not at all clear, but it helps to give depth and perspective to the whole pageant, and there certainly *are* ruffians like Menas, so that no doubt all is in order. As for the *Agamemnon*, it would cost me a very long paragraph to summarize in the shortest possible way the legendary material that Aeschylus actually uses: the rape of Helen, the expedition to Troy, and its success, the history of Cassandra, the murder of Agamemnon, and of Cassandra, even the quarrel in the previous generation between Agamemnon's father Atreus and his own brother. That will indicate the range of the material, but the plot is very brief. It is announced that Agamemnon is coming home, he comes, and brings with him the captive princess Cassandra; Clytemnestra his wife murders them both; she says that he deserved it, because he had sacrificed their daughter to Artemis in order that the expedition might proceed; then her paramour Aegisthus comes in to say that he deserved it, for a different reason. That is all. Aeschylus, like Shakespeare, had a long and complex story to work with. The difference is that Aeschylus tears his to bits, and with the bits he begins to construct a play about a certain conception of justice: roughly speaking, that retributive justice inflicted in plain revenge leads to chaos. His framework is not the story, but this conception. Those bits of the story which he does not want, the story of the war, for instance, or the seduction of Clytemnestra by Aegisthus, he throws away, and those which he does want he uses not in chronological order, but in the order that suits him. (He is able to treat the story in this way because his audience knew its main outline already. One great advantage in using myth was that the dramatist was saved the tedious business of exposition.) He is, in this special sense, creating something new, the Form is entirely under his own control. His theme, crime punished by crime that must be punished by crime, he states a first, a second, a third time, with ever increasing tension, and the result is a logical, beautiful and powerful structure. All

Greek plays are, in this way, built on a single conception, and nothing that does not directly contribute to it is admitted. In fact, in Greek plays it is Menas who is thrown overboard. Hence the power and clarity of the plays. There are said to be as many Hamlets as there are actors capable of playing the part; such a thing could not be said of any Greek tragedy. The relation between the meaning and the form is so logical that any wayward interpretation can be convincingly disproved. If it does not account for every detail of the play, it is wrong, for the true interpretation explains everything.

Such, I think, is the origin of the logic and clarity which are so obvious in the Greek sense of form. The artist has a very clear idea of what he is going to say, and is in complete command of his material. Equally obvious is the Greek love of symmetry. This has some interesting ramifications; we find the feeling for pattern and balance wherever we look. We may look first in one or two obvious places. Architecture we have already mentioned; the irregularity of plan displayed by nearly every Gothic cathedral suggests to our minds the idea of dynamic energy, of life; to the Greek mind it would be abhorrent, suggesting only imperfection. The perfect building, executed as conceived, will naturally be symmetrical. Or we may turn to Greek prose, with its passion for balance and antithesis, often indulged in to excess. In the good writers or speakers antithesis comes directly from the acuteness of intelligence which at once analyses an idea into its component parts. (A good example is an anecdote about Themistocles which it would be a pity not to quote somewhere in this book, so Hellenic is it. An envious man from the very unimportant island of Seriphus told Themistocles that he owed his fame not so much to his own merit as to the fact that he happened to be an Athenian. 'There is something in that,' said Themistocles; 'I should not have become famous had I been a Seriphian, nor would you, had you been an Athenian.') But sometimes, even in Thucydides, the second part of the antithesis is purely formal, and in the prose style elaborated by some of the Sophists, antithesis, emphasized by parallelism of all kinds, including rhyme, becomes inexpressibly tedious. The Greek stylistic vice was not incapable shapelessness but bogus formalism.

But the Greek not only liked his own creations to be symmetrical, or patterned; he also believed that the universe at large must be symmetrical. This was natural. In the works of Man, Reason and Perfection assume a symmetrical form; Man is part of Nature; therefore Nature too, being *ex hypothesi* based on Reason,[1] will be symmetrical.

Indications of the symmetry of Nature were not wanting. In the course of the year darkness balances light, and cold balances heat. Even the inconstant winds observe a general balance, and the lawful movements of the stars had long been known – except for the planets, 'the Wanderers'. Symmetry, Law, and Reason were different aspects of the same thing.

Therefore the Greek tended to impose pattern where it is in fact not to be found, just as he relied on Reason where he would have been better advised to use observation and deduction. The early geographers illustrate the first point. Herodotus in Egypt was immensely excited by the Nile, and made all the enquiries he could about its source. One man was able to tell him, at third hand, a story of certain adventurous youths of a tribe that lived near the Syrtis (the Gulf of Sutra) who struck southward through the Libyan desert and after a dangerous journey were carried off by little black men (the Pygmies); and past their city flowed a great river, running from west to east, with crocodiles in it. Herodotus' informant guessed that this was the Nile, 'and' says Herodotus, 'reason supports this'. The reason is natural symmetry, for as the Nile bisects Africa, so the Danube bisects Europe, and the mouths of the Danube are directly opposite the mouths of the Nile. The Danube rises in the far West, 'among the Celts, by the city Pyrene', says Herodotus, who had clearly heard the name Pyrenees, but turned them into a place or a people; what is more obvious than that the Nile, for its part, rises in the West too, and so has its source,

---

1. The Greek for Reason, in the present sense, is 'logos', from which the adjective 'logical'. 'Logos' is usually mistranslated 'word': it is rather 'speech', or, the idea which is conveyed by speech. 'In the beginning was the Word' really means 'In the beginning was the Conception'.

as well as its mouths, opposite that of the Danube? – This is entirely characteristic of the early stages of Greek geography; whoever made the earth of course made it properly, in symmetrical form.

The other point, that the Greeks used Logos where they should have used scientific methods, can be illustrated from a controversy in the history of Greek Medicine.

There are writers on Medicine who take, as the basis of their discussion, some hypothesis that they have arbitrarily chosen – The Hot and the Cold, the Wet and the Dry, whatever they think fit. Thus they reduce the number of the causes of diseases and death among men, making them the same in all cases. These writers are mistaken in many of their actual statements,[1] but their worst mistake is that it is a craft, and a most important one, that they are dealing with.

This is the beginning of an essay 'On Ancient Medicine' which has come down to us under the name of Hippocrates of Cos, the greatest figure in fifth-century medicine. Whether Hippocrates in fact wrote this essay is not known and is not important: the significant thing is the protest of the scientist against the *a priori* philosopher. The latter, descending into Medicine from the ampler regions of Natural Philosophy (as understood by them), were framing general 'hypotheses' – not scientific hypotheses, which are provisional theories formed to explain the facts observed, but unsupported generalizations more like the axioms of mathematics. This, our writer says later, is all very well with impenetrable mysteries like what goes on in the sky, or under the earth, but it is not the way to deal with a 'craft' (or an 'art', for the Greek word *technē* means both). The basis of Medicine, he goes on to say, has long been known, both its principle and its method. The method has led to many excellent discoveries, and what remains will be discovered, if a competent enquirer knows what has been learned already, and makes this the basis of further research. But the man is both the victim and the cause of error who rejects and despises all this and tries to prosecute enquiry in any other way. It is impossible: and I will prove that it is impossible.

1. The text is uncertain here.

That is to say, in a science where there was the possibility of building up a body of truth by observation and experiment, there were Greeks who could be scientific enough. We see this already in Thucydides' description of the Plague. He gives a minute description of its physical effects, and indeed of its mental and moral effects too, and introduces this description by saying 'Anyone, physician or layman, may say what he thinks about the probable origin of the plague, and the causes which he thinks were enough to produce so great a disorder. I, for my part, shall describe only what it was like, and record those symptoms which might enable it to be recognized again, if ever it should recur; for I was attacked by it myself, and personally observed others who suffered from it.'

This is the scientific attitude; Thucydides will have nothing to do with unsupported generalizations. And what could be more scientific in temper than the following passage from the *Precepts?*[1]

In Medicine one must pay attention not to plausible theorizing ('logismos'), but to experience and reason ('logos') together ... I agree that theorizing is to be approved, provided that it is based on facts, and systematically makes its deductions from what is observed ... But conclusions drawn by the unaided reason can hardly be serviceable; only those drawn from observed fact.

Of the careful observing of facts we have an excellent illustration in the *Epidemics*, apparently the case-book of a travelling physician. The writer is quite systematic. He first records the prevailing weather, then sets down the general course of the illnesses of his patients, mentioning the age, sex, and other details that might be relevant. I give the following typical example because it is short, and records an interesting place-name:

The young man who was lying ill at the Liars' Market took a fever after running, and unusual physical exertion. Day 1: bowels upset, many thin, bilious motions; urine thin, rather black; no sleep; thirsty. Day 2: all symptoms worse; excretions more unfavourable; no sleep; mental processes deranged; slight sweating. Day 3: uncomfortable, thirsty; nausea, much tossing about; distress, wandering in mind;

1. Hippocrates (Loeb edn., I, f.), edited by W. H. S. Jones.

extremities livid and cold; hypochondrium on both sides strained and rather flabby (?). Day 4: no sleep; a turn for the worse. Day 5: died. About 20.

There is a nineteenth-century criticism of the *Epidemics* (quoted by Dr Jones) which is interesting because it misses the whole point. It is to the effect that the author of the *Epidemics* is an inhuman spectator of human suffering that he does nothing to alleviate. In fact, he does once or twice mention his treatment – for example, 'Hot fomentations gave no relief' – but the point is that he is writing as a pathologist rather than as a physician and sticks to his point. The Greek, in this case, was more scientific than his modern critic realized.

These quotations make it clear that there were Greeks who understood and followed scientific procedure, but also that others used mere *a priori* methods. To quote Dr Jones: 'As the divine origin of disease was gradually discarded, another element, equally disturbing, and equally opposed to the progress of scientific medicine, asserted itself. Philosophy superseded religion. Greek philosophy sought for uniformity in the multiplicity of phenomena, and the desire to find this uniformity led to guesswork and neglect of fact in the attempt to frame a comprehensive theory. The same impulse which made Thales declare that all things are water led the writer of a treatise in the Hippocratic Corpus to maintain that all diseases are caused by air. As Daremberg says, the philosophers tried to explain nature while shutting their eyes.' – Not that the Greeks were peculiar in this. The human mind is much given to the thrilling exercise of leaping across chasms as if they were not there. The medieval theory of music, for instance, was sometimes bedevilled with the doctrine of the Trinity in a way that seems a little incongruous nowadays.

But let us not be too superior to those Greeks who 'shut their eyes'. They kept something else wide open, namely their minds, and although the eye-shutting retarded the growth of science, the mind-opening led to things perhaps equally important, metaphysics and mathematics.

Mathematics are perhaps the most characteristic of all the

Greek discoveries, and the one that excited them most. We shall be more understanding of those who shut their eyes to facts if first of all we keep in mind the Greek conviction that the Universe is a logical whole, and therefore simple (despite appearances) and probably symmetrical, and then try to imagine the impact on their minds of elementary mathematics.

It happens that I myself – if I may be personal for a moment – was enabled to do this by an insomnia-beguiling piece of mathematical research that I once did myself. (Mathematical readers are permitted to smile.) It occurred to me to wonder what was the difference between the square of a number and the product of its next-door neighbours. 10×10 proved to be 100, and $11 \times 9 = 99$ – one less. It was interesting to find that the difference between 6×6 and 7×5 was just the same, and with growing excitement I discovered, and algebraically proved, the law that this product must always be one less than the square. The next step was to consider the behaviour of next-door neighbours but one, and it was with great delight that I disclosed to myself a whole system of numerical behaviour of which my mathematical teachers had left me (I am glad to say) in complete ignorance. With increasing wonder I worked out the series $10 \times 10 = 100$; $9 \times 11 = 99$; $8 \times 12 = 96$; $7 \times 13 = 91$ ... and found that the differences were, successively, $1, 3, 5, 7$ .. the odd-number series. Even more marvellous was the discovery that if each successive product is subtracted from the original 100, there is produced the series $1, 4, 9, 16$ ... They had never told me, and I had never suspected, that Numbers play these grave and beautiful games with each other, from everlasting to everlasting, independently (apparently) of time, space and the human mind. It was an impressive peep into a new and a perfect universe.

Then I knew how the Pythagoreans felt when they made these same discoveries – in vain, so far as I had been concerned. The ultimate and simplifying Truth that the Ionians were trying to find in a physical Something was really Number. Did Heraclitus declare that everything is always changing? Here are things that do not change, entities that are eternal, free from the flesh that corrupts, independent of the imperfect senses, perfectly apprehensible through the mind. Moreover, since Number was conceived spatially, these mathematical entities had a quality that the Greek postulated of anything perfect: they were symmetrical, the Logos in them was a pattern. We may illustrate this by inverting the series stated above. The series of square numbers can be obtained by adding the successive odd numbers:

$$1^2 + 3 = 2^2; 2^2 + 5 = 3^2; 3^2 + 7 = 4^2 \ldots$$

To the Pythagoreans these facts were patterns – for their mathematical thinking was done in geometrical terms; hence 'square number':

The further Greek thought advanced into this new world, the more its instincts seemed to be proved right, that underneath the apparent variety there is simplicity; that Law rules, not Chance; that the universe is based on Reason, and that reasoning can disclose its inner reality. The road to the truth lies not through the senses but through the mind.

This belief was strengthened by Nature's habit of being geometrical. Some Pythagorean must have observed the geometrical structure of flowers and the larger crystals. We have no record of this, but we do catch echoes of the excitement caused when the school discovered the mathematical basis of the musical concords. To the completely unmathematical mind it still seems a miracle of coincidence that what the ear accepts as the same note an octave higher is produced by a string exactly half as long – the simplest case of a whole series of ratios which are also musical intervals. In this the Greek mind saw much more than a coincidence, and much more than an interesting fact in physics. The Greek mind (as we should put it) was given to arguing from analogy, to leaping across chasms, the real reason for this being his assumption that the whole universe, or Nature, is a unity – the physical, the moral and the religious universe together. If we remember this; if we remember how he thought of morality as a mean between opposites, a proper 'tuning', a harmony of the soul; if we remember the great part played in Greek education by 'Mousikê' (which included poetry and the dance); if we remember that mathematical relations were already being discovered in the physical universe – then we can understand how the Pythagoreans, excited by their researches into the properties of the tuned string, took a leap, and thought that they could find a mathematical basis for religion and morality too. They evolved a mystical doctrine of numbers, according to which God, or the Good, was 1 – Unity; Justice 4, the next square-number, and so on. It was a gallant attempt; but the history of man has shown since how much easier it is to master the physical than the moral universe.

Plato was an ardent student of mathematics: over the door of the Academy was inscribed

ΜΗΔΕΙΣ ΑΓΕΩΜΕΤΡΗΤΟΣ ΕΙΣΙΤΩ

which, being interpreted, means 'A Credit in Mathematics is required'; and one of his sayings was 'God is always doing Geometry' – a philosophic expression of the same instinct that moved Herodotus to conjecture what he did about the Nile. But with the mathematical impulse Plato combined Socrates' conviction that the proper study of mankind is Man, and the ultimate Good for Man. He inherited, too, Socrates' dialectical method, that is, the search through logical enquiry for the 'logos', the all-embracing definition, of the virtues. He believed, like Socrates, that Virtue is Knowledge; that a man who knows what virtue is will necessarily practise it, since virtue, being good, is necessarily preferable to what is bad. On this point it may be true that Socrates and Plato underestimated the weakness of the Will, but it is also true that we probably underestimate what they meant by 'knowledge'. Plato, like some of his predecessors, drew a sharp distinction between knowledge and opinion. Knowledge is not what a man has been told, shown or taught; it can be only what he has found out for himself by long and rigorous search. Moreover, only the permanent, not the transient, can be the material of knowledge; only what 'is', not the objects of sense which are always 'becoming' something else. Plato in fact reaches a position not

G

very far from that of the Psalmist who says 'The knowledge of God is the beginning of wisdom' – though he reaches this position by a very different road. The knowledge of 'what is' comes only through a life given up to intellectual striving, the introduction to which is the study of mathematics, for this leads the mind away from gross objects of sense to the contemplation of things more real. The unchanging Realities we can apprehend by the mind only: the senses can show us only transient and imperfect copies of Reality. Of the Realities, or the Ideas, the highest is The Good, and although Plato does not formally identify The Good with God, he speaks of its divine nature in such a way that formal identification would make but little difference.

Such is the Knowledge having which a man cannot do wrong; it is the knowledge of Being, of The Good, virtually of God. It is something much richer and wider than our current, purely intellectual 'knowledge', for a moral as well as an intellectual passion is its driving-force, and its object is the Truth that embraces everything; it belongs in fact to the same order of things, however different it may be in kind, as the Christian State of Grace. Here is the culmination of the search made by Greek thinkers for the inner reality, the 'logos'; The Word was God.

XI

MYTH AND RELIGION

THE object of this chapter is not to summarize a wide and very complex part of Greek life and thought, but simply to explain certain apparent contradictions which may be troubling the reader.

We have spent some time on developing the idea that the Greek instinctively looked for unity and order in the universe, and this might lead us to expect him to be a monotheist. Instead of that, we find him professing a most luxuriant polytheism. Even in classical times, in the days of the enlightenment poets seem to invent new gods without thinking twice about it: Hope, or Fear, or a dozen other such conceptions, can become Gods without surprising anybody, and we all know how St Paul (inaccurately translated by the Authorised Version) found the Athenians 'very god-fearing', but fearing a multiplicity of gods. Moreover we have seen, I hope, that the bulk of classical poetry and art is notably serious. It is very far from lacking in gaiety and charm; nevertheless the outstanding quality is a sense of moral responsibility. Yet the myths on which this art is based seem incredibly irresponsible. The innumerable stories of divine caprice, brutality, amorousness, might well give us the impression that the Greeks were a people who took their moral duties very lightly indeed. But the impression would be quite false.

These are two serious difficulties. The explanation is, to put it very briefly, that the Greek word 'theos' does not mean God; that, in early times, the connection between theology and morality was not what we think it ought to be – in fact it was virtually none whatever; and that we inevitably take the myths in the wrong spirit, and approach them from the wrong end, since we first meet them in their later and more trivial guise. We begin, whether we know it or not, with Ovid and his late-Greek authorities. To understand myth properly, we must begin at the beginning and not at the end.

Let us take polytheism first. The primitive Greek seems to have thought about the gods much as other primitive people do. Our life is in fact subject to external powers that we cannot control – the weather, for example – and these powers are 'theoi', gods. All we can do is to try to keep on good terms with them. These powers are quite indiscriminate; the rain falls on the just and on the unjust. Then there are other powers – or so we hope – that will protect us: gods of the tribe, clan, family, hearth. These, unseen partners in the social group, must be treated with scrupulous respect. To all the gods, sacrifice must be offered in the prescribed form; any irregularity may be irritating to them. It is not obvious that they are bound by the laws that govern human behaviour; in fact, it is obvious that some of them are not. That is to say, there is no essential connexion between theology and morality.

But the temper of the Greek people is shown by the way in which this primitive religion developed, still in prehistoric times. Among their Latin kinsmen the divine powers remained both multitudinous and anonymous, and ritual remained, so long as the religion persisted, a matter of observing with the most legalistic exactitude ancient formulae whose very meaning might have been forgotten. There was a barely imagined 'numen', which we can hardly translate by anything so definite as 'spirit', that concerned almost every action of a man's life, from his first wail as an infant to his final disappearance into the grave; and if the rites were observed in the exact form, nothing else mattered. Among the Greeks things developed very differently. In the first place, their lively dramatic and plastic sense inevitably made them picture the 'powers' in something like human form. The gods became, one might say, sublimated Kings. In the second place, the impulse towards unity and order reduced the number of gods and combined them into a family and a family council. One example of such combination will suffice. The great tribal or national god Zeus was already also the sky-god. There was too a deity Herkeios who protected a man's 'herkos' or farm-enclosure. These two gods became one, under the title Zeus Herkeios, Herkeios becoming only an adjective, a special aspect of Zeus in this particular function of defending the enclosure.

But this impulse went further. Even though some of the powers may seem to be lawless and at times manifestly in conflict with each other, nevertheless there is a regular rhythm in the universe which they may strain but never break. In other words, there is a power which is more powerful than the gods; the gods are not omnipotent. This shadowy power was called Ananke, 'what has to be', or Moira, 'the sharer-out'. This conception of a universal and impersonal power contains the germ both of religion and of science.

The next stage is the combination of theology with morality – not of course that the process was as clear and systematic as any short summary must suggest. The Greek could never respect forms as the Roman did. We can see at least two particular ways in which the gap between religion and morality was crossed. Sacrifice to the gods demanded strict ceremonial purity; for example, a man who had shed blood might not take part until he had been purified. It was natural that in time this divine demand for outward purity should be extended to inner purity. Again, certain offences which human law could not punish or men detect were placed under divine sanction. In primitive conditions the outlaw, the refugee, had no legal protection, and the humble person may not be able easily to obtain it. Therefore the suppliant, the guest, the beggar were regarded as the peculiar care of the gods. Perjury is an offence which it may be impossible to prove; therefore it is one which is peculiarly abhorrent to the gods. Above all, the Greeks refused, ultimately, to distinguish between Nature and human nature. The powers therefore that rule the physical universe must also rule the moral universe. By this time the gods have been spiritualized; Ananke or Moira are now not the superiors of Zeus, but the expression of his will, and other divine powers, like the Furies or Erinnyes who punish violence and injustice, are his loyal agents.

But was there no conflict between such a conception of Zeus and the myths which presented him as violent, irascible, amorous? There was indeed. But before we speak of the conflict, we had better find out how the myths came into existence.

Two kinds of myth do not concern us here, the historical or professedly historical, like the Trojan cycle, and tales like that of Perseus cutting off the Gorgon's head, which are folk-myth, *Märchen*, like the story of Jack and the Beanstalk. We are concerned with things like the overthrow and mutilation of Cronos by his son Zeus, and the enormous number of goddesses, nymphs and mortal women who were successfully loved by Zeus and Apollo. These are the stories which mislead us, and gave offence to the Greeks themselves in more reflective days. How did they arise?

In general, they were simply explanations of things, given colour and life because the Greeks could not help it.

They were explanations. There was an enormous number of existing religious practices and vaguely-remembered traditions

which called for explanation, and as the truth had been forgotten, fiction took its place. The preceding paragraphs
have given only a very imperfect idea of the complexity of
prehistoric religion in Greece. We spoke, in a general way, of
polytheism among the early Greeks – but let us reflect that
these 'early Greeks' were not a coherent nation, but tiny
pockets of people who pushed and jostled each other about for
centuries, settling here, resettling there, continually making
fresh contacts with new neighbours. Let us reflect too that
only highly developed religions are exclusive and intolerant –
religions like Judaism, Christianity, Mohammedanism. A
polytheistic religion is naturally hospitable to new gods. A
fragment of the early Greek race, settling down among or
upon new neighbours, would naturally continue its own
deities, but would honour also the deities already existing in
the locality. Thus – to take one example typical of thousands –
at Amyclae near Sparta there was a festival known as the
Hyacinthia in which both Hyacinth and Apollo were honoured. The chief feature of the sombre Hyacinth-ritual was the
pouring of libations into the ground; the second of the three
festival days was dedicated to Apollo, and was much more
cheerful. The remote origin of this double festival is undoubtedly that a new people worshipping the Olympian
Apollo settled in Amyclae among a people whose religion was
entirely different from their own, a people that worshipped an
earth-god and not a sky-god. Piety and prudence would both
forbid the neglect of the existing cult; old and new therefore
were combined. As the generations passed the origin of the
double cult was forgotten; indeed the very existence of earth-
gods was forgotten. But natural conservatism and piety kept
the rite alive. What then was it all about? To pour offerings
into the ground could now mean only one thing: they were
being offered to someone who was dead; and as Apollo had a
share in the festival of Hyacinth, the dead Hyacinth must have
been a dear friend to Apollo. Hence the explanatory story,
that Hyacinth was a youth whom Apollo loved, but accident-
ally slew with a discus that he was hurling. 'Hyacinthus', as
we have seen, is not a Greek word, neither is the worship of

an earth-god Greek. In this rite and story therefore we have a
record or a reflection of the fusion of two entirely different
cultures.

Very often the earlier deity was a goddess, in which case it
was natural to make her the wife of the incoming god. If he
was a god, like Hyacinthus, he might become his supplanter's
son – but that involved a mother, some local nymph or
goddess. This was natural, and very innocent; but as something
of the kind happened in very many of the innumerable valleys
and islands in which the Greeks settled, and as these local,
supplanting gods were more and more identified with Zeus or
Apollo, it began to appear that Zeus and Apollo had an enormous progeny by a very large number of favoured goddesses,
nymphs, or mortal women. But this divine amorousness was
the fortuitous result, not the intention, of the myths; and the
reason why it did not give immediate offence to religious sentiment was precisely that it was known to be only an explanation. It was not authoritative, dogmatic, educative; it was only
'what they say'. It was an explanation, and although it acquired
the weight of tradition it was an explanation which you could
take or leave. The essential thing was to honour the god in the
rite; nothing compelled you to believe the story about it.

But there was another type of myth, much cruder, that had
a different origin, though still intended as an explanation.
What for example could have led anyone to invent the story
about Zeus which gave such grave offence to later Greeks,
that Zeus overthrew by violence his father Cronos, and kept
him prisoner in the remotest depths of Hell? To put it very
briefly, myths like this are an attempt to grapple with the
origins of things, first of the physical universe, and then of
the gods. In the beginning was Chaos, 'yawning void'. Out of
Chaos came the broad, flat Earth, the true mother of all things,
gods as well as men. She produced Ouranos (Sky), and Earth
and Sky in union produced Night, Day, and a whole brood
of monstrous beings, these last being images of psychological
as well as of physical forces. The gradual emergence of order
out of confusion was naturally pictured in human terms. Why
did not Earth and Ouranos go on spawning such primitive

offspring? How did order come? Ouranos was overthrown
and enchained by a new and superior son, Cronos, and in the
fullness of time Cronos was similarly overthrown and superseded by Zeus, under whom the world and the moral order
which we know was brought about. That Cronos was a son of
Ouranos and Zeus a son of Cronos was quite incidental; there
was no one else of whom they could be the sons. It was only a
later and much more sophisticated age that could fasten on this
detail and begin to take offence at the 'unfilial' behaviour of
these gods.

Greek polytheism, then, was 'natural' religion, made more
complex and polytheistic by the fragmentation of the Greek
race, and by the fusion, at least in parts of Greece, of two
different kinds of religion, a religion that had to do with the
social group, and a religion that had to do with nature-worship.
The Greek instinct for unity and logic is seen in the creation
of the Olympian system presided over by Zeus the Father of
Gods and men: in this, Hellenic tribal and sky gods, apparently
non-Hellenic nature goddesses and gods, a whole multitude of
'daimones' (spirits, but not 'demons') like the Erinnyes or
'Avengers', and personified abstractions like Dikê ('Justice')
and Themis ('Law'), were united into a coherent system. This
instinct is seen too in the way in which morality, originally a
purely human and social concern, is placed under the protection of the gods; also in the unifying conception of Ananke or
Moira, originally superior to the gods, but later identified
with the Will of Zeus. The multitudinous myths were, by intention, explanations of this or that, inevitably given personal
and dramatic form by the lively Greek imagination.

But when religion and morality began to coincide, when
the gods became not only natural, social and psychological
powers, but moral powers too, the amoral element in myth
became a stumbling-block. It presented a challenge which was
taken up in different ways by the philosophers and by the
artists. The artists removed or forgot what they did not like,
and went on using the rest creatively; the philosophers swept
it all away. Already in the sixth century an Ionian philosopher
Xenophanes observed that if donkeys were religious they

would imagine their gods in the form of donkeys. So much for that anthropomorphism which was the very soul of myth. Even Euripides, though a poet, condemns 'the wretched tales of poets'. If a god does wrong, he is no god; if he desires anything, he can be no god, since God is perfect and complete. Plato utterly condemns the poets for publishing trivial, false and indeed wicked stories about the gods, such as that they fight with each other, or are overcome by emotions like grief, anger, mirth. Reluctantly, he will not allow Homer in his Republic, and he is very angry with the tragic poets for spreading unworthy ideas of the Deity.

It may well be that there were inferior tragic poets who deserved Plato's strictures, but so far as concerns the tragic poets whom we know, Plato's attack is absurd. It is the attack made on the artist by the philosopher who will not admit that there is any other road to the truth but his own. It is the attack of a severely intellectual philosopher who was also more of a poet than most poets have contrived to be; one who invented some of the profoundest and most beautiful of Greek myths.[1] 'There is a long-standing quarrel', says Plato, 'between philosophy and poetry.' So there was, on the part of the philosophers, and most of all in Plato's own soul.

But the poets were unconscious of it. Pindar, Aeschylus, Sophocles, Euripides were philosophical poets if ever there were such, and myth, even 'immoral' myth, was their natural medium. It is important to understand how they used it. Superficially, the dramatic poets wrote plays 'about' mythological personages; actually they did nothing of the sort. These men did not waste their own and the city's time playing with figures taken from a Noah's Ark – though something of the kind seems to have been assumed by critics who have written of their being 'embarrassed' by the myths they used. Nothing could be more false and less intelligent. They made their plays out of their own strivings with the religious, moral, philosophical problems of their time, and they used myth much as Shakespeare used Holinshed – and with just as much freedom. The story of Euripides' *Medea* is fairly well known: Medea,

1. See for example the last few pages of his *Gorgias*.

betrayed by her husband Jason, murders not only Jason's new Corinthian wife, but also her own and Jason's children. The central incident here, the murder of the children by their mother, was invented by Euripides; in earlier versions of the story they were killed by the people of Corinth. That is, in order to express his own idea, Euripides completely alters the myth – and his idea was not, as some modern producers seem to think, to create a part for a star tragic actress, nor yet to write a rather improbable psychological study, but to show how devastating, both to the immediate sufferer herself and to society at large, is passion uncontrolled by reason. Aeschylus similarly could use the most violent old myths and fill them with profound significance. In the *Prometheus* he uses the old cosmogonical story of the gods at war, of Prometheus defying Zeus and suffering in consequence age-long torment. In the *Oresteia*, the demand that Artemis makes of Agamemnon, that he should sacrifice to her his daughter, is a myth that comes down from remote days of human sacrifice; and the dealings of Apollo with Cassandra later in the play are not many degrees less shocking. Yet these myths are firmly built into two dramatic cycles – the one, alas, incomplete – which are among the supreme achievements of the human mind, dramas about the birth and growth of reason, order and mercy among gods and men alike.

So one could continue, showing how in all the dramatists, and in Pindar too in a rather different way, myth remained vital, filled now with deep religious or philosophic meaning. It was still in essence what it always had been, an explanation; but now, in the hands of these grave and powerful poets, it became an explanation of human life and of the human soul.

But the future of Greek religious thought lay neither with mythology nor with the Olympian gods nor yet with the more personal 'mystery' religions which were complementary to the Olympian cults. It lay with the philosophers. The Greek element in Christianity is considerable, and it derives from Plato. The Zeus of Aeschylus, pure and lofty as he is, was yet too much the god of the Greek polis to become the God of mankind, just as the God of the Jews could not become also the

God of the Gentiles without considerable change. It was Greek philosophy, notably Plato's conception of the absolute, eternal deity, which prepared the world for the reception of a universal religion.

So far as Greek myth is concerned some of Euripides' later plays show how the centre of gravity is shifting. Serious thought begins to run in purely philosophical channels. The day of high poetry is ending; the classical unity of myth and religion is breaking up. Towards the end of the fifth century, Euripides (as in the *Ion*, the *Iphigenia in Tauris*, and the *Helen*) begins to use myth satirically, playfully or romantically. We are now within hail of the final stage of Greek myth, the one which, thanks to the Hellenistic and the Roman poets, is the most familiar to us. The divorce of myth from thought was made complete by the effect of Alexander's conquests. To Greeks living in the new Greek or half-Greek cities of Egypt or Asia, among strangers and under a remote and powerful King, the immemorial gods and local deities of Greece, with their local rites, seemed far away and faded. As among us an interest in folk-lore arose when the folk had been uprooted from the countryside and herded into towns, so in the new Hellenistic age, when the Greeks were scattered and the old life came to an end, local legends and rites of the homeland were diligently sought out and catalogued, no longer living myth but only attractive relics. To them the poets and artists eagerly turned; learned poets – like some we know today – composing not for a living and visible polis, but for an educated public, wherever it could be found, scattered over the big new world. This, the Alexandrian age, is the time when mythology developed into a form of literary and artistic rabies, when pretty or scandalous stories of divine amours and surprising metamorphoses were told in elegant verse by poets who, poor men, found neither the inspiration nor the audience for anything more important. This is the age which intervenes between us and the classical Greeks, and gives the impression that the Greeks were incurable triflers. The serious thinkers of this age were not wanting, but they were its philosophers and scientists, not its poets. The mythologizing of these poets is at first charming, but it soon becomes an intolerable bore. It is dead; in Pindar, Aeschylus, Sophocles and Euripides it had been alive.

XII

LIFE AND CHARACTER

XENOPHON, who became leader of the Ten Thousand, was exiled from Athens for reasons which are not very clear. He had become a close personal friend of Agesilaus, King of Sparta, and Agesilaus found for him a small estate in the Peloponnesus, at a place called Scillus, close to Olympia – no bad place to live, if one could not live in Attica, for everybody went to Olympia, sooner or later. Here he must have written most of his books, including the *Anabasis*: and in the *Anabasis* – the account of Cyrus' expedition and its sequel – he makes occasion to describe his country-retreat. It is one of the very few descriptions we have of life in the country.

From the spoils that the Ten Thousand had won one-tenth was set aside for Apollo and Artemis, the generals severally being responsible for this. What Xenophon received for Apollo he dedicated at Delphi in the Treasury of the Athenians: what was due to Artemis of Ephesus ('Diana of the Ephesians') he left in charge of a certain Megabyzus, a priest to Artemis, as he himself was going off with Agesilaus and the rest of the Ten Thousand (now 8600) on a campaign against Thebes – and incidentally against Athens. But he survived the campaign, and Megabyzus, coming to watch the Olympic games, visited Xenophon in his country retreat hard by, and handed back to him the money due to Artemis. With it Xenophon bought some ground at a place indicated by Apollo at Delphi. 'As it happens a river Selinus runs through this property, and a river Selinus runs past Artemis' temple in Ephesus too, and in both there are fish and shell-fish. In the estate at Scillus there is hunting – all the game you could mention.' Out of the money Xenophon also built an altar and a temple, and on the produce of the property he laid an annual tithe to provide a sacrifice to the goddess: and all the citizens and the neighbours, with their wives, are invited to the festival. To those who come the goddess provides barley-meal, bread, wine, sweetmeats and a share of the animals sacrificed from the sacred pasture, and of those taken in the chase. For the sons of Xenophon and of the other citizens go hunting before the festival, and the men join in too if they like. The game is caught sometimes on the sacred ground, sometimes from Pholoê – boars, gazelles, and deer. The property is on the track from Sparta to Olympia, about two and a half miles from the temple of Zeus in Olympia. It comprises a meadow, and thickly-wooded hills which support pigs, goats, cows and horses, so that even the pack-animals of those who come to the feast have a good time. Around the temple itself has been planted an orchard with every possible fruit-tree in it. The temple is, on its small scale, like the one in Ephesus, and the statue is a copy in cypress-wood of the gold statue there. Beside the temple there is a pillar with this inscription: 'This property is dedicated to Artemis. He who has it and enjoys its produce must give a tithe every year, and from the surplus keep the temple in repair. If he does not do this, the goddess will see to it.'

It is a charming picture of one aspect of country life in one of the gentler parts of Greece. One can imagine that the 'citizens and neighbours' were a little puzzled by this very important stranger who settled in their midst – a man who had led those mercenaries back from the end of the world, and was on such good terms with Agesilaus of Sparta and was writing a book about it – other books too, so it was said, including one or two about a queer Athenian – nobody of importance, though Xenophon would often talk about him – a philosopher of sorts, it seemed, name of Socrates, or something of the kind. Though you wouldn't think there was much of this nonsense about Xenophon: a very religious man, very sensible and practical, though perhaps a bit fussy: he did set such store on having everything just so.

This appears very clearly from a very interesting little tract of his which goes under its Greek title of 'Economics', which means literally the management of the home and the estate. It

is very pleasantly put into the form of a dialogue between
Socrates and an Athenian country gentleman Ischomachus –
and for once it is the other man who does most of the talking.
Ischomachus has something to say about the training of a wife.
His own was not fifteen when he married her – Mediterranean
women do marry early – and had spent her childhood in strict
seclusion, that she might not know too much. She knew how
to make a garment out of wool, and how to supervise the servants at their spinning, but for the rest, Ischomachus instructed
her, first offering a sacrifice with prayers, in which the young
wife joined with truly Xenophontic piety. He pointed out to
her that he had chosen her, and her parents him, as the likeliest
partner to manage the joint house and to beget children to be
in every way excellent and to be the support of their old age.
His part is to look after what is outside the house – and presently we hear how the bailiff and the labourers are to be chosen,
trained and kept working loyally and happily – while her part
is to manage to the best advantage what he brings in: and God
has carefully differentiated the natures of men and women
accordingly; though in the moral virtues both are on the same
footing. The wife is compared with the queen bee. It is her
duty to manage so that what is intended for a year may not be
used up in a month, that garments shall be made for those who
need them, that the dried foods may be in proper condition
when they are wanted. More disagreeable, perhaps, will be the
duty of looking after the slaves when they are sick – but the
young wife banishes all his apprehensions here: 'This', she says,
'will be a most agreeable office, for those who are treated
well are likely to be grateful, and more attached to me than
before.'

The lesson continues with remarks on the training of the
women-servants in the domestic crafts: and then we come to
the house itself. It is arranged with great forethought, and with
no extravagance. Everything fits its purpose: each room seems
to invite what is put into it. Thus, the innermost room contains the most valuable rugs and vessels, being the most secure.
Corn is in the driest room, wine in the coolest, and such fine
vases and other works of art as we like to look at are kept in

the room with the most light. The house faces south, so that
the living-rooms catch the sun in winter and are shady in
summer (there being no doubt a slight colonnade outside).
Ischomachus is insistent on the order and tidiness. What would
an army or a chorus be like without strict order? He tells his
wife of a Phoenician ship he once saw: its multifarious tackle
was all stowed away in an incredibly small space – no bigger
than a decent-sized dining-room, but everything was accessible at a moment's notice, in the greatest emergency the
sailor could immediately lay his hand on whatever he wanted.
Tidiness is so excellent a thing in itself. Clothes, shoes, even
saucepans – how beautiful[1] they look when they are properly
arranged.

As to his own way of life, Ischomachus explains to Socrates
that he gets up early (this would certainly be at dawn) so that
if he wants to see anyone on business he is likely to find him in,
and has the advantage of the walk. (The implication is that this
is better than waiting until the forenoon and catching your
man in the market-place.) If he has no particular business in
town, the servant takes his horse out to the farm, while he himself walks, for the sake of the exercise; so much better than
walking up and down in one of the city colonnades. On the
farm he sees what the men are doing, and if he can think of any
improvement, he tells them. Then he mounts his horse and
rides, cross-country as if in war, except that he is careful not to
lame his horse. Then he gives his horse to the groom, and goes
back to town, sometimes walking, sometimes running, and
has a 'scrape-down' – for after exercise the athlete rubbed himself with oil and scraped off the mixture with a 'strigil', a
curved blade. After this, Ischomachus has his lunch – the first
food of the day – and is careful not to eat too much. What he
does with the rest of the day we do not hear: it was filled no
doubt with public and private business, and in talking with
people like Socrates. Socrates admires this way of life: 'No
wonder you are reckoned one of the best of our horsemen and
one of the richest of our citizens, seeing that you attend to both
these matters so diligently.' 'And yet', says Ischomachus, 'I am

1. 'Kalon', see p. 170.

not very popular.' – And there is no smile whatever on his face, and no very evident smile on Xenophon's.

How typical is all this? If we had a mass of such material with which to compare it, we might answer the question: but we haven't. My own guess is that it is not typical at all, quite apart from the fact that Ischomachus is a wealthy man. Something of the eighteenth century clings to Xenophon – his careful piety, his love of order, his eminent sobriety, his amiable prosiness. He found Spartan company congenial: it is a possibility that he served with the notorious Thirty Tyrants,[1] who terrorized Athens for a short time after the end of the Peloponnesian War. On the whole, not a typical Athenian, and it would be excessively simple-minded to suppose that the views on matrimony and the education of girls which he attributes to the not very sparkling Ischomachus represent standard Athenian practice.

But to this question we shall have to return. Two details which certainly are typical are the absence of breakfast and the close connexion between city and country life.

We have now seen a little of country life in the early fourth century, though it is through the eyes of a retired Major-General with a taste for history and for philosophy of no very arduous kind. Can we get really into the country, among the shepherds on the mountains, or the working farmer in some remote valley? It is surprisingly difficult. We have no records like those from monastery or manor-house which the medieval historian enjoys, and the city-state literature was never chatty or discursive. We hear of rustic festivals, not all of them as decorous as Xenophon's doubtless was: of ancient rustic superstitions and strange beliefs – for the wild parts of Greece remained very wild. In Arcadia it seems that so primitive a thing as human sacrifice could still be practised in the fifth century. Aristophanes – in the *Acharnians* and *Peace* notably, gives us a picture of the Attic peasant driven into the town by the Spartan occupation, and hating it: and in the *Acharnians* we meet two Harry Lauder figures, peasants from Thebes and Megara, badly hit by the war: but of detailed or even sustained descrip-

1. See p. 153.

tion there is nothing at all. We must go back two centuries or
more to Hesiod, confident that the picture of incessant work
and planning is not yet out of date, or we can go forward a
century to Theocritus and his tuneful shepherds, who have left
behind them a formidable literary progeny of Damons, Daph-
nides and Lycidae, but also real successors in the Greek shepherds of today, who, though they no longer improvise pun-
gent or graceful amoebean songs in hexameters, do at least
play on their pipes sometimes and create songs – or did, until
the war gave them something else to think about. The Theo-
critean shepherd is of course idealized, but in two of the more
realistic idylls (IV and V) the idealization may not be very
great. Theocritus VII gives a pleasant picture of a long walk
and a country picnic on a hot day in the island of Cos. Going
forward another four centuries to the writings of Dio Chryso-
stom, a fashionable orator converted to philosophy, we find a
detailed and a very sympathetic account of two families of
crofter-hunters who live entirely by themselves on some waste
land in a remote part of Euboea. Of these, one had never been
into 'the city' in his life: the other twice – and the account he
gives of it is most entertaining.[1]

Drama gives us an occasional thumb-nail sketch, more or less
vivid, of a rustic character – in Euripides' *Electra* the heroine
has been married off, by the wicked Aegisthus, to a blameless
peasant, that her children may have no pretensions to recover
the crown from the usurper. We see her at dawn carrying on
her head a pitcher of water from the spring, though her husband protests that there is no need for her to do this sort of
thing: 'but', she says, 'I do it because you have been so kind to
me. You have enough to do out of doors. I must look after the
house. It is pleasant to the man who labours to come home and
find everything in decent order.' Presently, when she has been
left alone for a while, to sing a lament for Agamemnon, the
Chorus appears, in the guise of girls who come to invite her to
the festival. 'No,' says Electra, 'I cannot dance and make
merry. And look at my unkempt hair and ragged clothes. Are

1. This is most readily accessible (in a condensed form) in J. A. K. Thom-
son's *The Greek Tradition*.

these worthy of Agamemnon, and of the Troy that he captured?' 'But the goddess is important. Come! I will lend you
an embroidered gown, and golden ornaments ...' But Orestes
turns up, her long-awaited brother, come with the faithful
Pylades to take vengeance on the murderers – but in no very
heroic spirit. He does not declare who he is, and Electra is
scared to death at seeing two armed men so near her house.
In due course the peasant returns, and he is scandalized at the
sight of his wife talking at the door with young men; this is
most unconventional and improper. Electra explains that they
are friends of her brother; they have come with a message from
Orestes – which is indeed all that Orestes has yet divulged.
'Then,' says the peasant, 'come in! My house is poor, but you
are welcome to what I have.' He goes in before them, which
gives Orestes an opportunity to make a delightful moralizing
speech on the theme You Never Can Tell. 'Take this man, a
common fellow: nothing to look at – but what nobility!' – the
point being that the royal Orestes himself – in this play – proves
singularly ignoble. The travellers enter the house, their slaves
carrying the luggage. The peasant reappears, and his wife hisses
at him: 'You fool! You know how poverty-stricken we are,
why did you invite these gentlemen in, so much above you in
station?' 'Well,' says this reasonable man, 'if they are gentlemen – and they seem to be – won't they be content with what
they find?' 'Since you have made this blunder, go and find my
old slave-attendant. He will be glad to hear that Orestes is still
alive, and he will give you something to feed them on.' 'Very
well. But go in and get things ready. When a woman is put to
it, she can find quite a lot to help out a meal. There's enough
indoors to feed them for one day. (Exit Electra.) It's a grand
thing to be rich! You can be generous to guests, and cure yourself when you fall sick. But so far as food goes it makes little
difference. A rich man can eat no more than a poor one.'
When the old slave comes, rather tired from the long climb –
for the peasant is no wealthy farmer of the plain – he brings a
lamb, some cheeses, some old wine – not very much, but sweet
and strong: very good for mixing with something weaker –
and wreaths of flowers, the graceful Hellenic equivalent of

evening-dress. But what is more to the point, he recognizes Orestes, so that the hero can hesitate no longer, and the play gathers speed for its grim and discreditable ending.

In the *Orestes* of Euripides we have reported to us an honest and downright speech made in the Argive Assembly by a working-farmer. Orestes is being tried for killing his mother and Aegisthus. Talthybius the herald got up, and made a crafty, indeterminate sort of speech. He is the type (says Euripides) that keeps in with the dominant faction, and he was always looking, with a half-smile, in the direction of Aegisthus' friends. Then Diomedes (the blunt soldier): 'Don't put them to death, but respect the sanctities by sending them into exile.' This provoked cheers and counter-cheers. The next speaker was vulgar, violent and torrential; he proposed death by stoning. 'The next urged the opposite: a man of courage, though nothing to look at; one who rarely comes to town, a working-farmer – and they are the men, no one else, who keep a country safe – but intelligent, quite willing to meet a man in argument, honest and above reproach.' He proposed that Orestes should be publicly crowned for avenging his father and killing an evil, godless and treacherous woman – and Euripides suggests that this proposal would have been accepted, if only Orestes had not been fool enough to speak in his own defence.

Euripides obviously admired the peasant type: in Sophocles we get not the type but the man. His messenger from Corinth in the *Oedipus Rex* is a shepherd who, years before, used to spend whole summers with his flocks high up on Cithaeron, as shepherds still do in Greece when the lower pastures dry up.

Three of these summers he spent with a shepherd from the other side of Cithaeron, from Thebes, a slave of the King there, Laius. Once the Theban turned up with a baby, and orders to expose it: but he could not bring himself to do this horrible thing, and the Corinthian took it. He gave it to his own king, who was childless, and gladly brought it up as his own. When the baby was a grown man he suddenly left Corinth and never came back, for a reason which the Corinthian shepherd never understood. Oedipus made his way to Thebes, and rendered the Thebans a great service, for which, Laius having just been killed by brigands, he was given the vacant throne, and married the Queen. Then, years after, the old King of Corinth died, and there was a talk of inviting Oedipus to succeed him. At once our shepherd sees his chance. He goes off to Thebes as fast as he can to be the first to bring the news to Oedipus: he can expect a handsome reward. Besides, he has another claim on Oedipus' favour; it was he who saved his life as a baby. So he comes into the play full of importance but very polite, very helpful, and quite certain that he is now a made man. But he stumbles out of the play an utterly broken man, for the result of his well-meant kindness to a helpless baby was that Oedipus grew up to kill his father and to marry his mother.

There is a common soldier in the *Antigone* who is very like this Corinthian – independent, a vivid talker, with a sort of clumsy subtlety of mind and a taste for paradox. He has to tell Creon that somebody has disobeyed him and buried the traitor's body. Creon flies into a terrible rage; he storms about treachery and corruption; then he rounds on the wretched Guard and tells him that if he does not produce the culprit he shall be hanged; that will teach him to take bribes!

Guard. May I say something? Or must I just go?

Creon. Don't you know yet that every word of yours offends me?

Guard. Where does it hurt you? In your ears or in your soul?

Creon. Why do you probe the seat of our displeasure?

Guard. I grieve only your ears; it is the culprit who grieves your mind.

Creon. Pah! You are nothing but a chatterbox.

Guard (brightly). Doesn't this prove that I didn't do this thing?

Creon. Yes you did! You have sold your soul for money.

Guard. Dear me! A terrible thing, when a man jumps to the wrong conclusion.

But the endless fascination of Sophocles is leading us too far from our theme. We were speaking of rustic life. The evidence is such as we have described, and there is not a great deal more. But before we turn to city life we may look at one tombstone. It was found in Acharnae, the Attic mountain-region from which the charcoal came, and it commemorates (presumably) an ex-slave. It is in plain prose, but for the literary (and metrical) touch of the Homeric epithet used with 'Athens'.

This fine memorial marks the grave of Mannês the son of Orymas.
He was the best Phrygian in Athens of the spacious dancing-floors.
And by Zeus I never saw a better wood-cutter than I am.
He was killed in the war.

Now we may plunge into the turbulent life of Athens, where the difficulty is not quite the scarcity of evidence, but rather its occasional and disconcerting gaps. What is the evidence? In literature there are first and foremost the plays of Aristophanes and the substantial remains of Menander's comedies (though these are outside our period); certain minor works of Xenophon – the *Economics* already mentioned, the *Memorabilia* (a Memoir of Socrates), the *Symposium* (Table-talk), and the *Revenues* (on Athenian public finance); the private (law-court) speeches of Demosthenes (not indeed all by Demosthenes, but that makes no difference); many lively scenes in Plato, and especially his marvellous *Symposium*; and the very acute and amusing *Characters* of Theophrastus, of which no one interested in humanity ought to remain in ignorance for ten minutes longer than he can help. All these make extremely good reading, though it must be said that some of their translators draw a veil of literary pomposity between the reader and the original. Among the other evidence is the large number of vases decorated with scenes from daily life, and some funeral sculptures and inscriptions.

It would be foolish to try to summarize all this in a few pages. Let us rather take a few general points, and bring in what precise information we can by the way.

'Call no man happy until he is dead.' We have met this maxim before, and even a superficial knowledge of Greek or Athenian life helps to explain its currency. Life, and consequently thought, were built very close to the bed-rock of Necessity, and a certain hardness, and therefore resilience, was the result. Local drought or floods could cause local famine. In 1930 it befell me to walk through the Peloponnesus. We were buying supplies in a village, and our guide warned us to buy extra bread because at the next village, half a day further on, they had had a wet harvest so that their bread was uneatable. So it was. The margin of life is so small, and the cost of transport so high, that a mischance like a bad harvest cannot be remedied.

Then there was war, bad enough for us, but in many ways worse for the Greek. In the *Memorabilia* Xenophon records a conversation between Socrates and a certain Aristarchus. Aristarchus had been a wealthy landowner, but all his property was in the occupation of the enemy, so that not only was his entire income gone, but in addition to that he had on his hands fourteen female relatives who had fled from the enemy. The modern state does its best to invent cushions of various kinds to soften such blows upon the individual: the Greek polis, with its rudimentary finances and its complete individualism, did not even attempt it. 'I don't know how to keep them alive,' said Aristarchus: 'I can't borrow, having no security: I can't sell my furniture, because nobody is buying.' Socrates suggested a simple solution. 'The women naturally know how to spin and make clothes. There is a market for clothes. Buy wool, and set them to work.' Aristarchus did, and came back later to say that the women were working with a will, were much more cheerful and amiable, and were making enough money to live on. His only complaint was that they accused him of living in idleness. 'Ah,' said Socrates, 'tell them the story of the sheep who complained that the watch-dog did nothing.'

Here is another war-story from Demosthenes LVI. A certain Euxitheus has been rejected on scrutiny by his fellow-demesmen as not being a lawfully-born Athenian. He appeals to the Court on the grounds that the decision was bad. If it stands, he is ruined; he will drop to the status of resident alien and as such will not be able to own property in land, and will be subject to certain other restrictions that might well take away his livelihood. (It is sometimes stated that such a man was liable to be sold as a slave, but this seems to be a mistake.) Part of the supporting evidence used against him was that his father had a foreign (non-Attic) accent – an interesting detail: all true Athenians, unlike all true Londoners, had the same accent, and were proud of it. But, says the plaintiff, my father was taken prisoner during the Peloponnesian War, was sold as a slave in Leucas (near Corfu), and remained there many years. Naturally the purity of his Attic suffered. He gained his release through an actor who happened to visit Leucas: his kinsmen here ransomed him, and he came back home. If the story is true, we may guess that the Athenian slave was able to meet the Athenian actor, and through him to let his relatives know where he was. If the story is not true, at least it is one which its inventor expected to be believed. But he seems to have produced testimony to its truth.

Apart from the chances of war there were risks by sea from pirates, particularly after the fall of the vigilant Athenian Empire. In Demosthenes LIII a man goes off in search of run-away slaves, is captured by a privateer, chained (to the great detriment of his legs), and sold in Aegina. The ransom is 26 minae, or 2,600 drachmae, and the drachma can be considered, in actual purchasing value, as something not far short of a pound, as pounds go nowadays. He comes to a friend, who pledges goods and property to help him raise the money. It is incidents of this sort which help us to understand the emphasis which the Greeks always laid on Friendship: in a world like this a man without friends was defenceless indeed.

Demosthenes LII contains a similar incident. A certain Lycon, of Heraclea, being about to sail to Libya, went to Pasion his banker,[1] with witnesses, reckoned up his balance (1,640 drachmae), and instructed Pasion to pay the money to Lycon's business-partner Cephisiades of Scyros, who was abroad on another business-trip. Since Pasion did not know Cephisiades, the two witnesses whom Lycon took with him were to identify him to the bank when he came to Athens. Lycon set sail, the ship was captured by pirates and Lycon, wounded by an arrow, died. The consul of Heraclea at Argos, where the privateer put in, took charge of Lycon's effects, and sometime later claimed this balance from the Bank, which had paid it to Cephisiades in accordance with Lycon's instructions.

1. For an interesting and lively account of banking see T. R. Glover's chapter on 'The House of Pasion' in his *From Pericles to Philip*.

The result of the case is, as usual, unknown – for the later scholars who preserved these speeches had no interest in them as documents: only as specimens of Demosthenes' style.

So we could continue for a long time, without even touching on the perils of revolution, with wholesale confiscation and murder or exile. From this particular malady Athens did not suffer as badly as certain other states, but in compensation she suffered – or rather, citizens worth attacking suffered – from a type of man whose Greek designation, 'sycophant', means very much more than the word does in modern languages. We have bitter complaints about this social pest from Aristophanes onwards. Xenophon (*Memorabilia*, II, 9) records a conversation between Socrates and a wealthy friend, Crito. Crito observed that it was very difficult for a man to live in peace: 'at this very moment people are bringing actions against me, not because I have done them any wrong, but because they think I would rather pay them money than have the trouble of going to court.' Socrates (as always, in the *Memorabilia*) is very practical. He suggested to Crito that he should cultivate the friendship of a certain Archedemus, a man of great ability and integrity, a good speaker, but poor, because he disdained easy roads to wealth. Crito therefore – note the gentlemanly procedure – made a practice of inviting Archedemus every time he offered a sacrifice, and when his crops came in, whether of corn, oil, wine, wool or anything else, he would send a portion to Archedemus. In return, Archedemus turned on some of these 'sycophants'. He discovered offences of which they had been guilty, and, with the help of other citizens whom they had blackmailed, pursued them mercilessly until they promised to let Crito alone, and in addition paid money to Archedemus. He was taunted with being a hanger-on of Crito, but his reply was 'Which is the more honourable, to be the friend of honest men and the enemy of the wicked, or to make honest men your enemies and the wicked your friends?'

We have a picture of such a person – Stephanus – in the highly disreputable and very readable speech *Against Neaera* (Demosthenes, LIX: probably not written by Demosthenes). In this violent attack Stephanus is described as a blackmailer living on the immoral earnings of his wife, whose various prostitute-daughters he has illegally married to Athenian citizens falsely representing them to be his own children, born of an Athenian mother. 'This fellow', says his prosecutor, 'was getting no income worth mentioning out of political life, for he was not yet one of the regular speakers, but only a sycophant, sitting near the platform and shouting, making indictments and laying informations for hire, putting his name to other men's proposals. Then Callistratus took him up' – Callistratus being one of the leading statesmen of the day; not a lucky one, for he was eventually condemned to death in a moment of popular indignation when a Thessalian upstart had actually carried out a naval raid on the Piraeus.

Accusations made in Athenian courts are not always to be implicitly believed; nevertheless complaints of conspiracy and corrupt evidence are so common, and in some cases so well supported by argument and evidence, that it cannot have been unknown. It could not have been difficult for determined and clever men to exploit in this way these amateur 'people's courts': a regular formula was, 'And you, gentlemen, were so completely deceived by these unprincipled blackguards that ...' For instance, Apollodorus, one of the accusers of Stephanus in this speech, tells this story. He was a member of the Boulê when the Assembly decided to send out its entire force to Olynthus. Apollodorus therefore proposed that, since Athens was at war, the surplus revenue should be diverted from the festival-fund to the war; this being in accordance with law, the proposal passed the Assembly without opposition. But Stephanus attacked it as unconstitutional: he produced false witness to sustain the charge that Apollodorus had been in debt to the Treasury for many years and therefore was debarred from making any motion in the Assembly, 'and by bringing forward many charges that were quite irrelevant he secured the verdict'. In spite of entreaties Stephanus proposed the enormous fine of 15 talents (which we may think of as something like £75,000), which, he says, was just five times what he possessed. If the fine were not paid within the year it would be doubled, and all his property confiscated: Apollodorus and his family would have been reduced to beggary, and no one would have married his daughter. However, the jury reduced the fine to one talent, which he was able to pay, though with difficulty. 'And for this', he says, 'I am grateful. And your indignation, gentlemen, is due not to the jury that was deceived, but to the one who deceived them. – And so', he adds, 'I have very good reason for bringing this present case against him.' Prosecutors speak very frankly of their desire for vengeance – for at least two reasons: the explanation, if believed, will free them from the suspicion of 'sycophancy', and to seek revenge was a matter of personal honour.

In the case of Euxitheus just mentioned there is an interesting story which seems to be true. The appellant (so he says) had given offence to a violent and unscrupulous politician called Eubulides, by giving testimony against him in a case which Eubulides lost by a very large majority. Eubulides' revenge was to contrive his expulsion from the register; if the plaintiff could be proved to have illegally crept on to the register, he was liable to be sold as a slave and to have his property confiscated. Eubulides' method sounds vaguely familiar. He happened to be a member of the Boulê, and as such convened a meeting of the deme to examine the register. Most of the day he wasted making speeches and framing resolutions, so that the actual voting did not begin until it was very late. By the time the plaintiff's name was called – apparently the whole thing was sprung on him suddenly – it was already dark, and most of the demesmen had gone home, for most of them actually resided in the deme,[1] and that was about four miles from the city. Practically none were left except men suborned by Eubulides, but in spite of the plaintiff's protests Eubulides insisted on taking a vote. 'There were not more than thirty who voted, but the votes on being counted came to more than sixty, so that we were all astonished.' And no wonder.

In reading these very interesting speeches we do well to remember two things. One is obvious enough, that more scoundrels are met in the law-courts than in general society. The other is the period to which they belong: the middle of

1. Membership of a deme went by ancestry, not residence.

the fourth century. In fact they give us detailed evidence for the argument put forward in our chapter on the 'Decline of the Polis': the complexity of life in Athens was such that the old amateur conception of the polis no longer worked properly. The theory of the constitution – like that of the American – was out of date.

Much could be said about the burdens and vexations in which public services involved the rich, and the anxieties and perils which a public office might bring upon a poor man, but other aspects of life claim our attention, and it would be a mistake to harp too long on the dangers of public life, since the normal and the uneventful is not recorded. Enough has been said to show that life, even in Athens, was not stultified by a humdrum security. Indeed, to turn from the civilized perfection of Sophocles and Plato to Greek life in the raw is to experience something like a mental dislocation.

Most men are interested in women, and most women in themselves. Let us therefore consider the position of women in Athens. It is the accepted view, challenged, so far as I know by nobody except A. W. Gomme,[1] that the Athenian woman lived in an almost Oriental seclusion, regarded with indifference, even contempt. The evidence is partly the direct evidence of literature, partly the inferior legal status of women. Literature shows us a wholly masculine society: domestic life plays no part. Old Comedy deals almost entirely with men (but for the extravaganzas of the *Lysistrata* and *Women in Parliament*); in Plato's dialogues the disputants are always men; the *Symposium* both of Plato and Xenophon make it quite plain that when a gentleman entertained guests the only women present were those who had no reputation to lose, except a professional one: indeed, in the Neaera – case testimony that one of the wives dined and drank with her husband's guests is given as presumptive evidence that she is a prostitute. The Athenian house was divided into the 'men's rooms' and the 'women's rooms': and the women's part was provided with bolts and bars (Xen., *Oeconom.*). Women did not go out except under surveillance, unless they were attending

1. In *Essays in History and Literature* (Blackwell, 1937).

one of the women's festivals. Twice in tragedy (Sophocles' *Electra* and *Antigone*) girls are brusquely told to go indoors, which is their proper place: Jebb, commenting on *Antigone* 579, quotes a poetic fragment: 'Nor permit her to be seen outside the house before her marriage', and he quotes from the *Lysistrata* of Aristophanes: 'It is difficult for a (married) woman to escape from home'. It was the man who did the shopping; he handed what he bought to his slave to carry. (The 'mean man' in Theophrastus carries it all home himself.) In the comedies of Menander (third century B.C.) the young man who has romantically fallen in love with a girl has invariably met her at a festival – the implication being that he has little chance of incurring this malady in ordinary social life. (Though we may remember that the staid Ischomachus 'chose' his young wife, so that presumably he had at least seen her, and we shall hear from Theophrastus that a young man might serenade his sweetheart.) Indeed, the romantic attachments that we do hear of are with boys and young men, and of these we hear very frequently: homosexual love was regarded as a normal thing and treated as frankly as heterosexual love. (Like the other sort, it had its higher and its lower aspect.) Plato has some fine passages describing the beauty and the modesty of young lads, and the tenderness and respect with which the men treated them.[1] Marriages were arranged by the girl's parents, and we have seen from our brief glance at Xenophon's Ischomachus that he at least took no very ecstatic view of matrimony. The wife is the domestic manager and little more: indeed, he expressly says that he prefers his young wife to be entirely ignorant, that he himself may teach her what he wishes her to know. The education of girls was omitted; for intelligent female company the Athenian turned to the well-educated class of foreign women, often Ionians, who were known as 'companions', hetaerae, women who occupied a position somewhere between the Athenian lady and the prostitute: Pericles' famous mistress Aspasia belonged to this class – her name, incidentally, meaning 'Welcome'! So we read in

1. Those who find this topic interesting or important are referred to Hans Licht, *Sexual Life in Ancient Greece*.

Demosthenes: 'Hetaerae we keep for the sake of pleasure: concubines (i.e. female slaves) for the daily care of our persons, wives to bear us legitimate children and to be the trusted guardians of our households.' And finally, no account of the position of women in Athens is complete without a reference to Pericles and Aristotle. Pericles said in his Funeral Speech: 'The best reputation a woman can have is not to be spoken of among men either for good or evil': and Aristotle holds (in the *Politics*) that by nature the male is superior, the female inferior, therefore the man rules and the woman is ruled.

Therefore, as I have said, it is almost unanimously held that the Athenian woman had very little freedom, some writers going so far as to speak of 'the contempt felt by the cultured Greeks for their wives'. It is orthodox to compare the repression of women in Athens with the freedom and respect which they enjoyed in Homeric society – and in historical Sparta.

This seems to be confirmed when we turn to the legal evidence. Women were not enfranchised: that is, they could not attend the Assembly, still less hold office. They could not own property: they could not conduct legal business: every female, from the day of birth to the day of her death, had to be the ward, so to speak, of her nearest male relative or her husband, and only through him did she enjoy any legal protection. The 'guardian' gave the woman in marriage – and a dowry with her: if there was a divorce, the dowry returned with the wife to the guardian. The legal provision most foreign to our ideas related to the daughter who was left sole heir to a father who had died intestate: the nearest male kinsman was entitled to claim her in marriage, and if married already he could divorce his own wife in order to marry the heiress. (It should be explained that in any case Attic law recognized marriage between uncle and niece, even between half-brother and half-sister). Alternatively, the nearest male kinsman became guardian to the heiress, and must give her in marriage, with a suitable dowry. In fact, a man who had no son and was not likely to have one, normally adopted one – not a male baby but a grown man – for example, a brother-in-law;

for the purpose of the adoption was not to indulge a sentiment or cure a psychosis, but to leave behind a proper head of the family to continue its legal existence and religious rites. But obviously many a man died before the adoption of a son appeared necessary: heiresses were left, and Isaeus (an orator who specialized in cases of disputed inheritance) assures us – or rather assures his audience, which may not be the same thing – that 'many a man has put away his wife' to marry an heiress. Apart from this special case, the laws of divorce applied to husbands and wives with reasonable, though not complete, impartiality: for instance – I quote Jebb's careful wording – 'a childless union could be dissolved at the instance of the wife's relatives'.

Does any more need to be said? When the legal evidence is added to the literary – and I think my necessarily brief summary represents both not unfairly – is it not quite clear that the Athenian treated his women with considerable indifference, for which 'contempt' may not be too harsh a substitute? Can we doubt on the evidence that in this pre-eminently masculine society women moved in so restricted a sphere that we may reasonably regard them as a 'depressed area'?

In detective stories there often comes a point where the detective is in possession of the facts, and sees that they lead to one conclusion. There is no doubt at all – except that we are still ten chapters from the end of the book. Accordingly, the detective feels a vague uneasiness: everything fits, yet it seems all wrong: there must be something, somewhere, which he has not yet discovered.

I confess that I feel rather like that detective. What is wrong is the picture it gives of the Athenian man. The Athenian had his faults, but pre-eminent among his better qualities were lively intelligence, sociability, humanity, and curiosity. To say that he habitually treated one-half of his own race with indifference, even contempt, does not, to my mind, make sense. It is difficult to see the Athenian as a Roman pater-familias, with a greater contempt for women than we attribute to the Roman.

To begin with, let us take a few general considerations that may induce in us a certain hesitation. As far as Greece is concerned, the most Hellenic of us is a foreigner, and we all of us know how wide of the mark even an intelligent foreigner's estimate can be. He sees undeniable facts – but misinterprets them because his own mental experience is different. Other facts he does not see. For example, I once had the advantage of having an analysis of the English character from a young German who was not a fool, and knew England tolerably well, both town and country. He told me, as something self-evident, that we play cricket for the good of our health: and when I mentioned in the course of the discussion the flowers which every cottager loves to grow, I found that he had supposed them to be wild flowers. Naturally, his picture of the Englishman was exceedingly funny. Similarly, every Frenchman has his mistress (evidence: French novels and plays), no Frenchman loves his wife (all French marriages are 'arranged'), there is no home-life in France (men congregate in cafés, which respectable women do not use); and the Frenchwoman's legal status is much lower than the Englishwoman's. Women in France therefore are less free, less respected and less influential than in England. – We used to hear this argument, and know how silly it is. The foreigner so easily misses the significant thing.

Another general point: the fallacy of assuming that anything for which we have no evidence (viz. home life) did not exist. It may have existed, or it may not: we do not know. – But is it possible that Greek literature should be so silent about domestic life if domestic life counted for anything? The answer expected is No: the true answer is Yes. In a modern literature the argument from silence would be very strong: in Greek literature it amounts to very little. We have noticed how Homer refrains from painting in the background which we expect, and gives us one which we do not expect; we have noticed how the dramatists are constructional rather than representational. In the *Agamemnon* Aeschylus does not show us the streets and the market, ordinary citizens' houses, goatherds, cooks and scullions about the palace. We do not infer that these did not exist, nor that Aeschylus had not an interest in such things. We can see at once that these things do not come into his play because there was no reason why they should. All classical Greek art had a very austere standard of relevance.

A related point is the subject-matter of the literature of the period. Unless we are on our guard, we instinctively think of Literature as including novels, biographies, letters, diaries – literature, in short, about individuals, either real or fictive. Classical Greek literature does not revolve around the individual; it is 'political'. Practically the only informal literature we have is Xenophon's *Memorabilia* and *Table Talk* (the *Symposium*), and these do not profess to give an intimate biography of Socrates, but deal explicitly with Socrates the philosopher. We find Xenophon's Ischomachus rather unromantic? To what has been said above on this point we may now add this, that Xenophon was not writing about Athenian married life; like Mrs Beeton, he was writing on Household Management.

Then there is a point very shrewdly made by Gomme, that our evidence is scanty, and we may easily misinterpret what we have. Gomme puts together some dozen dicta about women and marriage selected from nineteenth-century writers which would give a very false impression if we could not see them – as we can – against the whole background, and read them accordingly. Take Pericles' dictum, which has come re-echoing down the ages. It is typical of the disdain which the Athenians felt for women. Possibly. But suppose Gladstone had said, 'I do not care to hear a lady's name bandied about in general talk, whether for praise or dispraise': would that imply disdain, or an old-fashioned deference and courtesy?

Again, it is pointed out that it was common form in Athens to refer to a married woman not by her name (as it might be, Cleoboulê) but as 'Nicanor's wife'. The Athenian woman, poor thing, did not even have a known name, so obscure was she. Quite so: but among ourselves, when Sheila Jackson marries she becomes Mrs Clark: Sheila to her friends indeed, but Sheila Jackson to nobody. – We must be cautious.

My last general point is perhaps the most important. In discussing this topic, what are we really talking about? Are we comparing the position of women in Athens with the position of women in Manchester? Or are we trying to estimate the character of the Athenian, and of his civilization, on the basis (partly) of the position he allotted to his women? It makes a very great difference. If the former, then it is pertinent to say that the Manchester woman can vote and take a part in political life, while the Athenian woman could not. But if we say that because we give women the vote we are more enlightened and courteous than the Athenian, we are talking nonsense. We are comparing details in two pictures and ignoring the fact that the pictures are utterly different. If a woman in Manchester wants to go to London, she can do it on precisely the same terms as a man: she can buy her ticket, summer or winter, and the fare is the same for all. If an Athenian (male) wanted to go to Thebes, he could walk or ride a mule, and in winter the journey across the mountains was exhausting and perilous. If a woman wanted to go – it might be possible, by waiting for the proper season, but it would be a serious undertaking. It is perfectly reasonable, in a modern state, that women should be enfranchized. In the first place, civilization – to use the word for once in its improper sense – has made the physical differences between the sexes of very little political importance: women can use the train, bicycle, telephone, newspaper, on the same terms as men; and conversely the bank-clerk or don, provided that he is healthy, need not be stronger in muscle than the normal woman; he knows that there is no chance of his being required next week to march twenty miles under a baking sun in heavy armour, and then to fight as stoutly as the next man – or else imperil the next man's life. In the second place, the substance of politics and administration has changed. It is true that political decision then, as now, affected everyone regardless of age and sex, but the field which government covered was very much smaller, and concerned, in the main, matters which, inescapably, only men could judge from their own experience and execute by their own exertions. One reason why women have the vote today is that in many matters of current politics their judgment is likely to be as good as a man's, sometimes better, while in important matters their ignorance is not likely

H

to be greater. Nor should we forget what is probably an even more important difference. We think that it is normal to regard society as an aggregate of individuals. This is not normal from the historical point of view: it is a local development. The normal view is that society is an aggregation of families, each having its own responsible leader. This conception is not Greek only: it is also Roman, Indian, Chinese, Teutonic.

It is open to anyone to say that not for untold wealth would he have been a woman in Ancient Athens: perhaps one would not regret not having been an Athenian man either; for the polis, not to mention the ordinary conditions of life, made some extremely uncomfortable demands on him too. What is not sensible is to say to the Athenian: 'We treat women much better in Golders Green. Aren't you a bit of a blackguard?'

After this general discussion let us look at the evidence again. We will try to keep in mind the two separate questions: does the orthodox view correctly state the facts? and, if so, does it draw the correct deductions from them? That is, was the life of the Athenian woman restricted and stunted? and, if so, was the reason that the men regarded them with indifference or disdain?

We have seen that the literary evidence is too scanty, and, in a certain sense too one-sided, to give us any confidence that we have in it the complete picture. When a man gives a dinner, his wife does not appear. The Athenian gentleman liked masculine company – unlike the gentlemen of London, who have never even heard of a club which did not freely admit ladies. But did the Athenian play the host or the guest every evening of the year? And did the women not have their social occasions? Euripides was under the impression that they did: more than once he says things like, 'What an evil it is to have women coming into the house gossiping!' Did the Athenian, when he had no guests, dine alone, like some Cyclops in his cave? Did he never dream of talking to his wife about anything except the management of the household and the procreation of lawful children? Stephanus and Neaera once more raise their disreputable heads. Their prosecutor says, in his peroration, to the one, two or three hundred jurymen:

Gentlemen, if you acquit this woman, what will you say to your wives and daughters when you go home? They will ask where you have been. You will say, 'In the courts'. They will say, 'What was the case?' You of course will say, 'Against Neaera. She was accused of illegally marrying an Athenian, and of getting one of her daughters – a prostitute – married to Theogenes the archon. ...'

You will tell them all the details of the case, and you will tell them how carefully and completely the case was proved. When you have finished they will say, 'And what did you do?' And you will reply, 'We acquitted her'. – And *then* the fat will be in the fire!

It is perfectly natural – and that is the reason why I quote the passage. It is one of the very few scraps of evidence we have bearing on the ordinary relations of a man with his wife and daughters, and what happens is precisely what would happen today. The juryman is not expected to reply to his women: 'You forget yourselves! You are Athenian women, who should rarely be seen and never heard.'

Another literary scrap. In Xenophon's *Table Talk* one of the guests, Niceratus, has recently married. Niceratus knows Homer by heart, and explains to the company how much Homer has taught him – strategy, rhetoric, farming: all sorts of things. Then he says, turning pleasantly to his host, 'And there's another thing I've learned from Homer. Homer says somewhere: "An onion goes well with wine". We can test that here and now. Tell them to bring in some onions! You will enjoy the wine very much more.' 'Ah!' says another guest, 'Niceratus wants to go home smelling of onions so that his wife shall think that no one else has so much as thought of kissing him!' It is of course very slight, but it is precisely the sort of good-natured jest that one might hear any evening in an English club or a public-house.

But there is evidence, not yet mentioned, which is not so slight. It points in the same direction, and is unintelligible on the orthodox view. We happen to possess a large number of painted vases (fifth century) that portray domestic scenes, including some funerary-urns representing a dead wife as living, and taking farewell of her husband, children and slaves.

There are also sculptured tombstones – quite ordinary ones – showing similar scenes. These, in their noble and unaffected simplicity, are among the most moving things which Greece has left us. They rank with the Andromache passage in the *Iliad* which I paraphrased earlier. I quote from Gomme's essay a sentence which he quotes from an article on certain Athenian tombs.[1] 'Damasistratê and her husband clasp hands at parting. A child and a kinswoman stand beside the chair, but husband and wife have no eyes save for each other, and the calm intensity of their parting gaze answers all questionings as to the position of the wife and mother in Attic society.' Homer says, in a notable verse. 'There is nothing finer than when a man and his wife live together in true union' – ὁμοφρονέοντε, 'sharing the same thoughts'. If an illustrator of Homer wanted to illustrate this verse, he would automatically turn to these paintings and sculptures – made for a people who held women, especially wives, in slight esteem!

I will say no more about vases, but turn to Attic tragedy. One of its notable features is its splendid succession of tragic heroines – three Clytemnestras, four Electras, Tecmessa, Antigone, Ismene, Deianeira, Iocaste, Medea, Phaedra, Andromache, Hecuba, Helen. They differ in character, naturally, but all are vigorously drawn: none is a dummy. What is more, the vigorous, enterprising and intelligent character is commoner than the other sort. This, it may be said, is natural enough in drama. Perhaps so: but it is not inevitable that in Euripides the women, good or bad, should so often be more enterprising than the men. The clever woman who contrives something when the men are at a loss is almost a stock character in Euripides – Helen, for example, and Iphigenia (in the *Iphigenia in Tauris*). As for enterprise – 'Come!' says the old slave to the ill-used Creousa in the *Ion*, 'you must do something womanly. Take to the sword! Poison him!'[2] It is hard to believe that the dramatists never, even by accident, portrayed the stunted creatures among whom (we are to suppose) they actually lived, and got these vivid people out of books – from Homer. As if a modern dramatist turned from his despised contemporaries, drew his women from Chaucer or Shakespeare – and made a success of it. Euripides indeed makes women complain of what they suffer at men's hands – much of it as relevant to modern society as to ancient: he also makes many of his men suffer at the hands of vengeful and uncontrollable women. Some moderns accuse Euripides of being a feminist; ancient critics – with more reason, I think – called him a misogynist. At least, he did not think them negligible: nor did Aeschylus and Sophocles.

Now that we have positive reason for doubting at any rate the extreme doctrine of repression and disdain, let us, like the uneasy detective aforementioned, examine some of the evidence again. 'It is difficult for women to get out', says Jebb, quoting Aristophanes, in a note which otherwise deals with the very careful supervision of unmarried girls. The suggestion is that married women too were carefully kept indoors: and any classical scholar would remember that Xenophon speaks somewhere of putting bolts and bars on the door of the women's quarters. But if we actually turn up the passage in Aristophanes we get a rather different impression. It runs (a married woman is speaking): 'It's difficult for women to get out, what with dancing attendance on one's husband, keeping the servant-girl awake, bathing the baby, feeding it ...' We have heard not dissimilar things in our own time: the ogre has disappeared from this passage at least.

But she was not allowed out unless she had someone to keep an eye on her? The lively Theophrastus helps us here. With his habitual fineness of distinction Theophrastus describes three characters all of whom we might call 'mean'. The first of them is straightforwardly 'stingy': it is characteristic of him to come before quarter-day to collect sixpence due to him as interest on a loan, to turn the whole house upside-down if his wife has lost a threepenny bit, and to prevent a man from helping himself to a fig from his garden, or from picking up a date or olive in his orchard. Then there is, literally, 'the man of base gain', who gives short measure, feeds his slaves badly, and sponges on his friends in petty ways. But it is the third who concerns us at the moment. He does the family shopping, as the men regularly did, but instead of handing it to his slave to carry home, he carries it home himself, meat, vegetables and all, in a fold in his tunic: moreover, although his wife brought him a dowry of £5,000, he does not allow her to keep a maid, but when she goes out he hires a little girl from the women's market to attend her. This kind of meaness is 'aneleutheria', or 'conduct unbecoming a gentleman': Theophrastus defines it as 'a lack of self-respect where it involves money'. That is to say, for a lady to be properly attended when she went abroad was only her due. And I may add here, with a conventional apology for its coarseness, another detail from Theophrastus which contributes something material to our argument. One of his Characters is the Coarse Buffoon, 'who will stand by the door of the barber's shop and tell the world at large that he means to get drunk ... and when he sees a lady coming he will raise his dress and show his privy parts'. There were all sorts in the streets of Athens. There were perhaps very good reasons for not allowing girls to go about unguarded.

Then if we actually look at the bolts and bars passage, we find that their purpose is 'that the female slaves may not have babies without our knowledge,[1] and to prevent things being improperly taken out of the women's quarters': which may serve to remind us to what an extent the Greek home was also a factory. Quite apart from what we regard as 'domestic work', there was the making of clothes – from the raw wool, the grinding as well as the baking of the flour from the corn which the husband had brought in, the provision of food for the winter. We have in fact to think away most of our shops and the things that come in packets. Clearly the wife's position was one of great responsibility. Hollywood demonstrates to us, both by precept and example, that romantic love is the only possible basis for a happy and lasting marriage: was the Greek necessarily dull or cynical because he thought differently? He was aware of the force of 'romantic' love – and generally represented it as a destructive thing (see Sophocles, *Antigone*,

---

1. Both Xenophon and Aristotle remark that to have children made a decent slave more well-disposed to his owner. But a man does like to have some idea who is likely to be born in his house.

781 ff., and Euripides, *Medea*, 628 ff. 'When love is temperate, nothing is more enchanting: but save me from the other sort!')

But this is all very well: the man had his hetaerae and worse. What about that passage in the Neaera-speech? – what indeed? It is sometimes used as if it had all the authority of a state-document – but what is it? A remark made, in a disreputable case, by a pleader who is very much a man of the world to a jury of a hundred or more ordinary Athenians, very many of whom are there because the seven-and-sixpenny juror's fee pays the fishmongers' bill at the end of the week. 'Hetaerae indeed! Pretty slave-girls! Too expensive for the likes of us – but thank you for the compliment!' And in any case, what is the speaker actually saying? His whole argument is concerned to bring out the enormity of Stephanus' offence in foisting upon the body-politic alien and even tainted stock. This is not snobbery: it has its roots in the conception that the polis is a union of kinsmen. Therefore he says, 'Hetaerae and slave-girls are all very well, but when we come down to bed-rock, on which the existence of our polis depends, and the sustenance of our individual households, to whom do we turn? To our wives.' Far from implying contempt for the wife, this passage raises her beyond the reach of other women. It is in fact entirely in keeping with the evidence of the vase-paintings. It is our entirely different material and social background, and our inheritance of centuries of romance, which make us misread passages like these and then to try to argue away the evidence from painting and drama. Even so lively and sensitive a scholar as T. R. Glover represents Socrates as saying this to a friend: 'Is there anybody to whom you entrust more serious matters than to your wife – or to whom you talk less?'[1] But the plain meaning of the Greek is '... to whom you entrust more serious things, and with whom you have fewer arguments?' And the reason why he has fewer arguments with his wife is (by implication) that they are working together in partnership and understanding.

Boys were sent to school, taught to read and write, and educated in poetry, music and gymnastics: girls did not go to

1. Glover, *From Pericles to Philip*, 346; Xenophon, *Econ.*, III, 12.

school at all – another proof that the Athenian despised women and preferred dolts. The Athenian woman was illiterate and uneducated – so that when she went to the theatre and heard Antigone talking so nobly and intelligently, she must have opened her dull eyes in astonishment, wondering what sort of a creature this was, and how Sophocles could ever have imagined that a woman could be like that! It is obviously grotesque. It comes, again, from our confusing Athens with Manchester.

First, we are making an assumption which may or may not be true when we argue that because a girl did not go to school she was illiterate. Children have been known to pick up the art of reading at home, and what we know of Athenian intelligence and curiosity suggests that our assumption is unsafe. Secondly, those who cannot read today are sub-human, but that is not true of a society in which books are comparatively rare things. To the ordinary Athenian the ability to read was comparatively unimportant; conversation, debate, the theatre, much more than the written word, were the real sources of education. The boy was not sent to school to work for a certificate and thereby given 'educational advantages' (that is, qualifications for a job better than the manual work which we admire so much more than the Greeks). The Greek, in his perverse and limited way, sent the boys to school to be trained for manhood – in morals, manners and physique. Reading and writing were taught, but these rudiments could not have taken very long. The rest of the elementary curriculum was the learning of poetry and singing (mousikê), and physical training: mousikê was prized chiefly as a training in morals and in wisdom, and the moral influence of 'gymnastikê' was by no means overlooked.

What was the girl doing meanwhile? Being instructed by her mother in the arts of the female-citizen: if we say 'housework' it sounds degrading, but if we say Domestic Science it sounds eminently respectable; and we have seen how varied and responsible it was. To assume that she was taught nothing else is quite gratuitous, and the idea that her father would never discuss anything political with her is disproved by the Neaera-passage.

But did women have any opportunity of sharing in the real education that Athens offered? In the Assembly and law-courts, no – except at second-hand. What about the theatre? Were women admitted? This is a very interesting point. The evidence is various, clear and unanimous: they were. I quote one or two samples. Plato, denouncing poetry in general and tragedy in particular, calls it a kind of rhetoric addressed to 'boys, women and men, slaves and free citizens, without distinction'. This would be unintelligible if none but male citizens were admitted to the dramatic festivals. In the *Frogs* of Aristophanes Aeschylus is made to attack Euripides for his 'immorality'; Euripides, he says, has put on the stage such abandoned sluts 'that decent women have hanged themselves for shame'. Why should they, if they were carefully kept at home? The ancient *Life of Aeschylus* tells the story that the Chorus of Furies in the *Eumenides* was so terrific that boys died of fright and women had miscarriages – a silly enough tale, but whoever first told it obviously thought that women did attend the theatre.

The evidence is decisive, but 'in the treatment of this matter scholars appear to have been unduly biased by a preconceived opinion as to what was right and proper. Undoubtedly Athenian women were kept in a state of almost Oriental seclusion. And the old Attic comedy was pervaded by a coarseness which seems to make it utterly unfit for boys and women. For these reasons some writers have gone so far as to assert that they were never present at any dramatic performances whatsoever. Others, while not excluding them from tragedy, have declared that it was an impossibility that they should have been present at the performance of comedy.'[1] Impossible; *ganz unmöglich!* That is the end of the matter. But Haigh, though believing in Oriental seclusion, shows that the evidence disproves the notion that women could attend Tragedy but not Comedy. And even if we violate the evidence, we gain nothing, because the tragic tetralogy itself ended with the satyric play, of which the one surviving example (Euripides' *Cyclops*) contains jokes which would make the Stock Exchange turn pale. In this matter, then, there was an equality and a freedom

1. Haigh, *The Attic Theatre*, 3rd edition (by A. W. Pickard-Cambridge).

between the sexes inconceivable to us – though not perhaps to eighteenth-century Paris.[1]

It seems then – to sum up this discussion – that the evidence we have hardly warrants such phrases as 'kept in almost Oriental seclusion'. Scholars have not made a clear enough distinction between girls and married women, nor between conditions of life in Athens and Manchester, nor between Classical Greek and modern literature. Theocritus, in the early third century B.C., writes a lively mime describing how a Syracusan lady in Alexandria visits a friend and goes with her through the streets to a festival: and we are told, 'These are Dorian ladies: see how much more freedom they had than the Athenians'. The inference seems illegitimate. We ought rather to say, 'This poem was written in Alexandria, a cosmopolitan city, in an age when the city-state had come to an end, and politics were the concern of kings and their officials, not of the ordinary citizen. See therefore what different subjects the poets now write about. No longer do they confine themselves to matters which touch the life of the polis: instead, they actually begin to write about private and domestic life.'

But the doctrine of 'seclusion' has taken such a hold that when a married woman in Aristophanes tells us why it is hard for her to go out, we do not think it necessary to listen: we know already. And when we find perfectly good evidence that women went to the theatre – often to see plays which we should certainly not allow our women to see – we struggle against it. After this, the unconscious argument seems to run: 'If women had such a position among us, the reason would be masculine arrogance and repression: therefore, that was the reason in Athens. The Athenian certainly neglected and probably despised his women – unless they were foreigners and not too respectable.' Then we are surprised at the vases, and argue away the indications to be drawn from the women-characters in tragedy. We forget the physical conditions of Greek life, how primitive they were, and how such conditions necessarily distinguish sharply between the way of life and the interests of

1. It is true that comedy and the satyric drama were associated with 'religion' – and that it often removes all difficulties to call the same thing by a different name.

men and women. We are assured that the Athenian turned to the company of hetaerae because these women were educated and their wives were dolts. What innocence! Even among ourselves it is not unknown that the girl who lives alone in a small flat and takes her meals out may have a more active social life than the married woman. These hetaerae were adventuresses who had said No to the serious business of life. Of course they amused men – 'But, my dear fellow, one doesn't *marry* a woman like that'.

Similarly, we contemplate the legal disabilities of women, and particularly of the heiress. This, we say, proves how little the Athenian thought of the dignity of women. It proves nothing of the sort. It proves only what we knew before, how little the Athenian – or at any rate Athenian law, which may not be the same thing – thought of the convenience and interests of the individual in comparison with the interests of the social group – the family or the polis. The case of Apollodorus *v.* Polycles (Demosthenes) is worth mentioning in this connexion.

Apollodorus is a wealthy man of affairs, and a trierarch. The Assembly decides that a naval expedition is urgently necessary. The trierarchs are to bring their ships to the pier the next day, and to serve on them for six months. Has Apollodorus complicated business affairs on hand? Does he hear, during the six months, that his mother is dying? Is the crew allotted to him both insufficient and incompetent, so that if he wants a proper crew he must pay the men himself and take his chance of getting his money back? – That is all bad luck, but it makes no difference. Apollodorus can get a friend to look after his affairs for him – that is the sort of thing friends were for – and his mother can die without him. Apollodorus cannot leave his ship. No one would suggest that Apollodorus was as roughly treated as an heiress, but the principle is the same. Nor should we consider the position of the heiress without also considering the religious and social importance of the family, and the solemn responsibilities of the head of the family for the time being. The extinction of a family, and therefore of its religious cults, was a disaster, and the dissipation of its property hardly less calamitous. Let us then by all means feel sympathetic towards the heiress'—as we do towards those unsuccessful generals who were executed – but let us not too hastily assume that the law regarding them indicates contempt of women. After all, among the Romans at a comparable stage in their history, the Paterfamilias still legally possessed powers of life and death over members of his family. We must see the thing in its complete setting before we begin drawing inferences.

What can be said about the social life of the men? Here again we must remember the nature of our evidence: no Athenian ever set himself the task of drawing a picture of contemporary society – nor indeed of writing in such a way that such a picture emerges as a by-product. We have plenty of lively detail, but we have to be very careful how we generalize from it.

We know that politically Athens was 'exclusive'. The lines drawn between slave and free, alien and native, were sharp; it was difficult to cross them, and illegal assumption of superior political status was severely punished. It is natural for us to think that this political exclusiveness was accompanied by a similar social exclusiveness – but that seems to be quite wrong. 'Citizen' meant 'member', and 'membership' depended on birth. Only to reward exceptional services was 'membership' given to an alien – who after all was normally a 'member' of another state. 'Citizen' did not mean 'superior person'.

Indeed, one's general impression of Athenian society is that it was singularly free from barriers that depended on status, whether political or financial. At the beginning of Plato's *Republic* we have a very pleasant picture of old Cephalus. He was an alien (though a rich one), but he mixed freely in the best Athenian society. Socrates was poor, and of no distinguished family, but we find him dining with the great without any sort of embarrassment on either side, and talking, in the city, with rich aristocrats and artisans on precisely the same terms. And not only Socrates: Antisthenes, a fellow-guest in Xenophon's *Symposium*, is also a poor man. But this evidence is of course selective; Plato and Xenophon had no occasion to mention rich men who were unintelligent and snobs.

But there is other evidence. There is – to take the extreme case – the treatment of slaves. We know, from vase-painting and other sources, that real friendship between the slave and his owner was not uncommon: it all depended on the individuals concerned. Enslavement, after all, was a haphazard thing. Many a slave was a very decent and intelligent man, and the Athenians were sensible enough to distinguish between the status and the man. The slave who, by a common usage, worked out his own emancipation received the status of 'metic' or 'resident alien', and nothing suggests that he did not receive that place in society which his own character and talents could command. Only once in the extant forensic speeches is slave-origin used as a taunt, and that is by Apollodorus, whose own father Pasion had been the slave, the highly respected manager, and eventually the successor, of a banker, and then had been made a citizen.

Between rich and poor the political division became sharp enough, but how far was there a social division too? Certainly, one would say, not so far as among us. You could not tell that a given Athenian was 'no class' as soon as he opened his mouth, and, as we saw earlier, the essentials of education were available on the same terms to all. We get the impression that the Athenian was much more open-minded in his appraisal of men than we are – which in any case we ought to expect in a society much more exposed to sudden reversals of fortune.

For instance, Theophrastus' *Characters* analyse thirty separate faults or deficiencies: the pure snob is not among them. There is indeed the Petty-proud man. He keeps an Ethiopian slave: if he has a pet jackdaw he trains it to hop up and down a little ladder wearing a shield: when he has gone in procession with the other knights he swaggers about the town still wearing his riding-cloak and spurs: he has his hair cut rather too often: he keeps a pet monkey: he has a private wrestling-ground, and when he lends it for a match he is careful to arrive late, so that people will nudge each other and say 'That's the owner'. There is the Oligarchic man. He never goes out before midday (thus proving that he has nothing to do with anything so vulgar as business), wears his cloak with studied elegance, wears his hair and beard neither too long nor too short, and has antidemocratic political views. 'Let us have a committee of one – provided that he is a strong man'; 'We should keep these fellows in their place'. In these men there is indeed a certain lack of affability – as there is too in the Arrogant man, who won't speak until he is spoken to, and entertains men in his house but won't dine with them himself – but they are not the dreary money-snob.

We hear a lot about 'good form', and a lot about personal qualities. Sometimes we are tempted to think that if you were ugly, the man you met took it as a personal insult. So Apollodorus (Demosthenes XLV, 77): 'My face, my quick walk, my loud voice, do not, I think, make me one of fortune's favourites. They put me at a disadvantage, inasmuch as they annoy other people without doing me any good.' A deep voice was approved of, and a dignified walk, but excess of elegance (as we have seen) was ungentlemanly: it is the Petty-proud man who is at special pains to keep his teeth white: on the other hand it is the Disgusting man who has black ones. The Boor shows too much bare leg when he sits down, answers the door himself, sings in the (public) bath, and drives nails into his shoes; just as the Mean man (the *aneleutheros*) wears shoes that are all patches, and swears that they are stronger than horn. There is one character who sounds like a *nouveau-riche*: he is the Late-learner. This man, when he is 70 or more, learns poetry and has lessons in dancing, wrestling and riding: his fault is that he shows off unseasonably and unsuccessfully. There is no tinge of social superiority in the portrait. The silly man practises shooting and throwing the javelin with the youngsters, and offers to show the tutor how to do it, 'as if the tutor knew nothing about it either'.

Theophrastus is hard to leave, and I will not leave him without at least introducing the Officious man and the Slow and Stupid man, irrelevant though they may be. The Officious man will show you a short cut and get lost – very Hellenic this! – will 'try an experiment' by giving wine to a man whose doctor has forbidden it, and so will lay the poor fellow flat; and when he is taking an oath will remark to the bystanders,

'You know, this isn't the first time I have taken an oath'. The Slow and Stupid man tots up a bill, writes down the total, and says, 'What does it come to?' He is left alone in the theatre, fast asleep, when everyone else has gone. Somebody asks him if he knows how many funerals went along the Cemetery Road last month, and he replies, 'I only wish you and I had half as many'. And after dining unwisely he has to get up in the night to go to the public place, and on the return journey he goes into his neighbour's house by mistake, and is bitten by the dog.

But we must return to our argument, even though that means passing over the Tactless man, who serenades his sweet-heart when she is ill of a fever, calls on a man who has just come in from an exhausting journey and invites him to go for a walk, acts as arbitrator and sets the parties by the ears when their only desire is to be reconciled, and, 'when he is minded to dance, takes hold of another man who is not yet drunk'.

Poverty is of course deplored. For one thing, it renders a man unable to help his friends as he would wish. Euxitheus protests that his opponent has sneered at his mother because she sells ribbons in the market-place, 'contrary to the law, which allows a case for slander to be brought against anyone who makes it a reproach against a citizen, male or female, that he or she plies a trade in the market'. It is significant perhaps that a law (or clause) was necessary, but then, the market was a special case; it raised a presumption that you were something of a rascal. (Cf. *The Liars' Market*, p. 189.) The scoundrel who got up the case against Euxitheus urged too that his mother was a nurse. 'And what of that?' he says. 'Like many others we were badly hit by the war. Plenty of Athenian women are acting as nurses: I will give you names, if you like.'

We are often assured, with more or less of qualification, that the Greek despised manual work. The idea was dismissed by Zimmern (in his *Greek Commonwealth*) as 'grotesque', and the adjective, I think, was well-chosen. As in considering the treatment of women, we have to rid ourselves of certain contemporary notions before we properly appraise the Greek attitude. We have also to consider who our 'authorities' are, and what they were talking about. It is a modern habit to speak, in the tone of one uttering an incantation, of 'the workers'. The Greek was too simple-minded to think in chunks like this. He would want to know 'Working at what? And how?'

For example, we have it on the authority of Socrates (as reported by Xenophon, *Econ.* IV, 3) that some states (not Athens) forbid their citizens to engage in mechanical occupations. We at once think of the rule which the Amateur Rowing Association is said to have (or to have had), that no one who follows a 'menial occupation' can be an amateur oarsman. We are perhaps surprised to find such snobbery in Socrates, of all men: but if we look at the passage we shall find that it implies no snobbery at all. What leads up to it is this: 'Men do indeed speak ill of those occupations which are called handicrafts, and they are quite rightly held of little repute in communities, because they weaken the bodies of those who make their living at them by compelling them to sit and pass their days indoors. Some indeed work all the time by a fire. But when the body becomes effeminate the mind too is debilitated. Besides, these mechanical occupations leave a man no leisure to attend to his friends' interests, or the public interest. This class therefore cannot be of much use to his friends or defend his country. Indeed, some states, especially the most warlike, do not allow a citizen to engage in these handicraft occupations.'

When he was confronted with a proposition, the Greek, being simple-minded, did not as a rule ask whether it was reactionary, or popular, or 'deviationist': he was inclined to ask if it was true. States which, as it were, limited the franchise to those classes who were likely to be always ready for military service (among whom would certainly be included all farmers) may have taken a narrow view of a state's functions, but they cannot on this account be said to have despised manual work *per se*.

Suppose we apply Socrates' reasoning to our own times. As it happens, I have written most of this book sitting by the fire. If I had to march to Bridgwater next week I should faint by the wayside: certainly I should want to throw away my shield.

If I were called up for jury-service I should probably ask to be excused, on the grounds that my University could not continue without me. Socrates would no doubt find me extremely interesting as an individual, but he would think me a poor citizen and put my trade on his black-list. But it would be unsafe to conclude that Socrates 'despised intellectual work'. In fact, what he is objecting to is not menial work, but specialization. Work on the land meets with his warmest commendation. He does not sneer at 'the clod-hopper.'

And let us not forget that Socrates here is speaking politically, not socially – and he was not the sort to allow irrelevant considerations to interfere with an argument (nor were Plato and Aristotle either). We see a different side of Socrates in the *Memorabilia*, III, 10 – the Socrates who spent much of his time drifting into workshops or studios (for the two were hardly differentiated) and talking to the 'worker' about his trade. And, says Xenophon, they found his conversation very useful to them. Xenophon records a conversation with a certain corslet-maker, Pistias. 'What an admirable invention is the corslet! It gives protection where protection is needed, and yet doesn't prevent a man from using his arms. Tell me, Pistias, why do you charge more than other makers? Your corslets are no stronger, and they are made of the same materials'. Pistias explains that his are better proportioned. 'But suppose your customer is himself ill-proportioned?' Pistias explains that he makes them fit the individual. 'So that proportion', says Socrates, 'is not an absolute, but is relative to the wearer – And, of course, if they fit well, the weight is evenly distributed, and therefore less noticeable.' 'Exactly', says Pistias: 'that is the reason why I think that my work deserves a good price. But there are people who prefer a highly ornamented corslet.'

These workmen thought well both of themselves and of their trades. Vase-paintings – made for ordinary sale – often give us a scene in a workshop. Most frequently, as is only natural, they show us the potter's own operations, but other trades are illustrated too. English potters have often decorated their wares with butterflies, or with sweet country cottages: I am not aware that the factory itself has ever been put on a plate or a jug. There may be other reasons for this, but at least the fact that the Greek potter used his own trade for purposes of decoration suggests that there was no general social prejudice against it.

We hear, in the *Memorabilia*, of a certain Euthêrus, a man of property ruined by the war, like the Aristarchus whom we met earlier. He had taken on some manual work – what it was, we are not told – thinking this better than trying to sponge on friends. 'This is all very well,' says Socrates, 'but what will you do when you are too old for labouring? You had better find someone who wants an estate-manager – someone to superintend the labourers, supervise the harvest, and so on. A position like this will be much more useful to you when you are old.' Very sensible advice – and what does Euthêrus say? Something so fundamentally Hellenic that I have heard it from a Greek myself, from the proprietor of a small and failing restaurant in a small and decaying Greek town. While I was there, enjoying day by day his admirably cooked meals, he was forced to give in and to accept a job in a restaurant elsewhere. I began to express what good wishes my Modern Greek enabled me to express, but he cut me short and with a look and gesture of infinite bitterness he said: 'Hypállelos!', 'subordinate'. This is exactly what Euthêrus said. Euthêrus did not mind being a manual labourer, but to be a gentleman-bailiff ...! As the Bohn translator says, in his racy manner, 'I should with great reluctance, Socrates,' said he, 'submit to slavery.' Socrates points out that managing an estate is very like managing a city, and that is the opposite of a slave's job. Euthêrus is obstinate: 'I will not expose myself to anybody's censure.' 'That is difficult', says Socrates. 'But you must find someone who is not censorious – a fair-minded man, for whom you will be able to undertake tasks which are within your powers, and decline those which are not.' What Euthêrus did we do not know – but to be an estate-manager! Oh Zeus!

In fact the Greek attitude to work seems to have been a very sensible one: there is no such thing as 'work' in the abstract. Everything depends on what the job was – and particularly, on whether it left you your own master. The citizen did not mind working alongside slaves: the difference was that he could knock off and go to the Assembly, and the slave could not. Pistias could shut up shop when he liked: 'Back tomorrow'. He had an interesting trade, he could take a pride in his work, and if his customers did not like his goods they could go elsewhere. The Greeks appraised work: they were neither snobbish nor sentimental about it. When Aristotle said that menial and mechanical occupations unfit a man for citizenship, it is impossible to controvert him, on his own ground. It was not a prejudice: it was judgment, quite valid on his own premisses. Aristophanes lampoons Cleon as a violent and vulgar seller of hides – but he does not sneer at the sellers of hides who were not violent and vulgar. Of the son of his prosecutor Anytus, Socrates said (*Memorabilia*, 30), 'I don't think he will stay in the servile trade to which his father has put him' – apparently, again, selling hides; 'He is a lad of ability.' Exactly: he is a cut above that. In fact, the occupation that was generally looked down upon was selling by retail, and the reason for this was partly economic prejudice – such a person does not really do anything, but is a parasite – partly moral (*The Liars' Market*), and partly, one might almost say, aesthetic, for such a person does not make anything that demands skill or gives satisfaction. We have the term 'counter-jumper' ourselves: 'and' says Demosthenes[1] talking of more exalted dealers, 'in the world of commerce and finance it is thought quite remarkable if a man is both clever and honest.' In the later Greek world there are plenty of philosophers and writers who write with scorn about 'work', but that was a split world, which had invented 'culture'.

To bring this rather rambling chapter to an end we may perhaps ask if there are any general characteristics of the people which have not been mentioned, or have been insufficiently treated. There is certainly one.

The reader may perhaps have been startled that a litigant should openly admit that he is bringing a prosecution in order to be avenged on his opponent.[2] This is a motive which among us would be carefully concealed: indeed, it is one which the

1. Defending the banker Phormio.   2. See above, p. 218.

defence, not the prosecution, would seek to establish. Yet in the Greek courts it is proclaimed quite openly. It is a matter worth considering at some length.

Obviously, it is no explanation simply to say that the Greeks were vindictive. Perhaps they were – but why should such desire for revenge be regarded as a merit? For it certainly was, provided that the desire and the vengeance sought were not considered unreasonable. This is shown by the one character of Theophrastus which it is difficult for us to understand – the Ironical man. The word 'ironical' has completely changed its meaning. 'Irony' was the opposite of boasting and exaggeration, and being the opposite was equally a fault: for the Greek always knew what recent political history has taught, that the opposite of a bad man is not a good man, but a different sort of bad man. 'Irony' meant not only understatement, but also a lack of frankness, and dissembling of real motives, and a parade of false ones. Theophrastus' Ironical man is, then, among other things, that 'he goes up to his enemies to chat with them, instead of showing hatred. He will praise to their faces those whom he attacked behind their backs, and will sympathize with them in their defeats. He will show forgiveness to his revilers, and excuse things said against him.'[1] We can be quite certain that what Theophrastus is objecting to is not that the 'forgiveness' is insincere. As the braggart affects to be a much finer fellow than he is, so his opposite, the Ironical man, affects (among other things) to be much meaner than he is; and how can a man more clearly display meanness of mind than by affecting to forgive his enemies? Even to pretend to do this is disgusting: really to do it would be worse.

This is thoroughly Greek. 'Love your friends and hate your enemies' was a maxim which nobody before Socrates ever thought of challenging. Aristotle's pattern of nobility is the 'highminded man' or the 'man of great soul'. (The literal Latin equivalent, 'magnanimous', has acquired a different and most un-Aristotelian colour.) He, unlike the Ironical man, will be open both in his friendships and in his hatred, for concealment is a sign of fear.

1. Jebb's translation.

We can understand that insincerity is a bad thing: what we have also to understand is that to forgive your enemies is a bad thing, and to be revenged on them a plain duty.

This extremely unchristian morality arises partly out of the nature of Greek society, in which the group is socially more important than with us, and the individual less important. The individual is a member first of his family, then of his polis. A wrong done to him is a wrong done to his family or his polis, as the case may be, and he must avenge it in the interests of his family or his polis. We ourselves have a distant parallel in the strictness with which an official or trustee will administer funds: it is not for him to be generous with other people's money.

But much more important than this was the influence of the Greek sense of honour. The Greek was very sensitive to his standing among his fellows: he was zealous, and was expected to be zealous, in claiming what was due to him. Modesty was not highly regarded, and that Virtue is its own reward is a doctrine that the Greek would think mere foolishness. The reward of virtue (*aretê*, outstanding excellence) is the praise of one's fellows and of posterity. This runs right through Greek life and history, from the singular touchiness of the Homeric hero about his 'prize'. Here is a typical remark:

If you were to look at the ambitiousness of men, you would be surprised how irrational it is, unless you understood their passionate thirst for fame, 'to leave behind them', as the poet says, 'a name for all succeeding ages'. For this, they are ready to face any danger – even more than for their own children: to spend their substance, to endure any physical hardship, to give their lives for it. Why, do you imagine that Alcestis would have given her life for Admetus, or Achilles given his to avenge Patroclus, if they had not thought that their own aretê would be immortal – as indeed it is? No, the nobler a man is, the more is undying fame and immortal aretê the spring of his every action.

This is the wise Diotima, instructing Socrates in Plato's *Symposium*. It is normal Greek doctrine: we find it in philosophers, poets and political orators. Take the *Ethics* of Aristotle.

If we ourselves were to define 'greatness of soul', we should postulate certain qualities, these qualities to be continually shown in action: but we should not add that the man of great soul should be conscious of these qualities, still less that he should demand their public recognition. But what does Aristotle say? That the 'man of great soul' (or 'of great mind', or both) is one who regards himself as worthy of high things, and is in fact worthy of them. The man who overrates himself is conceited: the man who underrates himself is mean-minded: the man who is worthy only of small things and rates himself accordingly is sensible, but not high-minded. The particular object of his regard will be the highest thing that we know: that is, what we offer to the gods, namely Honour. He will naturally have all the virtues, otherwise he would not merit the highest honour. But he will not overestimate the value even of honour, still less of wealth and political power. These are inferior to honour, for men desire them for the sake of honour, and if a thing is desired for the sake of something else, it is necessarily inferior to that something else. He will not run risks for small ends, nor exert himself in small things, because he despises them: but he will run a great risk, and at a time of great danger will be reckless of his life, thinking that life is not worth living without honour. He will not be given to admiration, as there is nothing that strikes him as great.[1] He will not bear a grudge: he will prefer to overlook injuries. He will not care either to be praised or to praise. He will, of course, not talk about other men in a personal way, nor speak evil of others, not even of his enemies, except for the express purpose of insulting them.

Such is this philosopher's Great Man – and his greatness is shown partly in his indifference to the 'praise' which is the normal spur to action. (Socrates for example, says that the good general will put in the front rank the 'ambitious' men, 'those who will be ready to brave danger for the sake of praise'.) His greatness consists in his just appraisal both of external things and of himself. Unaffected modesty is not one of

1. As Balfour once said, 'Nothing matters very much, and very few things matter at all.'

his virtues. He regards above all things (but even so, not unduly) Honour – and what is this 'honour'? It is not the inner
compulsion which we mean by 'honour': the nearest Greek
word to that is *aidôs*, shame. The word that Aristotle uses here
is Timê, and it is significant that this word is also the normal
Greek for 'price' or 'value'. (The same root in fact turns up in
our word 'estimate'.) This indicates the importance which the
Greek attached to the public acknowledgement of one's qualities and one's services.

Now, it would be a mistake to suppose that the ordinary
Greek would necessarily admire this character as much as the
philosopher does: if a philosopher thought like the rest of us he
would not be much of a philosopher. Nevertheless, making due
allowance for philosophical thoroughness and abstraction, the
picture is entirely Greek, exaggerated though it is. Some of the
details suggest Pericles. (Pericles came home from a party one
night, escorted by one of his slaves with a torch, and followed
by a man who hurled abuse and insult at him all the way.
Pericles took no notice, but on reaching his own house he
turned to the slave and said, 'See the fellow home'.) What is
common to Aristotle's 'man of great soul' and the average
Greek is his lively sense of his own worth, and his desire for
'honour', that justice should be done to him.

This it is which does most to explain the unashamed desire
for revenge. A man owes it to himself to be revenged; to put
up with an injury would imply that the other man was 'better'
than you are.

Aristotle's character is unusual in this, that he does not bear
a grudge. But why not? Not because he thinks it morally
wrong, but because he judges this to be beneath him. He does
not forgive: he only despises and forgets. The ordinary Greek
did neither.

We have noticed how anxious the Greek was to have his
timê, his due meed of praise. He was – and is – essentially
emulous, ambitious, anxious to play his own hand. (Unless
this is understood, modern Greek politics are unintelligible.)
So, at every hand we meet the idea of 'contest', agôn. Those
things that we weakly translate 'Games' were, in Greek,

agônes: the dramatic festivals were agônes – contests in which poet was pitted against poet, actor against actor, chorêgus against chorêgus. Our word 'agony' is a direct development from agôn; it is the anguish of the struggle that reveals the man.

With all this goes personal ambition, which the Greek of superior talent often found it impossible to control. The best commentary on this is Thucydides' account of the two Greek leaders in the Persian War, Themistocles the Athenian, who engineered Salamis, and Pausanias, the Spartan commander at Plataea. Very soon after Plataea Pausanias was sent out with an allied fleet to liberate the islands, but he acted with a violence which alarmed the allies so much that they begged the Athenians to assume the leadership. The Spartans recalled Pausanias to answer charges of injustice to individuals and of intriguing with Persia; 'for he seemed to be behaving more like a tyrant than a commander' (Thuc. I, 95). As they sent no successor, the command fell to the Athenians by default. But Pausanias went out again, with a single ship, and presently was found in the Troad, intriguing with Persia. Again he was recalled. He obeyed, trusting to his royal position and wealth. Proof against him was lacking, but his contempt of the laws and his adoption of Persian manners looked suspicious. Moreover, he had presumed to inscribe his own name on the votive-offering which the Greeks had made to Delphi as thanksgiving for the victory. Helots asserted that he had been tampering with them, planning an insurrection. In the end, the ephors trapped him into confessing his dealings with Persia. To avoid arrest he took refuge in a temple, where he was starved to death.

But the evidence against Pausanias had implicated Themistocles. He too had given himself rather high and mighty airs, and was too much of a radical – and opportunist – to work comfortably with Aristeides, so that the safety-valve of ostracism was used, and it was Themistocles who was expelled. He went to Argos, the irreconcilable enemy of Sparta, and the Spartans were no doubt very glad to be able to inform against him in Athens. The Athenians sent a party to arrest him, but Themistocles was warned, and Thucydides (for once) does not disdain a romantic story. Themistocles fled first to Corcyra

(Corfu), thence to Adrastus, King of the Molossians, though they were not on friendly terms. Adrastus happened to be away from home, but Themistocles appealed as a suppliant to his wife. She told him to sit on the hearth, and gave him her child to hold. When Adrastus returned, Themistocles, as suppliant, could plead his case, which was: 'I did you an injury: but a man of honour avenges himself only on his equals, and in my present case I am helpless. Besides, I opposed you only in the matter of a request you made, whereas my present proposition to you is a matter of life and death.' It is piquant to find this subtle politician in so Homeric a setting. Adrastus protected him, until of his own wish Themistocles made his way to Asia, and sent a letter to Xerxes' son and successor: 'I did your father more harm than any other Greek, when he attacked us, but I also did him great service, dissuading the Greeks from cutting off his retreat. I am your friend. I can do you much service. I wish to wait a year, and then visit you.' The King approved, and during the year Themistocles learned all he could of the language and institutions of Persia. He became a great man with the King, governor of Magnesia in Asia, where he died at last of disease and was rewarded with a monument, 'though some say that he poisoned himself, when he found that he had promised the King more than he could perform'. The malicious touch is very Greek, but it seems most unlikely that so clever a man as Themistocles would ever have dug such a pit for himself. 'Such was the end of Pausanias the Spartan and of Themistocles the Athenian, who had been the most distinguished men of their time.'[1] Not for nothing does Greek tragedy speak as it does against hybris, and so often represent Hope as a snare and a temptation.

Finally, we must not forget that the Greeks were southerners. The serenity of Greek art, the poise of the Greek mind, and the safe Greek doctrine of the Golden Mean, encourages perhaps the idea that the Greek was an untroubled and passionless creature; and the idea is perhaps reinforced by conceptions drawn from seventeenth- and eighteenth-century neo-classicism, and conceivably from modern performances of Greek

1. Thucydides, I, 94-96, 128-138.

plays, in which dimly-robed women gather in sculpturesque groups on the stage and recite, in artificial and rather embarrassing unison, a lot of lugubrious mythology.

It is all wrong. Nothing that does not quiver with controlled excitement is Classical Greek – though it may be post-classical. If Aeschylus does not leave you excited and transfigured, you have not been getting Aeschylus. (It may be that it is impossible to get Aeschylus now without studying Aeschylus: that is another matter.)

Let us for a moment consider this matter of Greek plays. The dialogue-scenes give us no trouble: they are dramatic enough. It is what happens between them that chills the blood: the elegant group of maidens or old men reciting Swinburne, all at once. Those who find this dull should not blame the Greeks: they would not have endured it for five minutes. These choral odes were never spoken, but always sung: not only were they sung but they were also danced: and not only were they danced – as indeed they sometimes are in modern revivals – but they were danced in a circular dancing-floor nearly ninety feet in diameter. Now, it is roughly true that the only people today who know anything about Greek dancing are those who teach it: to try to reconstruct it from the few representations on vase-paintings is most hazardous, for the reason that vase-painters knew nothing and cared less about perspective: if they show a frieze-like procession that means only that a frieze-like procession made an effective decoration on a vase, not that the dance looked like this. But we have left the metre of the poetry, and that gives us at least the rhythm, and, as it were, the ground-floor plan of the music and the dance: and from these it is perfectly obvious that the dances were eloquent, varied, and, where necessary, tumultuous. From these we can see for example that the dance-sequences in Aeschylus tended to be architectural in conception: in Sophocles, extremely plastic. The story of the Chorus of Furies in the *Eumenides* (p. 233), though foolish, is testimony that Aeschylus was not dominated by ideas of neo-classic dignity; and testimony of a different sort is not hard to come by. For example, in that most stately and exciting play the *Seven Against Thebes*, the chorus enters in the character of women terrified to death by the enemy who are attacking the town. Aeschylus forgets that Greek Tragedy, particularly when written by Aeschylus, is statuesque: he forgets too that the Chorus always enters to the perfectly regular, anapaestic, 4–4 march-rhythm. He brings on this chorus to music the time-signature of which would be $\frac{3+5}{8}$ – and if any modern choreographer should want to represent tumult and disorder on the stage, let him try this! (If the reader is totally unmusical, let him count, in perfectly steady time, 1 – 2 – 3 – 1 – 2 – 3 – 4 – 5, and try to walk to it, taking a step each time he says 'one'.) Greek tragedy, in fact, is like modern opera inasmuch as it combines dramatic speech, poetry, music and ballet – in a ninety-foot circle. It is unlike opera inasmuch as it is always about something intrinsically important, and the words were not only audible, but also made sense.

This little disquisition shows, perhaps, that the Greeks did not make a point of being drab, but on the contrary demanded life, movement and colour. Indeed they coloured their statues, a discovery which came as a great shock to many modern scholars.

Let us take another illustration of the essentially passionate nature of the Greek. The Greek for 'love' we all know: erôs. Eros graces Piccadilly Circus, the god of Love, the Greek equivalent of Cupid. But how exact is the equivalence? 'Cupid' means 'desire', the related adjective 'cupidus' often means no more than 'greedy'. But 'erôs' has different associations: it means something like 'passionate joy', and can be used quite naturally in a context which has nothing to do with love. For example, Ajax, in Sophocles' play, is utterly disgraced and threatens to kill himself. Tecmessa his wife is in despair: so are Ajax's own men (the Chorus): they will be left defenceless against the malice of Ajax's enemies. But Ajax professes to be overborne by their entreaties: he will endure the disgrace, and live. Whereupon the chorus sings, and dances, an ode which begins with the words: 'I shiver with erôs: my abounding joy gives me wings'. Erôs is no Cupid; he is something which makes every nerve tingle.

The 'lover' is the erastês: and in the Funeral Speech the grave Pericles, 'the Olympian' as Aristophanes called him, said to the Athenians, 'You must be *erastae* of Athens.' That is, 'Let Athens be to you something that thrills you to the very marrow'. – Not the remark of a cold man.

The doctrine of the Mean is characteristically Greek, but it should not tempt us to think that the Greek was one who was hardly aware of the passions, a safe, anaesthetic, middle-of-the-road man. On the contrary, he valued the Mean so highly because he was prone to the extremes. It is we more sluggish Northerners who have a certain furtive admiration of extremes. The characteristic fault of bad English poetry – of some of the weaker Elizabethan drama, for instance, or of the stuff that Dryden wrote for Purcell – is furious bombast: it is as if the poet was trying to beat himself up into something like excitement. The typical Greek vice is rather a frigid elaboration. The Greek had little need to simulate passion. He sought control and balance because he needed them; he knew the extremes only too well. When he spoke of the Mean, the thought of the tuned string was never very far from his mind. The Mean did not imply the absence of tension and lack of passion, but the correct tension which gives out the true and clear note.

INDEX